THE LINGERING DEAD

Also by J. N. Duncan

Deadworld

The Vengeful Dead

THE LINGERING DEAD

J. N. Duncan

KENSINGTON PUBLISHING CORP.
http://www.kensingtonbooks.com

KENSINGTON BOOKS are published by

Kensington Publishing Corp.
119 West 40th Street
New York, NY 10018

All Kensington Titles, Imprints, and Distributed Lines are available at special quantity discounts for bulk purchases for sales promotions, premiums, fund-raising, and educational or institutional use.

Special book excerpts or customized printings can also be created to fit specific needs. For details, write or phone the office of the Kensington special sales manager: Kensington Publishing Corp., 119 West 40th Street, New York, NY 10018, attn: Special Sales Department, Phone: 1-800-221-2647.

ISBN-13: 978-0-7582-5565-5
ISBN-10: 0-7582-5565-9

First Mass Market Printing: April 2012

10 9 8 7 6 5 4 3 2 1

Printed in the United States of America

Acknowledgments

This was the most difficult book to write thus far, mostly due to time constraints and the stress that the real world can bring at times that can make everything else so difficult. A big thanks to Martin, my editor for editing on the fly to help me get this book finished on time, and to my agent, Ginger Clark for offering some timely, early feedback on the manuscript. A bigger thank you to my wife, (author Tracy Madison), who had to deal with my deadlines while I simultaneously looked for a new job. Vida, thank you for all of your efforts behind the scenes there at Kensington. Also, to the mysterious folks at the art department. I don't know who you are, but the covers get better every time, which makes me happy. Also, big thanks to everyone else who has supported and encouraged my writing along the way here. Writing stories is both a blessing and a wonder, which I hope to continue to do until I no longer can. Happy reading/writing everyone.

J.N. Duncan

Prologue

Jessica Davies's face was numb. The motorcycle helmet provided little protection against the cold October air, but she did not care. Hunkered down in the sidecar of Charlie's roaring machine, her gloved hands gripped the lip of the shell, and she squealed with fearful delight every time Charlie took a curve too fast and the wheel of the sidecar lifted off the ground. She was miles from nowhere with the coolest girl in the world and no clue where they were going. It was glorious, terrifying fun.

It sure beat the hell out of doing meth on Petey's dilapidated old couch that smelled like piss and vomit. There was more warmth in this wind-whipped sidecar than she ever got from his rusted out, charcoal hibachi. Not to mention the bonus of being miles away from his grimy hands and a mouth that tasted like rotted ass. Wherever Charlie was going, it had to be a million times better than that wretched dump.

The tree-lined highway gave way to another small town. Charlie eased off of the accelerator and they came to a stop at the single stoplight in the center of the town. Her pert, red mouth spread into a grin, and she stared down at Jessica through the gleaming, mirrored lenses of her aviator goggles. If the light was just so, Jessica swore she could see Charlie's otherworldly eyes behind them.

"Doing OK down there, Sis?"

Jessica nodded. "This is so fucking great! I love you." God! Where had that come from? But what else could this tingling, energized feeling be? No boy had ever managed to spark these sensations in her before. Warmth, comfort, desire. The feelings had been almost instantaneous. Charlie oozed cool out of every pore, and that little blond curlicue on her forehead was to die for. And the whole "sis" thing made her smile inside. They would be just like sisters.

The corner of Charlie's mouth curled up. "Good. We'll be home soon. Mom's making us lasagna."

"Sounds fabulous. My mom can't stand up long enough to cook anything."

Charlie's hand reached down and covered hers. "Well, mine will just love having you."

The heat from Charlie's hand seeped right through the glove, sending goose bumps up Jessica's arm. "Cool. I'll just be happy to have a place with heat."

She gave Jessica's hand a squeeze. "You'll love it here." The smile softened. "Trust me."

The light changed to green and Charlie turned them off the highway toward the edge of town, winding back toward the oak-lined hills. Jessica sat up straighter, watching the rustic, brick buildings rush by. It looked quaint, almost old-fashioned, and a far cry from the burned-out, South Side Chicago tenement she had been holed up in. Even in the frigid, dying light, the town looked peaceful.

On the back edge of town, an entire three blocks off of the highway, Charlie brought them to a drive heading up into a stand of oak and maple, a stark, black web of limbs shielding the lighted windows of a house. A simple, wooden signpost next to the mailbox read in white block letters: THATCHER'S MILL.

"You live in a mill?" Jessica shouted.

"A house, next to the mill, silly," she said. "My family has lived here for over a hundred years."

"Oh, wow." Jessica nodded and stared up the drive at the looming, two-story house. Over a hundred years. She couldn't remember ever living in a place longer than two. This was a place with real family. People who cared.

They rolled to a stop in the gravel drive that circled in front of the wood-sided house. A shingled roof overhung a wide screened porch running the length of the house. Jessica had barely managed to get her helmet off when the porch lights flooded the drive and the front door flew open.

"Charlie!" A woman came bustling across the porch and knocked open the screen door, the hem of her ankle-length dress balled up in one hand. A face-cracking smile reached nearly to the edges of the white bonnet on her head. "You brought her home!"

Charlie pushed the aviator goggles up onto her head and swung off the motorcycle. "Of course, Ma-ma. I always do."

Home. Her home. How did that work? Jessica returned Charlie's irresistible smile. "Brought me home?"

"Yes," Charlie said and reached down to take her hand. "My home is your home. You belong here now."

A corner of those still-perfect red lips curled up, and even in the halogen glow of the porch light, Jessica stared into those bright, iridescent eyes and knew the absolute truth of her words. The momentary knot in her stomach melted away. "I really do love you."

Charlie squeezed her hand, but then the exuberant clapping of Charlie's mother interrupted the moment. "Come on, girls. This is just so wonderful. Dinner is almost ready. Do you want to change, Charlie?"

"Um, yeah. We better. Becca smells a little ripe." She reached down and hooked her hands beneath Jessica's underarms and lifted her out of the sidecar.

Before she had an opportunity to say a word, Charlie's mother embraced her. She smelled of soap and garlic and a hint of lavender. "You had us so worried, Rebecca, love. I thought you'd died."

The hug left Jessica breathless, and then Charlie's husky whisper blew into her ear. "Just roll with it. I'll explain later." Charlie took her hand again. "Ma-ma, chill out. I told you everything was fine. So, go get the table ready. We'll be down in like fifteen."

The mother sobered up. "Of course, sweetie. Everything is almost ready, just the way you like it."

Charlie nodded toward the house. "Come on, Becca. Let's go clean up."

Jessica followed, Charlie's hand pulsing with warmth around hers. Inside, she was hit by a wall of heat from a wood-burning stove in the corner of the living room. It carried the scent of baked bread, garlic, and pasta sauce. A grandfather clock chimed that it was now five-thirty. The place was immaculate and so . . . old. Jessica marveled at the furnishings. It looked like she had just stepped into a Norman Rockwell painting.

A male voice yelled out from the kitchen. "Charlie? That you?"

"Yeah, I'm home, Pa-pa," she yelled back. "Just getting cleaned up. We'll be down in a few."

Across the dining room, where slender candles burned and a setting for four adorned the table, the kitchen door opened and a tall, fortyish man wearing crisp black pants and a white shirt smiled at them. His sleeves were rolled up and there was a dishcloth in his hand. "Rebecca?"

Charlie pulled her toward the stairs. "Yep. Just finish up. We'll be down in a minute."

Jessica leaned toward Charlie. "Who's Rebecca?"

"It's you, of course. Now come on. I'm hungry."

The bedroom took up one end of the upstairs, two expansive Persian rugs covering most of the floor. Parked on each one was a full-sized canopy bed, draped in silky, gauze curtains. An ornate, gold-inlaid chest pushed up against the foot of each. Tiffany lamps gave off a diffused glow from the nightstand of each bed. A faint scent of lavender suffused the air.

"Holy shit," Jessica said. "Is this really your room?"

Charlie walked over to a walk-in closet, disappearing inside. "Duh. But it's our room now. Your bed is on the left." She came out a moment later, a floor-length, deep blue dress in her hand. "Bathroom is at the end of the hall. Wash up and then change."

Jessica stifled a laugh. "Into that? But it's so . . ."

"What?" Charlie brought it over and tossed it on her new bed and then stepped up to Jessica, her face inches away. "Old? Is that what you were going to fucking say?"

The depthless eyes intensified, freezing Jessica in place. "N-no, not that. I'm sorry, Charlie. It's just not the kind of thing I usually—"

"It's Rebecca's," she snapped back. "It's yours. You are Rebecca now."

Jessica swallowed and nodded. "OK. That's cool. Is it because—"

Charlie grabbed her arms and walked her over to the bed. Jessica's toes barely brushed the floor. "Ow! Fuck, Charlie. That hurt."

The slap came out of nowhere, snapping Jessica's head sideways, which then was forcefully pulled back by Charlie's hand gripping her jaw. "You don't talk like that, not ever!" The twisted mouth abruptly softened. "Rebecca is a good girl. She doesn't talk like that. Got it?"

Jessica whispered, blinking away the tears, "Got it."

Charlie let go of her chin and sat down next to Jessica on the bed. "You are Rebecca while you're here. No more Jessica. You"—she smiled, leaning over to kiss her on the cheek—"are my sister now." Charlie reached into her pocket and pulled out the switchblade Jessica remembered from earlier in the day when Charlie threatened to castrate Petey if he mouthed off any more. The blade flipped open.

Jessica stared at the keen, shining blade. "What's that for?"

Charlie held out her other hand and drew the tip of it across her palm. A thin, dark line of blood oozed out. "Blood," she said. "We're sisters now, you and me. Now and forever, I swear upon this oath in blood."

"What do you mean?" Jessica stared in lurid fascination at the trickle of blood slipping down Charlie's wrist.

"Give me your hand." When Jessica hesitated, Charlie heaved a sigh. "Do I have to ask again?"

This was crazy. Jessica could not believe she was going to do it. She held out her hand. "Like blood sisters or something?" Charlie took her hand, the point of the blade pushing at the skin. Jessica wanted to watch, but could not pull her gaze away from Charlie's. Her hand seemed so far away.

Charlie's face softened. "Exactly. My sister, my blood."

Jessica felt the knife score her palm but could feel nothing. "You really want me to be your sister?" Their palms pressed together and Jessica gasped at the rush of tingling heat that washed through her, much like that moment when Charlie had first touched her, only this time it went right to places she had not expected it to go.

"Now and forever," Charlie whispered. "Our blood is one." She squeezed and Jessica felt a cold chill brush across her face. "Say it, Becca."

Her voice struggled up out of her throat, hollow and distant. "Now and forever. Our blood is one."

Charlie grinned and lifted Jessica's blood-smeared palm between them. "We'll be together. Always."

Jessica returned the smile. She was perfect. How could she feel so well suited to this girl? It was fate. It had to be. Then, Charlie's tongue brushed the skin of her hand, the lightest, feathery touch that traced its way across her palm. Jessica closed her eyes. It should not have felt so good. It made no sense, but nothing had ever felt so right as this. Charlie was her sister, now and forever.

When Jessica opened her eyes, the wound upon her palm was barely a pink line, and her skin shone white with a glistening sheen.

Chapter 1

Jackie walked back to the kitchen area of the new Special Investigations office to make herself yet another espresso, the third one in two hours. What else was there to do? Cynthia had everything in perfect order. She had spent the entire previous day nodding in agreement to every suggestion Cynthia made about setting up the office. It was a showroom office straight out of *Architectural Digest*, and Jackie wasn't even sure how to operate half the shit around her. All funded, of course, by everyone's favorite millionaire vampire, Nick Anderson.

Worst of all, they weren't actually doing anything yet. Her former FBI boss, Belgerman was having the "special flagged" cases sent over at some point during the day. Cynthia had offered to train her on the needed software programs, but the last thing Jackie wanted was to start her first full day on the job as the head of Special Investigations with lessons in just how underqualified she was to do it. She could not even handle sitting in her own office.

In a matter of days after being forced out of her FBI position thanks to her involvement in the death of a Chicago detective, Jackie had gone from a cubicle with barely enough room to turn around in to a three-hundred-square-foot cavern with its own bar and big screen television. Nick had even had them put in a floor-to-ceiling corkboard along one section of wall to mount her case info upon. The space completely overwhelmed. She felt like a child invading her parent's private space.

"Agent McManus!" Cynthia's voice rang throughout the office.

Thank, God! Jackie made her way toward the front, around the dividing wall to where Cynthia's grand, curving slab of mahogany greeted all who entered.

"Ms. Forrester," McManus said, with a more-than-friendly smile. "How are you today?"

He leaned against a dolly stacked four high with file boxes. Jackie's greeting froze upon her lips. "Shit, McManus. Tell me those aren't all full of files."

Laurel's voice interrupted her shock. *Look at that! I can't wait to see what's in there.*

"Nobody asked you," Jackie muttered.

McManus stood up straight. "What?"

"Nothing," Jackie said. She needed more practice at the whole notion of keeping internal and external conversations separate. It was getting really old.

"You talking to Agent Carpenter?" When Jackie rolled her eyes, McManus grinned and waved at Jackie. "Hey, Agent Carpenter. How are things going, um, in there?"

I'm good, thanks.

Jackie sighed. She really did not want to be the go-between while Laurel was riding around in her head. "Just quit, OK? It's too damn weird. How many files did you pack up?"

He shrugged. "Going by weight, I'd guess a few hundred at least."

"Lovely," Jackie said. *How many hours would it take to sort through all of that crap?*

Days. We'll need to build a database. Laurel was clearly far more excited by the prospect than Jackie.

"Just put them over there against the wall, Agent Mc-

Manus," Cynthia said and pointed. "We'll figure out where we want them later."

At that moment the door opened again, and in walked Nick, carrying a cardboard box with an Annabelle's Coffee Shop label emblazoned upon it. Shelby was on his heels. At least there would be pastries.

"Morning, everyone," Nick said. "I bear gifts. Agent McManus. Good to see you again." He set the box down on Cynthia's desk. "Help yourself if you like. Looks like we've finally got something to work on around here."

"*Pffft!*" Cynthia huffed, and opened the box. "Speak for yourself, cowboy. I've been busting ass all week long getting things ready for you guys."

Nick reached in after Cynthia and looked at Jackie. "Croissant?" The chocolate-filled pastry was offered before she had a chance to reply.

She wanted to turn it down for stubbornness' sake, but her stomach was rumbling. "Thanks."

"Take a breath, Jack," Shelby said, her softly glowing eyes twinkling with amusement. "This'll be fun. Aren't you at all interested in seeing what kind of craziness we'll find in those boxes?"

Through a mouthful of croissant, Jackie replied, "Do I have to answer that?"

Shelby walked by and patted her on the shoulder. "Relax, babe. This is where the real work begins." She held the bear claw in her mouth and picked up a box, heading around toward the back.

"Agent McManus? You're welcome to stay," Nick said.

"Much as I'd prefer the company, I've got to head uptown to meet with some gang taskforce people." He stared at Cynthia as he spoke. "You all have fun, and try not to work too hard. This place looks real rough."

"It's pure hell," Cynthia answered with a soft laugh.

McManus backed toward the door. "Good to see you all

again. Good luck with this stuff, Jack. Let me know what you come up with."

Jackie waved while she washed down her croissant. When the door closed, she eyed Cynthia. "Pretty sure he likes you."

"He's easy on the eyes, that's for sure," she said.

Shelby's voice rang from the back. "Ask him out for fuck's sake, Cyn. He was practically drooling on you."

Cynthia shrugged. "We'll see. I can wait."

"Waiting's for losers," Shelby yelled back.

Jackie turned away and walked back to find Shelby before either of them noticed the capital *L* glowing on her forehead. She had put Nick on hold for nearly a month now. Things had felt so great in those moments after their date, playing that magnificent organ at the Rockefeller Chapel. And then?

Yeah, and then what? Laurel wondered along with her. *You're going to lose him you keep this up, girl.*

Shut up, Laur. Nobody asked you.

Hey! Not my fault you keep forgetting to block me out. And don't get snippy. You know it's true. Unless you want to lose him, of course.

No! I don't want to lose . . . Jackie sighed. *Forget it. Can we not talk about this now? I'd rather bury myself in a bazillion weirdo cold-case files, thank-you-very-much.*

Oh, me too! This is going to be too cool.

Jackie bit off her response and stepped into their conference room, with its football-field-size table, where Shelby was already digging into the file box. Cynthia and Nick were close behind, donuts in hand.

She stared at the stacks of manila folders Shelby was heaping onto the table. "OK, so what have we got here?"

"Filed by date," Shelby said. "This box goes back to 2000."

Jackie picked up the folder from the nearest stack. "Which means we probably have thirty to forty years' worth of this shit to sift through." The first sheet of paper inside was a form, indicating nothing more than a phone conversation. "A Ms. Rose Shumway believes her next-door neighbor is a vampire and disposing of his victims in the weekly garbage. Local authorities contacted. No further information." Jackie turned the page over, and then checked the next sheet to make sure there was no continuation. "What the fuck? That's it? We get forty years of this?"

Nick grabbed a handful of folders and set the donuts down on the table. "I'm sure it's not all as bad as that. We'll find something, I'm sure."

Shelby waved her file at Jackie. "Bitch, bitch, bitch. Get up in the wrong bed this morning?"

"You know what?" Jackie's jaw clenched. God, she could be an ass. Shelby stared back, eyes wide with anticipation. It was not a fight Jackie would win. Ever. "Just read your fucking files. Find something useful."

Shelby grinned. "Ooo! She's being all bossy. I likey."

Jackie's hands gripped the file so tight they began to shake.

Let it go, hon, Laurel said with calm assurance. *She's just picking on you.*

"I'm fine," she mumbled and grabbed a stack of files. "I'll be in my office if you find something." She stormed out without waiting for a response.

Five minutes after slamming her office door closed and tossing the files across her desk, Jackie was kicked back in her chair with her eyes closed. First real day on the job and she was already getting a headache.

Someone knocked quietly on the door. "Jackie?" It was Nick, ready to tell her to relax, no doubt.

She wanted to ignore him. A pep talk was the last thing she needed.

Yes, you do. Let him in. Laurel's motherly tone was both kind and stern.

"You know what?" Jackie snapped. "Why don't you go bother someone else?

A sigh whispered through Jackie's head and Laurel stepped out of her body. Laurel gave her a sideways glance, walked out through the wall toward the conference room and was gone.

"All right, then," Nick said.

"No." Jackie groaned and sat back up. "Come in, damn it." Nick opened the door and entered the office. "I wasn't talking to you."

He walked up and placed his stack of files down on her desk. On top was another chocolate croissant. He sat down in one of the plush chairs across from her. "Sorry about Shelby there. She was just being—"

"A bitch?" Jackie cut in. "But no more than usual. Everything's getting on my nerves today, that's all."

"Anything I can do? Something else you need here to make things—"

"No! God, no. More than enough, Nick. Really. This is all kind of overwhelming. I mean look at this place." She waved her hand at the office space. "You'd think I was the CEO of Chrysler or something."

"Any reason we can't have the best for this? I mean, I could have them come back and set up a cubicle for you."

The slight twitch of smile, stretching the long scar along his jaw, dissipated Jackie's annoyance. "Don't get me wrong. This is an amazing space. I just feel . . ." She picked up the other croissant and took a bite. "I feel like I'm out of my element. This isn't me."

"Then make it yours," he said. "You do have a say, you know. You're the director of this operation."

Jackie sagged back in her chair. "Yeah. I know. Wish I knew what the hell that meant."

"It means what you make of it, Jackie. We're a team

here, at least I hope we are, but as director, you get final say on things."

Final say. What they did, what these powerful, nerve-wracking people did was on her shoulders. "You do realize how weird it is having me order you guys around?"

He shrugged. "Not really. You're more than smart and capable enough to do it."

Jackie sighed and sagged back in her chair. He didn't get it. "Thanks, but I have no idea what I'm doing. You guys are far more expert on this stuff than I am."

"Then we'll be the experts. Look, Jackie." He leaned forward, elbows resting on his knees. "I think you're right for this job because, one, you're a leader. You know how to take the reins on something and lead it where it needs to go. Even when you don't know, you have great instincts. Two, you have the guts to make hard choices when they need to be made. You won't back down when shit hits the fan. Trust me, you'll be fine. Give it some time."

She avoided his gaze. Her "guts" turned to mush if she did that for long. "You must have a lot of time on your hands then." When his smile broadened, Jackie laughed. "Fuck. You know what I mean. Right now, I don't think I could decide my way out of a paper bag."

Nick sat back. "OK, I have something easy for you to decide on then."

"What?"

"Thanksgiving," he said. "What do you want for Thanksgiving dinner?"

Thanksgiving? Shit, that was in two days. The previous eight years had been with Laurel's parents, which was kind of out of the question now. She had not given a single thought to it this year. "I hadn't really planned on doing much."

"You don't have to do anything," he replied. "All I need are your preferences. Turkey and stuffing? Ham? Rack of lamb?"

"So, I'm coming over for Thanksgiving dinner?"

"You had other plans?"

"Well, no, not really," she said. "It's just . . ." It sounded great and potentially intimate, which cranked down the screws on her stomach. "I guess I'm coming over. Do I need to bring anything?"

"No. Just your appetite. Cyn and Shel are coming. We usually do Thanksgiving together. I only need to know what you'd like."

The paranormal freak-show Thanksgiving. What could be better? At least there would be other people. "Is it possible for you to cook something I won't like?"

"I could try," he said. "Maybe bull's testicles or something."

Jackie snorted. "You've actually had those?"

"Among other things. Not my preferred body part, I'll admit."

And there it was again. Normal conversation turned disturbing because the guy drank blood to stay alive. She caught his gaze, wondering if he noticed the look on her face, and Jackie realized his reference may have had nothing to do with food. "Great. Surprise me then. You know I'll eat anything you cook. Think I'm ready to dig into these files now. How about you?"

Nick picked up a file from his stack, doing little to conceal the smirk on his face. "You're the boss."

After six hours, Jackie picked at a box of Chinese takeout, her eyes glazing over with weariness and frustration. The conference room table had been papered from one end to the other, stacks of notes and forms piled up by year. Some were far bigger than others, but they had potential cases going back to 1971. Many were ridiculous notes like Ms. Shumway's, certain to be nothing, but others had a definite creep value that made Jackie wonder. Everyone had pulled aside those they thought might hold some kind of value. There were dozens, perhaps over a hundred. Jackie gave it her best unfocused stare and continued to eat her shrimp-fried rice.

Shelby plopped the rest of pot sticker in her mouth. "So. Any ideas on how you want to sort through those, Jackie?"

"No. How about a random number?"

"I saw a few interesting ones," Cynthia added.

Shelby reached up and pulled one out of the middle of the stack, floating it across the table toward her. Jackie watched it drift to the floor. "Well, that's one down. Any other ideas, anyone?"

Nick sipped on a beer, his booted feet crossed up on the end of the table. "It would make sense to either start with the most recent or ones that are closest to us."

"I think we should go through this stack of good ones and rank them from most to least likely to be legitimate paranormal incidents," Cynthia said.

Jackie nodded. Cynthia, ever the practical one, was probably right. Jackie leaned over and picked up the sheaf of paper from the floor. It was one she had come across during the blur of afternoon reading. Unlike all of the other ones she had read, this one had actually come from a former FBI agent. The note was handwritten, dated August 12, 1993. It stated, rather simply:

Thatcher's Mill. I was travelling to Chicago for a workshop when I drove through this little, rustic town just south of Dubuque. This place had more ghosts in it than I've ever felt before, by a factor of ten to one. Remarkable and completely unnerving. Will have to investigate this if opportunity arises or we ever decide to look into paranormal events.

FBI Agent. If they were going to get any kind of reliable source material, what could be better than a fellow agent? "Laur?" Laurel, who now walked freely around the room, moved over from the corner behind Shelby. "What do you make of this one? You recognize the name?"

Laurel took a moment to read the note. "No, but we should contact her. I know there are other agents with abilities. It's just not common knowledge."

Jackie slapped the paper down on the table. That was good enough for her. "There we go. Thatcher's Mill. It's full of ghosts. Should be great fun."

Shelby threw her arms up in the air. "The boss has spoken!"

"Shelby?"

She grinned at Jackie. "Yes, babe?"

"Bite my ass."

"Now you're getting the hang of it."

Chapter 2

Jackie tousled and fluffed her hair for the umpteenth time. No matter how hard she tried, the scar along the side of her head remained visible to some degree. The short, ruffled, auburn hair just was not long enough yet. A month after Rosa had nearly killed her, and short of wearing a damn baseball hat, she could do nothing to disguise the hideous pink ribbon of flesh that ran above her left ear. As if she wasn't scarred enough on the inside.

And what did it matter anyway? Jackie gave herself the finger in her bathroom mirror and marched back out into the living room. The phone was ringing. She rolled her eyes at the familiar number on Caller ID.

"What's up, Shelby?"

"Hey, babe. You want me to pick you up? I'm heading out to Nick's in about an hour. You're practically on the way."

Jackie absently rubbed at her scalp. "Nah, you go ahead. Not sure I'm going."

"What? The fuck you aren't," Shelby said, snapping in Jackie's ear.

"My head's killing me." Which was not a lie in a round-about sort of way. "And I just got up, so I won't be ready—"

"Oh, bullshit! When have you ever taken more than five minutes to get ready for anything? Take some damn Tylenol and quit being a chicken shit. It'll be fun, and Nick's holiday meals will make your panties wet."

Jackie cringed at the thought. Walking around Nick's with wet panties was the last thing she needed to be doing. Nothing on her end would be inspiring such reactions from Mr. I'm-a-bazillionaire-who-does-everything-like-a-rock-star. Hell, she couldn't even make herself look like a semi-attractive, non-brain-damaged woman.

"I'm not being a chicken shit," she said. "I'm just not up for it right now."

"Babe, you can't even lie good over the phone. What's the damn problem? This is the first holiday in ages that I've seen Nick actually excited to have. He wants you there."

And that fact still, after nearly two months, made no sense to her. What the hell did he see in a clearly washed-up, drunken, mutilated, bitch of an FBI agent? It was stupid. Clearly he was just desperate, having been without anyone for so long. She was just the first woman handy. Now that he was no longer consumed by Drake, who had slaughtered his family and tormented him for a century, the entire world was open to him. Nick Anderson had his choice of women, who were all quite obviously more put together than she was.

"He just wants somebody there, Shelby. It could be me or any other woman," she said. "He's just happy things are over and he can get his life back."

Shelby huffed. "I'll be there in an hour. Laur can help you pick something out. Fight me on this and I'll make you even more miserable."

"Shel—" the phone clicked off in her ear. "Fuck."

The cold whisper of Deadworld blew through her, and Jackie involuntarily shivered as Laurel came knocking. She turned toward the feeling of death that crept across her skin anytime a ghost was around and saw Laurel's transparent, washed-out figure standing before her. The folded arms and roll of her eyes said it all.

"You can't bail on this, hon," she said and eased down

the short hall toward the bedroom. "Come on. I'll help you pick out something suitable to wear."

"I'm not dressing up for this, Laur."

"You aren't going to," she hollered from the bedroom. "I said suitable, not dress up."

Jackie groaned and trudged after her. It did not matter one iota what she wore. The result would end up being the same. Upon entering her bedroom, she picked up a half-empty wine glass on the dresser and drained the rest of its contents. It was going to be a long day.

After donning the gray, knee-length skirt and navy-blue, silk blouse, minus a bra at Laurel's insistence, Jackie found herself once again staring at her disfigured head in the mirror. On the counter was the makeup case Laurel had bought for her some Christmas or birthday in the distant past, most of the items still in their plastic wrap.

"No amount of lipstick is going to cover up this gaping hole on the side of my head," Jackie said.

"Your hair is fine," Laurel replied, sitting on the toilet seat beside the counter, looking over the color choices in the case. "You want Nick to see the scar."

"What? It's fucking hideous! I look like an escapee from a mental hospital."

"It's a reminder that you almost died, and the fact Nick almost did too in saving you. Life is precious. Make the most of it, hon."

"So, we're being sneaky and toying with his mind." Jackie picked up the lipstick Laurel's finger was poking in and out of. "Plum Brulé? Really?"

"Dark and luxuriant," Laurel said. "Very kissable color, and of course we're being sneaky. What kind of question is that?"

"God. What are you, sixteen?" Jackie turned up the lipstick dial and stared reluctantly at the dark red cone of lipstick.

"Shut up." Laurel swiped at Jackie, her hand passing

through Jackie's bicep. "I never got to do anything like this with you before."

"I hate cosmetics, you know—"

"A date, you idiot."

"This isn't a date! It's fucking Thanksgiving dinner." She waved the lipstick at Laurel. "Did Shelby say anything to Nick? Is there some plan going on here that I should know about?"

Laurel laughed. "Nothing so sinister as that. Would you relax, please? Put on your lipstick." She got up and walked behind Jackie. "Just, you know, after we leave, you might have . . . an opportunity with Nick."

Jackie pulled the lipstick away from her mouth before the snort of laughter made her draw a line across her face. "Opportunity? I'm leaving when you guys do. Don't get your hopes up." She leaned back toward the mirror and began to apply the lipstick again, focusing hard on keeping her hand still. They were going to leave her alone with Nick? How could something be both compelling and utterly terrifying at the same time?

The silence lasted so long Jackie finally glanced at Laurel's reflection in the mirror, whose mouth had creased into a thin, annoyed line. "What?"

"Why can't you give yourself a chance?"

"I'm going, aren't I?"

"Hon? Don't be a shit. You know what I mean."

She stuffed the lipstick back into the cap. Her mouth now looked like an autonomous creature, completely beyond her control. *Kissable, my ass.* "You do realize that the only reason he has any interest in me is because we nearly died together. It's that whole . . . whatever the hell it's called, hero complex or something." She slammed the lipstick back into its case. "He doesn't actually want me. It's just the idea of me he likes."

Laurel stepped up close behind Jackie, her hands reaching out, ready to embrace and then let them fall back to her sides. "Then show him the idea is worth the reality. I happen to know the real you, hon. You're worth the effort."

"Bullshit." Jackie threw up her hands and turned away, walking out toward the bedroom to find her shoes. "And you don't count. You . . . um . . . you just don't count."

She followed Jackie, moving until she stood directly through Jackie as she leaned down into the closet. "Why, because I'm a girl?"

Jackie yanked her shoes up through Laurel's legs, stepped over to the bed and sat down. "No! Of course not." She shoved one foot into the low-heeled, black-and blue-trimmed leather pumps. Jackie could not even recall when she had worn them last. "You've been with me practically every day for over eight years, Laur. You know what a pain in the fucking ass I can be. Let's face it, I'm not the easiest person to be around."

"But I fell in love with you anyway," Laurel said, voice softening.

"And couldn't tell me because you knew I'd totally freak out." Jackie slipped on the other shoe and stomped back out to the living room. She could not handle looking at Laurel while talking about this.

Laurel followed on her heels. "That's not the only reason. Look." Jackie was picking up her jacket off the top of her piano when she felt the icy chill of Laurel's hand dragging through her shoulder. "Look at me, Jackie."

She closed her eyes and took a deep breath before turning around. "What, Laur? Let's face it. I'm pretty much a walking fuck-up, and—"

"No!" The ghostly finger poked through Jackie's ribs. "You've had fucked-up things happen to you. That doesn't make you a fuck-up. So stop that, right now. Sweet Mother of us all, you're frustrating."

Jackie nodded. "See? Point proven. And let's face it. Nick isn't going to last eight years trying to find the soft, pretty spot on the inside."

"Not if you don't drop your prickly little walls for more than two seconds."

She shrugged into her jacket, pulling it snug with a huff. "Won't matter. You know he'll take one deep look with those weird, glowy eyes, and see nothing that he wants."

"Oh, bullshit," Laurel said. "He's already seen you at your worst, and what do you know! He's still around."

There was a chime on Jackie's doorbell. "Damn it. Shel's early." She walked over to the door and buzzed Shelby in before turning back to Laurel. "Seeing it and experiencing it are totally different things."

Laurel was silent for a moment. The sound of Shelby's muffled voice could be heard singing outside the door. "This is all about sleeping with him, isn't it? You're afraid you'll flip out on him."

The door swung open and Shelby bounced into the living room. "Happy Thanksgiving, girls! We ready to . . . OK, now what?"

Jackie gave Laurel a stern look. "Nothing. Let's go." She grabbed her keys off of the entry table and made for the door. The last thing she wanted to get into was a discussion about sex with Nick or the breakdown after Laurel had died or, God forbid, both. Because, truth be told, Laurel had hit it square on the head. Any pleasurable thoughts about sliding beneath the sheets with Nick morphed into a bloody, freak-out disaster, and once that happened, he would be long gone.

Out on the stairs leading down to the street, Laurel quietly stepped into her body. "You're worrying too much, hon. That won't ever happen again."

"Not discussing it, Laur," she whispered. "And keep Shel out of it."

"What was that, babe?" Shelby chimed in from directly behind.

Jackie's heart skipped a beat. The woman walked on air.

Jackie forced a smile onto her face. "Nothing. Just looking forward to good food and good beer."

Shelby brushed by and opened the door leading out, giving Jackie a fleeting kiss on the cheek as she passed. "You'll have to come over one of these days so I can teach you how to properly lie. You really are terrible at it."

Jackie made sure to bump her going out, but refused to look into those smiling, bottomless eyes. "Up yours."

Chapter 3

Charlie opened the door to the Thatcher's Mill Police Department and wrinkled her nose. Why did the place always smell like a cat had pissed in the corner somewhere? The open entry room of the small brick building two blocks off of Main Street held several wooden chairs and a long, narrow bench, upon which sat the gray, dim form of Rebecca. Charlie stepped over to her, a wistful smile forming on her lips and reached out to brush her hand over the girl's hair. The wide, staring eyes closed for a moment when she did. The price one paid when asking the law for help.

"Ms. Thatcher!" Elinore, the tawny-haired receptionist, said. "What a pleasant surprise. I wasn't expecting you." Crumbs from the holiday cornbread leftovers in her hand crusted the corners of her mouth.

"Are you ever, Eli?" Charlie said, rolling her eyes. "I need a word with Elton. See that nobody disturbs us."

"Of course, Ms. Thatcher."

Charlie marched through the reception area, or rather around the reception desk, and stepped into Elton Carson's office. She waved at the cigarette smoke that hung like fog in the air. "Damn it, Elton. I thought I said to keep the fucking cigarettes out of your office. I hate that shit."

He hastily brought his feet down off of his desk and

stubbed out the butt in the already full ashtray. "Sorry, Ms. Thatcher. Old habits." He smiled, wiping his hand across the strands of hair still left on his head. "What brings you to the office today? I wasn't expecting you until our usual meet."

"I've heard by more than one person that Rachel Crenshaw is moving up to Dubuque to live with her boyfriend." Charlie stepped forward and placed her hands on the edge of his desk. "Can you substantiate that rumor?"

Carson shrugged. "Could be, I guess. That college boyfriend of hers has been down here more than a few times to visit, if you know what I'm saying."

"So, she's fucking a visitor," Charlie said. That always produced problems, without fail.

The police chief licked his upper lip, dragging the tip of his tongue across the pencil thin smear of mustache. "It would appear so, Ms.—"

Charlie's hand flicked out with hummingbird speed, her delicate hand flicking the disgusting tongue before it could be pulled back into his mouth.

"Ow!" He dabbed at his tongue with the back of his hand, checking for blood. "Christ, Charlie. What was that for?"

"For being a lecherous shit," she said. The man was far more foul than his father. At least he had given due respect for the law and was tolerable to look at. His son was a snake, living in the dank, dark world of rocks better left unturned. Carson's son was thirteen now, and looked to be far more like his grandfather.

"But I wasn't . . ." He sighed and averted his gaze from hers. "Sorry, Ms. Thatcher. It won't happen again."

She laughed at that. "Of course it will, Elton. God, at least have the balls to admit your lust for me. Your embarrassment only pisses me off."

"Sorry. Really. I don't mean—"

Charlie jumped over the desk, a deft gymnastic maneuver, vaulting and landing beside him. The switchblade was in her hand before her feet had hit the ground. She pressed it to his throat, grabbing his chin with the other hand to force him to face her. "Can you deal with the college boy? I don't want him around here anymore."

He nodded. "Of course."

She pushed away from him, the blade scoring the soft flesh of his neck enough to draw blood. Several red tears of blood welled up from the split in the skin. "Show me you're an adequate lawman, Elton. Perhaps I'll include a bonus in your paycheck."

Carson gulped and managed a feeble laugh. "Don't really want your money, Charlie."

Charlie grinned back. "See? Nice and direct and honest." She reached down and wiped the blood up with a finger, bringing it up to her lips and sucking it clean with deliberate slowness. "Take care of that boy."

"Consider it done," he said and pulled a handkerchief from his pocket.

Charlie stopped him and traced her finger back across his neck once again, sealing the wound up as she went. She smiled at Carson as his eyes fluttered shut and then slapped him hard once across the face. "Next time I come in here and you're smoking, you're going to be eating those fucking things. Got it?"

He rubbed gingerly at his cheek. "Yeah, damn it. I got it."

"Good." Charlie spun on her heel and walked out, annoyance gradually turning to excitement. It was time to give Becca the present she had had made for her.

Up the hill at her house, Charlie clomped down the stairs into the basement, where Becca was helping Ma-ma wash the week's clothes. The stench of soap and bleach was strong in the air. Ma-ma was pinning clothes up on the lines back by the trap doors, which were open, letting the cold November air clear the room. Becca ran a dark, sudsy piece of cloth over the washboard and dunked it into the tub of soapy water.

"Sis! I thought you were going to be gone until afternoon." She smiled and waved her fingers at her.

Charlie returned the smile. The charm was finally starting to hold. The girl was more resilient than most, which boded well for when the time came to try. She had to be tough, but more importantly, she had to believe and she had to love. Charlie walked over to Becca and kissed her on the cheek.

"You guys are almost done. I didn't think you'd finish before lunch time."

Ma-ma walked over and squeezed Becca's shoulder. "Your sister knows how to work up a storm. Make sure you get some lotion on those hands, sweetie. That bleach will do the devil's work on your skin."

Charlie looked up at her mother. "Turkey leftover sandwiches for lunch, Ma-ma. Twenty minutes."

"Of course, dear. Just the way you like them."

Rebecca fed the garment through the roller to squeeze out the water and then handed it over. "Here, Ma-ma."

When she reached to grab the next article of clothing from the basket, Charlie grabbed her hand. It was still wet, but she could feel the dry skin forming on the knuckles. "Ma-ma's right. That bleach is trashing your hands." She brought it up to her mouth, pressing her lips to the base knuckle of the index finger. When she pulled it away, the skin was smooth and untarnished. Becca stared up at her with wide eyes. "Come on," she said. "You can finish up after lunch. I have something for you."

Rebecca beamed. "Really? What is it?

Charlie took her hand and pulled Rebecca to her feet. "Come on. I just know you'll love it."

They hurried up the stairs, hand in hand, through the kitchen filled with the smell of freshly baked bread where Charlie grabbed her travel satchel, and then up the stairs again to their bedroom. They sat down on the impeccably made bed, with its Victorian lace pillows and hand-crocheted blankets, where Rebecca fidgeted with excitement.

She folded her legs up cross-legged on the bed, bouncing with anticipation. "What is it, Charlie?

From out of the satchel, Charlie withdrew a paper-wrapped package, tied in a bow with a piece of twine. She slapped at Rebecca's crossed legs. "Put your legs down. Ladies do not sit like that."

She immediately unfolded them and let her feet dangle toward the floor. "Oh, of course. Sorry." Rebecca stared at the package in Charlie's lap. "Open it, already!" She giggled. "This is so exciting."

Charlie smiled. It was just like it had been, that sunny fall day in 1896, when her father had brought home a similar package, wrapped in paper and twine, and both of them had sat in nervous anticipation on the living room sofa, watching him undo the twine and pull the secret surprise from the paper. Only it had not been much of a surprise at that point, having become something of an annual, family tradition.

The twine sprang loose from its tightly wound bow and Charlie pulled it off, carefully unfolding the paper to reveal the tissue-wrapped contents. It was a polished wooden box, about half the size of an ordinary shoebox, delicately inlaid and hand-painted on top with a scene of two young girls running through a meadow, carefree and hand in hand.

"Oh, Charlie! It's so pretty. What is it?"

She lifted the lid, the hinges inside bringing up the painted porcelain figurine of the two girls from the painting, posed together in a dance. Charlie reached down and turned the delicate, golden key on the side, winding up the music box to play.

"It's us," she said. "Old Man Wilkens makes them. He's a woodworker, and quite good actually. His papa taught him all he knows, and he was the best in the world." Classical music chimed away as the two figures turned in unison, and Charlie handed it to Rebecca. "Here. You can add it to our collection."

Rebecca gingerly took the box into her lap. "Our collection?" She stared lovingly at the gift, uncomprehending for a moment, but then her eyes widened with realization and she looked across the room at the mahogany curios cabinet in the corner, the glass shelves inside filled with similar boxes. "Oh! We collect them." She nodded as if in complete understanding. "Of course. How wonderful. Charlie, it's beautiful. Thank you." Her arms reached out and embraced Charlie, squeezing her tightly. "I love you so much."

Charlie closed her eyes and breathed in the sweet scent of her hair. Yes, things were all coming together so well. It was all so perfect, like it had once been and would be again. "I love you, too, Becca." She pulled back and kissed Rebecca, taking the blade from her pocket and grasping her hand. "Sisters forever and always?"

Rebecca stared lovingly at Charlie. Her smile could not get any bigger. "Forever and always, Sis." She turned her palm over in Charlie's hand, offering it to her without thought.

The blade delicately scored Rebecca's palm and Charlie brought it to her mouth, sucking at the blood that welled forth. She could taste the love in that energy that filled her, and a part of her wanted to keep drinking until the last of that feeling filled every part of her and every last drop of blood was gone.

Then the cold touch of the dead brushed across her. Charlie traced her tongue over the wound, sealing the skin, and dropped Rebecca's hand. Someone was approaching. Someone strong with the energy of the dead, a feeling she had not felt in over a hundred years.

"Charlie?" Rebecca's smile faded. "What's the matter?"

Her stomach knotted in panic, and Charlie leaped to her feet. "I just remembered something. I need to go."

She groaned. "Oh, but why?"

"Stay here!" She took Rebecca's face in her hands, eyes aglow with power. "Do not leave the house or even open the door until I get back."

She nodded. "OK. What's wrong, Charlie?"

"Nothing. Just stay in the house and do not answer the door if anyone comes."

Charlie bolted out the door and down the stairs. "Pa-pa! Ma-ma! Come here now."

A vampire was coming and she needed to leave.

Chapter 4

Feeling good. I'm feeling good. This is going OK, I think. And while a part of her truly was enjoying the moment, savoring Nick's arm draped across the back of the couch, her head cradled into the crook of his elbow, the butterflies in Jackie's stomach danced to a different tune, ignoring the Falcons–Colts game on the television, and the casual banter that went with it. They wanted to know what was going to happen when everyone decided to leave. *Are you staying or going? You going to spend the night with Nick or be a coward chicken-shit again and bail?*

Jackie's brain could not let go of the doubt or steer itself clear of all the paranoid pathways the evening might take. Every thought of his hands roaming her body or her legs wrapped around his waist came plagued with visions of drunken breakdowns or worse, just being plain lousy in bed.

At thirty-two, she had been with more than her fair share of men, but she could remember almost none of them or, more importantly, what she had done. Her sex life consisted of a sixteen-year-long string of drunken, one-night stands. Jackie had no clear idea of what sober, clear-headed sex might be like, and the thought terrified her. And then there was Nick.

What would he expect? What would he want from her?

He had witnessed the end of her meltdown and probably had a pretty good idea of what had been going on there. Was he into that kind of thing? Was she? Jackie could not remember if and what she had liked. Would Nick want a taste of her blood? Was sex tied up in all of that with him?

The questions turned and squirmed in Jackie's gut, refusing to let her be. This not knowing, not being able to grasp onto anything solid was surely going to kill her. Of course, she could just ask him, but . . . yeah. No.

"Coffee, babe?"

Shelby's hand brushed across her shoulder and Jackie startled against Nick. "I don't know! Wait. What?"

Shelby laughed. "Coffee. Do you want another coffee? I'll make you one before Cyn and I head out if you want."

Head out? "You guys are leaving already?" She glanced over at the television, which was now showing the postgame show. *It's over? How'd that happen so fast? It was halftime just a minute ago.*

"Babe, it's after eleven," Shelby said, patting Jackie's shoulder. "I've got Black Friday sales to hit up in the morning, and Cyn is going with me, isn't that right, hon?"

"Wouldn't miss it," she replied over her shoulder as she headed toward the kitchen. "You can come with, if you want, Jackie." Her smile was flip. "We're hitting up Kohl's at four AM."

"That sounds . . ."

Nick casually watched her out of the corner of his eye. Laurel stared at her from the other couch, eyebrows raised. The butterflies in her stomach chanted in unison. *Get out now! Run, girl! Run!* "That sounds like a nightmare. Think I'll pass."

Shelby's grin widened. "That's what I thought you'd say."

Yeah, well I sure didn't. Guess I'm staying with you tonight, Nick. How's that sound? Nick gave her one of his faint half-smiles, stretching the scar along his jaw line, and she looked away. *I wasn't implying anything.* Another part of her, swimming furiously against the onrushing current of paranoia and fear, wholeheartedly disagreed. At the moment, it was not faring so well, and Laurel's reassuring smile provided no extra boost of confidence.

Nick stood up, pushing to his feet, and Jackie felt the cool, vacuous absence of the arm that had been draped behind her head. A shiver went down her spine. The cavalry was riding off into the sunset without her. No hope of rescue after this point. They were not coming back for her. There would be no Laurel to save her from herself on this. She watched Shelby pour a shot of Kahlua into her coffee, and wished that it was the other way around.

Jackie got up to say good-bye to them, and Shelby whispered in her ear when she hugged her. "You're safe here."

Laurel passed through her, pausing briefly. *You want me to stay?*

Yes! But you can't. I can do this. I want to. I need to, Laur.

There was a reassuring surge of warmth that enveloped Jackie. *I know, hon. And please, just try to relax. This is supposed to be enjoyable.*

I know, I know. I'm trying. Just hurry up and go, please. Before I change my mind.

The door opened, letting in the bone-chilling cold of Deadworld for a moment and then Laurel was gone. At the same time, Nick closed the front door behind Shelby and Cynthia, and the soft thud had Jackie's heart jumping in an instant of panic. She almost sloshed her coffee all over the slate floor.

Nick waved his hand at the doorway, his smile casual. "You can still escape."

No. My only escape is here. She licked her lips and took a sip of the coffee. "No. I'll take your food over shopping any day."

He laughed. "Good to know." Nick turned to face her, his eyes gazing directly into hers.

Jackie's breath hitched in her lungs for a moment, but she forced herself to return the look. "What?"

"I'm glad you're here," he said.

Those words were so loaded with potential meaning that Jackie found herself speechless. What to say to that? She was glad to be there as well, or at least glad she had faced down the quivering nerves in her gut and decided to stay, with all of the implicit consequences of that action. Jackie knew precisely where Nick wanted this night to end up, but his steady gaze did not swarm over her with lust. His eyes were as patient and unreadable as ever. Any decisions to be made, any steps forward would be on her shoulders. Her voice, however, refused to cooperate.

Nick put his hand out between them, an invitation breaking the awkward silence. "How about a little piano time?"

That was a familiar step she could handle. Jackie reached out and placed her hand in his, dwarfed by the size of it. "Sounds good to me."

Up in the loft, Nick turned on a floor lamp beside the piano and sat down, placing his coffee cup on a coaster.

Jackie set hers next to his, matching cups, steaming away. *Matching. Just like a couple.* Her heart began to thump a bit harder. *I can do this. I can. It's just a normal date. A simple, normal date.* The sort of date she had not had. Ever. Jackie slowly let out her breath and sat down next to Nick.

"Any preferences?" he asked.

She shook her head. "No. Anything is good. Everything you play sounds wonderful." *Good at every damn thing in the world, and I don't even know if I can do the one thing I was good at anymore.*

Nick's hands froze over the keys. "You OK, Jackie?"

She looked up at the calm, questioning expression on his face, and the momentary panic in her chest subsided. "Yeah, of course. Why wouldn't I be?" Jackie flashed him a smile, hoping it looked more authentic than it felt. "Play."

He did, and the tension in her chest eased. He truly was a

gifted pianist, though perhaps less impressive with the God-given talent and a century to practice. After a few minutes, the song changed to something Jackie recognized, and Nick nodded toward her.

"Play," he said.

"I'm no match for—"

"Not a contest," he replied. "Come on. I like playing with you."

Jackie glanced quickly up at him, but Nick was already focused back on the piano. She was looking for things where there shouldn't be. Not everything was innuendo. *Quit trying so damn hard, idiot. Just do this.*

She put her hands on the keys and took a deep breath. Nerves had her missing a couple of notes, but a few moments later Jackie fell into the rhythm of the song. Their hands moved in tandem, following one another, playing off one another, and Jackie was surprised, just as before, that it came so easy to sit here as a team, two parts of a whole making a single piece of wonderful music together.

When the song finished, Nick laid his hand across her thigh. "You see? You're better than you think, Jackie."

"I'm so out of practice. I don't really play enough." Despite the coolness of his skin, warmth flooded through Jackie's thighs, spreading from one to the other. Tension and nerves could not hide the truth.

He patted her thigh, causing Jackie to flinch, and got to his feet. "Come on. I've got something for you."

Jackie watched him walk over to the archway leading into the library, a large room extending over the bedroom wing of the house, full of nooks and seating areas formed from row upon row of bookshelves. "What is it?"

He motioned for her. "Come and find out."

"You don't need to give me anything, Nick." *I'm here aren't I? No bribes are necessary now. You can just jump my bones and get this all over with.*

"You'll like this. Trust me."

Jackie followed him into the room, decorated with old Victorian-style couches and chairs, antique tables and Tiffany lamps. When he flicked the light switch, the whole space was suffused with the warm glow of light from a pair of chandeliers. Nick pointed to a love seat tucked into an alcove of shelves.

"Sit. I'll be right there." He walked further into the room, stopping at a bookcase covered by a glass door.

God, I don't need a book. She had not read one in over a year, the last being something about crime-scene forensics. But she could play along. Maybe it was his idea of being romantic. Obviously there were worse plays to make, and she had seen most of them, even if she could not remember them at all.

Jackie sat on the edge of the love seat, hands folded in her lap, and waited. A curtained window looked out into the night; rivulets of water trickled down the windowpane. It was quiet enough that she could hear the faint patter of the rain against the glass. Nick returned with a stack of several leather-bound tomes and set them on the coffee table in front of her.

"Your choice," he said, "to inspire practice."

She picked up the book on top and read the gold-embossed title, *Mozart: Sheet Music.* Jackie eyed Nick curiously, who gave her an easy smile. When she opened the cover, Jackie found what the title indicated, pages and pages of sheet music, encased in clear, protective sleeves. The pages were yellowed, some cracked around the edges, and clearly old. It hit her then what she must be looking at.

"Wait. Are these originals?"

He nodded, his smile broadening. "Some of them. Most are handwritten copies, but some of them are the originals."

"Oh, my God." Jackie traced her fingers over the notes. "Shouldn't these be in a museum somewhere?"

Nick shrugged. "They could be, but I like them where I

can see them and use them on occasion. It makes the piece feel a bit more . . . real, I suppose."

"Wow, Nick. I couldn't take any of these. God, they must be priceless."

"You can, and you will," he said. "They're mine after all. I can do with them what I wish, and I wish for you to make use of them. If you'd like to, of course."

"But—" *I have nothing to give you in return. I haven't been around long enough to collect shit like this. Give me a few decades to catch up, and maybe.* The butterflies began to stir once again, agitated and nervous.

"But nothing," Nick replied. "If you see one you'd like, take it. Think of it as borrowing from the library."

Jackie laughed. "I don't have a card."

"Think I can make an exception just this once," he said. "Perk of having an in with the librarian."

She leaned back and turned to him, suppressing a chuckle. Inside, the butterflies beat furious wings in an effort to escape. *Shit. Here we go. I know what I'm doing. I've done this a million fucking times.* Jackie smiled. *I just can't remember ever doing this right.* "So, I have an in, do I?"

Nick's arm reached behind her and settled on the back of the love seat, close enough that her hair brushed across the flesh of his arm. Goose bumps erupted across the nape of her neck and danced down her spine. "Ms. Rutledge, I believe you've been *in* with the librarian since day one."

She leaned toward him. If that wasn't an invitation, then she did not know what one was. She licked her dry lips and replied softly. "Rough edges and all that, huh?"

The crows'-feet around his eyes deepened. "Something like that."

Nick's mouth was soft and inviting as always, never pushing forward. The pace and momentum of this moment was hers to make, and Jackie swallowed back the pangs of uncertainty. Beneath the foggy effects of the Kahlua, thoughts of how, what, and why receded into the background. They did not exist. Things just happened and the controls of the ship were left to turn where they may. In Jackie's dark sea, one never knew what monsters might swim up out of the depths.

But now, with hands firmly gripping the controls, Jackie felt her quivering palms unsure of where to guide things. She was the *Titanic* in a sea of approaching icebergs, pristine caps covering old, dangerous behemoths beneath.

Keep moving forward. Just push past all of this, you chicken shit. It's just a little sex, and he looks good, smells good, tastes good, and that mouth knows what it's doing. Jackie hooked her hand around the back of Nick's head and pressed harder into him. *Nothing weird here. Nothing.*

Nick's hand splayed across the small of her back, pulling her closer, and the other came up to cup her cheek. Confined in the embrace of a man who had drunk half of her blood, Jackie drew back a few inches.

"Nick . . ." *You don't want my blood do you?*

His thumb brushed across her cheek, the eerie, soft glow of his eyes locking on to hers. "You want to take this down to someplace more comfortable?"

God, those eyes! He could charm her into doing almost anything he wanted, bring out any dark need he might plumb from the depths of her mind. The butterflies had grown teeth, were gnawing away at her insides. They knew what was coming. They knew with or without charms where this path was leading. *No! This won't go there. I'm sober, clearheaded, and in control. I'm not that person anymore. I won't freak out.* The butterflies did not stop their frantic efforts to escape. Give it time. Normal was never on this menu.

"I'm comfortable right here," she said. "It is a love seat." *Fuck, I really said that, didn't I?*

"It is indeed," Nick replied, not missing a beat. "You are small, so I don't think space is a requirement here."

Jackie let a nervous laugh escape and buried her face

against his chest. "Fuck you," she mumbled. "It's more than enough." *I may not have double D's, but they're there, goddammit.*

"Hey," Nick said, and curled a finger beneath her chin to lift her face back up. "You *are* more than enough."

If only. She reached up and put her hands on his shoulders and swung a leg over his so that she straddled his lap. *Just do this girl. Don't stop, don't think, just do it.* The hard ridge pressing up beneath her was a good indication the sheriff was not lying at least. *He wants this. It's not just years of build-up getting released on the handiest body available. God knows I've been a handy body.* She put her hands down on the firm, swimmer's pecs. *Maybe he does just want the easy lay.*

Nick's hands slipped around her waist and wandered up beneath her blouse, pushing the smooth, blue silk across her breasts. Her nipples swelled against his palms as he continued to push the blouse up and she sucked in her breath. A shiver coursed through her.

He pushed her arms up and pulled the blouse over her head, dropping it to the floor. Jackie suppressed the urge to cross her arms over her chest and placed her hands back on Nick's chest. His hips shifted subtly beneath her.

"You're sure about this, Jackie?" He traced a finger lightly down between her breasts. "I know Shelby and Laurel have been—"

"No!" She pinned his hand to her chest. *Fuck, Nick! Talk later. Don't make me think about . . . everything.* Jackie heaved a sigh. "No. I want this. I think—" she glanced down between them "—that you want it, too."

Nick smiled. "Very much."

"So just shut up." Jackie pulled his hand away and leaned down to kiss him, pressing her hips down against him. "Please. Let's just . . . fuck. OK?" *Jackie, you sound like a freaking slut. This is going all wrong. I've done this a million times. Pull it together.*

One hand slipped around to the small of her back, pushing her down even harder against the firmness of his cock. The other brushed lightly through her hair, skimming over the pink scar on Jackie's scalp. "I cede to your demands."

She kissed him again, trying to savor the touch of his hands roaming over her body, but every time he hit a hip bone or brushed over a rib, Jackie wanted to cringe. *Too thin. I look like a damn anorexic. A skinny, scarred up, scared little teenager who doesn't have a clue what the fuck she is doing.* Jackie sandwiched Nick's face between her hands and kissed him with more force, biting on his lip, and darting her tongue into his mouth. *Just keep going. Go, go, go.*

A hand slid across her stomach and down beneath the band of her panties, cupping her, a finger sliding between the folds. It felt wonderful, but Jackie realized with horror that she just wasn't very wet down there. *Too nervous. Fuck, I can't relax. He's going to think I'm not interested.*

"Take off your shirt," she demanded, pushing herself upright. Jackie grabbed at it, pulling it up across his stomach. "No fair that I'm the only one losing their clothes here."

The hand withdrew from between her thighs and Nick removed his shirt. "Better?"

I'm blowing this. God, I need a fucking drink. Jackie fumbled at Nick's pants and unbuttoned the jeans. "Almost."

He arched up his hips and let her pull the jeans down until he could step out of them, and then pulled her underwear down to add to the pile. Nick stared up at her, hands folded over the tight, swimmer's belly. One corner of his mouth curled up. "Enough?"

Jackie wanted to pause and stare. He wasn't ripped by any stretch, but the muscles were all firm, lean lines flowing over his body. Nick Anderson was a very good-looking man. Her hands began to tremble. *Stop. Please body, don't fail me now.* "Not quite."

Nick slipped his hands into the boxers and pushed them down over his thighs, revealing just how ready he was for her. "Better?"

Warmth flooded through her. So much for not being wet. *OK, I can do that.* One hundred and eighty years had not hurt Nick Anderson in the slightest. Jackie reached down and pulled the boxers all of the way off, finding her face parked not more than two feet away from a damn fine cock. *Climb on top? Blowjob? What would he want? Do I even give good head? I've done it a thousand times, I'm sure. Fuck. Do I even like doing it? What if I suck at it? I'll bet Shelby could throat the whole damn thing. God, the bitch. Nick's going to be disappointed after that. How do I live up to the goddess of all things sex?*

"Jackie?" Nick reached up to her. "Come here."

He'll be fucking the rookie, like some anxiety-ridden teen, except this teen isn't so nice and sweet and tight anymore. She's been used a thousand times, fucked six ways to Sunday, like some street corner whore.

Her shaking hand disappeared in Nick's and he pulled her forward until she lay across his chest. He cupped her cheek and kissed her lightly. "What's wrong?"

"Wrong? Nothing's wrong. I'm fine," she said in a rush. "Do you think something's wrong?" *He's having doubts, knows I'm not right for him, knows this won't work! He always sees right through me, knows I'm just a goddamn fuck-up.* A voice, distant, laughing and mean, whispered up from the dark sea of memory. *You're just like her, always will be. A dumb, fucking whore who hates herself even more than she hates me.*

Nick brushed his thumb across her cheek, and to Jackie's horror, felt the warm smear of tears between them. "You're worried and stressed. I want this to be enjoyable for both of us. So, maybe if we curl up here for while and relax? Just get more comfortable being together."

"No, no," she replied, pushing herself back up, feeling

the breadth of his cock sliding against her. "I'm good, really. I need to do this." She reached behind and grabbed a hold of Nick, pulling his cock upright and settling herself against it. "It's all good. I'm fine." Letting go, Jackie pushed herself down, letting the length of him bury itself inside her, and was rewarded with Nick's quiet groan. "See? All good."

"Jackie. I don't think—"

"We're good, Nick. Doesn't that feel good?" *See? Just normal old sex. A nice fuck.* But the look on his face said otherwise. His mouth was no longer relaxed into that sexy, easy smile. The creases around his eyes had deepened with concern. But worst of all, the hard warmth of him had eased. He was losing interest. Jackie worked her hips harder, stroking up and down along the shaft.

"It does, trust me," he said. "But this isn't right, Jackie. I want this to be right."

The butterflies began to bleed out, fluttering with rampant glee through her body. "It . . . it is right." Her chest began to tighten, pressing down on a heart that thumped a frantic beat. Jackie clamped her thighs around Nick, driving herself against him. *I'm good. I can make this good. I'm not like her anymore.* "Just . . . just . . . just go with . . ." The air was catching in her lungs, making it hard to breathe, to talk. He felt great inside her, filling her, driving away those furious, panicked butterflies pinned within the walls of her chest.

Nick implored. "Jackie, stop. Please."

The taste of salty tears stung Jackie's mouth. "No . . . we . . ." Where was the air? The fucking butterflies had used it all up. "It's . . . OK."

"Jackie!" Nick's hands clamped around her arms. "You're starting to hyperventilate. Stop."

She jerked away, tumbling off of him and fell to the floor. That warm fulfillment was abruptly a cold, empty void. *It's all empty in there. Cold, dead, and useless.* Nick reached for her, but Jackie batted his hands away. *Leave me alone!* She wanted to say it, but the words would not come out. She couldn't breathe. Her chest had collapsed in on itself, and she was left gasping like a beached fish.

Nick knelt down on the floor and placed his hands on her shoulders. Jackie grabbed at them, tried to slap them away, but even though his grip was light, his arms were immovable iron rods. "Jackie! Slow, deep breaths. You're having a panic attack. Calm down. You're all right."

She vigorously shook her head. *No. Fuck, no!* She pushed her hand against her chest. It hurt like hell. "Not . . . panicking."

"Yes, you are," he said. "You need to calm down and try to take some deep breaths."

Jackie tried to pull away. This could not be happening. She kept her gaze turned away from his, not wanting to see the expression on his face. Pity? Disgust? Amusement? All three perhaps? She had to get out of there. "Let me . . . go."

The large hands clasped around her face, forcing her to look at him. "Jackie? Look at me." When she refused, they clamped a bit tighter. "Look at me, please."

She did finally, gasping like a winded sprinter. "Sorry . . . I'm . . . so . . . sorry."

"Stop it. You're OK," he said, voice deepening, becoming melodic. "Your breathing is slowing. Your chest is relaxing. You're going to be fine, Jackie." The thumbs of his hands brushed at the tears running down her cheeks. "Let's just take it easy. Slow down and relax."

Nick's irisless eyes glowed, pulsing to the slowing beat of her heart. She could see that cold, gray door to the dead within the depths of those eyes. The pain in her chest began to ease. "Nick." Jackie tried to pull away. "What are you doing?"

"Helping you relax. We can get back to all of this later. Just take it easy, Jackie. Deep breaths."

It dawned on her then. Vampire mojo. He was charming

her. "Stop! Stop it." Jackie kicked at him, jerking her head free of his grasp. He dropped his hands and sighed with disappointment.

"It's OK, Jackie. I just want—"

"Fuck you," she yelled and grabbed her blouse from off of the floor. "Fucking vampire mojo bullshit." *I don't need your goddamn pity.* The scar at her elbow, where Nick had cut her to drink her blood suddenly ached. Jackie thrust her arms through the sleeves of her blouse and realized she had put it on backward, but she did not care. She had to get the hell out of there. Her panties were still on the floor, beneath Nick's legs and her pumps were downstairs. Jackie brushed at the tear streaks on her face. "I have to go. I'm sorry, Nick. I just can't do . . . this."

She ran, nearly falling down the stairs going to the entry. Her purse lay on a table by the door. Jackie snagged it and grabbed at the door, fumbling with the lock. Behind her at the top of the stairs, Nick's voice implored.

"Jackie, please don't go. This is all . . . it's all right."

The lock finally opened and Jackie yanked the door open. She glanced back up at Nick, standing there in all his naked glory. *It's not all right. I can't do this . . . normal shit. I can't be normal.* Her chest was tightening up again. She had to escape before she disintegrated into a blubbering mess on the floor.

"No, Nick," she said and blinked away more tears. "It's not all right. I'm sorry, really. I'm just . . . I have to go."

She slammed the door behind her and bolted for the car, bare feet soaking up the cold November rain. The door opened before she could get into the car, and Nick's silhouette stood behind the screen door, watching her. After three tries, her trembling hand finally got the key into the ignition, and Jackie gunned the engine, spinning the wheels backing out of the drive. Once on the road, she fumbled in her purse for the cell and punched in the last number she would have ever expected to call.

The other end picked up after four rings. A sleepy, confused voice answered. “Jackie?”

“Tillie?” Jackie swallowed, trying to keep the blubbering stammer out of her voice. “I need to see you.”

“What time . . . Jackie, it’s after—”

“Please, Tillie!”

“What’s wrong? Where are you?”

“I’m . . . I’m on my way home.”

“All right,” she said. “I can meet you there. What happened?”

Jackie hung up without answering, wiping at the tears streaming down her face, and blew through a stop sign on the rain-slick road. *My worst nightmare is what happened.*

Chapter 5

"Dear, you called me in a panic," Tillie said. "I've never heard you so . . . frightened before. Nothing you've told me so far," she said with a sympathetic shrug, "says why you were so scared. Did he hurt you?"

Jackie hung her head once again. Here it came. "No."

"Threaten you in some way?"

She groaned. "No, nothing like that."

"Then what was it, Jackie? Help me understand."

Heat flushed into her face. "I tried to sleep with him."

"Oh," Tillie said quietly. "That did not go well, I take it?"

Jackie rubbed her hands over her face. *God, how to explain this mess?* "Not unless chest pains and hyperventilating means good sex."

"Oh, dear," Tillie said. "That sounds like you had a panic attack."

"Yeah, something like that. Nick said the same thing. I couldn't breathe, Tillie. I thought I was going to pass out."

"What did Nick do?"

"He tried to use his vampire-voodoo-charm bullshit on me," Jackie said. Anger knotted up her stomach again at the thought. "So I left."

Tillie leaned across the coffee table and placed her hand

on Jackie's knee. "That does sound frightening, Jackie. I'm sorry you had to experience that."

She nodded. "Yeah, me too. Probably thinks I'm bat-shit crazy now."

"You aren't," Tillie replied. "I think you're just afraid to let him in."

Jackie laughed. "Oh, I let him in all right."

Tillie gave her a stern look. "Emotionally, dear. Afraid to let him see the real you."

"The real me." Jackie flopped back against the couch. "Not even sure *I* want to see the real me."

"And therein lies your problem," Tillie said, and patted Jackie's knee. "How can anyone get to know you if you're afraid to know yourself?"

Jackie groaned. "I know, I know. But what if . . ." She sighed, took a deep breath and then slowly let it out. "What if he doesn't like what he sees? What if nobody does?"

"They don't matter, dear. It's more important that you like what you see. So, the question is, when you look at Jackie Rutledge, what do you see?"

Not what you'd hope to. "I don't know. I—" She stopped when the cold rush of Deadworld swept through her. Laurel was coming. "Shit. Laur, not now, please."

Laurel did not make her typical, casual entrance, stepping through the veil between the living and the dead. She tumbled in, like a runner who abruptly catches her toe on a crack in the sidewalk, rolling across the living room floor, through the piano and out into the hall. Jackie leaped to her feet.

"Laur? What the hell?"

On her feet as well, Tillie laid a hand on Jackie's arm. "What is it? What's wrong?"

A moment later, Laurel stepped back through the wall into the living room. She readjusted her blouse while looking furtively around the room. "That was a little too . . . Dr.

Erikson? Why is . . ." She looked back and forth between Jackie and Tillie. "Oh, no. Hon, what happened with Nick?"

"Laur, why are you here?" Jackie demanded. Could she never have a breakdown in peace?

"Laurel is here?" Tillie asked, stepping away from Jackie to the middle of the room, looking around curiously. "Where is she?"

Jackie threw up her hands in frustration. "Yes, she's here. Maybe we could have a group therapy session."

"I'm so sorry," Laurel said. "I didn't have any choice. I need to stay with you for a while."

"What? Why?"

"That thing is back," Laurel said. "It almost got me."

The idea that Laurel'd had a spat with Shelby went out the window. "What are you talking about?"

"The Spindly Man," she replied. "That green-eyed thing is here." Laurel pointed up over Jackie's head. "On the other side."

"We knew that." Jackie followed the line of her finger but saw nothing. "Was it chasing you?"

"No, hon. You don't understand." Her hand swept across the room. "It's here on the other side. Right outside of your apartment. I think it's looking for you."

Jackie's knees suddenly went weak and she collapsed back onto the couch. She remembered that lanky, quill-covered monster as clear as the day she saw it crossing that bridge in Deadworld, when those, eerie green orbs turned their focus on her. "Well, shit."

Tillie stepped over to the couch and sat down next to her. "What is it, dear? What's wrong?"

Jackie shook her head in disbelief, staring blankly at the wall, her hands clasped together on top of her head. "Everything. I think we're done for now. I need to get out of here."

* * *

Three hard knocks on the office door startled Jackie awake. She nearly tipped her chair over backward jerking her feet off the desk. She had seen Tillie off and driven around aimlessly, blasting random radio stations on the stereo, until she had found herself near the office. Even Laurel's usual soothing words had done little to settle her nerves or her stomach, and she'd wandered the office while Jackie downed another shot of tequila from the office bar and fell asleep staring at the ceiling of her office. The clock on Jackie's desk phone now read 8:30 AM. Three hours of sleep. Fabulous.

"Jackie? You in there?" It was Shelby's voice, and not the happy-go-lucky tone Jackie was used to.

"Yeah, one sec," she said. Jackie grabbed the almost-empty tequila bottle and dropped it in the garbage under her desk. Her mouth felt full of tainted cotton balls, and her head swam loosely upon her neck when she got to her feet.

When she unlocked the door, Shelby pushed in before she could even pull it open. She carried a duffle, slung over one shoulder, which she unceremoniously dumped on the floor beside the door as she marched in. It took Jackie a moment to realize that it was her duffle.

Jackie stared down at the bag. "What's going on?"

Shelby handed her a large cup of coffee from Annabelle's. "Here. We're starting that case today."

Jackie took a sip of the delightful, hot black-gold. "We are?" What the hell was going on? "What happened to Monday?"

"Freaky alien monster thing hovering around your apartment is what happened," Shelby said. "We're getting out of town for a couple of days to see if it goes away." She pointed at the duffle. "Laur helped me snag some of your clothes. Nick is getting the plane fueled, and we're meeting him out there at ten. So, let McManus know or whatever needs to happen, and let's get the fuck out of here, OK? OK. Let me know if you need anything before we go, and put on some perfume. You smell like a distillery." She turned around and left.

Jackie watched her go, too stunned to even snap back at her. Knocking Shelby Fontaine off-kilter took some doing. The Spindly Man had unnerved her, and that was a good enough answer right there as to how serious this was. And Nick was fueling up the plane. What plane? When did they get a plane?

Cynthia was out front assembling folders on her desk, and clearly had been doing so for a while. Jackie eyed the groups of papers going into each folder. "How long you been here, Cynthia?"

"Oh, an hour or so, I guess," she said. "Just putting together what we have on Thatcher's Mill for you all to take and read on the plane. Not sure how much of it is useful, but it's what I've been able to pull up on short notice."

"I'll call McManus and get him and the geeks on it before we go," Jackie said. Cynthia nodded and pulled another stack of papers from the printer. "Cynthia, you might want to go to my apartment and see if you can—"

"I don't know what it is, Jackie," she replied. "All I can tell you is, that thing isn't dead and it isn't human." She looked up at Jackie with a wan smile on her face. "And yes, it freaks me out, too."

"Hmm, yeah. You could say that," Jackie said. "Could you tell if it has malicious intent?"

She shrugged. "It isn't human, Jackie. I don't know." She stepped over and brushed her fingers across Jackie's hand. "And I'm sorry last night didn't work out."

Jackie rolled her eyes, but could tell the feeling was genuine. "Could be worse." Though how was not something Jackie could imagine.

Cynthia laughed. "Isn't that always the case? Well, anyway. I hope it does. Your auras are a good match."

Auras. What the hell did that mean? They both glow red or something? Jackie did not feel like talking about it now.

She had to figure out how she was going to ride on a plane with Nick without throwing up.

"Cynthia, how long have you known Nick?"

She stopped and set the papers down on her desk, and stared at Jackie for what seemed like a minute. "I've known and loved him for years, Jackie. He's one of the best people I've ever known. If you can't trust him, then there's nobody you can."

Not quite what she was going to ask, but still enough to impress. It was just weird how these people all seemed interconnected. She nodded.". Thank you."

"And, Jackie?" she said. "If you have any questions about anything, you know, psychic, please ask me anything. I'm more than happy to help you come to grips with all of this. I can't imagine how hard this has been."

Jackie gave her a fleeting smile. "If you can figure out what the hell that thing is on the other side, that would be great." She turned away, knowing there was no answer to that one yet, and walked back toward her office to figure out what she would need to take on this trip.

An hour later, they were on their way to Midway Airport. Shelby kept glancing into the review mirror.

"If I didn't know better, I'd think we were being followed," she said.

Jackie sat up in the backseat and looked out the back window. "Really? Where?"

"That blue Jeep a couple cars back," Shelby replied. "We're almost to Midway, so we'll see in a minute."

Jackie's first thought was FBI, but it was not a government vehicle, and from what Belgerman had told her, the investigation into her actions involving the death of Detective Morgan were done and/or shelved. Chicago PD had been pissed about the whole thing, but it all quieted down once it was made public that she was no longer an active agent. For all they knew, she had been fired.

They pulled off of Sixty-Third Street into the hangar

area for private aircraft. The Jeep slowed up behind them in the turn lane but then continued on after they crossed traffic. Jackie got a good look at the driver as they pulled away.

"Shit. I know that guy," she said, disgusted.

"FBI?" Shelby wondered. "Chicago PD?"

"No." Jackie shook her head in disbelief. "It's a fucking reporter."

"What?" Shelby and Cynthia chimed in together.

"He was investigating the Tannenbaum fire," Jackie replied. "He wanted to know how I got from there to the hospital quicker than the ambulance did."

"That the same guy who showed up at your apartment?"

Jackie watched the Jeep disappear as they pulled in between the hangars. "Yeah. He doesn't seem to be leaving well enough alone."

Laurel's voice sounded off in her head. *If he thinks he has something, he won't let it go if he's any good.*

Jackie turned back to face the front. *I know. Let's hope he sucks.* He did not strike her as being some glorified story chaser, though. She would see him again, no doubt about it.

They pulled up outside a corrugated metal hangar, right next to Nick's purple Porsche. Shelby popped the trunk lid of Cynthia's car and stepped out. Jackie sat staring at the gray metal wall, knowing that somewhere on the other side was Nick Anderson, the last person in the world she wanted to see or talk to at this moment.

Hon, trust me on this. Nick is going to feel just as awkward about this as you do.

Doubt it. Jackie finally opened the door and stepped out to pick up her bag. She took a deep breath and let it out in a rush. They were starting their first case. This was a new deal, a new lease, a fresh start, and yet she had never felt more frazzled and at loose ends then she did at this moment.

God, I'm so not ready for this, Laur. What the hell am I doing?

You're leading a case, just like you've always done, Laurel told her.

And you know as well as I that this is not *like anything I've ever done.*

Concept is still the same, hon. Work the case, utilize your resources, and put your coworkers to work. Solve the crime.

If there was even a crime to solve. Who knew what the hell they were getting into? Still, Laurel was right. As fucked up as everything was, it was still a case. She knew how to work with that.

At the hangar door, Jackie stopped. Nick stood in the middle of the hangar by the stairs leading up into a sleek, white Learjet with a thick, purple strip running down the side. Emblazoned in matching elegant purple lettering, "SPECIAL INVESTIGATIONS, INC." ran down the side from wing to tail.

Shelby's laughter echoed throughout the hangar. "Nice touch, babe. I feel so *Criminal Minds* now."

"Good grief," Jackie whispered. "This is insane."

Shush, Laurel chided. *Just enjoy the ride. Our sheriff can burn his money anyway he wants to.*

Jackie shook her head and forced her feet to move forward. *Just nod and get on the plane. No need to say a word.* Nick smiled and nodded at Shelby and Cynthia as they climbed up the stairs into the plane. His smile sagged as Jackie came up to meet him.

"Jackie," he said quietly and bowed his head in acknowledgment.

She could not look him in the eye or anywhere near his face for that matter. With her hand gripped even tighter on her shoulder bag, Jackie increased her pace and strode passed him. "Hey, Nick," she muttered and went up the steps two at a time and disappeared into the dark confines of the plane.

The Lear seated sixteen, four groups of paired, leather

seats facing each other. A bar and kitchenette separated them further, making it eight in front and eight in the back. Jackie chose the seat farthest away from the door, hoping everyone would just leave her alone on the flight so she could get herself organized in some way or another. Shelby ruined that by plopping down in the seats across from her, stretching her legs across both seats.

Her elbow propped on the armrest, chin in hand, Shelby smiled at her. “Can’t ignore him forever, boss.”

“I realize that, Shelby. Thank you.” She made no effort to hide the sarcasm.

“Longer you take, the worse it’ll be, trust me,” she replied.

“I know!” Jackie snapped back, trying to keep her voice down. “Can you just leave it alone, please? It isn’t any of your goddamn business.”

“It is if you can’t effectively communicate with your team,” she said in a harsh whisper, the smile vanishing from her lips. “Flight’s about twenty-five minutes. Figure it out, Jack.” Shelby reached over and gave Jackie’s knee a firm squeeze and then got back to her feet, moving up front to sit with Nick.

She heard Laurel grumble inside her head. *She’s right, hon. Even if she’s being a bitch about it.*

Jackie slumped against the side of the plane and closed her eyes as the plane rushed down the runway for takeoff. *At least we agree on something.*

Chapter 6

The brief squeal of wheels touching down jarred Jackie out of her doze. It seemed she had only just shut her eyes, but now it was time to get busy. The squirming, nagging fear in her gut had to be buried, pushed down into the depths where she could ignore it. Any luck and it would just go away.

Jackie paused by Nick, who stood at the door of the plane as they all stepped off. She let out the breath pent up in her lungs. "Ready to roll on this, Nick?"

He looked down at her in silence for so long, Jackie was afraid he might not bother to answer her. Finally, he nodded. "I am. You?"

"Nope. We'll figure it out as we go," she said and headed for the steps.

A cold wind swirled around the airfield, little more than a single strip of concrete and one corrugated metal hangar. The ground was damp from an earlier rain. Jackie looked around, half expecting there to be a limo waiting for them.

"Do we have a car?" she asked.

"Should be by the main office," Nick said, coming up behind her.

"Pretty out here—" Cynthia began.

"Great," Jackie said. "Let's go."

They all followed in silence, shoes splashing through the puddles on the tarmac. Once they reached the squat, flat-roofed main office, Jackie walked through the door and made her way toward the front. Outside, she spotted the rental car and walked over to the Ford Explorer to wait for Nick to bring the keys.

You OK, hon? Laurel wondered.

"I'm fine," Jackie said quietly. "Just trying to . . . shift gears here."

Just remember, this isn't the FBI anymore.

"No need to remind me of that," Jackie said. What they were, exactly, remained to be seen. When Nick got to the SUV, Jackie held out her hand. "I want to drive."

He dangled the keys over her outstretched palm. "You know where we're going?"

She snatched them out of his fingers. "Not really."

"Oh, let her drive, babe," Shelby said, and tossed her bag over the backseat into the back. "She needs to be able to control *something*."

Jackie pointed a finger at her as she opened the driver's side door. "Not helping." She did not need every last one of her foibles brought to light for them to discuss. It was bad enough that they all knew what they did.

Once out on the highway, Cynthia rode shotgun and informed her, via the GPS, that they were about twenty minutes away from Thatcher's Mill. Jackie took another deep breath. She was getting tired of trying to constantly relieve the tension in her gut.

"So, let's go over what little we know and what we want to do," she said. "Sound good?" When nobody offered up any other options, she continued. "We have a town with more than its fair share of ghosts, which obviously I'm not sure what that even means."

Nick cleared his throat. "Town that size, you would be lucky to find three or four at any given time."

That sounds about right, Laurel agreed.

"So, let's say for the sake of argument that we're looking at five times that number, fifteen to twenty ghosts. What could that mean?"

"Likely an incident of mass death," Cynthia replied, "but the little bit of digging I've been able to do hasn't pulled up anything like that."

"How far back did you go?" Shelby asked.

"Back to the turn of the century," Cyn said. "Doesn't mean something didn't happen of course, but I didn't see anything that got noted anywhere."

"Someone or something could be keeping them around," Nick added. "Sometimes one tormented soul will draw others to it, like a magnet."

"Misery loves company," Jackie said.

"Something like that," he replied.

There was an awkward few seconds of silence, until Shelby broke it. "Laur, baby. Come out of Jackie's head and sit with me."

Jackie sighed. This was exactly what she signed up for. Laurel hesitated. *Go, for Christ's sake. I'm fine.* She slipped out, sending a cool shiver down Jackie's spine. "What about a killer?" she offered. "Could we have a serial killer on our hands?"

Cynthia shook her head. "No reports of linked murders of any kind in the area. At least nothing that has popped up on anyone's radar."

They were getting nowhere with this. "So, lots of possibilities but no corroborating information of any kind at this point. Which means, we need to cruise the town and canvas the locals."

"And see if we can talk to any of the ghosts," Nick added.

"I'll check that out," Laurel said. "That's kind of my thing now."

Shelby snickered at her. "Laurel Carpenter, Ghost Detective."

"Oh," Cynthia said. "I'd watch that."

"If you could see them," Shelby replied.

The three of them laughed. Jackie frowned in an effort to hide the smile creeping onto her face. Damn them. There was nothing amusing about any of this. In the rearview mirror, Jackie could see the corner of Nick's mouth curl up as he shook his head. It was better than nerve-wracking silence at least.

The two-lane, shoulderless road wound its way through rolling hills and scattered fields, little more than wet dirt and groves of dark, spider-webbed branches collecting water from the low-slung sky. They were in the middle of bum-fuck nowhere, with nary a coffee or pastry shop to be seen. Somewhere off to the east, the Mississippi wound its way south through Iowa farmland. It was not difficult to imagine ghosts wandering aimlessly over this landscape.

They finally passed a sign that said THATCHER'S MILL, 2 MILES. Jackie had the feeling that a couple of hours in the podunk and they would be on the road back, having wasted a perfectly good Friday that she could have spent curled up on her couch doing a whole lot of nothing.

"You realize this could be a complete waste of time," she said to no one in particular. "This is a ten-year-old lead we're following up on."

"So what?" Shelby said. "It's a good way to get our feet wet. We'll figure out what's worth going out on and what's not."

"I suppose," Jackie replied.

The Ford crossed a bridge over a shallow creek, where a sign welcomed them to Thatcher's Mill. Up ahead, Jackie could see the main street, lined with old brick, two- and three-story buildings, and not much beyond that, the highway exiting the town and disappearing around a tree-covered hill. The brightly colored sign of the local diner could be seen on a corner up ahead, and Jackie had half a mind to stop there first, just so she could get some coffee in her system.

Then someone stepped out in the path of the SUV, forcing Jackie to swerve and slam on the brakes. She caught some gravel on the side of the road and slid sideways off onto the shoulder.

"Holy shit!" She leaped out of the SUV, scanning the road for a body. There was nothing to be seen.

"She's over there," Nick said, pointing behind the Explorer, but he made no effort to move.

Jackie spun on her heel and then froze. It was a woman all right, light and wispy as fog. She curled around behind their car and continued to walk toward the edge of town. Now that she was aware of its presence, Jackie could feel the cool whisper of Deadworld, faint but there. Her heartbeat finally began to slow.

"OK, that about caused a heart attack," she said.

Shelby laughed and laid a hand upon her shoulder. "Takes a while to get used to that. I've almost dumped my bike a couple of times, not realizing until too late what I was about to hit."

Laurel followed the ghost for a few steps, calling out to her and then stopped. "She's not even aware. Strange."

"Or doesn't care," Nick said. He turned back to the car. "Well, that's one. Wonder how many more we'll find?"

On the edge of the road, Laurel stared off into the heart of the town. "There's more," she said. "I can feel them."

"How many?" Jackie wondered and climbed back into the driver's seat. "A lot?"

Laurel shrugged and walked through the door and back to her spot. "Can't tell. Let's drive through town and see."

Once back on the road, Jackie eased them into town at a brisk twenty miles per hour. Cynthia pointed out the next one, lingering on a street corner outside the diner. Laurel spotted another above the feed store behind a window. Another crossed the road, clipping the front corner of the

SUV, and Jackie felt the bone-deep twinge of the dead. By the time they reached the far side of Main Street, they had spotted ten. She circled back down a side street, parallel to the highway and then crossed back over to the other side to follow a second street back up.

There were only about eight blocks worth of town in Thatcher's Mill, a few hundred people at the most. Jackie finally pulled into a spot on the street outside the diner. She wanted more than coffee now. Cynthia had been keeping notes.

"How many?" Jackie asked.

"Assuming we didn't duplicate any," Cyn said, rechecking her tally, "about thirty-five."

"Goddamn," Shelby said. "What the fuck is going on in this place?"

Nick sat on the edge of his seat, feet dangling out to the ground. He stared blankly toward the edge of town. "Anyone else notice they were mostly women?"

Cynthia tapped her notepad. "Thirty-one of them were female. That can't be good."

"Thirty-one?" Jackie leaned over and looked at Cynthia's notes. "Almost ninety percent. You're right, that isn't good." They all got out without saying a word. "Yeah, that's what I figured." So much for the quick trip. It was time to call up the Geekroom over at the FBI and get Hauser moving on this.

Nick closed his door and, instead of heading into the diner, walked out into the middle of Main Street. A car slowed and honked at him, swerving around his still figure. His hands were on his hips, head cocked slightly to the side while he made a slow, 360-degree turn.

Shelby leaned against the SUV, arms crossed over her chest. "What is it, babe?"

Jackie walked out to where he stood. This was not a look she had seen on him before. "You see something, Nick? Or sense something?"

His gaze abruptly refocused and he looked down at her, face etched with concern. "I've been here before."

Jackie pursed her lips. "Why is that making you look so worried?"

"I'm not sure," he said. "It was a long time ago, 1890s I think."

"So, something happened here back then?"

"Maybe. I was chasing down Drake at the time."

Shelby stood up straight. "Drake was here?"

"Passed through, anyway," Nick replied. "He might've killed someone here."

Jackie closed her eyes for a moment and then turned back toward the diner. "Great. Nearly die, lose my job, fly hundreds of miles away, and we still run into the fucker."

Cynthia held the door open to the diner for her. "It was a hundred years ago. Surely it can't be related to what's going on now."

Jackie marched past her and into the diner. "Don't bet on it."

Chapter 7

The coffee, somewhere between FBI swill and Nick's decadent mud, soothed the tense knot in Jackie's stomach. It still boggled her mind that they had somehow picked a case in a town where Drake had been. It could be nothing at all, but dozens of ghosts and a vampire who took pleasure in creating them did not seem coincidental to her at all, even if it was one hundred years ago.

Shelby, the little wench, had pushed herself into the booth next to Cynthia, leaving the empty space next to Jackie as the only spot for Nick to sit. He had slipped in without a word and artfully kept his body from touching hers, though it did not matter. Even inches away, it felt to Jackie as though he was pressing up against her.

"So," Shelby said, leaning against Cynthia and sipping her water, "what's the agenda, boss?"

How the hell was she supposed to know that? "I was hoping you had some bright ideas. I can get Hauser to dig up some info about this place, find out if anything out of the ordinary has gone on here. Maybe we can have a word with the local law enforcement."

"Get the law out of your head, babe," she replied. "If you've got a place with ghosts, what are you going to hear?"

Hear? Of course. "Ghost stories. This place should have a million of them. Speaking of which, where did Laur go?"

"She went poking around to see if she could talk to any of them," Shelby said.

"That will be our best source," Nick added. "Those that have been here a long time may not remember much of anything, but any recently dead should remember what happened."

The waitress, a forty-something woman with her hair pulled up and pinned with a pen, stopped by to refill Nick's and Jackie's coffees. "More ghosthunters, eh?"

Jackie sat up straight. "We're not . . ." She took a deep breath. "We heard there were an unusual number of, um, hauntings in this area."

The waitress snorted. "You and every other freak with an EMF meter."

"Look, Miss—" Jackie clenched her fists. She was not about to get labeled as a group of circus clowns trying to prove the existence of ghosts.

"Ma'am," Nick said with his charming half-smile. His hand rested on Jackie's thigh, patting it a couple of times in warning. "We're not here to run tests for paranormal activity. We already know there are ghosts here. We're researchers. We're here to find out why."

"Oh!" Her terse face relaxed into a smile, not entirely friendly. "Well, I'll give you a sound piece of local advice then." She leaned over and topped off Nick's coffee. "It's wise to leave the Thatcher's Mill curse alone."

"Molly!" The balding, bearded cook yelled out at them from the grill. "Quit your infernal blabbing. They don't want to listen to your BS."

Molly frowned and whipped her head around. "Curse ain't no bullshit, Tucker! Just advising the good folk here to do what's best for them."

"Look like they can take care of themselves, woman. Take their damn order and leave them alone."

"Sorry," Molly said, shaking her head. "Old prick's in a mood today. You all looking for some lunch or just sipping coffee while you figure out where to find your ghosts?"

"Already found them," Jackie said, giving her best fake smile. "I'll take a cinnamon roll or Danish or whatever pastry sort of thing you have back there."

Molly stared at Jackie for a moment before turning her gaze back to Nick. "What about you, handsome? What'll it be?"

"Roast beef sandwich," he said. "Have you seen any of the Mill's ghosts, Molly?"

"Course I have." She laughed. "Everyone here has at one time or another."

"Coconut cream pie," Shelby added. "So, what's this curse all about?"

"For you?" Molly nodded at Cynthia, who sipped her hot tea and shook her head.

"Just the tea, thanks."

"Thatcher's curse," Molly said, pulling the pen from her hair to write down their order. "Once born here, you never leave, even after you're dead."

Tucker leaned over the diner's counter. "Damn it, Molly. Leave the poor folk alone."

Nick waved him off. "It's all good, sir. We're just out from the University of Chicago doing some research on local ghost stories. Your town seems to have a few."

Tucker chuckled. "More than a few, but I'd keep looking if I were you. Most folk around here don't like your type prying into things. Private, quiet people who don't like to be reminded about unsavory things like dead girls walking their streets, if you understand what I'm saying."

Tucker went back to his grill, and Molly walked back to deal with their order. Nick took a sip of his coffee, and Shelby grinned, giving him a salute with her water glass. "Nice one, babe."

"And more or less true, other than the U of C part," he said quietly over the top of his cup.

"I could've handled that just fine," Jackie muttered.

"Oh, come on." Shelby laughed. "You'd have reamed her a new one. Let's face it, boss, subtlety is not one of your strong points."

Jackie downed more of her coffee. "Fuck you." They all snickered at her, and Jackie reluctantly smirked in return.

They were halfway through their food when Laurel returned from her initial foray into the town. "I really don't like this place."

Jackie swallowed her mouthful of Danish. "Found something?"

"No," she said. "That's the problem. None of the spirits I could get to talk had anything to say. A couple were looking for someone but they weren't sure who. None of them had any inkling of moving on. I didn't really press any of the ones I found, because I just wanted to get a feeling for what was going on, but I got the disturbing sense that they have no idea why they're here."

They all looked perplexed at Laurel, except Jackie, who had no idea what the significance of Laurel's findings were. "I take it this is unusual?"

"Certainly strange," Cynthia said.

"We'll need to talk to as many as we can," Nick said. "If they are all like that, then we likely have someone around here that is influencing them."

"Why would someone want to do that?" Jackie wondered.

Nick shrugged. "I don't know. Ghosts linger for a purpose. If they don't have one, they move on. So, on the surface this makes little sense."

"What about the curse?" Cynthia asked. "Could someone have done that to this town?"

"Wait. What?" Jackie blinked in disbelief. "You're taking that whole thing seriously?"

Laurel absently tapped at her lip, lost in thought. "A powerful witch might be able to do something like that."

"Seriously?" Jackie stared at her. "Curses are real?"

"Oh, definitely," Cynthia replied. "But this would be something special. Your average witch doesn't play around with the dead. I'll have to make a couple of calls to some friends and see what they have to say on it."

Jackie shook her head. "This is beyond me. I don't know the first thing about handling a situation like this."

"We handle it like any other case would be handled," Nick said. "We ask questions, dig a little deeper, and do some research."

"This isn't like any other case," Jackie insisted. "I don't know what the hell to do with stuff like this."

"Bullshit," Shelby said. "And it's not all on you, babe. We're a team, remember? We all have our areas of expertise here. Make use of them."

Jackie sagged back against the seat. She could apply the only experience she had, which was leading a team of field agents in an effort to solve a crime and catch a criminal. It couldn't be that different, right? "OK, so we go talk to the ghosts. Cynthia, contact your witch people. I'll get Hauser to run us a quick criminal history on the area and see if anything pops. Nick, Shelby, and Laur, canvas the town for as many ghosts as you can find, and I'll go have a word with the local law and see if they have any insight into this."

Shelby shuddered. "Listen to her being all leaderlike. Gives me goose bumps."

"Shel," Nick said, clearly as exasperated by her as Jackie felt, "leave it be."

"And the sheriff being all protective of his lady," she said, smiling through the last bite of her pie. "It makes me all fuzzy inside."

Jackie dug a twenty out of her wallet and slapped it down on the table. "Such a bitch. Move, Nick, before I do something stupid and get my ass kicked." Nick stood up to let her out. Shelby snickered away while Cynthia tried very hard to hide the smirk on her face. "Everyone go deal with your shit. We'll meet back here in a couple of hours and compare notes."

Jackie could see Nick's hand wavering by her arm, ready to calm and console, but she wanted nothing to do with any of them at the moment. Jackie pushed passed him and headed for the door, dialing in Hauser's number and realizing too late that she had not bothered to ask if anyone knew where the local law was located.

Hauser was just what she needed after getting her nerves Shelby-fied once again. "Hauser! You wouldn't believe how good it is to hear your voice."

"Jack! How's my favorite agent in hiding?"

"Seen better days, that's for sure," she said, climbing into the SUV. "I passed along some info to McManus this morning about a place—"

"Thatcher's Mill?" he cut in. "Yeah, got that earlier this morning. So, how's the new gig? Got something interesting going on already?"

"It's . . . weird," she replied. "Running a case with no actual crime is just odd. I'm out of my element."

"I'm sure you'll find someone to kick the crap out of." He laughed in her ear. "Only a matter of time."

She watched Shelby and Nick walk out of the diner. Wasn't that the truth? "Yeah. Anyway."

"Well, speaking of no crime, Thatcher's Mill is one strange place," Hauser said.

Jackie's heart skipped a beat. "You got something already?"

"I ran a quick background on the place after McManus called. Just your typical check, common data, that sort of thing."

"OK, and?"

"You're in the safest town in the world, from what I can tell."

"What? This place is crawling with ghosts. I find that hard to believe."

"Well, they didn't get there by getting killed by anyone," he said. "The place has no record of violent crime, like ever."

"What do you mean, none? How far back did you go?"

"Far back as records are digitized," he replied. "There isn't a single record of a homicide or assault or even disturbing the peace for as far back as you want to look. I even did a quick newspaper search and not a thing."

"How is that possible?"

"Either you're surrounded by the nicest people on the planet, or someone is neglecting to keep very good records."

"Huh," Jackie said, stunned for a moment. One person didn't not keep records for decades. That required a chain of events and willful complicity by a number of people. A number of people had clearly died in this town, and if what she had learned was actually true, the deaths were not all by natural causes. "OK, my curiosity is piqued. This is something I can deal with. Can you give me an address for the local law here?"

"Coming right up, Jack," Hauser said. "By the way, we all miss you around here."

Jackie smiled. "I miss you guys, too."

The local police station was two blocks away in a one-story, red brick building. It did not look big enough to hold a single jail cell. A lone police car was parked along the street out front. The glass front door was emblazoned with bright red letters THATCHER'S MILL POLICE DEPT. and when Jackie stepped in, she tripped a dangling bell overhead, signaling everyone that she had arrived. A reception desk sat immediately to the right, behind which was a plump, heavily mascaraed woman in her fifties, looking more ready for the town picnic in her bright, flowery dress than for doing anything related to law enforcement.

The rest of the reception area was lined with several chairs and a wooden bench, upon which sat a young, see-through woman. The general, faint but pervasive sense of Deadworld in this town disguised the fact that she was sitting right there. There had to be a way to focus that ability better. The last thing Jackie needed was to be surprised by a ghost at every turn. Jackie stared at the young woman, who sat arrow-straight with her hands folded neatly in her lap, like she was waiting to be called for something. After a few seconds of staring, her eyes slowly turned to focus on Jackie.

"Can I help you?" the receptionist said with appropriately feigned politeness.

The woman, or perhaps she was a teen, Jackie could not tell for sure, stared in silence at Jackie for several more seconds before returning her blank stare to somewhere across the room.

"Excuse me. May I help you with something?"

Jackie cleared her throat and faced the receptionist, feeling that the ghost's gaze had most certainly returned to her. "Yeah, I'd like to speak with the chief or officer in charge, if I may."

She gave Jackie a casual look-over. "Can I ask what this is pertaining to?"

Jackie's hand itched to reach for the badge. No authority whatsoever now. She was just Jackie Rutledge, Director of Special Investigations, Inc. It did not have the same ring to it.

"I'm a researcher from the University of Chicago, doing a project on ghosts, and—"

"Oh!" She looked at Jackie with wide-eyed surprise and then shook her head. "We don't have any ghosts around here. That's just a bunch of folklore phooey and nonsense drummed up to get tourists through here."

Jackie shrugged and put on her best fake smile. "That

may very well be the case, but I was actually wanting to ask the chief about something more law-enforcement related."

The woman heaved a sigh. "Ah, well then. Chief Carson can probably answer that. Is there a problem?"

"No, no," Jackie reassured. "It's just part of the research we're doing. Thatcher's Mill has some very peculiar crime rates compared to the surrounding areas, and with all the stories of ghosts around here, my team wanted to check it out."

"You have a team?" Her brow wrinkled in confusion.

Jackie resisted the urge to roll her eyes. This was going so well. "Look, I don't want to waste the chief's time any more than I have to. I swear this won't take long."

A door on the far side of the room behind the receptionist swung open. "Goddamn, Elinore. She'd be done asking her questions by now if you'd just hollered at me in the first place."

"Sorry, Chief," she said, attempting to look like she was actually doing something. "I figured you might be busy."

He shook his head. "Busy listening to you gab." He walked around her desk and put out his hand, a twisted, smarmy smile on his face. "Chief Carson. What can I do for you, Ms. Rutledge? Something about the Mill's crime rates?"

Jackie took the hand, pasty and clammy, in hers. He had to be in his fifties, given the thinned out strands of hair slicked back over his scalp and the paunch overhanging his belt. The pencil-thin mustache over his lip looked like it had been drawn on with makeup.

"Jackie Rutledge. And I'm glad to meet the local law for a town with the lowest crime rate in the world. You must be proud."

Carson's hand dropped away, and the leering smile vanished. "Who'd you say you were with, Ms. Rutledge?"

"I didn't," she said. "I'm leading a research team from the University of Chicago on incidents of paranormal activity in this region. Thatcher's Mill seems to have more than its share of ghost stories, but little in the way of crimes to account for their source. Our research put your town on the top of our list. So"—she waved her hand across the room, turning to see if the young woman was still sitting on the bench. She still sat there, staring straight through her—"we're here, trying to make sense of our data."

It sounded like good bullshit. She was going to have to get everyone on the same page about just what the hell they were doing in the town. Conflicting stories would only make these folk more suspicious.

Carson thrust his hands into his pockets. "And what data is that?"

"From what we could find, there hasn't been a homicide in this town as far back as we can look up records, not even an assault," Jackie said, carefully watching his face for reactions. "That just seems to defy the odds, so I was hoping you might be able to clue me in as to what the story is here."

"Story?" His mouth worked in silence for a moment, making the mustache look like a worm crawling across his face. "No story, really. We're just peaceful folk around here, and I run a tight ship. Folk here know the law and like to keep things . . . peaceful."

"What about the chief before you?" Jackie asked. "He ran things just as tightly as you do?"

He laughed, his belly jiggling atop his belt. "If anything, Ms. Rutledge, my father ran things tighter than I do now, and his father before him."

That explained the conspiracy of cover-up, if there indeed was one. "So, there hasn't ever been an actual murder in this town as far back as you know of?"

"That's right," he said, taking a step closer to her, pushing the edges of her personal space. "We're good folk here, who look after each other and mind their own business."

Jackie stood her ground and smiled with no fake friendliness this time. "If I didn't know better, Chief Carson, I'd say you were warning me off."

The wormy smile broadened into a gap-toothed grin. "Just saying, Ms. Rutledge. Folk don't take much to having strangers digging into their business. Your—team is it?—is likely better off moving on to the next town and not wasting your time."

"I see," Jackie said. *Smarmy little shit.* "Well, I'll take your advice up with my team and see what they have to say. We wouldn't want to be upsetting the fine folk of Thatcher's Mill."

"You seem like a smart girl, Ms. Rutledge. I'm sure they'll listen."

And why don't you just say, "Get the hell out of my town," you pasty coward? "Thanks for your time, Chief. Have a good day."

Jackie spun on her heel and stepped toward the door, catching the young woman sitting on the bench out of the corner of her eye. She had not moved, but her shadowed, lifeless eyes followed her out.

Chapter 8

Nick slapped down a ten-dollar bill on the counter. "Thank you for your time, Mr. Pratt." He took another sip from the cream soda made by the drug store's old-fashioned soda fountain. "I haven't had a soda this good in years." He turned and walked away, while the elderly gentleman, wearing an apron with his name inscribed on the front, swiped the bill up off of the counter.

"It's a two-dollar drink, Mr. Anderson," he said.

"Keep the change, worth every penny." Nick stepped through the jingling door and stood beneath the awning, watching a light rain soak the pavement. That was now the third person to lie about the ghosts of Thatcher's Mill, every one of which had hurried away from his presence. The ghosts had been more than wary. They had wanted nothing to do with him.

He pulled out his cell and hit the button for Shelby, while surveying the street. The diner on the corner across from him catered to a handful of locals. To his right, a dairy truck rolled by on the main highway, water spraying up from its tires. To the left, Thatcher's Mill Road stretched off to the east, leading to the edge of the town some four blocks away. There, a drive, shrouded in a stand of oak and maple, wound up the hill, where a plume of smoke dissipated into the low rolling gloom of the sky from a brick chimney barely visible across the tops of the trees.

"Any luck, babe?" Shelby asked.

"I haven't been able to get a single spirit to stick around long enough to chat," he replied. "And I just got lied to about them for the third time in three tries. Something is very off with this place."

Her sarcastic bark of laughter rang in his ear. "Gee, you think? Same problem here. I just about decked the cranky old fuck at the hardware store. I swear, if I hear one more person call me 'Missy' again, I'll scream."

Nick slurped down the last of his cream soda, dropped it in the trash can outside the door, and began to walk east. What was so familiar about this town? He had done more than just pass through here so many years ago. Every corner and building gave him a twinge of déjà vu. He had roamed these streets, lingered in this little town for more than his usual night before moving along the path in his quest for Drake.

"Nick?"

"Yeah?"

"What is it?"

"Nothing," he said. "Just trying to remember why I was here a century ago. It's all a blur, but I stopped here when I was on Drake's trail."

"You stopped in a thousand little backwater towns," she said. "How are you supposed to remember every damn one of them?"

"I know, but there was something else here. I stayed here, maybe for only a day or two longer than usual, but there was a reason. I just can't remember what it was, damn it all."

"You're just getting old, babe."

"Tell me about it."

"Don't get morose on me, cowboy," Shelby snapped

back. "I hate when you brood. Don't worry. Jackie will come around. Just give her some time."

Nick sighed. "I wasn't even thinking about that." *Not actively at least, but thanks for bringing that up.*

"You should be," she said. "Give her space, but don't let her go. She needs you."

"Yes, Mother Meddlesome. Now how about butting out for a while and focusing on the task at hand. I'll be back at the diner in ten minutes."

"OK, I'm almost there. Cyn and Jackie are already waiting."

"Good," Nick said. "You all can plan our wedding." He clicked off before she could reply and shoved the phone back into his pocket. Getting the last word in with her was one of the small pleasures in life.

But it was a poison pill, of course, as the thought brought up actual images in his head of being married to the small, feisty woman who rode into town on her own personal baggage train. The notes of their piano duet echoed in his mind, and that continually fleeting look of almost happiness on her face, when her eyes opened from their perpetual gloom and lit up with the spark of life, a spark he had ignited. If only there weren't so many things in the way that kept it from catching fire and coming to life.

Nick stopped at the end of the road, where two brick posts marked the edge of the drive winding up the hill. A metal placard on one read simply THATCHER'S MILL. He closed his eyes against the spattering rain and caught the faint whiff of smoke drifting down upon the wind. It was a town where the dead fled and the living wanted nothing to do with him. Just like . . .

His eyes snapped open. She wanted nothing to do with him. Over a hundred years ago, on this very hill, in that very house hidden among the trees, a young woman had wanted nothing to do with him. Yes, he remembered now.

Thatcher's Mill flooded up from the depths of Nick's memory.

The mare came to an uneasy stop, her shoes clopping hollowly on the wooden planks of the bridge. The welcome sign read THATCHER'S MILL. Nick leaned over and patted the mare's neck. "Easy, girl. I can feel him, too."

His stomach grumbled. It had been a long, hard two days' ride up along the Mississippi, following Drake's trail. Worse, it had been nearly two days since he had drank any blood. He needed to find someone suitable soon. With a little more coaxing, he nudged the horse back into motion and trotted back onto the muddy road leading into town.

The taint of Drake was the strongest he had felt in months. Not since Kansas City, when he had actually spotted him at the train station but had been too late to board the train. The feeling did not have quite that potency, but he had been here, perhaps just hours before. Even the steady drizzle could not wash away the stench of that man.

Not surprisingly, the town looked empty. Shutters were closed, lamps were extinguished, curtains were drawn, and doors were shut. People were hiding. Nick knew that feeling all too well. It also meant the law had fled from or been killed by Drake. He had stamped his indelible mark of blood upon this place. In the center of town, at the single crossroad, he had a drugstore, saloon, feed store, and the sheriff's to choose from. Nick rode over to the sheriff's and swung off the horse, tying her loosely to the hitching post out front.

Once under the eave, Nick removed his hat and shook the water from it before stepping inside. The single jail cell was empty, as was the rest of the sparsely furnished room. A six-slot gun case on the wall behind the desk was missing two rifles. A town full of holed up folk and a missing sheriff. The situation did not bode well at all. In the stillness of the room, Nick pondered his next move when his overly sensitive hearing caught the faint sound of a wail. It was more a scream of anguish, immediately knotting up his stomach. He had heard that familiar cry far too many times in his thirty years of crisscrossing the country in his endless pursuit of Cornelius Drake. It was the keen of sorrow, the howl of loss for the dead.

Back on his horse, Nick made his way east, past the glass storefront of the drugstore, splashing his way up the rutted road toward the edge of a tree-covered hill that overlooked the town. He caught movement out of the corner of his eye, a face poking through a pulled-back, lace curtain in the window of a sod-covered house. The look was one of curiosity and fear.

Through the trees, he could see the house, built in a clearing partway up the hill. There was a millhouse off to its right, fed by the stream he had crossed coming into town. Every step increased that sense of death he had felt upon entering the town.

The scream echoed down through the trees to him once again, fading into sobs, the sound of a girl or young woman full of mourning and rage. Nick urged the mare up the hill.

Two hundred yards up the road, the trees thinned to reveal a wide clearing. There, a sturdy farmhouse had been built, whitewashed with green shutters on the windows. Here was the money of the town, the Thatchers if Nick were to hazard a guess. On the far side of the clearing was the mill, where he could see the waterwheel churning slowly with the current of the stream. In front of the door, a body lay sprawled in the mud, unmoving. Halted in the center, surveying the scene, Nick caught the unmistakable, muffled sound of a rifle being cocked. From the broken front window, he watched the dark steel of the barrel slide across the sash, pointed in his direction.

“Ma’am?” Nick called out. “I’m U.S. Marshal Nicholas

Anderson. You needn't fear me. I mean you no harm. I come to offer my—"

A flash exploded from the barrel of the rifle and Nick flinched. The mare jumped, rearing back and nearly dumping him onto the ground. Before she could spook any further, he dismounted and grabbed the reins, keeping the horse between him and the window just in case.

"Ma'am, are you hurt? Does anyone need medical attention?"

"They're all dead!" a young, female voice cried out. "He killed them all. What are you doing here?"

Nick slowly walked his horse toward the front door. "Ma'am, what is your name?" He kept a careful eye on the rifle barrel that followed his every move. It shook with unsteady hands. The last thing he wanted was to get shot from an anxious squeeze of the trigger.

"Charlotte," she said. "Charlotte Thatcher."

"Are you hurt, Charlotte?

The gun sagged, tipping the barrel toward the sky. "I don't know. There's . . . there's so much blood."

Nick stopped several feet from the door. He was close enough now to see that the girl was no longer peering out the window. "I'm coming in, Charlotte. I'm here to help." He was met with the sound of choked sobbing. Nick tied off the mare and stepped up onto the porch. The front door was ajar. After easing the door open, he peered around the door jam and saw Charlotte sitting on the floor, face buried in her hands, her slight body shaking with the force of it.

Add another name to the list of people torn apart and ruined by the man he could not stop.

She was barefoot, her spun-wool dress ripped open halfway down the front. The white lace of the collar had been stained the rusty-red color of blood. Her hands were smeared with it. Strands of matted hair fell around her face.

Nick knelt down next to her. "Charlotte," he said quietly. "Let me see if he's hurt you."

When his fingers brushed her arm, Charlotte's hands dropped away, her eyes wide and blind with terror. She scrambled away from him, one hand instinctively clutching at her torn dress. "No, no! Stay away. You stay away from me."

Squatted down on his toes, Nick paused, saying nothing until those wild eyes refocused. "Charlotte. I need to see if you're bleeding." Finally she nodded, and Nick scooted closer, offering his hand to her until she took it. The slender fingers were buried in his and he held it firmly, trying to reassure her, while the other pushed up the sleeve of her dress, to check her arm, and then prodding and squeezing gently to check for broken bones and lacerations. Other than a small cut over her left eye, Charlotte appeared to be unharmed physically, unless Drake had forced himself upon her as well, but Nick was not about to pursue that avenue at this moment.

"All right, Charlotte," Nick said. "Let's get you over to that sofa, and cleaned up a bit. Would you like some water?"

When he released her hand, Charlotte latched onto his with both of hers. "Everyone is dead. Nobody stopped him."

Nick pulled her up and guided her over to the sofa. "I know. He's an evil man, Charlotte." After she sagged back against the cushion, Nick sat down in the chair next to her. "Where are your parents? Are they here in the house?"

She nodded, sniffled, and pointed at the staircase. "They're dead."

Nick already knew. This was not the first time Drake had left a lone survivor for him to find. "Is there anyone else? Brothers? Sisters? Hired help?"

Charlotte blinked at him in silence, eyes pooling with tears, and then she looked down to her lap, where one hand picked absently at the fingernails of the other. The tears began to drop one by one onto her dress. "Becca."

"Is that your sister?"

The hand continued to pick while the tears soaked into the wool. "Not no more." She looked back up at him, despair and incomprehension molding her face. "Nobody tried." Charlotte's voice crumbled. "I didn't . . . know . . ."—she shrugged, lip quivering, and wiped at her running nose—"what to do."

Nick picked up a blanket from off the shelf beneath the couch's end table and unfolded it, draping it over Charlotte's legs. "Stay right here, Charlotte. Can you do that? I want to have a look around and see if anyone is still alive."

Charlotte nodded and reached out toward his face until her fingers brushed across his cheek and then fell back to her lap. "Becca's dead."

He patted her knee and stood up. "I'm sorry, Charlotte. Truly, I am."

The mother was in the pantry, her head barely attached to her body thanks to a severe slice to the throat. Blood had sprayed across the wall and floor. Why he simply shot some victims and at other times rended the flesh from their bodies, Nick still did not fathom. He suspected that those who were reminders of something from his past inspired this insane kind of blood lust. Nick had stopped trying to decipher the meaning long ago. The man was smart enough to know what he was doing and never followed any kind of discernible pattern.

The father had been bled out in the tub, with long, thin slices through the veins of his arms and legs. The hilt of a knife still protruded from his chest. And it was in one of the bedrooms that Nick found the remains of what once was Becca. He sagged against the doorway when he saw her, sprawled on the blood-soaked sheets of her bed, her insides spilled out. It was an all-too-familiar image from his past, and Nick was about to turn away, when it occurred to him that he was looking at Charlotte. Becca had not just been her sister. They were twins.

Nick rubbed a hand over his face and shook his head. "God damn you, Cornelius." He turned quickly away. There was no point in lingering there any longer. Back downstairs he stooped before Charlotte. "I need to check the mill and then I will return to help you and find someone in town who can take care of you."

Charlotte nodded, but said nothing.

The body outside of the mill appeared to be a sheriff's deputy. He had a single, dark hole in the middle of his forehead. His gun remained holstered. Nick reached down and closed the man's eyelids, to shield his dead eyes from the rain. At the door to the mill, he kicked the mud off of his boots and stepped inside. The room was stocked with barrels of grain. Sacks of flour lined a shelf along one wall, and on the opposite, a water wheel lurched against the current of water running through the slough beneath the floor. In the center of the room, the milling machinery groaned with the effort of movement from the wheel.

It took a moment for Nick to realize that the ragged movement of the gears was due to the fact that someone was stuck in them.

The hard soles of his boots echoed across the floor planks as he made his way over to the figure that sagged against the wooden housing of the millstones. The man's arm was threaded through the metal cogs, what remained of his hand dangling by ligaments and flesh coming out the other side. He sat on his knees, unable to fall any closer to the ground, soaking in his own blood. When Nick knelt beside him, he could see the sheriff's star pinned to the shirt inside his coat. Somebody at least had tried to save the Thatchers.

Short of cutting off the arm, there was little Nick could do here. "My apologies, Sheriff. Had I been able to warn you, I would have gladly told you to run for your life."

At the sound of his voice, the sheriff groaned, his eyes opening a crack.

Ah, dear God, he's still alive! "Sheriff. I wish I could have helped you. This man you fought . . . I'm sorry. You had no chance. He is inhuman."

The sheriff only groaned again and closed his eyes once more. He was close to death, Nick could see that. There was too much blood on the floor. Cutting off the arm would only end things that much sooner, and time was short. He was in sore need of blood. The call of the dead was getting stronger by the minute now.

Nick pulled the straight razor from the inside pocket of his duster. "Forgive me, Sheriff. I can only offer this small mercy."

With one deft slash, Nick opened the man's neck. He would be dead in moments, but the blood Nick could take in that small time would get him through the next few days. The loss of pressure from so much blood loss already, gave him only a few seconds before the last sigh of breath from the sheriff's lungs escaped him, but Nick drank what he could, feeling the energy of the man's life flow into him, pushing back against that yawning door in his soul that continually threatened to pull him through.

Finished, Nick withdrew a handkerchief from his pocket and wiped the blood from his mouth. When he stood, the unmistakable creak of the floorboards greeted him. There in the doorway stood Charlotte.

"Ms. Thatcher," he said quietly. "This is not a sight for such young eyes."

The rifle shook in her hands, braced against her shoulder and pointed at his chest. "Monster!" she hissed. "You're one of them."

Yes. He was, doomed to a hellish existence spawned from the hands of something created by the devil himself. Nick folded the handkerchief and tucked it back in his pocket. At this point, he hoped her fear and rage would again send her aim awry.

"There is no need for that, ma'am," he said, attempting to sooth away her terror. "You can put the gun down. I will not harm you."

Charlotte stared at him in silence for several seconds, the gun wavering over his body. Nick held her gaze, hoping that his sway would be enough. For a moment, he thought the bright, teary eyes were losing their fire, but then the handle of the rifle popped.

Her lips barely moved. "You will die."

The muzzle burst to life, and Nick smiled grimly at the whimsical hand of Fate, as he attempted to turn and felt the burn of metal rending his flesh.

Chapter 9

Nick practically stormed into the diner, his short hair dark and slick with water. He did not appear angry from what Jackie could tell, but then he was always difficult to read. Once again, Shelby had sat next to Cynthia, leaving him no choice other than to plop his wet body down next to hers. He leaned forward, arms resting on the table.

"I finally remembered why this place felt so familiar," he said in a hushed voice. "Drake murdered a family here, a husband, wife, and a daughter. The second daughter survived. They lived up the hill on the edge of town at the mill that the town is named for."

Jackie felt the hollow ball of nerves in her gut tighten. *Christ. How many people had that thing killed?* "And you think that had something to do with what is going on here?"

He sat back up and heaved a sigh. "Perhaps."

Cynthia waved a suggestive finger at Nick. "That might explain the source of the curse."

Molly, the waitress, chose that moment to stop by with her pot of coffee. She reached out without asking and filled Nick's cup. Jackie shoved hers over for a warm-up.

"Wouldn't even talk about that around here if I were you," she said. "It's not safe."

Jackie pulled her coffee cup back. "Safe for who?"

"Anyone," the waitress whispered and moved along before anyone could reply without raising their voices and being heard throughout the restaurant.

"We need to talk to her," Jackie said. "Alone."

"And we need to talk," Nick said, and for a terrifying moment, Jackie thought he meant about them. "But not here. Everyone in this town seems to be wary of our presence."

"Got that right," Shelby said. "Ghosts and otherwise. Every time I mentioned the word 'ghost' everyone just clammed up and did their best to shoo me away."

"And their chief of police is an asshole," Jackie added. "I thought for a minute he might try to escort me to the edge of town."

Nick said, "So, do we want to stay close by or fly back home?"

Laurel stepped out of Deadworld, and pushed directly on Jackie. *Let me in, please!*

Shelby smiled at Jackie. "Well, that took long enough. I thought there wasn't much to see over there?"

Let's head back, hon. That thing is coming.

What? The spindly fucker? It followed us?

Yes! And I'm pretty sure it's you, not us, that it's following.

"We're going back home," Jackie said, the decision made within one stuttering heartbeat. "That . . . whatever the hell it is followed me."

Shelby slammed her hand down on the table. "Fuck."

Nick stared at Jackie for several seconds, mouth tightening into a frown, and then got to his feet. "She's right, let's head back. If it took several hours for it to catch up to us, we'll have several to figure something out once we're back."

Jackie slid out and followed close behind Nick. What they could possibly figure out in that time remained to be seen. What did one do with strange alien beings following you around via a parallel, dead universe?

Jackie let Nick drive. As much as she hated giving up

vehicular control, her hands were damp and fidgety. Worse, though, was the fear that she might abruptly see those glowing green eyes appear in the middle of the road and swerve everyone to their doom. She stared off into the low-swept gloom, and listened to the others discuss probable causes to this town. The stupid thing was, they could just leave it. There was no apparent crime. They had no authority to investigate, make arrests, conduct searches, or anything. They were just a group of civilians digging into a potential problem. It could be anything or nothing at all, but Jackie had a firm feeling that it was far from nothing.

Five minutes into their flight home, Jackie's cell phone rang. It was McManus.

"Hey, Jack," he said. "You all have a problem back here."

Shit! What else could go wrong with this day? "Great. Just what I wanted to hear. What's up?"

"Looks like someone broke into your office."

"You're shitting me." Jackie wanted to hurl the phone across the cabin. "How bad is it?"

"A broken window, but from what we can tell, nothing's been taken. You'll have to come by to make sure."

"Goddammit. You're not making my day any better, McManus."

"Sorry," he replied. "You guys find something out there?"

"Maybe, I don't know. A lot of ghost shit we don't understand. We need to get some more intel on the place."

"Hauser should be working on it."

"He is. I'm sure he'll dig up something. He always does."

"You going to be coming by, then?"

"Yeah, guess we are. An hour or so, I'd guess."

"Cool. Sorry, Jack. I'll see you then."

Jackie clicked off her phone. Everyone was now giving her an expectant look. "Someone may have broke into the office," she said and shoved the phone into her pocket. "We need to go by and check it out."

McManus was sitting on the edge of Cynthia's desk when they walked in. "Hey, you guys. How was the trip?"

"Bad enough without having to deal with this crap," Jackie said. "Any leads on who did this?"

He shrugged. "Still very little. I was hoping you all had your security system operational before you left."

"Cyn," Nick said, "pull up the security cameras and see what's there."

She was already around the desk when he said it. Jackie and Shelby walked down the hall toward the back offices. A quick, cursory look-over verified what McManus had said earlier. Other than a broken window in the conference room, nothing appeared to be missing or out of place. Back in the front, McManus leaned over Cynthia's shoulder on one side, while Nick stood behind looking down at the computer screen.

Jackie stopped next to him. "Find anything?"

Nick pointed at the screen. "See for yourself."

The intruder, wearing jeans, a black leather jacket, and a ski mask, climbed in through the broken window and then stopped to look at the files they had stacked on the conference table. He then pulled out a digital camera and began to take pictures.

"Who gives a shit about these old files?" Jackie wondered. Who could possibly know that they even had them?

"Good question," McManus said.

The intruder walked out of the room and came up to the front, where he proceeded to attempt to get onto Cynthia's computer.

"Not a hacker, that's for sure," Shelby commented.

Cynthia glanced up and smiled. "He'd never guess my password anyway."

After about a minute, the man gave up and wandered back down the hall, taking more pictures as he went. In Jackie's office, he stood in the middle and did a slow turn before walking over to her case board. He looked over what little information was there, copies of what they had on Thatcher's Mill, and took several more pictures. He then proceeded to hastily make his exit back out through the broken window.

"Pictures of what we're doing," Jackie said. "Why?"

McManus stood back up, his hand brushing across Cynthia's arm. "Thanks, Cynthia. In and out in under five minutes. Security company arrived in six. So, he knew what he was doing."

"Not a professional, though," Nick added. "And not sure what he was looking for."

"He wanted to know what we were doing," Shelby said. "Like Jackie said, why? And who would care? Nobody except FBI has any idea about what we're up to."

Jackie pointed an accusing finger at the computer screen with the frozen image of the man climbing out the window. "That fucking reporter! The shit followed us to the airport."

"Reporter?" McManus said. "What reporter?"

Nick nodded. "The one from your apartment. That would make sense."

"He found a discrepancy at the Tannenbaum fire," Jackie said. "Thinks we're covering up something."

"And now the strange FBI agent is working for an even stranger organization called Special Investigations." Shelby chuckled. "No wonder he's curious. I'd be wondering, too, given what he knows."

"Who is this reporter?" McManus asked. "I'll track him down for you and see what he's up to—unofficially, of course."

"He wants a story," Jackie said. "It's what they all want. You know what? Just leave the asshole alone for now.

There's nothing for him to find. He wants a conspiracy and cover-up, but he won't believe the truth even if he finds it."

Nick gave her an arched eyebrow. "Breaking and entering, Jackie. You want to just give that to him?"

"He'll show up again," she said. "We'll have words when he does."

Shelby snorted. "I'll bet." She picked up her purse off of the desk. "Should let me talk to him. He won't come around anymore after that."

"No voodoo mojo bullshit, Shelby!" Jackie demanded. She took a breath and wiped from her mind the image of Nick's hands holding her face the night before, his depthless eyes glowing with the gray fog of the dead. "Last thing he needs is to figure out the things we're capable of."

"Then let me arrest him," McManus said. "You don't need this kind of thing going on, not to mention that it's, you know, against the law."

"Not worth it," Jackie said. "All he did was break a window. He'll pay for that, but I'm not tossing a guy in jail for wanting answers."

McManus nodded. "OK, fair enough. You let me know otherwise, though."

"Can we go now?" Jackie said. "I'm starving and tired and want a break from all of this crap."

"I've got steaks," Nick said. "We could figure out what we're doing while I grill."

"Beer?" Shelby asked.

Nick smiled. "Of course. Jackie?"

She really just wanted to go home, but they did need to figure out what to do next, and her fridge was back to its cartons of Chinese and other things past their expiration dates. And this time she would make sure to go when the others did. And Nick was grilling steak. She was salivating at the mere thought of it.

Jackie glanced up at him. "Steaks sound great."

He turned to McManus. "Welcome to join us, McManus.

We can fill you in on what we've found and you can help us plan out next steps."

"Um," he said, and then caught Cynthia looking up at him from her chair. Jackie watched Shelby poke him in the back. Did the woman ever *not* stick her fingers into other people's business? "Sure. It's too late for me to get anything done back at HQ anyway."

"Sweet," Shelby said and bounded toward the door. "Cookout at Nick's."

Jackie rolled her eyes and nudged Nick. "Don't you ever want to smack her? Even just a little?"

A smile tugged at the corners of his mouth. "Every day."

Chapter 10

The smell of steaks on the grill wafted in through the screen door and Jackie's stomach grumbled. The cold beer was doing little to alleviate her hunger. She sat at the dining room table, staring out through the glass windows at Nick, who stood shrouded in the glow of the porch light and swirling smoke. At times he would turn and gaze in at them through the glass; if the angle was right, she would catch a glimpse of those glowing eyes, faint but discernible if you knew what you were looking for.

He had not said a word all day about anything that had happened, not even a hint of how he was feeling about it all. He had not shied away from her or avoided her gaze. Either he was doing an admirable job of giving her space or he had no feelings about what had happened. But how could that be? She had completely flipped out on him, embarrassed them both, and undoubtedly left him disappointed he'd ever involved himself with her. He was doing a fantastic job of moving on with things and just letting it be. Damn him.

"Yo, babe," Shelby said, snapping her fingers in front of Jackie. "Earth to Jackie. You with us?"

Jackie turned back to the others gathered at the table

with her and what little information they had spread out before them. "Sorry. We ready?"

McManus, sitting across from her and next to Cynthia, set his cell down on the table. "You're on speaker, Hauser. What have you got?"

"Hey everyone. I'm just digging back into this stuff again," he said. "Sorry I couldn't do more earlier, but I can't make this high on my priority list at this point."

"That's OK, Hauser," Jackie replied. "We don't even have a real case at this point."

"I'll put some extra time on it here after hours because I love you so much."

Shelby made a dismissive sound and Hauser laughed. "We love you, too, Ms. Fontaine, but I think you scare most of us down here in the lab. No offense."

She huffed. "What have I done to scare you boys?"

"Oh, pretty much everything, I'd guess."

Everyone laughed at that. Jackie shook her head.

"So, nothing new since this morning?" Jackie asked.

"Nothing criminal," Hauser replied. "It is a strange little town, though."

"Tell me something I don't know," Jackie said.

"Most of the families there have been living in Thatcher's for generations. Very few people have moved in or out from what I can tell. In fact, the population hasn't varied by more than a few people for decades."

Jackie had no idea if that fact meant anything. "That doesn't happen much, I take it?

"It's statistically possible," Hauser said, "but highly improbable. It smacks of population control if you ask me."

Control. The wormy smile of Chief Carson flashed in her mind. "Can you look into the police department there? Their police chief gave me a bad vibe." Not to mention the ghost that stared at her the entire time.

"Sure. Anything else you guys want me to dig into, besides my general poking around?"

"Death certificates," Shelby added.

"Of the townsfolk?" Hauser asked.

"Yes. We want to know who has died there over the past century," she said.

Hauser chuckled. "Hundred years? Not sure I can track it down that far back, but will see what I can do. Am I looking for something particular?"

"Age of death," Shelby replied, as Jackie was about to add the same suggestion. "A list of how old everyone was who died there."

"How is that going to help you?" Hauser asked.

"A bunch of ghosts, Hauser," Jackie replied. "They all look roughly the same age, and we're betting death records aren't going to match up."

"Wow, sounds cool. You guys get all the fun stuff."

Nick came in carrying a platter of steaming, grilled rib eyes and foil-wrapped potatoes.

"Hardly," Jackie said. "We've got steaks to eat here, Hauser. We'll talk later."

A few minutes later, they were all gathered around the table, digging into succulent meat and butter and sour cream-drenched potatoes.

McManus waved his fork at Jackie, chewing away on a mouthful of food. When he finally swallowed, he said, "How is it you haven't married this guy yet, Jack? People have killed for food this good. Seriously, Nick, this may be the best steak I've ever had."

He smiled. "All in the seasoning. It's a secret recipe I got from my cook days."

"Covert mission, Jack. Do it."

Jackie gave McManus a halfhearted smile and kept eating her food. Married. Now there was a joke. How about making it through until the next morning? That would be a worthy goal. Pathetic perhaps, but a success nonetheless. There was some more friendly banter, but everyone was focused mostly on the food until the plates were clean. Nick then made them coffee, and tea for Cynthia, while McManus and Shelby continued on their beers.

"Did we get anything new from the FBI?" Nick wondered after everyone was settled back at the table again.

Jackie shrugged. "Only that the population of the town hasn't changed in decades. Hauser's looking into the police chief and gathering up stats on death certificates."

"Well then, what is next on our agenda?" Nick asked. "I assume we're all in agreement that this is worth pursuing further?"

"Should have Laur here," Jackie said. "She's over waiting to see if that thing comes back."

"What thing?" McManus said.

"Long story, McManus." Jackie waved him off, hoping he would let it slide. "Nothing you can do about it right now anyway."

"Hope it stays that way," Cynthia added.

Jackie quickly continued. "Anyway, what do we do now? We don't have a whole lot to go on other than some suspicions and a bunch of ghosts where there shouldn't be any. Other than trying to find someone who will talk, I'm open to suggestions."

McManus's cell rang again and he immediately put it on speaker. "That was quick, Hauser."

"Hey, we aim to please down here," he said. "Still digging, but I ran the certificates for you, since that was a quick and easy thing. What specifically do you want to know?"

Jackie thought for a second. "Young women. How many women, fifteen to twenty-four, have died there in the past hundred years?"

"Sure. Iowa goes back to 1880's on these. One sec," he said, and there was silence for a few moments. They all stared at the phone in anticipation. "OK, looks like twenty-six, but only three of those are after 1950."

"That's it? You sure, Hauser?" Jackie asked.

"Stats don't lie, Jack. It may not account for every last one of them, but assuming the records were filed, it should be pretty accurate."

"Thanks. That was potentially helpful," she said. *And not in the way that I'd hoped. This is going nowhere good.*

After Hauser clicked off, everyone was silent for a moment.

"The numbers don't add up?" McManus said.

"We counted thirty-six ghosts in Thatcher's Mill," Jackie replied, "thirty-one of which were female, and most of them young women. That was just all we could find in a couple of hours walking around."

"This is not good, I take it?"

"No," Nick answered. "It's not. Young women have died there that are likely unaccounted for through the records."

McManus sat back, hands folded behind his head. "You telling me that someone has been bringing women to Thatcher's Mill and killing them?"

"Given the little we know so far, it's a good possibility," Nick said. "But it could've been fifty years ago for all we can tell. We were unable to get any information from the ghosts there."

"They wouldn't talk?"

"They were all very reluctant to say anything at all."

"I think some of them were flat-out afraid to talk," Shelby added. "It was very weird."

"But it was a place attacked by Drake a century ago," Nick added. "That fact may or may not be involved here."

"Really?" McManus nodded. "Sounds like a lot of loose ends and theories that need to be verified."

"We're going back," Jackie said. "Tomorrow." They had no choice. It could all turn out to be nothing, but her gut told her that was not the case. Some or all of those ghosts walking around in Thatcher's Mill had been killed by someone, and her suspicions told her that it was still going on.

"Executive decision!" Shelby stated. "I'm really curious now what the hell is going on there."

Cynthia took a quiet sip of her tea. "Could all of those women been killed by someone?"

"The second you find something, you call me, Jack," McManus said. "You don't have any authority to do anything."

"No need to remind me of that," Jackie said. "I'm well aware of my current situation."

An awkward silence followed, finally broken up by Shelby. "Who's up for a little pool? No need to get all serious until tomorrow."

"You any good?" McManus wondered.

"Enough to kick your ass, Agent McManus," she said, grinning.

"Sweet. How about you, Jack? Up for a little FBI versus the civilians?"

She shook her head. "No, go ahead. I'm not in the mood."

"Oh, come on, babe. Have a little—"

"Not in the mood!" Jackie snapped back.

"Fine." She raised a placating hand up between them. "Go be all broody." She turned back to McManus. "Care to put a little money where your mouth is, McManus?"

He stood up. "I think I have a few lonely bills in my wallet looking for some company."

Cynthia joined them, and Nick moved toward the kitchen. "Think I'll get things cleaned up here first."

Left alone, Jackie grabbed her coffee and went out on the expansive back deck. The rain had stopped and moon-crusted clouds drifted by, obscuring and then revealing the night sky. Hopping a ride on one of those clouds and drifting away for a while sounded like the best thing in the world at the moment. Everything felt so unsettled. Her nerves danced on pins and needles. Nothing was as it should be or had been. She needed to get a rhythm back in her life, somehow, because all of her old routines had been stomped into the ground. The wheels were spinning, and nothing in her life right now gave her any traction.

Her cell picked that moment of quiet to ring in her pocket, buzzing against her thigh and Jackie nearly knocked her coffee cup off the deck railing. Her eyes rolled to the heavens when she saw caller ID. Tillie.

"Dr. Erikson," she said, trying in vain not to sound too exasperated. "How are you?"

"I called to ask you the same thing, dear. I left on such an awkward note last night."

"Story of my life right now. I'm fine . . ." Jackie took a deep breath. "OK, not so fine, really. I'm stressed out, but it's manageable."

"Have you talked with Nick about what happened?"

She turned and leaned against the rail to see Nick walking toward the sliding glass door, coffee in hand. Shit. "Not yet. I don't think I'm ready to go there."

"I believe it's important that you do, Jackie," Tillie said, her voice softening. "Don't let him push you, though. Anything, whatever it is, should be at your discretion, when you're ready."

Push me. I don't think he'll push this at all if I've learned anything about the man. "Not sure I'll ever be ready for that."

"Dear, you will. Trust me. Trust yourself."

The door opened and Nick stepped out. "Thanks for the call, Tillie. I need to go." She hung up without waiting for a reply.

Nick stopped a few feet away. "Long first day, Agent Rutledge. It was an interesting one, to say the least."

"No kidding," she said. "Thanks for cooking by the way. It was really good, as always."

He shrugged, a faint smile on his shadowed face, set off by the dim gray glow in the depths of his eyes. "Have to keep the crew well fed."

"You know, Nick, leading this group is kind of redundant. I'm the least skilled when it comes to this supernatural crap."

Nick stepped up and leaned against the rail beside her. "Those aren't the skills required for the job, and those skills will grow with experience. You may think this ridiculous, but I have a feeling you will find that you have more ability with regard to the supernatural than all of us put together."

Her coffee went down wrong when she tried to laugh that off and Jackie ended up coughing. "Yeah, right. I don't have a clue, Nick, about anything at the moment."

"I know I've said this before, but it takes time, and we can all help you with it, if you'll trust us enough, and you have the desire."

Trust and desire. Those were tricky concepts, and even more so when put together. And then there was that lingering elephant dancing between them. "I don't know, Nick. I didn't want any of this . . . stuff. I don't want . . ." She sighed, at a loss to explain or even wanting to.

"Me?" Nick asked quietly.

It took a second for the question to sink in. "What? No, I wasn't trying to say that, and I don't really want to talk about that now." *Please don't go there. Please don't.*

He nodded. "I understand. I do, but I'd like to say something, and you don't have to respond or say anything, just be willing to listen."

God, here it comes. Jackie turned and looked up into that calm, still face, the porch light reflecting off the smooth, new skin of the scar along his jaw. "OK. I'm listening."

"First off, I wanted to apologize—"

"Nick, no." Jackie laid her hand against his chest. "No apologies. You didn't do a damn thing wrong."

He stared down at her in silence until her hand dropped away, and gave Jackie a pained smile. "I'm sorry that I didn't stop things sooner. I could tell it was difficult before things ever got to the point they did. I've known this was hard for you from day one. I don't understand it all, and I don't need to, but I'd like to. I didn't stop things sooner last night because I had hopes that when I woke up this morning, you'd being lying in bed next to me."

Jackie hung her head, staring down at the deck in silence. *Me too.*

"Jackie," he said, and remained silent until she looked back up. "Whatever it is, whatever you need . . . take your time. We aren't in any hurry, and I'm not going anywhere. If, in the end, the answer is 'no,' then just tell me. There's no obligation here. You don't owe me for saving your life or anything else. If what I am interferes too much, then I get that, too." Nick thrust his hands into his pockets and let out his breath in a rush. "When you get down to it, it's pretty simple. I like you, Jackie, enough that I do want you waking up next to me in the morning, but I also consider you a friend, and life has done you no favors of late. As your friend, I want you to take care of yourself and be healthy and alive. To me that's more important than any of this other stuff between us." He picked up his coffee cup off the railing and took a drink. "OK?"

What to say to that? Jackie nodded. "OK." The tension that had knotted up her stomach when he began this speech faded by the time he was done. Last night had not made him think she was a complete nut job, even if she was. "Thanks for that, Nick." She chuckled. "I don't think I've ever heard you talk that much at one time."

He turned and leaned against the rail. "It needed to

be said. Something like last night was not meant to break us."

Jackie was not quite sure how to take that, but she had to agree. She did not want it to break them, to get in the way of everything else. Her hand settled on top of his. "My coffee's cold. Warm it up?" For now at least, that dancing elephant had pranced off into the shadows.

Chapter 11

Margolin pulled up under the streetlight in front of the Thatcher's Mill diner and shut off the headlights of his car. He leaned forward against the steering wheel and stared out at the smattering of lit windows curtained off against the night. It looked like your typical rural town, like a thousand others scattered around the Midwest. Not a creepy thing about it.

He recalled the note, pinned to the bulletin board in Special Investigations' office, over a decade old, speaking to the inordinate amount of ghostly activity in the area. The questions had been running through his head for the past four hours. Why were they here? What possible interest could they have in a bunch of ghosts? And why the hell was a former FBI agent working for that company?

Inside the diner, Margolin stepped up to the counter and sat down on a stool. The dinner crowd had gone, and there were only two others seated in the room. The waitress, who was busy cleaning up behind the counter, gave him an exasperated smile. Someone was ready to go home.

"What can I get for you?"

"Some coffee," he said, "and how about a piece of pie?"

"Pumpkin or apple?"

"What do you recommend?"

"Apple's made here," she said.

"Apple it is, then."

He waited in silence while she got the pie and warmed it up in a microwave. She put a scoop of ice cream on the side and brought it over with the coffee pot. "Anything else for you?"

"Actually, I have a question," Margolin said.

The woman rolled her eyes. "I'm off at ten, and no." With that, she sashayed back over to her cleaning.

Margolin laughed. "Thanks, but not what I wanted to ask."

"Ah. Well." She gave him a fleeting smile. "Too bad. You're cute and I probably would've changed my mind."

"Good God, Molly," came the cook's voice from the back. "I pay you to work, not flirt."

"Oh, you be quiet, Tucker," she yelled over the counter. "It's called customer relations."

"Do your relating on your own time, woman," he sniped back.

Margolin grinned. "Molly, is it? Well, Molly, I was hoping you might have—"

The loud rumble of a motorcycle engine cut him off. He turned and looked out the window to see a polished piece of fabulous chrome and fire-engine-red paint roll to a stop in front of his car. Someone hardly big enough to be riding the thing swung her lithe little leg over the seat and came marching up to the door. The door jangled the overhanging bell and slammed back against the wall, and in walked a pistol-whip of a young woman, her head covered in an old-fashioned aviator style hat with goggles perched on top of her head. Her black army boots moved soundlessly across the floor.

"Tucker! Molly!" She stopped when she caught Margolin staring at her. "Eat your dessert, pretty boy."

"What's up, Charlie?" Tucker stepped out from the

kitchen, wiping his hands on his apron. "Not your usual night out. Something wrong?"

Pretty boy? Margolin could not recall ever having been called that, except maybe by his grandmother when he was seven. This woman—though woman might be stretching it, she did not look much older than sixteen—had a very authoritative look about her. Having interviewed hundreds of people over the years, Margolin could usually tell someone's character just by how that person stood and looked at others, and this motorcycle chick had "boss" written all over her. It struck Margolin as very peculiar in someone who looked so young. He made a mental note: *older than she looks.*

"I just spoke with Chief Carson," she said, stopping at the cash register on the end of the counter and folding her hands over the top of it. "He says some people were here earlier, looking for something."

"Oh!" Molly exclaimed, waving a finger at Charlie. "It was them ghosthunters, four of them I think it was."

Margolin sat bolt upright. *Answered that question. And why are you suddenly so anxious, Molly? Little motorcycle chick makes you nervous?* "You know, I happen to be looking for them, too."

Charlie's head pivoted with the slow precision of a wind-up doll until her gaze fell upon Margolin. She lay her cheek down against her arm and arched her brows. "Do you now? And just who are you, pretty boy?"

He had a handy retort, but it faded away somewhere between his brain and mouth. Those big, hooded, hazel eyes were haunting. Something about them looked off. They were exceptionally bright, even for the lit room they were in. "I'm a journalist, from Chicago. I'm following a story on this group and was hoping to find out why they came here to Thatcher's Mill. Something to do with ghosts, I think."

"Really," Charlie said. "Chicago?"

"It's true," Molly said. "They wanted to know why there were so many ghosts here."

"I see," Charlie pushed herself up from the register. "Molly, why don't you close up. I believe the diner is closing a few minutes early tonight." She walked toward Margolin, who got a very unsettling feeling in his gut about this woman, yet he could not take his eyes off of her. "Tom," she said to the man who had been reading his paper over coffee in the corner booth, "best you be heading home now."

He folded up his paper and scrambled to his feet. "Sure thing, Ms. Thatcher. Lovely to see you, as always."

She flashed a smile at him before refocusing on Margolin. "So, pretty boy, what is your name?"

He leaned away from the counter as she approached. There was something incredibly dangerous in that smile of hers. "Margolin. Philip Margolin. You can call me Margolin."

"Philip Margolin," she said, lingering longer on the *ph* sound. "Why don't you come sit with me and tell me about these ghosthunter people from Chicago."

He slid off the stool before even considering his answer. "You seem to have some authority around here, Charlie."

Again, the fleeting smile rolled across her face, leaving no pleasantness in its wake. "That I do, Philip." She drifted across to a booth and sat down, watching Molly lock up the door behind the fleeing Tom. "Sit, please. Molly? Some tea, if you would."

Margolin slipped into the seat across the table from her. Who the hell was this chick? He could see the allure, but these people were falling all over themselves. She folded her hands together and rested her chin upon them, staring at him in silence as Molly slid the cup of hot water dangling a teabag string before her. Charlie did not acknowledge her presence. Margolin got the unnerving sense that he had stepped into a bad, teen mob show on the CW.

"So, Philip," she said and reached down to bob her

teabag in the cup, "tell me about these ghosthunters you're looking for."

Actually, I'm more interested in who you are, lady. Once again, though, the thought did not quite reach his mouth. Her question was innocent enough. "Honestly, I don't know a whole lot about them, other than I believe they're involved in some kind of FBI cover-up."

The hand let go of the tea bag and she stared at him, not moving for several seconds. "The FBI? That is interesting. Why do you think that?"

I should be trading information here, seeing what she might know about why they're here. "The woman, Agent Jackie Rutledge—"

"Agent!" The cool, seductive demeanor vanished for a split second, but then Charlie smiled and picked up her tea. "She is an FBI agent?"

Margolin wagged a finger at her. "Was. That's the operative word here. She got fired for killing a Chicago cop, and is now with this group called Special Investigations. I found out through my, um, resources, that they're digging through old FBI files, looking for something. They came here, and I'm trying to find out why."

"Old files? That is curious," she said, demurely sipping at her tea. "There have been no significant crimes in Thatcher's Mill for years."

Margolin chuckled. "You hardly look old enough to know about crimes that happened here years ago."

The smile vanished as easily as it had come. "Looks can be deceiving, Phillip. I'm quite familiar with what goes on in my town."

Whoa. My town? That hit a sore spot. This chick is not what she seems. Creepy little bitch. "So, what do you think they're looking for then? What's with the ghosts?"

Charlie set down her tea, and the smile returned. "Old stories, passed down over generations, nothing more. It brings in the tourists and the occasional crackpot looking to prove the existence of the paranormal."

"These people are hardly crackpots, Charlie," Margolin said. "They're up to something."

"Perhaps," she said, "that is why they harassed Chief Carson today." Her hand slipped across the table, reaching for his, a single finger tracing lightly across its back. "You have your suspicions, I suspect. You are a big city journalist after all."

Margolin looked down at the finger brushing over his skin, suppressing the shudder of goose bumps that ran up his arm. *Wow. This chick is smooth. Definitely not a teen.* "If I were to guess, I'd say they're looking for someone, maybe someone involved in this cover-up they're perpetrating. You know," he said, "you have the brightest eyes I've ever seen. They almost glow."

Her finger continued to trace its circle on the back of his hand. "Family trait. Like them, do you?"

"They're quite stunning, actually." *Shit! Is this going where I think it is? Or is she just playing me? And why do I care?* Questions could be dealt with the morning after.

"Thank you." Her head cocked to one side while those big, dark eyes studied him. "Perhaps we can help one another, Phillip. Would you like to help me with these people?"

"You know I would," he replied. "How can you help me?"

Charlie's hand covered his, and Margolin felt his cock begin to harden. "I have a certain influence around here. I can . . . make things happen. If they come back—"

"When," Margolin said. "If they're digging, they'll be back." *And in the meantime maybe we can get to know one another a little better.*

She nodded. "When they come back, would you like to help me deal with them? I believe we could have a mutually beneficial relationship here. Maybe you'll even get your story."

"I'd like that. How shall I contact you, Charlie?"

"There's a bed and breakfast a mile up the highway. You can stay there," she said, and withdrew her hand from his. The separation created a hollow ache in his chest. "We'll be in touch."

Oh, I'd like to touch you all right. Jesus Christ, this girl has it going on. I'm clearly not getting out of the city enough. "You want me to contact you when they get back in town?"

Charlie slid out of the booth and stood next to him. Her hand reached out to caress his cheek. "You're such a pretty boy. We'll keep this between us, OK? Our little secret?"

Margolin nodded. *Who can say no to that face? What an amazing beauty.* "Sure thing. We'll get these bastards, don't you worry."

"I'm not worried." Her finger brushed across his lips. "We will."

Chapter 12

After a relatively restful night—meaning Jackie had actually slept for more than three hours without waking up from a nightmare that involved blood, death, Nick, Laurel, her mom, or some combination of all of the above—she woke to the simple, blaring beep of her alarm clock. Bickerstaff padded up from the foot of the bed and rubbed his face against hers.

Jackie slapped her hand over the clock, swatting at it until she hit the off switch. She sneezed. "Damn it, Bickers! Get down." The cat leaped to the floor when she threw back the covers and sat up. In her reading chair in the corner of the room, sat Laurel's pale, ethereal figure. "Laur? How long you been sitting there?"

She smiled and shrugged. "A while. You were sleeping so peacefully. I couldn't bear to wake you up."

Jackie rubbed her hands over her face, digging out the sleep from the corner of her eyes. "Which means you have something you want to tell me?"

Laurel grimaced. "It came back, hon. That thing is just hanging out on the other side, waiting for you. I know it is."

"Shit." Jackie slammed her hands down on the bed, got to her feet, and headed to the bathroom. "I mean, maybe it doesn't matter. If I never cross over again, it might just go away."

"Which is fine," Laurel replied, passing through the bedroom wall and into the bathroom. "At which point I'm more concerned it might get me. I can't directly leave you or get to you anymore, hon. Do you really want to have to travel every time I come or go?"

"No," Jackie said. "That wouldn't be ideal, but Laur?" She pulled off her pajama top and reached into the shower to turn on the hot water. "I'm not going to go over and tell that creepy fucker to leave me alone. For now, we'll just have to deal with the fact that some alien porcupine bastard is following me around. Maybe we'll all figure out a plan to deal with it, but right now the thought of that thing freaks the hell out of me. I've got enough on my plate."

"Can I ask how things are with Nick?"

"No," Jackie replied. "I'm actually dealing with it though, sort of. So don't worry.

Laurel nodded. "I know. Enjoy your shower. This is going to be a long day."

Shelby picked her up at seven-thirty and they were all sitting at the conference table with coffee, Annabelle's pastries, and Hauser on the speakerphone.

"A bunch of shiny, happy people living there in Thatcher's Mill, guys," Hauser said by way of greeting. "I haven't found any discrepancies to indicate record tampering. The Thatcher family on the other hand, is . . . well, honestly, I'm not even sure what to make of this info."

Jackie washed down her chocolate croissant with now-lukewarm coffee. Hauser being unsure meant she was going to have no clue. "That bad, Hauser?"

"It's not bad, per se," he said. "Just, well, get this. Robert Thatcher married Mildred Wilcott about five years ago.

Wilcott took the family name and then also had her first name changed to Beverly."

"First name, too?" Jackie asked. That was odd.

"Her name was Mildred," Shelby said. "I'd be so inclined as well."

Cynthia slapped her across the arm. "Shut up. You're so mean."

Shelby stuck her tongue out at her. "Just honest. Mildred is simply dreadful."

"Anyway," Hauser said loudly, "now it gets weird. Robert Thatcher was born Isaac Larson. He changed his name when he married his first wife, Beverly Thatcher."

"Say what?" That was a new one on Jackie. "The second wife took the name of the first wife? That's pretty damn creepy. Why would anyone want to do that?"

"Assuming they wanted to," Nick replied.

Hauser chuckled. "Oh, it keeps going. I've found seven Thatchers so far who joined the family and became either Beverly or Robert Thatcher. They really do want to keep the family names alive. It'll be fun to see how far back this goes."

Nick sighed, both hands wrapped around his coffee mug on the table. "It will be the Thatchers who ran the mill in the 1890s. I'll bet you anything that's where the chain starts."

Together, Shelby and Jackie said, in the same exasperated tone, "Drake."

"Wonder if that has something to do with the curse that got mentioned?" Cynthia said.

Shelby laughed. "Cursed to become a Thatcher? That's . . ." She turned to Cynthia. "Is that possible, Cyn?"

"Something like that? Not likely. Not without help," she said. "A curse is more subtle."

"So, someone is coercing them," Nick added. "Why is having the Thatchers around so important?"

"Why don't we go ask them?" Jackie said.

"Yeah, you'll have to," Hauser said. "Apparently there's no home phone."

"None?" Jackie found that hard to believe. "No cell service either?"

"Not that I can find," he replied. "If something comes up, I'll let you know. In the meantime, I'll keep looking as much as I can. Other priorities, FBI stuff." He paused for a moment. "Sorry, Jack."

"No need, Hauser. Thanks," she said.

"It might be after hours or lunch break, but I'll keep seeing what I can dig up. Glad to help my favorite *agent*."

The speaker went silent. Jackie grimaced. "Wipe those looks off your faces right now." Their pity was the last thing she needed or wanted. "I'm here by choice. Nobody forced me to do this, so just . . . don't."

"All right," Nick said. "Fair enough. Are we heading back to Thatcher's Mill, then?"

Jackie downed the last of her coffee. It would be a while before she had any of the good stuff. "Yes. Let's see what other weirdness we can dig up in that ghost town."

They were in Thatcher's Mill before noon. Jackie slowed as they crossed the bridge again, wary this time of any lingering dead strolling across the road. Now that she knew they were there, the ghosts were not difficult to pick up on. She counted five with just a cursory look around Main Street.

"Still a party in the Mill," Shelby said. "Really curious why they're all here."

"Maybe the Thatchers will give us a clue," Jackie said. "I also think that ass-hat police chief knows something. I'm going to have a little talk with him again."

Shelby reached over and slapped Nick on the shoulder. "Don't you just love her when she gets all firm like that?"

Nick turned and looked back at her, eyes narrowed. "Actually, yes. I do."

Jackie's head whipped around, eyes wide. Shelby snorted but said nothing. For once she had no rejoinder. Nick turned back, one corner of his mouth curled up in a smile and gave Jackie a hard, amused stare before refocusing on the road ahead. *What the hell was that all about? Did he actually just say what I think he did?*

"The Thatchers' place is on the edge of town," he said. "Turn right at the diner."

Main Street had the feel of a ghost town. Jackie saw more ghosts than actual living people out on the street. Even though it was a cool and blustery November day, she expected there would be more activity. It was also the post-Thanksgiving weekend, and she did not see a single Christmas decoration. "Anyone else find it odd that there isn't a single Christmas decoration up anywhere?"

They reached the end of the street and began to ascend the drive up to the Thatchers'. Nick leaned forward in his seat, studying the buildings up ahead with an intense gaze.

Jackie glanced over at him, wondering what was going through his mind. "You were up here before, weren't you?"

"Yes," he said, barely audible. "This is where Drake and I left our mark."

"You?"

"Let's just say the surviving Thatcher thought Drake and I one and the same," he replied.

"Do tell," Shelby said. "Do I know this story, babe?"

His reply was simple and final. "No."

The drive leveled off, coming out of the leafless, tree-lined drive into a large, open turnaround. The farmhouse was painted a soft yellow, with white shutters, and a screened-in porch ran the length of the house. The bushes along the beds in front were trimmed to hedge-like perfection. Jackie even noticed there was a rooster weathervane on the roof. Off to the right of the house was the mill. From her angle she could just see the top of the wheel turning in the water. That building was also in impeccable condition. The whole place smacked of a backcountry tourist spot. She half expected to see gifts for sale in the window.

"Not quite the haunted house I was expecting," she said.

"No, but it's haunted all right," Cynthia said. "Can you feel it? It's more intense than the town by far."

She's not kidding, Laurel added. *Blessed Mother, there's a lot of death here. The wall between us is very thin here, hon. We may not want to stay here long.*

Jackie stopped and turned off the Explorer. "What do you mean?"

Meaning that thing can't be far and we don't know what it's capable of.

"About what?" Nick asked.

Why did things always have to be complicated? "Laurel just mentioned that things are pretty thin here between us and Deadworld," said Jackie.

"If a lot of people have died here, that makes perfect sense," Nick replied.

"And that Spindly Man is following me around. We might not want to hang out here for very long is all Laur is saying. Can't say I disagree."

Nick nodded. "Good point. We'll try and keep this brief. I have no more desire than you do to confront whatever that thing is."

Shelby opened her door and stepped out. "Might have to at some point."

"Only when we have to," Nick said. "And right now, we don't. You want to go check out the mill, Shel?"

"Just don't go in," Jackie added quickly. "I'd rather not get called on for breaking and entering."

"Would I do that?" asked Shelby.

"Yes," everyone said together.

She waved them off and began walking toward the mill. "I hate you all."

Jackie began to walk toward the screen door when the front door opened. A man's feet echoed across the floorboards until he pushed open the screen and came down the steps. He wore a dark brown wool suit, white shirt, and a bowtie. Jackie had to do a double take. Yes, it was a brown and red plaid bowtie. His close-cropped hair was parted down the side and smoothed over with some kind of hair product. Round glasses gave him the look of an accountant, a very antiquated "I use an abacus" sort of accountant.

The man stopped a good ten feet from them. "May I help you? I was not expecting any visitors."

Jackie took a step forward. "Mr. Thatcher? Robert Thatcher?"

"I am," he said. "And who might you be, if I may be so bold?"

She took another step forward and thrust out her hand. "My name is Jackie Rutledge. My colleagues and I are from the University of Chicago."

He glanced suspiciously down at her hand. "Professors are you, then? What could possibly bring you to our small neck of the woods, Ms. Rutledge? Chicago is quite the journey from here." Robert turned and looked over at Shelby. "Excuse me, ma'am? What are you doing over there?"

Shelby waved and yelled back. "Just looking. It's a lovely mill. Does it still work?"

"Of course," he said, giving Shelby a confused look. "Why wouldn't it work? It's been making our flour for years."

Makes his own flour? Jackie could not quite fathom that. Was he Amish or something? "Mr. Thatcher, we are in the area exploring the history of ghost stories in the rural Midwest. As you can imagine—"

"Ghosts! Schools are studying such things these days?" He gave her a disgusted wrinkle of his nose. "What happened to literature and mathematics? Honestly! What an absurd thing to study. And you came up here to ask me about ghosts?" He laughed. "That's preposterous."

So is your fucking tie, she wanted to say, but the sound of Laurel clearing her throat rather loudly in her head made her bite her tongue. "Be that as it may," she said, forcing her voice to remain calm, "we wanted to see if you knew anything about the many ghosts that wander Thatcher's Mill or if you'd heard anything about the curse of Thatcher's Mill. We've heard a number of stories."

"Curse? In the Mill? Surely you jest," he said, clearly offended. "We're a plain and practical folk here, Ms. Rutledge. Curses are the work of heathens and you will not find any of them in this town."

Jackie forced a smile. "I did not mean to offend, Mr. Thatcher. How long have you lived here in Thatcher's Mill?" From over the top of Robert's head, Jackie caught movement on the edge of her vision. Someone was looking down at them through an upstairs window.

"The Thatchers have been here for decades, as you might well imagine," he replied. "Surely educated folk like yourselves would know this?"

Surely, I'm going smack you upside the head, you little twerp. "I meant you, Mr. Thatcher. How long have you personally lived here?"

"Why, I grew up here, as you might expect."

"Mr. Thatcher," Jackie said and pushed her hands into her pockets before they involuntarily reached out to throttle him. "We happen to know you married Beverly Thatcher and came to Thatcher's Mill five years ago."

"I most certainly did not," he snapped back. "I married my lovely Beverly seventeen years ago this past July. I may have married into the family, but I am a Thatcher through and through, thank you very much." He took a step back. "I believe I shall take offense at your presence upon my property now. I politely ask that you leave. Have a good day." Robert gave her a curt nod, spun on his heel, and marched back into the house. The door slammed, followed by the click of the deadbolt being turned into place.

"What the hell was that?" Jackie stared at the house in disbelief. "Does he even know what century he's living in?"

"We should get off his property," Nick said, "before he decides to call upon the police chief."

Jackie spun around and stomped toward the car. "Nothing a badge and a gun wouldn't deal with."

Hon, quit. It's fine. We've learned something. Let's go from there and move on, Laurel said.

Oh, well that's just preposterous, Jackie replied in her best imitation snotty voice. *People don't give you shit for being an FBI agent.*

Laurel huffed. *Then don't let them give you shit for hunting ghosts. Own your work, hon. Be proud of it. You're skilled in ways nobody else is.*

Jackie slammed the door shut and started up the Explorer. *That's the problem. Nobody else gets it, so it's just a fucking joke. Pisses me off. Anyway. I'm just being bitchy. He annoyed the crap out of me.* "Did anyone else see someone in the upstairs window?"

"A girl," Nick replied. "Fourteen or fifteen perhaps."

Shelby grunted. "Did we hear anything about kids?"

"And why would he lie about his past to us?" Jackie wondered. "Marrying someone and changing your name isn't illegal."

"Have to admit," Cynthia said, "that changing both your first and last name is a little strange."

"But worth getting all offended over?" Jackie didn't buy it. Something was really off with the guy, besides the stuffy suit.

"Call up Hauser," Nick said. "I want to see if he can tell us what the names of the Thatchers were back when I was here."

I'm going to stay here for a bit, hon, Laurel said. *Maybe there's a spirit who will actually have something to say. I'll come back down to the diner shortly.*

Jackie talked with Hauser, who said he would need a

little time to find out the old Thatcher names, but he quickly looked up census information on the current Thatchers, which listed only the Robert and Beverly Thatcher living at the residence.

"OK, then," Shelby said, as Jackie pulled the Explorer up along the curb next to the drug store. "So who's the girl?"

"Could be a relative for all we know," Jackie replied, getting out of the SUV. "But I'll bet we can find out quick enough. I want a coffee, and then maybe we can canvas the town again. Surely someone around here is willing to say something."

"They might be afraid to talk to us," Nick said.

"Everyone?" She could not believe that. People liked to gossip about strange goings on in their neighborhoods. This town should be no different. "Someone around here will talk. We just have to find them."

"We might try neighboring towns, too," Cynthia added. "They might have some interesting things to say about this place."

Jackie led them across the street to the diner, feeling horribly conspicuous on the nearly deserted streets. A young woman stepped out of a wall behind the diner and crossed the street, her eyes following them as they passed one another. Jackie waved.

"Hi there," she said, but kept walking. Maybe questioning was the wrong tack to take with these ghosts. Perhaps, if they just realized someone else noticed them, one of them might eventually take an interest on their own. They might be dead, but they were still human, and humans were curious creatures.

"What was that about?" Shelby wondered.

"A little reverse psychology," Jackie said, and pulled open the diner door.

"Oh." Shelby nodded. "Oh! Smart girl. See, I knew you were the boss for a reason."

When they sat down, Molly came by a minute later and

wordlessly poured coffee and set down water. She purposefully avoided eye contact.

Nick took a drink of his coffee after she walked away. “Not pleased we’re back, obviously.”

“Getting the clear impression that nobody around here takes much to strangers,” Jackie said.

“Conspiracy of silence,” Cynthia said.

Molly brought back menus and set them on the edge of the table. Jackie smiled up at her. “Molly, mind if I ask you a question?”

She stopped, her shoulders sagging in exasperation. “I have nothing to say about any ghosts in Thatcher’s. You folk should just move on to some other town.”

Really? Changing your tune already, Molly? Have words with the police chief perhaps? “Actually, I just wanted to know who the Thatcher’s daughter was?”

Molly heaved a sigh. “Which one?”

More than one. “Well, um . . .”

“Long, dark hair,” Nick said. “Teenager, about fifteen or so.”

She looked at them in silence for a moment. “That would be Rebecca Thatcher,” she replied. “Now, if you’ll excuse me, I’ve got other customers.”

There was one other customer in the diner. Jackie frowned. “She’s going to be useful.”

“So,” Nick said. “How does one go about having a daughter with no record of her living there?”

“Previous marriage?” Cynthia suggested.

“Not if you’ve been married for seventeen years and grew up here,” Jackie replied. “Think we need to get an accurate record of just who these Thatchers were before they were Thatchers.”

“I think you’re right,” Shelby said. “Something ain’t right up on the hill.”

Jackie felt the familiar cold breeze of Laurel returning. She glided through the kitchen and sat down between

Cynthia and Shelby. Jackie raised an eyebrow at her. "That was quick."

She shrugged. "Nobody had much to say, and our favorite alien is back. I did get a name, though, from one of the spirits. Rebecca. Her name was Rebecca."

Jackie just about spit her coffee back into the cup. "Really. Well, that is some interesting news."

Nick sat frozen, staring at his cup, his gaze far off and empty. "Interesting indeed."

"What is it, babe?" Shelby asked. "I know that look, and I never like it."

"When I was here . . . back then," he said. "The girl I tried to help, the survivor from Drake's attack, she had a twin sister. Rebecca."

They all looked at each other in stunned silence. The little nagging feeling of wrongness about this whole situation abruptly blossomed into a hollow pit of dread in Jackie's gut. "No shit."

"Well," Cynthia said. "Can't say that sounds good at all."

The door bell chimed as someone walked into the diner. Shelby sighed and downed the rest of her water. "Maybe you ought to tell us that story now, babe."

"Well, well," a voice rang out right behind Jackie's ear, startling her, "what's a former FBI agent doing in a little town like Thatcher's Mill?"

Jackie wheeled around and stared up at the source of the familiar voice. It took a second to register who she was looking at before her stomach knotted up in agitation. "Margolin."

He gave her an unwelcoming grin. "Ms. Rutledge. Fancy meeting you here."

Chapter 13

Jackie got to her feet, her small frame inches away from Margolin, who towered a good six inches over her. "What the hell are you doing here?"

"Might ask you the same question," he said. "Imagine my surprise when a little birdie told me you were heading out this way. So, what's Special Investigations doing in the middle of bum-fuck nowhere?"

She inched forward, bumping into him and forcing Margolin to take a step back. "The airport is twenty miles away, you shithead. How'd you know we were here?"

"I know a thing or two about investigation," he said. "Not that hard."

Jackie felt Nick slide out and stand up behind her. "I got this, Nick. He's just a reporter."

"Hey!" Tucker yelled from behind the counter. "Take your problems outside. I doubt Chief Carson would take kindly to a fight in here."

"And Mr. Anderson," Margolin said, the smile still on his face, "CEO of Bloodwork Industries, philanthropist to the Chicago arts community, and oddly, a PI on the side, helping people with paranormal problems. An interesting team"—his gaze roamed over Cynthia and Shelby—"to say the least."

"You have a point to any of this? Before I decide to throw you out on your ass?" Jackie said. If he had something, he would have said it already. Reporters were antsy like that in general. He was fishing. Though she might have to give him one good shot regardless.

Margolin chuckled. "You aren't an agent anymore, Ms. Rutledge, at least *officially*. So you have no authority to be throwing me anywhere."

She stepped forward again, staying in his face. "Who said I need authority? It would be a civic service."

The smile faded somewhat. "I'm not here to pick a fight with you, Rutledge. I just want to know what you're investigating here."

"None of your fucking business," Jackie said.

"Anything to do with all of the ghosts around here?"

Sonofabitch. There would be no getting rid of him now. "You've seen some ghosts then? Maybe you could point them out for us, help us out."

"Hey, you guys are the Ghostbusters. Isn't that your job?"

Ghostbusters? Weaselly motherfucker. Jackie cocked her fist and started to swing, only to lurch off balance when Nick's hand grabbed her wrist and halted all forward momentum.

"Not worth it, Jackie," Nick said, barely above whisper.

"The big, bad PI going to do your dirty work for you?" Margolin did, however, take another step back.

Purposefully egging me on. The little bastard is picking a fight for some reason, and he knows we could kick his ass. What the hell is he up to? Just then, a Thatcher's Mill police car rolled up in front of the diner and Chief Carson stepped out.

Shelby sounded amused behind her. "Well, well. Isn't that convenient?"

"Great." Jackie took a step back and bumped into Nick, who had not moved. "Last thing we need right now."

"Think it's time we put a little space between us and the Mill," Nick replied.

The diner's door jingled as Carson walked in, the dark worm on his lip following the frown of his mouth. "You folks having a problem here?"

Margolin moved toward Carson. "Hey, I was just asking what they were doing here, and she got all up in my face over it."

"Tucker!" Carson yelled. "What's going on?"

The cook walked out to the counter. "Pretty much what the newsboy said, though I can't say much for his attitude either."

"I see," Carson said, leaning against the cash register at the end of the counter. "Perhaps I was a bit too subtle with my suggestion yesterday, Ms. Rutledge. Then again, you didn't strike me as the type to heed good advice when you heard it."

Jackie started to retort, but managed to cut herself off before saying something too stupid to recover from. Not having a badge was proving difficult. "Our research isn't done yet, Chief Carson. When it is, we'll be out of your hair. As it is, no laws have been broken, nor do we intend to be breaking any, unless newsboy here decides to take a swing at me. We'll be on our way, though."

Carson folded his arms over his chest. "Be that as it may, I don't believe the good folk of Thatcher's Mill appreciate or want you to be researching their town. I suggest once again that you take your team elsewhere to conduct your business. It's not wanted around here. Is that a littler clearer for you, Ms. Rutledge?"

She felt Nick's hand resting against the small of her back, a gentle warning to leave this alone. She did not want to leave it alone. In another life, she would not have left it alone at all.

Laurel took the opportunity to ease herself into Jackie's

head. *Hon, I know. Let's just get out of here. We'll figure out what to do later.*

This civilian stuff is bullshit, Jackie told her. *I want my damn badge and gun.* Jackie walked toward the door, making sure to step on Margolin's toes as she went by, and paused next to Carson. "I got the message before, Chief. I'm a smart girl. Smart enough to know this town is hiding something. So I don't give a shit how clear you are. We'll be back." Without waiting for his reply, Jackie pushed open the door and left.

Back in the Explorer, Jackie forced herself to go the speed limit as she guided them out of town and toward the airport.

"I think we can count him as an enemy now," Cynthia said. "He gave me the creeps."

"He wasn't our friend to begin with," Jackie said. "This whole town is giving me the creeps."

"OK," Shelby replied. "Back to more important matters. What was it Laur said about one of the ghosts being named Rebecca? Coincidence?"

"Not likely," Nick replied. "What are the odds we have a girl named Rebecca Thatcher, a dead girl at the Thatcher's named Rebecca, and a Rebecca Thatcher who died over one hundred years ago?"

"Slim to none," Jackie said. "Maybe we can find something in the county records?"

"And who's the other sister?" Shelby wondered. "Who was it back then, babe?"

"Charlotte," Nick said. "Her name was Charlotte."

"Care to tell us that story? We've got some time to kill here."

"Yeah." He sighed. "Guess I'd better."

"And make it the short version. You know how long-winded you can get."

Jackie caught Nick shaking his head out of the corner of her eye and smiled. "Oh, yeah. A real blowhard, our Nick." He gave her a sidelong glance, the corner of his mouth curving into a smile.

"All right, then," he replied. "The CNN version of Nick's trip to Thatcher's Mill."

Surprisingly enough, he finished by the time they got to the airport, and once again, Jackie realized just how different a life this man must have compared to everyone else in the world. It was difficult to imagine how many bodies had fallen in the wake of his pursuit of that monster, Drake. She could relate to the singular purpose of tracking him down, just not the part about finally catching him. Somewhere out there, her stepfather Carl still lived and breathed, and God only knew how many lives he had ruined beyond hers and her mother's. Only Nick had never stopped, never been given the choice really, and she had. At some point, Jackie had given up her pursuit, and only held on to vague hopes that, some day, he would pop up on her radar again. If she never made it back to the FBI, however, even those small hopes would be gone.

Shelby's hand reached over the seat and squeezed Nick's shoulder. "Goes without saying, I guess, that I'm sorry, babe. Tough price for only trying to help."

He shrugged. "Is what it is, and that was over a hundred years ago."

"Still, no fun to have it all dredged back up," Cynthia said. "Figures, this would be the one case we manage to pick out of the stack."

"Karma," Shelby replied. "Maybe we were supposed to come back. It is beginning to seem like there's a correlation of some kind."

So it would seem. Jackie had to agree. This went beyond mere coincidence. "Let's see if Hauser has anything more for us. We need a bigger picture. There's a link to all of these ghosts there somewhere, and I don't think we're going to find it by going door to door."

"One has to wonder," Nick said, "why everyone would be so unwilling to talk about the ghosts. Most small towns would milk this kind of thing for all the tourism dollars they could get their hands on."

"Which means there's a reason they don't want anyone to dig," Jackie replied. "So let's keep digging until we find something. I want to go back with something, anything that I can shove up that chief's ass."

Shelby laughed and opened the door. "A girl after my own heart."

Back in the air headed toward home, they got Hauser back on the speakerphone. "Give us good news, Hauser," Jackie said.

"Hey, beautiful. Not so sure about good." He laughed. "How about more weirdness, because that's all I'm finding."

Jackie sipped on the good coffee Nick had brewed on the plane's built-in machine. "That's what we expected anyway. Shoot."

"I've compiled all of the vital records I could find, and it would appear that if you were born in Thatcher's Mill, you died there as well. Nobody has moved into or out of that place in decades, except those Thatcher men and women, which I guess explains the consistency in population over the years."

"An island unto themselves," Cynthia said.

"Pretty much," Hauser replied. "And like I said before, everyone there has died either from an accident or natural causes."

"Hauser," Jackie said. "Can you tell me how many girls named Rebecca have been born there?"

"Sure, one sec." There was silence for a moment before he returned. "Two, according to official records."

"Figured as much. How about the Thatchers? Can you tell me how many Thatcher children have been born over the past century?"

"Yep. There were . . . two. Charlotte and Rebecca."

"That's it? They've been there over a hundred years and never had any kids?"

"According to the records."

Nick frowned. "That doesn't add up. What are the ages of death on the Thatchers?"

"Let's see here." Jackie could hear the clacking of Hauser's keyboard in the background. "Forty-two, thirty-five, thirty-seven, twenty-nine, thirty-two. Man, I wouldn't want to marry into that family."

"So," Shelby wondered, "who is the kid living there with them now?"

"Laur?" Jackie asked. "Could that ghost you talked to be the Rebecca Thatcher who died back when Nick was there?"

"Possibly," she replied. "She looked the part, had on a pretty, old-fashioned wool dress with lace trim."

"As did some of the other female ghosts we saw," Nick said.

Shelby nodded. "The ones I saw as well."

It made no sense. "All of those ghosts can't be from that era," Jackie said. "And there weren't enough deaths in the appropriate age range to account for them all."

"Exactly," Nick replied. "So, if nobody has moved into Thatcher's Mill besides the Thatchers, where did these girls come from and why is there no record of them?"

"And Robert Thatcher was dressed up old school as well," Jackie said.

"Yes," Shelby replied. "Which means it's safe to assume that our current Rebecca Thatcher is, too."

"So the Rebecca that Laur talked to may not be the original Rebecca at all," Jackie said.

Cynthia brought her hand to her mouth, eyes wide. "Could some of those other ghosts be Rebeccas, too?"

"Holy shit," Shelby exclaimed. "We should have some Roberts, Beverlys, and Charlottes, too."

"The Thatcher's Mill curse," Cynthia said. "It kind of makes some sense."

"Curse, my ass," Jackie replied. "Thatchers are dying for a reason. We just don't know why yet."

"Damn, this is great stuff," Hauser piped in. "You guys get the coolest cases."

"Hardly," Jackie said. "Hauser, how long has the police chief, Carson, been on the job?"

"Sec. I'll check."

Jackie got up to pace. She wished she had her board to look at. "Let's assume for the moment that Thatchers have been dying at an absurd rate for years, and that it isn't some stupid curse afflicting them all." She stopped and laid a hand on Cynthia's shoulder. "Sorry, Cyn. No offense."

She smiled. "None taken."

"Seventeen years," Hauser said. "Carson has been chief for seventeen years."

"Great, thanks," Jackie replied. "So, it's probably safe to assume that they haven't all died of natural causes or accidents."

"That would be beyond coincidence," Nick said.

"OK then," she continued, "why would they all be listed as such on their death certificates?"

"Because," Shelby replied, "the coroner falsified the documents."

"Or didn't even do autopsies," Nick added. "If there's no indication of suspicious death, then no autopsy would be performed unless requested."

"We need to have a word with the coroner, then," Jackie said, "which we can't do until tomorrow." Another thought suddenly occurred to Jackie. "Hey, Hauser, one more thing."

"Shoot."

"Run obituaries on the Thatchers and see if there are any," she said.

"Gotcha."

Jackie ran the fingers of her hand through her hair. They were missing a key element here. Someone or something had to be making this all happen. "All right, so we have the Thatcher family—Mom, Dad, Rebecca, and Charlotte. Rebecca dies, for whatever reason, her ghost haunts the house, and then, sometime later, a new, unknown Rebecca shows up and assumes the new daughter role."

"Given what we know," Nick said, "that does sound plausible."

"So, someone tracked down and brought a new Rebecca into the family," Jackie said and groaned in frustration. "Why? What's so important about maintaining the semblance of the Thatcher family?"

"And what if their deaths aren't natural?" Shelby asked. "What if they're being killed off?"

"Why would you kill off people you went to the effort of finding and bringing into the family?" Cynthia asked.

"Because they don't fit the mold," Jackie said. "Beverly isn't the right Beverly. Rebecca just isn't acting the way Rebecca should."

"Or they try to leave," Shelby said.

"So, we're back to who in Thatcher's Mill would want or need the Thatchers to be there," Jackie said. "And not just be there, either, but maintain their original state from a hundred years ago." She plopped back down in her seat next to Nick. "God, this is fucked up. Maybe I'm way off base with all of this."

"Hey," Hauser's voice crackled through the speaker, "no obits on the Thatchers other than the original from 1897.

Not a single paper in the area has ever mentioned a Thatcher dying."

Jackie leaned forward, pointing her finger at the speakerphone. "Which makes sense if you're trying to cover up their deaths, and that's not easy to do unless you're in a position of authority to make it happen."

"Chief Carson," Nick said.

"Whose father was chief and his father before him," Jackie said. "He told me that. We need to see those police records." They'd also been up to the Mill to chat with the Thatchers. If Carson knew and was involved in this, he would be suspicious. "We also need to find out who this Rebecca is. If we're right, someone's missing a teenage daughter."

"If we're right," Shelby said, "that town could be full of missing daughters."

"We're going to need some surveillance gear before we go back," Nick said, "if we're going to stake out the Thatchers'."

Jackie downed the last of her coffee. A town full of missing daughters. Years of them, and all dead. What had they gotten themselves into? "We're going back tonight. If we've stirred up what I think we have, then that family is in danger."

Chapter 14

"Jack, don't do anything stupid," McManus said. "You're pushing it with surveillance."

Her retort died before it even got started. She could make no claims to not doing stupid things. "We need proof, McManus. Belgerman won't OK you coming in unless there's something concrete. If we can find out who that girl is, we've got kidnapping. All we need is a clean photo so we can run her."

"Not really," he replied. "You just have a girl pretending to belong to another family. Still have to show she was taken there forcibly."

"Oh, come on. You really think a girl is going to come in from out of town and just decide to settle in with a new family?"

"We've seen weirder things, Jack."

Could not argue with that. "Still, with a dead girl going by the same name, I'm going to assume something very wrong is going on in Thatcher's Mill."

"I'm with you, for sure," he said. "You've got something fucked up going on there. Just please don't jump the gun. You're a civilian. If shit hits the fan, call me in."

Civilian. Thanks for the reminder. "Soon as we have something. Thanks, McManus."

"Hey, no problem. I knew you'd make something of this situation, Jack. You're too good not to. Talk to you soon."

Jackie hung up and leaned back in her desk chair. She stared at her board, running through the events of the past couple of days, trying to make better sense of what was going on. McManus's words weighed on her. What if there was no force involved at all? What if these people came into the Thatcher family and wanted to stay? Then they would be left attempting to prove murder, a much tougher proposition, especially as a civilian. They needed to get hold of the records. If they could show forged police reports or autopsy records, it would be enough to bring the rest of them in. The real authorities.

She rubbed her hands over her face. With a little effort, she could still feel the badge in her jacket pocket, the snug fit of the holster beneath her arm. They were symbols of the authority she once had, and hopefully would again. But was she really that much less without them? Was she little more than a weapon and a shiny badge?

Quit it, hon. You're more than a badge and gun.

Yeah, I've clearly got it going on with this life now.

Transition is hard. You can't expect to just slide right into a new life without any complications. It doesn't work that way.

My whole life has become one big complication.

Are you speaking personally or professionally? Because professionally, I see how this might work great for you. I saw you on the plane. You were getting into this just like you did as an agent. I could feel that excitement in you, hon. This is a real, legitimate case. Ghosts or not, this is no joke.

I know, I know. Working this as a civilian just limits me in ways I'm not used to.

So? We change tactics. Subtlety can be just as effective as strong-arming people. You have other tools at your disposal now. We'll figure out new ways to do things.

You're right, of course. I just miss how things were.

You're better now. Stronger.

Wish I felt that way. I can't even manage to have a real date without falling to pieces.

Laurel sighed. *You'll figure that out, too. Nick's a patient guy. Just tell him what you want. He'll gladly take whatever you have to offer.*

Laur? What if—

A knock on the door interrupted them, and Shelby opened it, sticking her head in around the edge. "We got Chinese. Conference room."

Go eat. I can tell you're hungry, and no 'what ifs.' You have lots to offer.

It was show-and-tell over dinner, as Nick brought out the equipment he had gathered for the nighttime excursion to Thatcher's Mill. There was camo gear, long-range photographic equipment, infrared goggles, and tranquilizer guns.

Jackie swallowed a mouthful of shrimp-fried rice. "You just happened to have all of this handy?"

"I am a PI," he said, and smiled, "who happens to have money. It was part of our initial procurement for the new Special Investigations. You never know what a situation might call for."

"You have a secret stash of spy equipment somewhere?" She was trying to be glib, but Nick's smile answered the question. "Shit, Nick. I hope it's all legal."

The smile broadened. "Pretty much."

She laughed. "I want to see it. Why didn't I know about this?"

Cynthia folded her hands on the table. "You did, Jackie. It was in the packet of info I gave you on your first day here."

Laurel snickered inside Jackie's head. *Paperwork. Get used to it.*

Shut up, you.

Nick pushed his carton of food aside. "Cyn, you have the map set up?"

She grabbed a remote off of the table and pushed a button. A large LED screen on the far wall lit up. It was an overhead map of Thatcher's Mill.

Nick laid out the vantage points from which they could have unobstructed views of the house and how best to reach them. They would need to get pretty close in order to avoid the trees. Even without the foliage, it would be too dense for a clear photo op, and they needed clear views of all the windows. They would come in from the north this time so they would not have to come in on Main Street and increase the risk of being seen.

"That all looks good," Jackie said. "Any luck and we're in and out in an hour, but let's assume neither girl goes looking out any windows on her own volition."

"Then we knock on the damn door," Shelby said. "Wouldn't hurt to try asking them anyway. We might not need the photos at all."

"I hate putting those girls at any more risk than we have to," Jackie said.

"We'll ask about the police chief," Nick said. "Keep the topic off of the family. We might get an indication if he's a threat to them."

Jackie pointed her fork at Nick. "That's good. We need to check into him regardless. That's as good a starting point as any." She scraped at the bottom of her carton, fishing out the last bits of shrimp among the rice. The plan was simple, straightforward, and ran a decent chance of not getting screwed up over something random or stupid.

Shelby had her feet kicked up on the table while she finished off her beer, and Laurel sat quietly beside her in a chair. Talk about an odd couple. How frustrating would it be to be in love with someone you pretty much could have no physical contact with? Laurel looked across the table at Jackie and smiled, and she glanced away. A lump of guilt balled up in her throat, and she swept aside the image of Laurel lying on that stainless steel table, arm hanging limply over the side with its single trail of blood running down from the crook in her arm, and the echo of Drake's laughter resounding through that cavernous warehouse.

Jackie tossed the fork into her carton and pushed it away. "So, when do we leave?"

They assembled their gear and headed for the airport, Cynthia remaining behind for quick informational access via the computer, plus the fact that she had no training or experience with these sorts of operations. Once on the plane, Jackie leaned against the fuselage and stared out at the darkening skies. *Laur? How much do you love Shelby?*

How much? That's kind of a relative question, don't you think? Why?

I don't know. I just can't imagine how hard this must all be for you, putting up with all of my bullshit and then being in love with someone you can't really interact with at all.

We interact a lot, actually. We watch movies, play games, talk about books, tell each other our life stories. Other than the fact that we can't physically touch, we have a pretty normal relationship, I think.

Don't you miss it though, not being able to touch her, hold hands, any of that kind of stuff?

I'd be lying if I said I didn't. I miss it more than anything else, but it is what it is, hon. I'll take what I can get because this is the fate the Blessed Mother has given me.

Jackie was silent for a long moment. *I wish it could've been different for you, Laur. I'm sorry.*

Don't be. You had no control over that, so quit going there. No more blame. I'm actually pretty happy all things considered.

Jackie closed her eyes. *I just wish there was something I could do for you. You've done so much for me.*

"You all right, Jackie?" Nick asked.

She opened her eyes, finding Nick staring at her from

across the table between them. "Yeah, thanks. I'm fine." He kept watching her, the hint of a smile on his face. He knew she was bullshitting him, but respectfully declined to press the matter any further. "What's your favorite book?"

The smile vanished. He gave her a perplexed look. "Favorite book? Why do you ask?"

"No reason, just curious I guess," she said. "You have a library in your house. I was wondering if you had a favorite book in there."

"I have a signed first edition of Stoker's *Dracula*. He signed it for me himself." Nick laughed at Jackie's slack-jawed disbelief. "I know, a bit ironic, don't you think?"

Jackie tried to keep a straight face, but could not. She began to laugh. "That's . . . God, I don't even know what to say to that."

Shelby walked by as the FASTEN SEATBELT light dinged on. She patted Nick on the shoulder. "Vampires have a twisted sense of humor, don't they, babe?"

"I thought it an appropriate purchase at the time."

Jackie sat back up and buckled her seatbelt, still chuckling. "Actually, I think that's kind of awesome. I would've never guessed that in a million years."

Shelby's voice floated up from the back of the plane. "That's OK. We'll wait."

Laurel giggled away inside Jackie's head. *I forgot about that. She makes me laugh.*

Jackie watched Nick shaking his head at Shelby's remark. *I suppose she does at that.*

They landed at the Dubuque airport, instead of the tiny airfield to the south, so they could approach from the north. Nick drove this time, pulling off the highway on the north edge of Thatcher's Mill behind the local barbershop. The spot only obscured them from the main road, so they hoped that nobody would come wandering around. Given what Jackie had seen thus far, the odds were good no foot traffic would happen upon the SUV.

After gathering up their equipment, they moved to the base of the hill, which provided some cover as they walked among the heavy blanket of leaves through the stand of oak and maple. Nick led them up the hill, his large pack slung over his back, when they got in sight of the drive leading up to the Thatcher's. Jackie could see the house, lit up from a porch light and the soft glow emanating through the curtained windows. They were making their way to a low embankment at the edge of the clearing that would allow them some relative, low-lying cover.

"Right up there," Nick said in a hushed voice, pointing to a spot between two tree trunks that stood only a few feet apart. "That should give us a good view of the whole front of the house."

Jackie nodded, eyeing the spot, and began to trudge forward again when, one by one, all of the lights in the house winked out. "What the hell?" Finally, the porch light went out, leaving them in almost complete darkness. "Could they have alarms out here?"

"Possible," Nick said, "but unlikely. Robert Thatcher did not strike me as the high-tech type. Maybe someone saw movement down here. We'll wait a few minutes and see what happens. Let's crawl up to the spot."

He dropped down into a crouch, hugging the ground as much as possible, and Jackie followed suit. The house vanished from sight over the edge of the embankment until they reached the edge and could see over once again. A soft breeze sifted through the trees, but things were otherwise silent and unmoving. Nick shrugged out of his pack and began to unload equipment.

"Here," he said, and handed her and Shelby night-vision

binoculars. "You two see if you can spot anything while I get the camera situated."

Jackie pulled them up to her face and peered out, everything becoming suffused in a green glow. No curtains were pulled aside. No figures stood watching in the windows. "It's seven-thirty. Could they have just gone to bed?" In answer to her question, something cold ran down her spine. The breeze shifted, stirring the leaves on the ground in front of them. Jackie swore she heard someone whispering. "Did you guys—?"

"Yeah," Shelby said. "What the fuck is going on here?"

Someone called for her, Laurel said. *For Rebecca. I'm going to go in there in and look. Back in a minute.*

"Laur, wait!" But it was too late. Laurel had stepped out of her body and was now walking across the clearing toward the house. Out of the corner of her eye, Jackie saw something else, a wisp of fog shifting across the ground, until she realized it was another ghost.

"Over there," Nick said, pointing toward the Mill. It was yet another ghostly figure moving toward the house.

"Laur!" Shelby called in a harsh whisper. She turned to Jackie. "What's going on?"

"She said someone called for Rebecca. She's going to check it out."

"Shit." Shelby stood up and whispered out toward the house, "Laur, get back here."

It was too late though. Laurel was already going up the porch steps. Jackie scanned the house but could still see no movement. "Damn it. Now what?"

Another ghost came up from behind, passing by them within a few feet and Jackie nearly jumped out of her skin. Yet another appeared over by the mill building.

"Interesting," Nick said. "That answers our question about multiple Rebeccas."

"OK, but who the hell just called them over?"

Nick stared intently at the house. "I don't know. There's so much spiritual energy floating around here, I can't tell."

Jackie reached into the side pocket of the pack and pulled out one of the tranquilizer guns. "It's time to find out," she said. "Watch my back." She crawled up out of the undergrowth and stepped out into the clearing, marching purposefully across the packed dirt and gravel toward the front door.

"Jackie!" Nick called out. "Get back here."

She ignored him and kept moving, gripping the pistol tighter to calm her trembling hand. Laurel could be walking into trouble and she was not about to let her do it alone. At the top of the steps, she found the screen door to the porch locked, and with one deft punch, thrust the end of the pistol through the screen mesh. Jackie reached in and undid the lock, yanked open the door and moved quickly to the front door.

"Robert Thatcher!" She pounded on the front door. "I know you're in there." She hammered on it again. "Mr. Thatcher, I'd like a word—"

Laurel's familiar cold presence abruptly bled through the door and into Jackie's body. *Go, Jackie! Now! She called Carson up here.*

"Shit." She waited a moment, hoping that Thatcher would open the door, but he did not. Instead, one of the ghosts stepped through the wall and stopped next to her, staring in silence, her face unexpressive. Jackie forced a smile upon her lips. "Hello." The ghost merely stood there, eyes frozen upon her. Then another came through, blocking the door. Impassive as the other, she simply stared, whether at her or through her, Jackie could not tell. It was unsettling. When another came up from the opposite end of the porch and approached, Jackie decided that was enough. She spun on her heel and fled back off the porch, heading for Nick and Shelby. *Laur, what the hell was that?*

It was the sister. She saw me.

"What?"

"Jackie," Nick said, grabbing her by the arm as she hopped down over the embankment. "What are you doing?"

"Let's go," she snapped back. "Carson's coming."

"Ah, hell," Shelby said.

"All right," Nick replied. "Back down the hill."

They shuffled and skipped their way down the hillside. Twice, Nick grabbed Jackie by a handful of shirt to keep her from tumbling down. As they threaded their way along the edge of the wood toward the Explorer, the red and blue flashing lights of Carson's police car sped up the drive toward the Thatcher's.

They slammed the doors shut as Nick gunned the engine, backing lightless out of their space and onto Main Street.

"Well, that was a fucking bust," Shelby yelled, slapping the back of Nick's headrest hard enough to jolt him in the seat.

I saw her, Laurel said. *Rebecca. I got a good look.*

"Laur got a solid look at her. We'll get a sketch done," Jackie said. "And I think we have a new lead."

Nick flipped on the lights when he took off up the highway, illuminating a sedan parked across the street about one hundred feet away. Someone stood against it, leaning on the hood of the car, watching them.

As the Explorer passed him by, the man waved, grinning. It was Margolin.

Jackie just shook her head in disgust. "Sonofabitch."

Chapter 15

Jackie flopped onto the bed in her room of the Fairfield Inn, Dubuque. She rubbed her hands over her face and groaned at the sweet feel of the comforter her body sank into.

"Call me in the morning," she said. "I don't think I can move now."

Shelby walked out of the bathroom, brushing her hair. "Tempting. Sure you don't want to trade to Nick's room?"

Jackie growled in reply. "Do you ever stop?"

"When life has suitably resolved itself to my satisfaction," Shelby said and flashed a smile.

Jackie flipped her off. "Well, I'm screwed then. I don't think my brain is capable of resolution."

"Then quit using your brain so much," she stated. "Quit thinking about every last thing that might or could go wrong."

"Easy for you to say," Jackie replied. "You've probably already done everything that might or could go wrong or right for that matter."

Shelby fell onto the other bed. "I'll tell you something, sweetie. Experience isn't always what it's cracked up to be. Believe me. I would trade many things back to experience the newness of something all over again. You don't appreciate it until it's gone."

"Thanks," Jackie said, "but I'd just as soon skip the irony aspects of life."

The cold chill of Deadworld wafted through the room and Laurel returned. "Irony is good for you, and Spindly Man is here. I'm almost getting used to this cat-and-mouse stuff."

"Speaking of new experiences," Jackie said, "what the hell are we going to do about that thing? Not that I plan to ever cross over again, but if we ever had some . . . issue, I do not want to run into that thing."

A knock came at the door, and Shelby sat up. "No fucking clue, babe. It worries me though."

Great. The Queen of No Worries showing a twinge of something Jackie had not seen before. Fear.

Shelby let Nick in and walked back into the room with him. He set the laptop down on the desk and sat down. "You doing all right, Jackie?"

"Tired," she said, "and wishing things would go right just once for us . . . for um, Special Investigations." She pointed a finger at Shelby, who smiled at her with a raised eyebrow but said nothing.

Nick eyed them both for a second before continuing. "I wouldn't say things didn't go right, just not as planned. We did, after all, learn new information."

"Laur got a good read on Rebecca," Jackie said, "which we can hopefully translate into a decent likeness. I'll call McManus and see if he can arrange a sketch artist for us."

"Laurel," Nick said, "how did the sister react when you showed up?"

"Surprised," she replied, "and then angry. That's when she dialed up Carson."

"What exactly did she say? Do you remember?" Nick wondered.

"Something like, 'Carson, we've got a situation up here,' or close to it. It certainly did not sound like your panicked 911 call."

"So, Carson has a connection with the Charlotte sister," Nick said. "And someone called those ghosts to the house."

"Why would someone do that?" Jackie asked. "We need to find out about the sisters. We need to know who they really are. Once we can prove they don't belong there, I think I can get McManus in on this, so we can get the damn authority we need to properly investigate."

"I agree," Nick said. "We can find out about the parents though. Their name changes are legal record. We should see if we can find out where they came from and how they ended up in Thatcher's Mill in the first place. Jackie, how soon do you think we can get a sketch of Rebecca and Charlotte worked up?"

"I'll call McManus and see what he can arrange," she said.

"I had another thought," Nick said. "What if we ask that reporter to help us to find out about them."

"Margolin?" Jackie could not believe he would suggest that. "Why would that asshole want to help us? He . . . oh, you're right, Nick. He just wants a damn story. Let him think we want to give him one."

"Keep your enemies close at hand," Shelby said.

"He's not part of the ghosthunters invading the town," Nick added. "He might be able to talk to some folk who would otherwise not talk to us."

"Shouldn't be hard to track him down," Jackie said. "He seems to be following us wherever we go. Let me touch base with McManus here before we do anything else."

McManus got her the number for the sketch artist, someone not at all familiar with her working situation, and Jackie updated him on their progress. A call to Hauser got her Margolin's cell phone number, and then Nick reminded her to call Cynthia and fill her in. Pat Taggert, the sketch artist, set up an appointment for them tomorrow afternoon, and gave her an e-mail to send as many preliminary details as she could.

Margolin picked up his phone on the first ring. "Margolin," he said.

"Hello, Margolin," Jackie said.

"Agent Rutledge! This is a surprise. To what do I owe the pleasure of your phone call?"

Jackie gripped the phone tighter. She wanted nothing more than to tell the ass-hat off. "I want to put your ability to be a fucking pain in the ass to some use. If you're interested in a story, that is."

He was silent for several seconds. "Always looking for the story, Rutledge, but then you know that. So, what gives? Last time we chatted you were ready to plant your fist in my face."

"Can't say that feeling has changed much, but the good people of Thatcher's Mill aren't real keen on talking to a group of ghosthunters."

He laughed. "I don't think anyone around here much cares for you. You wore out your welcome pretty fast. It's that charming way you have about you."

She covered the mouthpiece and pulled the phone away from her ear. "When this is all done, can I kill him? Please?" Nick smiled at her and Shelby giggled. Jackie put the phone back to her ear. "Putting my charming ways aside for a moment, I think you can help us figure this story out."

"Really?" He sounded skeptical. "You're just going to give me the story? Why do I feel like there's some twist in here you're not mentioning?"

Jackie sighed. "Look. I don't like you. Honestly, I hate reporters, but you are apparently good at what you do, and we could use some information. If you can find it for us and it helps us resolve this situation, I'll give you the story."

Another pause. Could he actually turn down such an invitation? "OK, I'm game. I'll listen to what you have to say at least. Where do you want to meet?"

"I've got something to check on in the morning," she

replied. "We'll meet you there at the diner for lunch, and no, I'm not buying."

Margolin chuckled. "I'll bet you get all the guys, Rutledge. Diner. Noon. I'll see you there."

Jackie clicked off and dropped her phone on the bed. "Ugh. I really hate that guy. We're meeting him for lunch at the diner tomorrow. That work?"

"Should be fine," Nick said. "That gives us time to go through reports from the medical examiner in the morning. Laurel, you want to give us descriptions so we can send the artist the info? Maybe by tomorrow afternoon we'll start to have a few answers."

They compiled the list and sent it off, by which time it was nearly ten. Shelby had pizza delivered from a place that, thank the gods, the Blessed Mother, and anyone else worthy of thanks, also delivered beer. Settled into Jackie's head again, Laurel pined over the sausage, onion, and feta.

That pizza and beer looks so good. I think food is one of those things I miss the most.

It's just pizza, Jackie said. *Kind of ordinary, too, far as that goes. The beer, though, that really hits the spot.* She popped the top on a second one. *Even this crap stuff is good sometimes.*

It's another one of those things you don't notice until it's gone.

Jackie felt badly for her. It was difficult to imagine existing in the state Laurel did, to have no physical body, no real sensations to speak of. She wanted to help her. *Laur, do you think you'd be able to taste things if you were me? You know, if you had control of my body?*

Oh! I don't really know. I haven't had opportunity to try it out and see.

You want to? Try, I mean. I can let you take over for a few and see how that works.

Really? Oh, hon, that would be sweet of you. I don't want

to stress you out over a piece of pizza, though. I know how much you hate that sense of not being yourself.

What could a few minutes hurt? It was a small enough sacrifice to bring Laurel some happiness, even if only temporary. *Let's go for it. Have a slice. I'll be fine.*

Hon, are you sure? I don't want—

"I'm going to let Laur take me over for a few minutes so she can have a slice of pizza," Jackie said. "Just, you know, warning you, in case I start praying to the Blessed Mother over my pizza or want to give Nick a tarot reading or something.

You're a snot. Maybe I'll go sit in Nick's lap while I eat.

Don't you even!

Nick eyed her curiously. "You sure about this, Jackie? You know what you're doing?"

Jackie shrugged. "No, but Laur deserves no less." *OK. Let's do this. Push or pull or hit the magic button.*

Laurel did, nudging at that indeterminate place inside Jackie where body and soul joined forces, where the bonds had been snapped by Deadworld and now seemed held together by little more than Velcro. The world made a subtle shift, and in one blink of an eye, Jackie found herself watching the world from a distance, peering through someone else's body, only it was hers.

Jackie listened to her voice moan at the first bite of the pizza. She could tell her mouth moved, but whether it held pizza or a clod of dirt, she could not tell. The beer bottle came up to her lips to wash it down, and she heard herself laugh.

"Oh, this beer really is wonderfully bad."

The laughter began to melt into sniffling, and Jackie realized her vision had blurred slightly, her eyes blinking rapidly to quell the tears.

Wait. Laur? Are you crying? What's wrong?

"No, it's fine," she said, laughing again. "It just tastes so good. I really missed this."

Shelby looked at her, at Laurel, her head tilted at an odd angle. There was a look there Jackie had never seen before. Shelby swung her legs off the bed and fell to the floor on her knees in front of Jackie, hands resting on her knees, though she could not feel the pressure of the fingers there.

"Are you really there, sweetie?" Jackie watched her view bob up and down several times and then watched her hands come up to cup Shelby's face. A single tear rolled down her cheek.

Laurel brushed the tear away with the thumb of Jackie's hand. "I am. Your skin is even softer than I remember."

"Kiss me," Shelby whispered. "Before Jackie changes her mind."

Hey now! Wench. Laurel hesitated, inching forward an inch, but doing little more than letting Jackie's fingers brush across the features of Shelby's face. *Oh, good grief. Go ahead, Laur. Kiss her.*

Jackie leaned toward Shelby, head tilting to the side, and then the world went dark, burying Jackie in effusive, whispered proclamations, little gasps of pleasure, and the soft, suckling sound of flesh.

And then the darkness was swept aside in tide of green, an eerie, phosphorescent glow. The thin wall between worlds buckled and pulsed with an unfamiliar energy.

Laur? Something's wrong here.

No, hon. It's perfect. Thank you.

Another voice, thin and hollow, an asthmatic old man sounding off through a crackling megaphone, rang in her ears. *At last. You've come at last.*

Laur! Jackie pushed away from the strange, frightening voice, pulling at Laurel's vibrant energy, until she found the connection to her own body again. The green glow faded away and Jackie found herself pulling away from those full, red lips.

Shelby's brow furrowed with confusion. "Jackie?" She

rocked back on her heels. "Why'd you have to ruin . . . what's wrong?"

Jackie leaped up from the bed, knocking Shelby onto her butt, half expecting there to be a residual, glowing green spot left behind by whatever that thing was that had beckoned to her from the other side.

Nick came to her side, his hand gripping her arm, steadying her. "Jackie? What happened?"

She pointed at the bed, finger shaking uncontrollably. "It was that thing, the spindly whatever-the-fuck-it-is thing."

Nick looked over her shoulder at the spot on the bed where she had sat. "Did it do something to you?"

"No." Jackie let out a long, shaky breath. "It was trying to come through, I think. It talked." Her whole body was trembling now, and Jackie leaned back against Nick for support. "Damn it, Nick. It wants me for something."

"Shit." Shelby stood up from the floor. "Clearly, we have to figure out what to do about that thing."

Jackie laughed. "Yeah, well I'm open to suggestions, other than going over and having a chat."

Nick's hand settled on her shoulder. "I don't know. We have no idea what we're dealing with."

She walked over and grabbed another beer. "All I know is that ghosts on the other side are terrified of it. That's enough for me."

Shelby sighed, clearly frustrated—mostly, Jackie suspected, from losing her opportunity with Laurel. "I vote for some sleep. It's going to be a long day tomorrow."

Sleep? Jackie's heart rate had yet to return to normal. "Probably a good idea. I'm stepping out for some air first."

"I love you, baby," Shelby said, looking Jackie in the eye.

Jackie turned away. "She loves you, too, and I really wish you'd stop doing that, Shel. It weirds me out."

Shelby reached out and turned Jackie's face back to her own, smiling and kissing her briefly. "I love you, too, so don't feel bad."

"Gee thanks," Jackie said, shaking her head and walking toward the door. "Stepping out now."

She does, Laurel said. *She likes you a great deal.*

I know. It's just odd having her look at me to look at you, and the way she looks. It's unnerving.

Laurel chuckled. *I love that look. It makes me all squishy inside.*

Just try not to squish on me while you're in there, OK?

Jackie stepped out of the main lobby, stood outside the main door, and sipped on her beer. The cool air felt wonderful on her face. Sadly, there was little to look at for soothing her nerves, with an Olive Garden across the parking lot on one side and a doctor's office on the other. The wet asphalt reflected streetlights, but at least it was not raining.

How had life gotten so strange? Who knew it actually drifted so far from the center? Six weeks ago, she was just a plain old FBI agent, catching bad guys. Now her partner lived in her head, she was trying to date a vampire, and she was dealing with a town full of ghosts. Who had fucked with the highway signs of life and sent her down this dark, freak-show road?

The sliding entry door came to life, making Jackie jump. Nick stepped up beside her, beer in hand. "How are you doing?"

"I'm fine, for now at least," she said. "It's just . . . I don't know, Nick. This thing on the other side, it scares me. Ghosts and vampires, I can deal with, or at least I'm beginning to, but this? I don't like things I can't make sense of. At least ghosts and vampires are human."

"Me either," he said and draped an arm around her shoulders. "Would it help if I said that thing scares me, too?"

She laughed. "Not really. You and Shelby are supposed to be the experts on this dead stuff."

"It might not be dead," he replied. "You're a living soul

that can open the door to the dead. It's a unique ability, and I'm wondering if whatever it is can sense that."

"What are you saying?"

"I'm not sure," he said. "I'm just hypothesizing, trying to figure this out, but I wonder if it wants you for what you can do."

She turned and looked up at him. "You think it wants to come here? To cross over?"

"Maybe. I don't know, but it's certainly a possibility. Perhaps it's trapped there."

"God." Jackie drained down the last half of her beer. "I can't imagine letting that thing loose among the living. Who knows what it is or what it can do?"

"Exactly," he replied. "But, if it were here, maybe we could deal with it."

"Or not," Jackie said. She tried to wipe the image of those glowing green eyes from her mind. "Do you want to take that chance?"

"No," he said. "I don't, but I don't want you living in fear for the rest of your life either."

"Shit." Jackie had not even gone there. She laughed nervously. "Thanks for that. I hadn't even considered that it might never leave me alone."

He reached up, cupping her cheek with his hand, and Jackie leaned into the comfort of it. "We'll figure it out. Somehow."

"I hope so."

Nick leaned down and kissed her, soft and fleeting. "We will."

Jackie opened her eyes, staring up into the depthless, faint glow of his. Nick's stolid, firm voice always sounded reassuring, no matter what was said. "Again?"

He smiled, a soft curl of his mouth. "We will," he said and kissed her again, longer and deeper than the last.

Chapter 16

Who were they? Charlotte continued to brush through Rebecca's hair, yanking through the tangles and ignoring her gasps of pain. Ma-ma and Pa-pa were downstairs polishing and dusting things that did not need it in order to avoid her wrath. Carson said they were a group of ghosthunters, come to check out Thatcher's Mill, but this was no ordinary group of hunters, if that was even what they were, not when one was a former FBI agent. Ghost-hunters did not come to town with their own ghosts either, especially one as self-aware as that one had been. That one had actually *seen* her and bolted the moment she realized that she had been recognized.

That meant she likely knew what Charlotte was. The living were easy enough to dupe, but the dead knew. They could feel it. That reporter was convinced they were using the ghosthunter guise as a cover for something else. So why else would they be here if not to investigate her? If the FBI were somehow involved, then some serious problems could be coming her way. People like that had access to information, and Charlotte knew that a little digging into the town of Thatcher's Mill would turn up a lot of strange things, like why the Thatchers had two daughters they shouldn't actually have.

"Ow, Sis!" Rebecca finally yelped after Charlotte pulled through a particularly stubborn tangle.

"Hush," she replied into her ear. "Quit being such a baby."

"Are you still angry with me?"

Charlotte sighed. "No. I wasn't angry with you in the first place. I was angry at the woman who came to the door."

"Do you really think she's here to take me away?" Rebecca asked in a quiet, fearful voice.

Charlotte smiled and kissed the soft, exposed part of Rebecca's shoulder. "I was just upset when I said that. I'm not really sure why she was here, but I can't discount that possibility."

"But why?" she replied. "Why would she want to take me away from my family? I haven't done anything wrong, have I?"

Charlotte swallowed the warm knot in her throat. Jessica had become one with her so much easier than many of the others. It was as though she truly did belong. The effort required to entrench the belief that this was truly her family and where she belonged had been slight. Jessica wanted to be here, wanted to be Rebecca, and that had always been half the battle. There were times, especially late at night when they each lay in their beds after the lights had been turned off, and they talked in quiet voices about the mundane activities of the day or when they might again go for a ride on the motorcycle or walk up through the woods to where the stream fed into a pool, and they could lose their clothes and splash each other in the cold waters, that Charlotte could almost forget that this was not the real Rebecca. It had been so long since she had found someone who slipped so easily into the new persona.

She was probably ready, if it came to that, to try the next step and become her sister in the way that mattered most. Charlotte had hoped for more time, had wanted more, but these strangers in town were threatening that. If they somehow managed to find out who Rebecca really was, then they might bring her real mother here, and when Jessica failed to recognize her or have any interest in going back to her old life, things would become difficult. Worse, Rebecca might want to return to being Jessica, and that would not be allowed to happen. Not when her best chance at having her sister back in fifty years had come along. Charlotte would not allow that to happen.

Charlotte set the brush down on the bed. "You've done nothing wrong at all, Sis. They have no reason to take you away from me. Unless, of course, you would want to go."

She turned to look at Charlotte with a wide, watery stare. "I would never leave you. I'd rather die!" Rebecca threw her arms around Charlotte and hugged her tightly, sniffling into her shoulder.

"You're so sweet," Charlotte said and kissed her head. "We'll be together forever, Sis. I would kill anyone who tried to take you away."

"Oh! I would, too," she said, pulling her head up. "You're the only thing in the world that matters to me."

Charlotte reached up and brushed the tear off of Rebecca's cheek with her thumb. "Likewise."

Perhaps it was time after all. Why take the chance these people would find nothing and leave them alone? She thought the likelihood of that to be low. One did not come to Thatcher's Mill by happenstance to look for ghosts. Everything added up to them focusing on her, which meant they would have to be dealt with somehow, preferably a subtle little influence to leave town. And if they did find out who she had here at her house and everything blew up in her face? If she couldn't take them down, then she might be forced into the unthinkable situation of leaving and starting over.

No. She knew without a doubt that starting over was not an option. This life, this place, these people were hers. If someone was going to try and take that away, then she would take them all down with her. The end of her would be the end of Thatcher's Mill.

"What are you thinking, Sis?" Rebecca asked, wiping at her tear-filled eyes.

"A lot of things," she replied absently. Her gaze refocused on Rebecca. "How much do you love me, Bec? I mean, really, how much?"

Her big, brown eyes blinked several times in silence. "More than anything," she whispered.

Charlotte took Rebecca's face in her hands. "More than life itself? Would you be willing to die for me?"

There was only the briefest hesitation. "More than anything," she repeated.

She kissed Rebecca hard on the mouth. "Good. You are my sister in blood. Do you want to be my sister in spirit, too?"

The wide-eyed stare narrowed. "But we are sisters in spirit. I don't understand what you mean."

"It means . . ." She slid her hands down and took Rebecca's in her own. "It means that I died for you once, a long time ago, but I came back because I could not leave you behind. I loved you so much that even death could not take me."

Rebecca blinked away tears, her lower lip trembling. "I would die for you. Our bond is stronger than death."

She squeezed Rebecca's hands. "Do you believe so? Truly?"

She nodded emphatically. "How could death be stronger than love?"

Charlotte smiled and wiped a tear off her own cheek. "So very true, Sis. So very true." She reached into her pocket and pulled out the small switchblade. "When death comes, we will be stronger, together forever."

Rebecca threw her arms around Charlotte again. "Forever, Sis! We are—" The words cut off with a sharp gasp and she pulled away, staring down at her stomach, where the slowly blossoming red flower of blood began to creep across her dress. She looked back up at Charlotte with wide-eyed incredulity. "Charlie?"

"Hush," she said and eased her back on the bed. "Conserve your strength. Death is coming and our love shall keep it at bay."

"I'm bleeding," she replied, still in disbelief.

Charlotte looked down at her, tasting the energy of her upon the air, the sweet force of life seeping out of the wound in her stomach. "I know. It will all be fixed soon enough. Just be still and breathe."

"It hurts, Sis!"

"Do you trust me?"

"I do, but—"

"Then lie still," she said more forcefully and Rebecca eased back down. "Do you think I would let you die?"

"No, but . . . I don't understand." She grimaced and brought her hands up to the wound.

"Don't touch it," Charlotte insisted. "Just be still. I mean it. Think about us, our bond together, sisters in blood, and the fact that nothing, *nothing* in this world can break it." She reached down and clasped Rebecca's hand. "Even death cannot break it, no matter how strongly it says your time has come, I will always be with you, Sis." She leaned over, eyes pulsing with a swell of power. "Even in death, I shall never leave you. Our love is stronger than death, Becca. You must have faith."

"I don't want to die," she replied, wincing in pain.

"Do you want to be with me forever, Sis?"

Rebecca nodded at Charlotte.

"Then we must show death that it cannot win over love. I defeated it for you. Now it's time for you to prove that you love me and want me more than anything in this world." Charlotte stood up straight and turned toward the hall door. "Ma-ma! Come now!"

"Sis?" Rebecca's face was beginning to lose some color now. "I'm afraid."

Charlotte spun back to her and leaned over, placing a hand on each of Rebecca's shoulders, pushing her down against the mattress. "No fear! Death feeds on fear. Fear will let it get you and take you away from me. You must be strong, and I will be here with you to fight him, Sis. When he comes, I will be with you."

Light footsteps could be heard moving quickly down the hallway before the door swung open. Beverly stuck her head around the edge of the door and gave them a pensive look. "What is it, sweetheart? Did you girls need some tea or maybe—" She stopped when her gaze finally recognized what was going on. "Oh, dear Lord! What's happened to Rebecca?"

"Ma-ma, sit down, here, next to Rebecca," Charlotte said, pointing and motioning with her finger. After Beverly rushed over and sat down on the other side of the bed next to Rebecca, Charlotte grabbed her wrist when she tried to look at the wound in Rebecca's abdomen.

"Ma-ma?" Rebecca said in a sleepy voice. "I'm going to be with Charlie forever."

Charlotte tightened her grip on Beverly's arm until she gasped and looked away from Rebecca. "Ma-ma, Rebecca is bleeding to death, and she needs some more blood now. Are you willing to give her some?"

Beverly looked down at Rebecca and then back again. "Of course, but don't you think we should call an ambulance?"

"We don't have time," Charlotte replied and pulled out her blade again. "Will you give her some? You won't feel a thing, I promise."

"If she needs me, then, of course," she said. "I'd do anything for you girls."

With a quick flash of steel, Charlotte opened up a deep, inch-long cut into the veins on Beverly's wrist, who gasped but said nothing. "See, Ma-ma, you can't feel a thing, can you?"

"No, sweetie, it's OK," she replied.

"Good. I love you." She pulled the arm toward Rebecca, dripping a trail of blood across the spread. "Lay down here next to her and put the blood to her mouth, just like we used to do."

Beverly slid up next to Rebecca on one side, while Charlotte settled in against her on the other; Rebecca gave them a pleasant moan and then made a face at the taste of blood on her lips. Charlotte pinned the wrist to Rebecca's mouth so she had little choice.

"Drink, Sis," she said. "You must. Blood has the energy of life within it, and you need more to fight off death when he comes. Life and love, Bec. Look at me." Her head turned enough so she could see, and Charlotte held her gaze, putting on her best, most dazzling smile. "Let's show them all that our love is the most powerful of all."

Charlotte kept the wrist clamped down over her mouth with one hand, while the other gently brushed at the hair falling across her forehead. Beverly murmured reassurances. She reached out, feeling the energy of her fading slowly, weakening the bond between the physical reality and her soul. With the piece of Rebecca's soul flowing through her veins, Charlotte could make the connection to her easily enough. The key element on her part would be timing. The other would all be on Rebecca and her will to stave off the pull of death. The cold push of the other side was beginning to seep through.

Rebecca tried to say something, spluttering against the wound pressed to her mouth, as rivulets of blood spilled out across her cheek. Charlotte hushed her. "Drink, Sis. It's almost time. Be ready. I'm right here with you. Always."

After dozens of attempts, Charlotte had learned that she could not force them to fight. She had tried many different ways of charming, of trying to build a high level of emotional need and desire to stay with the living, but she had come to realize that in the end, it was still just a charm, a forced response, and death did not capitulate to such fakery. She could only build up a genuine desire and love, create a real bond, and believe herself that this girl was her sister come back to her. This Rebecca was the closest she had felt in so long. Other than convincing her that she was Rebecca and not Jessica Davies, the rest had come almost too easy.

"How much more?" Beverly asked, her voice strained.

"Until she is done, Ma-ma," she replied in a harsh whisper. "Do not speak again." A cool shiver ran down her spine. The dead were coming to make Rebecca their own. She refocused on Rebecca, whose mouth did little to drink the blood spilling from Beverly's wrist, and took one of her hands in her own. Charlotte squeezed it. "I love you, Sis. I will stand with you against him. Death cannot win." She kissed Rebecca's cheek, leaving a bloody smear across the skin. "Our love is stronger."

Charlotte pulled upon her reserves of power, built upon the blood of the townsfolk, and waited for the proper moment. That door would open and she would stick her proverbial foot in the door, keeping it open for as long as she might, funneling the energy through her bond with Rebecca and hoping against hope that she would see and utilize her own reserves to keep that hungry spectre of death sated. In the end, though, it would be Rebecca's will to turn back to the living, because once that door opened, the call of the spirit world was nearly irresistible.

As if she knew it was coming, Rebecca's hand squeezed hers at that moment when death arrived, and Charlotte fed the hungry monster with all she could afford to give. The pull of the other side was always compelling, such an easy thing to give in to. It came with such a sense of peace and release, but Charlotte knew better. She had been over there, where spirits roamed the cold, gray wastes, lost and aimless. Where they went after that, she could not see or tell, but if anyone knew the truth of what lay beyond this world of the living, consuming blood might not sound so appalling.

She felt Rebecca drawing toward the door, like fog into a vacuum, an alluring compulsion. This time, unlike the others, Charlotte did not demand she fight or resist, but only infused her power into Rebecca's mind, giving her the ability to see what the other side was pulling away, separating the soul from the last vestiges of the material body. Need and demand had always failed. No matter how strong it might be, such things did not influence death. This time would be throwing away all of the influence she had grown accustomed to, setting aside what she had become and be only what she had been once, long ago, a sister to the other half of her life.

"I love you, Sis," she whispered in Rebecca's ear. "You are a part of me I can't live without. I need you here, Bec." She swallowed down the lump in her throat. "I only live for you, so please come back to me."

The energy shifted then, a subtle change in flavor. Rebecca's life energy began to blend, tainted with Beverly's, and the flow of energy through the door thickened and slowed. Charlotte pressed Beverly's wrist more firmly against Rebecca's mouth. The time was now if it was going to take hold. It was up to Rebecca to realize what was happening, to take the energy being given to her and use it to pull that door back to the point where the life force only trickled away and blood would feed the cold pull of death.

Charlotte continued to whisper into Rebecca's ear, the seconds ticking down like minutes. It would happen at any moment now, the choice made to either fight or go, and as much as she wanted to shout encouragements at her, to force her own will upon her, Charlotte refrained, remembering those last moments over a hundred years hence, when the smiling preacher man had licked the blood from his fingers while she had cradled Rebecca much like she did now and sucked upon the blood seeping from the gash in her neck.

Rebecca spluttered and coughed, eyes fluttering open, and Charlotte propped herself up next to her, digging her fingers into the wound upon Beverly's wrist, who now lay unresponsive on the other side of Rebecca, her breath shallow. "Oh, Bec! Drink, Sis. Pull it in and feed that monster. Come back to me."

Rebecca sucked upon the wound, her own hands coming up now to grasp ahold, pulling hard upon it, her eyes still closed. Charlotte placed her hands over the soaked stain on her stomach and directed her energies there, binding and healing the flesh there. A minute, perhaps two later, and it was done, as quickly as it had begun.

Rebecca pulled the wrist away from her mouth, eyes blinking rapidly, confused and filled with fear. "Sis? What . . . what happened. How? I don't understand."

Charlotte covered her face in kisses, laughing with hysterical disbelief. "You're back! We did it! Love does conquer death. I told you. I told you, Sis!"

She smiled at Charlotte, wiping the blood from her mouth. "I feel . . . strange." She turned and saw Beverly lying still next to her. "Ma-ma? It worked!"

Charlotte reached up and turned Rebecca's face back to hers. "She sacrificed herself for you, Sis. Ma-ma's dead."

"But . . . what will Pa-pa say?"

"Pa-pa will understand," she said and smiled. "Everything is going to be OK now. We're going to be together forever."

Chapter 17

It would take them longer than the morning to go through the medical examiner's files, situated in downtown Dubuque. Jackie leaned over Shelby's shoulder at the computer screen. "Six years isn't much of a window to look at."

"You want to thumb through file cabinets trying to find Thatcher's Mill residents?" Shelby asked. "Without knowing names, we're kind of screwed."

Jackie stood up straight, hands on her hips. Through the office window she could see Dr. Kirby Mathews staring at them with arms folded over his chest and a scowl on his wrinkled face. "How soon you think he'll be calling down to Carson to let him know we're snooping around?"

"That old fart?" Shelby turned and waved her fingers at the man, whose scowl deepened even more. Could a man's face look any more like the bark of a tree? "Probably has already."

Nick opened a file drawer on the other side of the room. "I can look up Thatcher at least," he said.

After an hour, Jackie was convinced that it likely would not matter how long they spent looking at files. Every last one of them was the same. The people of Thatcher's Mill all died from natural causes, just as Hauser had stated. Every form was filled out and signed by Carson and Mathews. As far as they could tell, they were all in order, not a letter or word out of place.

"What could Carson have on this guy to get him to sign off on all of these, no questions asked?" Jackie wondered.

Shelby turned off the monitor, having finished their exploration of the files. She waved her hands dramatically in front of Jackie. "It's the Thatcher's Mill Curse."

Jackie huffed in frustration. "Such bullshit."

Nick set the stack of Thatcher files on top of the cabinet. "At least this should stir up Carson's ire. It'll be interesting to see what he has to say to us the next time we see him."

"Which should be soon," Jackie said. "After yesterday, he's probably parked on Main Street waiting for us to drive into town."

"Wouldn't hurt to have a few words with him anyway," Nick added. "See what he says if we accuse him of being involved in the Thatcher cover-up."

"Have half a mind to go confront the Thatchers directly and just ask the sisters who the hell they really are," Jackie said. "What's the worst that can happen?"

"They could have Carson arrest your ass," Shelby replied. "We really don't need to deal with that on top of everything else."

"Arrest me for what? Knocking on their door?"

"You think he actually needs an excuse?" Shelby replied. "If he's involved at all, he'll arrest you for breathing wrong."

"I think it's prudent for us to continue to work behind the scenes as much as possible," Nick said. "Let's wait until we have some proof of wrongdoing before we start confronting people."

Jackie frowned. "Let's go. You guys are no fun at all."

They hit up a Starbucks for coffees before heading south toward Thatcher's Mill. Jackie filled in McManus by phone, who said he would pass along the information through the appropriate channels to see that Dr. Mathews was looked into. He was looking forward to hooking up with them in the afternoon for the sketch-artist appointment. Hauser, on the other hand, had more information on the strangest town in America. Jackie put him on speakerphone so everyone could hear.

"It just gets weirder and weirder," he said, a gleeful tone to his voice. At least someone appeared to be enjoying this investigation. "Not only is your local chief of police a generational position passed down through the family, every position I can dig up info on is the same way. The mayor, your local volunteer fire department, the town electrician, the local diner, everything I look at is handed down to the next generation. It's like the town never changes."

"And how likely is that?" Jackie asked, knowing the answer already. It wasn't.

"Exactly," Hauser said. "The only odd ones out are the Thatchers. Those daughters of theirs don't exist, at least not on any official records. Everyone else I've tracked has maintained a consistent family size. If it grew, someone died. If Smith married a Jones, then a Smith married a Jones in the next generation. This is some cool shit you've stumbled upon, Jack."

"Not the choice of words, I'd use," Jackie said. "Have you actually found anything illegal for us to make use of?"

"Sadly, no," he replied. "Anything put on computer that I can access looks legit."

"You suck, Hauser," she said. "Focus on Chief Carson and the Thatcher girls. They're the key to all of this, and thanks for all the help."

He laughed. "No problem, Jack. We live for the freaky stuff down here."

They rounded a bend in the highway and Thatcher's Mill

came into view, looking so utterly ordinary and quaint beneath a now clear November sky.

"Someone has to be doing this," Shelby said. "There's no way a town just does this on its own."

"Or a group of someones," Jackie said. "How the hell do you garner that kind of control over so many people? One person couldn't do this. It's been going on far too long."

"I could," Nick said, staring out the window at the nearly empty town streets. "Shelby could."

Jackie turned to him in disbelief. "A vampire? But . . . wait. Wouldn't we have felt one by now?"

Shelby snorted. "If they stepped into Deadworld maybe. There's so much spiritual energy saturating this place, you'd be lucky to notice if they were standing right next to you."

"I would," Jackie muttered, staring up at the Thatcher house through the spider web of trees. "It's always the eyes that give it away, even with your funny contacts."

"You have a bit of an advantage there," Nick said. "Most people don't understand what they're seeing even when they do look."

The thought of another vampire chilled Jackie to the bone. The image of the Thatcher house from the night before filled her head, with the ghosts drifting across the ground toward the house. Drake had been able to do that, to use them in order to gain power. Nick had done it to save their lives. "God, I hope you're wrong."

Shelby turned off of Main Street and parked next to the diner. She turned and looked back at Nick. "You think it's Charlotte, don't you, babe?"

He was silent for a long moment. "Possibly. I want to see the picture Laurel describes first. It might tell me for sure."

"Then let's go," Jackie said. "There's no point in talking to Margolin now." Suddenly, she wanted to be very far away from this place.

"No," Nick replied. "We talk to him. He's been here for

two days now. There's a chance he's met whoever it is. He might know something."

Jackie took out her cell and dialed Margolin's number. He picked up on the second ring. "Margolin?"

"Agent Rutledge," he said, sounding pleased. "You're here early. Afraid to get out of the car?"

"What?" Jackie turned around and saw Margolin standing on the corner outside the diner's door. He waved.

"Thought you might get here early," he said. "So, let's talk."

"Asshole." Jackie clicked off the phone and shoved open the door. "He's here."

"I see that," Shelby replied. "You know, for a reporter, he's actually kind of cute."

"Yeah, well." Jackie stepped out onto the sidewalk. "He may be one of those people I don't mind if you bleed a little."

"You're so sweet." Shelby stepped out and Nick joined her. "You should keep this one, babe. She's got attitude."

"I'd be careful," Nick replied. "That attitude is going to punch you in the mouth."

She laughed. "Already tried. Isn't that right, Jackie?"

Nick looked across the top of the Explorer at her with a curious expression, and Jackie bit off her retort. "Let's go before I try again."

Inside the diner, Shelby slid in next to Margolin and gave him her charming, come-hither smile. "Hello, Margolin. Shelby Fontaine, but I guess you know that already."

Jackie moved in across from him, pleased to see Margolin shift away from Shelby, turning so that he could face her more. Molly the waitress approached, coffee pot in hand, face pulled taut into a what Jackie swore was a sneer. She walked by without stopping. *What the hell was that?*

"OK, Ghostbusters," Margolin said. "This is your dime. What've you got for me?"

How about I wipe that smarmy grin off of your face? Laurel's presence began to come forward.

Yes, I know! Don't worry. I've got this. "That depends on you, Margolin," Jackie said. "I'm not going to spoon-feed you a story. If you want to take, you're going to have to give."

"What did you have in mind?"

Jackie wanted to smile at Shelby, who kept inching in on Margolin's personal space. He could not wedge himself into the corner of the booth any further. "What it comes down to is this, Margolin. You want to know what we're doing here, then help us find out more about Charlotte and Rebecca Thatcher."

"The Thatcher girls?" He sounded surprised. "This is about them? You're kidding, right? They're like, fourteen. They're these old-fashioned sweethearts."

"And they're not actually Thatchers," Jackie said. It was time to take a risk. "Officially, neither one of them exists. We're trying to find out why and exactly who they are."

"That makes no sense," he said. "Charlie's a wonderful girl, loves her family. Why would you be going after her?"

"Mr. Margolin," Nick said. "We're not after anyone. We're trying to find out what happened in this town. There are things going on here that aren't normal, but we know that much of what has happened here revolves around what happened to the Thatchers. They may be in danger if we don't get to the bottom of this soon."

Good play, Nick. Work on his sympathies. Shelby leaned into him, her hand sliding across the table until it touched Margolin's.

"They might get killed," she said in a soft voice.

Margolin laughed and pulled his hand away. "You guys trying to scare me? Who's going to kill them? The only danger around here to the Thatchers is you all. What were you doing up there last night?"

"Trying to get a picture of the Thatcher girls," Jackie said. "Despite what you might think, Margolin, there is no hidden FBI conspiracy going on here. We aren't FBI. We're investigating a paranormal occurrence in Thatcher's Mill."

The easy smile dissolved into a smirk. "And who gave you the case?"

Jackie sagged back in the seat. "Oh, I don't know, Phil, who do you think? It was right there on the file box."

"All right, then," he said. "What's the FBI want with Thatcher's Mill? Why do you want to ruin this poor girl's life with your invasion of her life?"

Jackie spluttered. "Invasion? What the hell did she tell you? We haven't done a damn thing to them."

"Nice try, Rutledge," he snapped back. "You've been threatening—"

Sirens interrupted him, followed by the screech of tires and the flashing red and blue of police lights. Carson's car lurched to a stop behind the Explorer.

Jackie sighed. So much for Margolin. The fucking twerp. "Great. Everyone's favorite backwoods cop. This should be fun."

Nick slid out of the booth. "We need to lay low on this and get out of here."

Jackie could hear Carson's door slam shut. As much as she wanted to jump in his face over this mess, she knew Nick was right. The guy would arrest any or all of them on a whim, and they could not afford such a setback at this point, not with the possibility of those girls being in danger or Rebecca at least. She prayed Nick was wrong about the whole vampire angle.

"I'd suggest leaving them alone," Margolin said. "They aren't your story."

She ignored him, heading for the door. Molly the waitress stood at the cash register, a smug look on her face. “Don’t come back now.”

Jackie resisted the urge to slap her. Whatever happened to small town friendliness? Tucker, the cook, leaned against the entry back to the kitchen, arms folded across his chest, a similar acrimonious smile on his face. Once outside, she found Carson standing behind the Explorer, ticket book in hand.

“A problem, Chief Carson?” she asked.

“Besides you three? No,” he replied. “Getting kind of tired of you poking around in our affairs, Ms. Rutledge. Folks aren’t happy, and when my town isn’t happy, I’m not happy.”

“And the ticket?”

He pointed down at the sidewalk. “You’re over a foot from the curb.”

“We were just heading out,” she said.

He ripped off a copy of the ticket and handed it to her. “Good. See that you don’t come back.”

Jackie glanced at the ticket. The fine was five hundred dollars. “Jesus Christ! Five hundred for a parking violation?”

“We enforce our laws around here,” he said. “I see you again and maybe you’ll see what we do for harassment charges.”

The ticket crumpled up in her fist. “You threatening me, Carson?”

He stuffed the ticket pad back into his pocket and that thin line of a mustache twisted up into a smile. “It’s no threat. You’ve worn out your welcome here, all of you. Come back and I’ll see to it you spend a night in my cozy little cell.”

Nick stopped at her side, his hand settling gently on the back of her arm. “Let’s go, Jackie. This is trouble we don’t need.”

"That's right," Carson said. "I'm trouble you don't need. Might try listening to your man there, Ms. Rutledge."

Jackie jerked her arm away from Nick. "*When* I come back, Carson, you better hope Rebecca Thatcher is still alive, because if anything has happened to her, I'm coming after you first."

The worm on his lip drifted back down. "Rebecca? You think I have a problem with the Thatchers?" He laughed, the belly hanging over his belt jiggling with mirth. "You guys are dumber than I thought."

Shelby suddenly appeared between them, and Jackie's forward momentum carried her into Shelby's back. "You'll have to excuse, Ms. Rutledge," she said. "She has some authority issues."

Nick slipped his hand around Jackie's arm more firmly this time. "Jackie, leave this. Let's go."

Hon, this isn't the time or place, Laurel said. *Don't jeopardize the case for this. He'll get what's coming.*

Jackie turned away and marched around to the front of the car. "He's going down," she said and yanked open the door. "Got that, Carson? Your days as a cop are numbered."

"You might see that she has a little more respect for authority," Carson said.

Jackie watched Nick walk by in the rearview mirror and stop in front of Carson, standing nearly a head above him. "She has a great deal of respect for the law," he said. "We just have no respect for you, Chief Carson. Good day."

Shelby climbed into the driver's seat. "What a prick. Just take a breath, babe. I want to punch the little fucker just as much as you do."

Nick finally climbed in. "All right. Let's get out of here, before I decide Jackie was right and we beat the life out of that sorry excuse for a cop."

The Explorer wheeled around and Carson stared them down. "Stay out of my town," he yelled.

Chapter 18

Jackie breathed in the sweet, familiar scents of FBI headquarters, picked up a Styrofoam cup of horrid coffee for old time's sake, and made the rounds of the office to say hello to anyone who was there. She had really hoped to see Belgerman, to fill him in personally on how things were going, but he was out for meetings. His presence would have been a comfort.

She gave McManus the rundown, who looked worried after hearing about the run-in with Carson.

"You're going back, aren't you?" he asked.

"Of course, we are," Jackie said. "We aren't done yet."

"And if he arrests you? You realize you're out of our jurisdiction over there. That's the Omaha office's area. They'll have to get you out."

That might be an issue. Jackie did not really know anyone there. "What if things pan out the way we're thinking?"

"If you verify the paranormal activity, Belgerman should intervene," he said. "It'll take me a few hours to get there regardless."

"Then I'll just have to avoid getting arrested, won't I?" She smiled at his look of consternation. "Look. If we can prove a kidnapping or, God forbid, Charlotte Thatcher is a vampire, you should be able to get authority to move in and help, right?"

"Yes," he replied. "Just don't jump the gun, Jack. I really don't want to deal with dragging your butt out of jail."

"Don't worry. It'll be fine."

He rolled his eyes at her. "Yeah. This is me not worrying."

There was a knock on the conference room door, and the sketch artist came in.

Laur? You ready for this?

Of course. This will be fun.

Jackie smiled up at the bespectacled, rumpled man who carried nothing more than a laptop case. "Hi there. Ready to draw?"

There was actually no drawing at all, so thinking of the guy as a sketch artist had been something of a misnomer. After setting up the program, he led Jackie through an endless spectrum of questions, guided at narrowing down the details of Rebecca from the neck up. Jackie had never seen anyone operate this program before in person, so it was fascinating to see the generic face on the screen gradually morph into the likeness of the girl they were hoping to positively identify. An hour and two vile cups of coffee later, Laurel was finally satisfied with the image on the screen.

That's really close. At least as much as I can remember. Now for Charlotte?

Yeah, just give me a few minutes here.

She had the image sent down to Hauser to run against possible missing persons reports and had him run it on general description for as far back as the computers would allow within two hundred miles of Thatcher's Mill. If their theory held, they might get lucky and get a couple of hits on other girls who had disappeared over the years who matched Rebecca's general description.

When she was ready, they began working on Charlotte Thatcher's likeness. It was done about forty-five minutes later. Nick and Shelby were seated with them over the final fifteen minutes of the routine of relaying Laurel's information. Toward the end, Nick began to add some of his own alterations.

Jackie watched him point and make suggestions with growing trepidation. "It's her, isn't it, Nick. You can remember the details after so long?"

"It's the sort of thing that gets burned into your memory," Nick replied. "You tend to remember those who've tried to kill you."

An image of Morgan flashed through her mind, leering over her with wild-eyed madness, right before his possessed body had smashed her head against the floor and then bled out next to her. She would never forget that face. "So, is it her?"

"I can't be one hundred percent sure until I see her in person, but . . ."—he sagged back in his chair, face grim with regret— "it sure looks like Charlotte Thatcher."

"Fuck." Vampires. Bloody, fucking vampires. "We have to be sure. This will change everything we've been doing."

The images were put onto a memory stick and handed to Jackie. The image modeler, as he liked to call himself, closed up the laptop. "Will you be needing anything else?"

McManus got up and shook his hand. "No, thanks, Pat. You've been a big help." When he was gone, McManus sat back down. "So. What's the next step?"

"We have to go see Charlotte Thatcher," Jackie said. "It's the only way to verify the truth here."

"And if it's true?" he asked.

Jackie's reply was interrupted by her phone. It was Hauser.

"Got something for you here, Jack. You might want to come down here and see."

"On our way." She clicked off the phone and got up. "Hauser's got something. Let's go see what it is."

The geek room was its usual, dimly lit cavern aglow with computer screens. Several of the geeks hollered at Jackie and waved, who sheepishly waved back amid Shelby's chuckling. Hauser saved her, though, by waving them into his office, where his long, arcing desk housed three large computer screens.

Hauser surprised Jackie with a warm embrace. "Good to see you, Jack! Looking your usual, worn-out self, I see."

"Sleep is for lazy, computer geeks," she said. "It's nice to see you all again."

He plopped down in his chair. "Yeah, well you will owe me a six pack after you see this. I think we finally got something for you."

They gathered behind Hauser, who had one screen displaying a map with numerous red dots scattered across its surface, while the other had a picture of Rebecca Thatcher. It was displayed as part of the usual missing persons release police departments issued.

"Holy shit," Shelby exclaimed. "There she is. Jessica Davies of Madison, Wisconsin."

Jackie pointed at the other screen. "What's with all the points of interest on the map, Hauser?"

"Those," he said with a smile, "are hits on missing persons reports matching the general description you gave me on this Rebecca girl. That's twenty year's worth."

"Damn. How many are there?"

"Forty-seven," he said, "but I haven't gone through them all yet to see if any can be weeded out. Notice a nice little pattern there?

Thatcher's Mill made a near perfect bull's-eye in the center of the red dots. "Even if half those victims are unrelated, that's a Rebecca a year for the past twenty years. Fuck. She could have a hundred victims." The thought knotted her stomach. They could have one of the worst serial killers of all time on their hands.

"If it is indeed Charlotte," Nick replied, "you're probably right."

Jackie turned to him at the sound of his voice. He stared at the map on the screen or rather seemed to be staring through it to some far-off place. Shelby laid a hand on his shoulder.

"You had no idea back then, babe. You couldn't have known," Shelby said.

Hauser looked up at them, confused. "Known what? What am I missing here?"

"I think I did," Nick said quietly. "I just didn't want to believe it."

"Nothing, Hauser," Jackie replied. "Can you run the other girl just in case and then send it all over to Cynthia. We'll want this on our files at the office."

"Sure thing, Jack. This get you what you need?"

"I think so. I'll buy you that six-pack when we're done," she said. "We should get going."

Back in the elevator, McManus was worried. "Jack, you guys aren't about to go after another vampire, are you?"

"We need to verify this," she said. "I don't want to bring you guys in and have it all blow up in our faces. We've got that reporter, who isn't very sympathetic to our work, watching our every move."

"I don't like this," he said. "Belgerman won't either."

"I know," Jackie replied, "but I can't blow this on the first case. If we're wrong, this whole thing would turn into one, big clusterfuck."

"You call the second you know. Don't try anything without backup."

"Hey, I've learned my lesson on that one, don't worry."

Shelby snorted with laughter at that and McManus shook his head. "See this face? This is my worried face again."

Once out to the car, Shelby turned to Nick, jabbing a threatening finger at him. "Get over this right now, babe. You tried to help her then, and you couldn't. It's done. She's not that girl anymore."

"No," he said, his voice barely a whisper. "She's not."

Silence enveloped them and Jackie had no idea what to say to him. In her head, Laurel sighed. *Poor guy. This is going to be harder for him.*

What do you mean? This is going to be difficult for everyone if we're right.

Oh, I think we are, but the last time Nick saw this girl, she was still just a girl who had probably just been changed by Drake. Her family had been slaughtered. She was terrified and angry and Nick couldn't help her.

She tried to kill him, Jackie pointed out.

Because she saw what he was and took him for the same monster as Drake.

It's not like she gave him much choice in the matter.

Hon, would you have regrets, knowing what kind of life she had in store for her, knowing if given the chance you could have saved her from that fate?

Shelby gunned the engine, muttering under her breath and squealed the tires taking them out of the parking garage. Nick continued to stare out the window, lost in thought.

Shit. OK, I get it, Jackie conceded.

Do you? If she's what we think, having done what she's done, become what she has become, we're going to have to destroy her. We can't put her in jail.

Jackie sighed. *Yeah, I know.*

At the office, Cynthia had pizzas waiting. Nick said little, only grabbed a stainless steel bottle of synthetic blood and walked off to his office.

Cynthia watched him walk down the hall and shut the door to his office behind him. "What's going on?"

Shelby waved in his general direction and chomped down on a piece of pizza. "He's being a morose jackass is what he's doing."

"Oh." She carefully pulled off a slice of pizza and set it on her plate. "Why?"

"Because Charlotte Thatcher is a vampire and he's going to have to kill her."

Cynthia turned and looked down the hall. "Isn't that . . . ?"

"Yep." Shelby nodded. "One and the same. I just hope he can when it gets down to it, because it's going to take all of us to pull this off."

"Nick wouldn't do that to us," Jackie said. There was no way.

"Not purposefully," Shelby replied. She tossed two more slices of pizza on her plate. "I'm going to go cool off for a few, while our cowboy pulls his head out. Then maybe we can figure something out." She marched off leaving Jackie and Cynthia at the front desk. Jackie sat down heavily into one of the visitor chairs across from the desk and ate her pizza.

"Long day?" Cynthia asked.

She shrugged. "No longer than any other. I was rather pleased with our progress until about an hour ago."

"He'll come around, don't worry," Cynthia said. "I've seen him get like this before."

"Charlotte has probably killed dozens of young women," Jackie said. "You lose your rights to whatever you were when that happens, so Nick shouldn't be stressing on this one."

"Is it ever that simple?" Cynthia wondered.

"No." Jackie knew enough, had seen enough to know it was never simple. "It's not. You don't do this kind of job for simple answers, but I know what you mean, Cyn. It's always worse when you know things could've been different. I can certainly relate to that."

Cynthia gave her a sympathetic smile. "You should go talk to him."

She nearly choked on her pizza. "And say what? I don't know what to say to him about something like this."

"You don't have to," she said. "Sometimes just being there is enough."

Shit. I should go, shouldn't I?

Laurel said nothing and stepped out of her body and into the office. "I'm going to go sit with Shel for a few minutes and soothe some ruffled feathers."

Cynthia smiled and waved. "Hi, Laurel. Good to see you."

Jackie watched Laurel's body drift off through the walls. Cynthia only watched her in silent expectation. Finally Jackie huffed and dropped her pizza onto her plate and set it on the chair. "Fine. Print out that stuff McManus sent, would you, Cyn, and, you know, hold my calls."

She laughed. "Sure thing, boss."

For several minutes, Jackie did just what Cynthia had suggested—sat in Nick's office just being there. Beyond the wan smile when she entered, he said nothing. Jackie sipped on the Coke she had got with the pizza and tried not to fidget. As always, Nick looked unreadable, his face relaxed and expressionless in the dim light creeping in around the blinds. These were not the kinds of situations Jackie could relate to. Laurel had always been the one there for her, not the other way around. What would she say in such a situation?

"You tried to do the right thing," Jackie said quietly. "Back then, I mean. It's all we can do, and hope it turns out good in the end."

Nick finished off the last of his blood drink and set the bottle on his desk. "It's a bit ironic don't you think? To become the thing that ruined you only to have the monster return to finish the job."

"God, Nick. You aren't a monster," she said. "Far from it."

"Tell that to Charlotte Thatcher."

She rubbed her hands over her face. There was no easy way around this situation. "Even if we could just stop her from doing whatever it is she's doing, she's likely killed dozens of innocent people over the years. We can't let that slide."

"I've killed a few over the years, too, Jackie," he replied.

"That's different. Those people . . . deserved it."

He smiled. "Playing a little loose with the semantics aren't you?"

"OK, screw the semantics," she said. "The point is, you aren't a monster or evil or a sociopath. You did what you had to because you had no choice, and you made the best of what was available at the time."

"And so did Charlotte," he said. Nick groaned with frustration or perhaps just plain tiredness and got to his feet. "But you're right, and I know it. Choices were made and we must make the best of what's available."

Somehow, his words gave Jackie no sense of comfort. "Nick . . ."

He stepped around the desk and offered Jackie his hand. She took it and he pulled Jackie to her feet. "Thank you for coming in. I'm a brooding man who tends to dwell on things best left alone."

Jackie squeezed his hand. "You're a lawman who hates when the right thing to do doesn't fix all of the wrongs done, and I couldn't agree with you more."

His smile deepened the creases around his eyes, and Jackie felt the soft brush of his fingers tickle her throat until they tipped her chin up. "One could get to like a woman such as yourself, Ms. Rutledge." Nick's mouth came down to hers and lingered there for several seconds.

Jackie pressed back, sucking in her breath when he finally pulled away. Her pulse thumped rapidly in her chest. She had reached out, and he had actually reached back. Jackie grinned at Nick. It was a feeling she could get used to.

Nick's eyebrows arched. "What?"

She laughed. "Nothing. Let's go figure out what our next step is."

Chapter 19

The chairs in her office sat in a half circle in front of Jackie's case board. All of their current information was pinned up there, which to Jackie did not look like much. In reality, at the moment, they had no real proof of anything. The entire case was built on circumstantial evidence, conjecture, and postulation. Even if they got Charlotte into the system, assuming she was actually guilty of anything, a judge would laugh them right out of court.

They needed either a confession of guilt from Charlotte or some actual evidence that a murder had been committed or Jessica Davies to admit she had been kidnapped. The more they went over what they had, however, the more likely it seemed that they would get none of these things.

"What I still don't get," Jackie said, "is why? If our scenario is accurate, Charlotte has been collecting, and discarding, Mom, Dad, and Sister for over a hundred years. What is she not getting from them?"

"Because nobody is like the original," Shelby replied.

"Can you charm someone into being someone else?" Jackie wondered.

"With enough power behind it," Nick said, "you can get someone to do anything."

"Even kill themselves? Could every one of these girls have been talked into committing suicide?"

"Blessed Mother," Cynthia said with a gasp. "Perish the thought."

"Very unlikely," Nick replied. "That's one aspect of the will that is very difficult to overcome. Unless of course the person wanted to." Driven to suicide? Jackie swallowed hard. She was all too familiar with how that worked, having seen it first hand with her mother. "Let's assume mass suicide is not happening for the moment, look at the idea that Charlotte has Jessica charmed into thinking she's Rebecca. Could you remove it?" Jackie asked.

"Hmm." Nick rubbed at his jaw in thought. "I've never had opportunity to try."

"Me either," Shelby added, "but what if it turns out she's there of her own free will? We'd lose any advantage we have now, and it might put Rebecca at immediate risk. We can't force her to leave."

She was right. Jackie nodded. "So we're back to my original idea."

"Which I'll say again that I don't like at all," Nick replied.

Jackie frowned at him. "You two can't get near her. I can. I'll be wired and you'll be two minutes away."

He shook his head. "Two minutes won't be fast enough if there's a problem, and she's already spooked by our presence. We're a threat."

"Margolin was our only other possibility," Jackie said, "and he's clearly already chatted with Charlotte and is convinced we're up to no good. So, I think we're left with one choice, and that's me. Any luck and I can get Jessica by herself."

"We can't rely on luck with this," Nick replied, leaning forward and resting his arms upon his knees. "What are you going to say to her? How will you step through that door and convince her you aren't a threat?"

"By not focusing on her," Jackie said. "I'll play the kidnapping angle, wanting to find out that Rebecca is there of her own free will, which assuming she's charmed, she'll gladly do. If it works, we leave and let her think we've gone, get Margolin out of town, and then I go back, get Jessica out of there, and see if you can break Charlotte's hold on her."

"Sounds good to me," Shelby said.

Nick stared hard at Shelby. "And if it doesn't work?"

"Then we get Jackie out of there," she said. "Babe, there is no low-risk scenario with this. The first hint of trouble and we move in, and to be honest, I don't think Charlotte will do anything. She wants to keep her little world intact."

Nick heaved a sigh and stood up, clearly not happy with any of this. "This is also the same girl who put a bullet in my chest."

"We just won't let that happen then, will we?" Shelby said.

"Easier said than done," Nick replied and strode out of the room.

There was a moment of awkward silence, then Cynthia said in a quiet voice, "I'm worried, too. This sounds really risky."

I'm going with you, Laurel said. *I might be able to help in a pinch.*

Thanks, Laur. I was hoping you'd say that.

It was very risky, and stepping into the house of a vampire was the last thing she wanted to do, but like Shelby, Jackie did not think Charlotte would risk exposure if she could help it, not when she knew that two other vampires were waiting in the wings. "We knew there would be risks with this job, and we'll stay in constant contact, Cyn. If shit hits the fan, you get McManus on this immediately."

"I never thought we'd have vampires to deal with again," she said.

"Yeah, me either," Jackie replied.

* * *

It took them an hour to get ready and head out to the plane. Jackie's wireless mic was tucked into her bra and the tiny earpiece into her ear. She had a fully loaded tranquilizer gun and stun grenades, if push came to shove. She hoped this run would last no more than five minutes: talk to Charlotte, confirm she was a vamp, talk to Jessica, and let her say she was there of her own free will. Hello, sorry to bother you, thanks, and good-bye. Piece of cake.

On the road down to the Mill, Nick laid his hand on Jackie's thigh and she nearly jumped out of her skin. "Nervous?"

"Actually, I'm pretty good with the whole vampire thing now," she said. "I'm good."

Both Shelby and Nick chuckled at that one. He patted her leg. "You'll do fine. I'd be more worried if she didn't make you nervous."

"I think terrified would be a better term," Jackie said. "If we're wrong about her . . . just be ready, please."

"My foot will be on the pedal, babe," Shelby replied. "First whiff of trouble and we'll be on our way."

They rounded the final bend before town and Shelby killed the headlights and pulled off to the shoulder of the road. They would not risk getting spotted by Carson or Margolin this time unless absolutely necessary.

Jackie took a deep breath and let it out slowly. "OK. You come with horn blasting if there's trouble."

Nick's hand cupped her face and turned her to face him, where he leaned over and gave her a quick, hard kiss. "Good luck, Jackie, and please, please be careful."

"God, you're so cute sometimes, babe." Shelby turned, reached over and grabbed Jackie's hand, squeezing it tightly. "No gung-ho, super-agent bullshit, girl. Stick to the plan and let's be home before midnight."

Jackie opened the door and stepped out into the crisp,

night air. “I’m not trying squat against that girl.” *Not if I can help it, anyway.*

Her boots ground across the gravel until she hit the long grass off the side of the road. Another fifty feet and she was in the tree line, weaving in and out at the base of the hill until she had made her way around the east side of the town and stood directly below the Thatcher house. The town itself was mostly dark, a jagged shadow against the hills on the other side with sporadically blinking, yellow eyes. Silence cloaked her like fog. Between her position and the edge of town, Jackie caught sight of a wispy figure drifting through the shrubs of someone’s backyard. She had to quell the notion that it might spot her and go zipping up the hill to warn Charlotte.

Hon, we’re fine. It won’t bother us.

I know. Just jumpy. It’s so fucking quiet around here.

All of these dead scare the living things away.

“How you doing, Jackie?” Nick’s voice boomed in her ear, and Jackie practically jumped out of her boots.

“Christ, Nick,” Jackie said in a harsh whisper, “turn down the volume.”

“Sorry,” he replied softly. “Better?”

“Yeah. I’m heading up the hill now.”

In the silence, her feet crunching their way over twigs and underbrush, Jackie was sure the noise would alert everyone within a mile of her location, but the porch light up above remained on and no police lights came flashing from below. When she reached the top and stepped into the clearing, Jackie stopped and took a deep breath, double-checking to make sure her gun was properly situated and the stun grenades would detach themselves easily from the side of her belt. There were no signs of activity from inside the house.

“OK, I’m up top,” she said, “heading for the door now.”

“Anything unusual?” Nick asked.

“No, nothing,” she replied.

There were no signs of ghosts in the yard this time as she walked across the packed-gravel circle drive in front of the house. A pair of wooden rockers sat idly behind the screen windows of the porch, which Jackie half-expected to begin moving of their own accord. When she reached the wooden steps going up to the screen door her boots creaked on the planks, and Jackie froze, fist poised to knock, waiting to see if any reaction came from inside.

Do you feel that? Laurel whispered in her head. *She's in there.*

Jackie paused, reaching out for that sense of the dead. The ghosts were so frequent and dense in this town that she had gotten used to the feeling of their presence all around them, but when she actually looked and focused, Jackie felt it, too—a more intense thrum of energy..

Yeah, I can feel her. "Here goes nothing."

The rapping of her fist on the porch door sounded like gunfire in the still night air. She waited a good fifteen seconds before repeating. Another fifteen seconds and Jackie tried one more time. She felt the faint thump of footsteps through the soles of her boots. A moment later, the curtain hanging in the front door window separated a couple of inches, but Jackie could not make out who it was.

She hit the door again. "Charlotte Thatcher? This is Jackie Rutledge from Special Investigations. I'd like to ask you—"

The door opened. A slight figure stood silhouetted against the soft lamplight from inside. The short hair, forming a smooth shell around her head, indicated to Jackie that it could only be one person.

"What?" she asked sharply. "You want to ask me what?" Her voice was petulant, and Christ, but it sounded young.

"I'm here on behalf of my team to inquire about the welfare of Jessica Davies."

There was a brief pause. "There is nobody here by that name."

"Your sister, Charlotte," Jackie said.

"My sister is Rebecca Thatcher," she replied. "There is nobody here by the name of Jessica Davies. If that is all you came to harass me about at this late hour, then I bid you goodnight." She stepped back into the house and began to close the door.

"Charlotte! If you can't prove to me that Jessica is here of her own free will, we'll be forced to inform the FBI about possible kidnapping charges."

The door, halfway closed, swung wide open and Charlotte marched across the porch to the screen door. Jackie felt the sudden surge of Deadworld energy enveloping her.

Jackie! Be careful, Laurel said, pushing at the boundaries of Jackie's mind, ready to spring out against Charlotte.

Jackie took a step back, on the off chance Charlotte would attempt to fling the screen door open against her, but Charlotte stopped at the door, glaring through the screen, her shadowed face offset by the flare of glowing eyes. They narrowed into thin slits.

"You're carrying a ghost inside of you," she said, sounding more curious than surprised. "How . . . interesting. Where are the others?"

Nick's voice sounded worried in her ear. "Jackie? Watch yourself. I don't like her tone."

Jackie managed to hold her ground. *Me either.* "Nearby. Look, Charlotte, we have no qualms with you, if Jessica is here of her own free will. She's a missing person from Madison, Wisconsin, and we can't leave until we know she's not a prisoner here."

"Perhaps you did not hear me the first time," Charlotte said, her voice low and angry. "There is no one here by that name."

Another figure appeared in the doorway, her silhouette a near mirror image to Charlotte's. "Who is it, Charlie?"

"Becca!" Charlotte whirled away from the door. "I said to stay inside."

"I am," she replied, startled by Charlotte's abrupt attack.

"I was just curious . . . who is she?" Rebecca hesitantly stepped onto the porch. "She feels funny."

Feels? Jackie gave Rebecca a harder look. Why would she say that? Even Nick's voice repeated the statement in her ear. He was as confused by it as she was.

A sharp gasp rang through her head. Laurel's pressure on her, waiting on the edge to bust out, quickly receded. *Jackie?* Laurel's voice was tinged with fear. *Her eyes.*

Jackie saw it at the same moment. They weren't as bright as Charlotte's but they had the same definite, eerie gray glow to them. *Oh, shit! She turned her.*

"She feels," Charlotte said, "like someone who was just leaving. Isn't that right, Ms. Rutledge?" The screen door pushed open and Charlotte stepped out.

Jackie took a couple of steps back and reached into her coat, fumbling for one of the stun grenades, just in case this went south in a hurry. "How are you, Jessica? Do you want to go home?"

"Jackie?" Nick said. "There's some activity in the town. Let's call this."

Good idea, hon. Charlotte's good will is deteriorating fast. Let's go.

Jessica's head cocked to one side, accented by the odd angle of her eyes. "But I am home. I don't understand. Who's Jessica, Sis?"

"An old friend," Charlotte said and moved down the steps. "Now go back inside like I asked. Our uninvited guest was just leaving and not coming back."

Each step forward pushed Jackie back. She could not tell if it was fear or common sense that made her keep her distance. "Jessica! If you're in trouble, we can help you."

"Trouble?" If anything, her confusion had intensified. "Did something happen, Sis?"

"It's about to," Charlotte replied. She stopped and pointed a stern finger at Jessica. "Now get back in the house!"

"Get out of there!" Nick yelled in Jackie's ear. "We're heading for the drive."

Jackie palmed the grenade in her hand. "Apparently, Ms. Thatcher, your sister is well. Our information was in error."

Hon? Drop the bomb. Run.

The finger that had been pointing at Jessica swiveled around to Jackie. "Coming to my town was an error, Ms. Rutledge. You *will* leave and not come back. You *will* forget you ever came or that you *ever* met me. Do you understand?"

A wave of cold deluged Jackie, numbing her brain. *God . . . fucking . . . damn.*

"She's charming you, Jackie! Stun her. Get the hell out."

Laurel leaped out as Jackie staggered back, flying right at Charlotte with a scream that would impress any banshee. She did little to Charlotte, other than pass directly through her, but the moment was enough to startle, and that broke the icy vice that had clamped down on Jackie's brain.

She dropped the grenade, releasing the handle and bolted. Fist fights, gun battles, even the previous craziness holding baby ghosts in her uterus were all preferable to having the dead, wonky eyes boring into her soul. That was a line that no longer got crossed.

One-point-eight seconds later, the ground shook and a wall of air slammed into Jackie, throwing her forward. She tucked her shoulder, turned into a roll, hit the gravel with a thud, and was back on her feet, ears ringing so loudly, she could not hear Nick's voice yelling in her ear. At the bottom of the hill, she could see a pair of headlights coming up the drive. Without looking to see what had happened to Charlotte, Jackie ran like hell.

A high-pitched, childish scream pierced the night air. There was no pain in the sound, only rage. Jackie knew there was no chance in hell of outrunning Charlotte. She only hoped that she could reach the Explorer before Charlotte reached her. A hundred feet down the drive, Shelby slid to a stop, swinging the car around 270 degrees. Nick leaped out as she approached, eyes ablaze.

"Get in!" shouted Nick.

Jackie practically dove in, bouncing off the back of the front seat. Behind her, Jackie heard a chilling word, from a voice turned down an octave from the cute, fourteen-year-old she had just talked to. The petulance and haughtiness from before had turned into something Jackie did not recognize.

"You!"

Jackie sat up. Nick still stood outside of the door. "Nick! Let's go."

"Good evening, Ms. Thatcher," Nick said.

"Damn it, Nick!" Shelby yelled. "Get in."

"You!" Charlotte screamed this time.

"It's time you stopped this madness, Charlotte," Nick said. "Let the town go."

"Fuck, Nick," Shelby said. "Carson's coming."

Jackie looked down the hill. In the center of town, red and blue lights flashed off the buildings of Main Street. Through the trees off the side of the road, Jackie caught a glimpse of foggy gray moving up the hill. The ghosts were coming again.

"This is my town," Charlotte said. "You abandoned it, and now—"

"Sis?" Jessica stood at the top of the drive. "Who are these people?"

Charlotte whirled about. "Becca! Back in the house."

Seizing the chance, Jackie leaned out the door and grabbed Nick by the jacket. "Get the fuck in the car, Nick."

Shelby was spinning the tires on the gravel before he was even inside, dragging his feet along the ground before he could pull himself inside. Out the back window, Jackie could see little in the darkness at the top of the drive other than the faint glow of Charlotte's eyes. At the bottom, Shelby hit the street going at least fifty. At the end, where the road ran into Main Street, Carson's police car skidded around the corner, illuminating the last thing any of them hoped to see. A crowd had gathered in the street.

Backlit by the glaring, swirling lights, Jackie stared in disbelief at the shadowy crowd walking toward them. It was straight out of a bad horror movie. More stunning, she could see the black silhouettes of guns in their hands.

Shelby realized it at the same moment. "Fucking hell! They're armed."

To emphasize the realization, the front window of the Explorer erupted in a shower of pebbled glass, and Jackie threw up her arms to shield her face. Shelby spun the wheel, throwing the Explorer off the road between the pharmacy and Tom's Shoes, a space barely wider than the SUV. It smashed into and over a pair of garbage cans, through a stack of wooden crates, and finally burst out behind in the parking lot for the Main Street businesses. The police car entered a moment later.

"He'll chase us all the way to the damn airport," Shelby said.

Jackie crawled over into the back and grabbed her other stun grenade. "Let him get closer. This should knock him off the road." She reached for the latch and pushed up the rear window. "About fifty feet, Shel."

Shelby slowed out of the parking lot, tires still screeching on the asphalt as the Explorer oriented itself on the main highway. Carson was speeding across the parking lot now, catching up quickly. With 1.8 seconds, it would not take much. Jackie just needed him sliding out of the driveway and onto the road behind them. Roll the grenade into the middle of the road at the right time and let him drive right over it.

Jackie pulled the pin and waited. *Almost there. And . . .*

"Shit!" Shelby yelled. The Explorer lurched sideways and suddenly braked.

The momentum sent Jackie flying against the back seat.

Her elbow smacked into the side window, and the grenade tumbled forward to the floor.

"Out," Jackie exclaimed, and scrambled to get out the back window. She was halfway over, straddling the tailgate when the grenade detonated. The concussion propelled her out and she hit the pavement back first, knocking the wind from her lungs. A couple of rolls and she found herself face down in the middle of Main Street. Tires screeched impossibly close and Jackie struggled to push herself back up to her knees.

"Hold it right there, Ms. Rutledge," Carson yelled in her ear. "You're under arrest."

Jackie turned her head and found the barrel of his gun a few inches from her face. "Chief Carson," she said and tried to smile. Her mouth hurt and she could taste blood. "Just the worm I wanted to see."

There were footsteps on the pavement, and then Nick's voice. "Jackie! Are you all right?"

"Don't even think about it," Carson said. "Keep your hands where I can see them."

Jackie slumped back over, her head swimming. It was time to bring in the cavalry.

Chapter 20

The dashboard of the vehicle cracked beneath the force of Nick's fist. Shelby let go of the wheel and set her hand on Nick's thigh. "We have to wait for McManus, babe. We can't risk Charlotte sensing our presence and putting Jackie in danger. We can't."

"She's in danger regardless," he said.

"Carson won't do anything to her other than be an annoying shit," she replied. "And Charlotte will leave her alone as long as she believes her town isn't threatened."

"We can't assume that, Shel. Charlotte's got strangers who know who and what she is. She has been threatened, and the source of that is sitting right in the town jail."

"Babe, hate to say this, but she's not the threat. You are," she replied. "The second you stepped out of the car back on the hill, she knew who you were."

Nick sagged back in the seat and closed his eyes. He could still see Charlotte, flying down the hill toward Jackie and then coming to a dead stop when he stepped out of the SUV. She had known instantly. A century later and the memory of his brief time in her life had not dulled.

He sighed. "A mistake. One that Jackie cannot suffer for."

"And the best thing to do is stay the hell away until McManus gets here. Hell, I'm more worried about the fucking townsfolk. They were coming after us with guns in case you didn't notice. That girl's control over this place is insane."

"They failed her," Nick said. "Drake destroyed her family and she's never let them move on."

Shelby shook her head. "That doesn't matter anymore. Babe, I get the guilt. Really, I do, but this is a fucking bad situation. We have to stop her before shit really hits the fan."

She was right, of course. This was way beyond just stopping Charlotte. The entire town was at risk, one big powder keg waiting to blow up on them. And Jackie was stuck right in the middle of it. Nick pulled out his phone and punched in Hauser's number. After a moment he had the number he needed.

They had just pulled into the parking lot for the private hangar space at Dubuque's airport. Shelby eyed him curiously. "Margolin? You think he'll help us?"

"He's going to," Nick said. "Margolin? Nick Anderson, here."

"Well," Margolin said, "you guys sure do provide some good cover copy."

"No thanks to your lack of involvement," Nick replied. "You've been playing the wrong side, Margolin."

"Is that so? Your recent actions seem to have proven my point," he said. "Can't say going after Charlotte again was a wise move."

"You want the real story, Margolin?" Nick asked. "You won't be able to print it, but I'll give you the real story."

"I can print any story I want," Margolin said. "But I am curious why you think that."

"Because nobody would believe it," Nick said. "Because people don't believe in the kinds of things we're involved with, and you would be laughed right off your paper."

There was a moment of silence. "I'm assuming there's a catch in all of this? You want me to fabricate some dirt on the Thatchers?"

"I want you to stake out the Thatcher's Mill police station,"

Nick said. "I want you to keep an eye on anyone going into or out of there until we get back."

"And?"

"That's it," Nick said. "You call me the second anyone leaves or enters that building, no matter who it is, and I'll tell you all about the fact that you're sitting in a town being controlled by a vampire."

Margolin's bark of laughter rang in Nick's ear. "Vampires? You can't be . . ." He laughed again. "You think Charlotte Thatcher is a vampire? Oh, that's rich." Nick said nothing in reply. "You're serious. Why in the world would you believe that girl is a vampire?"

"Because I saw her turn into one back in 1897 when I came through Thatcher's Mill the first time."

Shelby stared at him. "Nick, what are you doing?"

"The first? Wait," Margolin began, then paused. "That was a hundred and ten years ago."

"Yes," Nick said. "I was in pursuit of the man responsible for the Tannenbaum fire."

"Hold on. Hold on a second. Are you telling me the guy in Chicago—"

"A vampire," Nick replied. "He killed Charlotte Thatcher's family and made her into a vampire, just like he did to me thirty years prior."

"So . . . you're a vampire, too." Nick could hear the disbelief in Margolin's voice, but it was still having the desired effect. Curiosity.

"I am," Nick said. "You want the rest of the story, though, you'll have to help me. Ms. Rutledge is not safe in that jail. If anyone goes into or out of that building, you must let me know."

"Or?" Margolin asked. "I'm going to guess there's an implied threat here somewhere. I'm not stupid, Mr. Anderson."

"No, you aren't," Nick said. "You're just likely under the thrall of Ms. Thatcher. She's a threat to anyone in that town, and especially Ms. Rutledge. I'm giving you one chance here to do the right thing and help me ensure her safety."

"Or?"

"Or the next time I see you, Margolin," Nick said slowly. "I will show you exactly what a vampire is capable of." He gave Margolin his number. "One chance. Choose now."

He chuckled. "Just like that, Mr. Anderson? Play watchdog or have you drink my blood?"

"Something like that, yes. Good-bye, Margolin." Nick clicked off and shoved the phone back in his pocket.

Shelby squeezed his thigh. "Nice play, babe. You going to make good on that threat?"

Nick propped his elbow on the windowsill and rested his head on his hand. "Count on it."

It was an agonizing seventy-three minutes before McManus's plane arrived. Three times Nick pulled out his phone to call Carson. On the third, Shelby yanked it out of his hand.

"Don't," she said. "It won't accomplish a damn thing. I'm sure she's fine, and Laurel is with her."

"Glad you're so sure of things," Nick bit back. "Carson is in Charlotte's back pocket. She could have him walk up and shoot her right in the goddamned cell."

"But he won't, because Charlotte wants her town. She wants her people, and bringing down the wrath of outside law enforcement is the last thing she wants."

Nick sat in silence for several seconds. He knew this was the case, but there was a time, when any house of cards reached its limit and adding one more card would cause it to topple. "I pray she doesn't realize the wrath of the outside law is already on its way."

She slapped the phone back into his hand. "Babe, nobody prays to the gods of the badge and gun."

"I hope it doesn't come to that," he said.

"Me too." She leaned over and glanced out the window. "Oh, look! I think the law has arrived a little early."

Nick leaned forward and saw the Learjet making its approach. He hoped it would be early enough.

A second car was waiting out by the tarmac for McManus. They would not be going in the same car since Nick and Shelby could not risk entering the town when McManus did. He jumped off the steps of the plane the moment they were down and walked quickly over to greet them.

"I got out here as quickly as I could," he said, glancing down at his watch. "County sheriff knows I'm coming in, so regardless of how this goes down, I'm calling them in as soon as we're done, hopefully with Jack on this side of the bars."

Nick nodded and followed him as he took off immediately for his car. "McManus, you realize what sort of situation they might be walking into?"

"I know," he replied. "Not a good one. They know it's a hostile situation, and I told them to keep a low profile until the rest of us get out of here. We've got about two hours until they do. Pernetti, and despite Jack's opinion, he knows what he's doing, is pulling together the team. If we don't have Jack out before then, it'll be the team's call on what to do next. This is a new gig for us, Mr. Anderson. We're kind of winging it."

Nick thrust his hands into his pockets. This whole thing could so easily go wrong in so many ways. Worse, it may have already. "We're right behind you," he said.

If they had any doubts about McManus's sense of urgency, his disregard for traffic safety and the rules of the road erased them. Even Shelby had to work to keep up with him. Nick was thankful for the speed at which he got them there, but when she pulled their car off to the side of the road a mile short of town, Nick's stomach began to tighten.

Shelby's fist popped him in the shoulder. "Quit worrying. We've got this. McManus will have her out in no time."

"Five minutes," Nick said. "If he hasn't called in five minutes, we're going in."

She grinned. "Fair enough, Sheriff."

Nick stared at his watch and then back to his phone, counting each and every second. Two minutes later he swore under his breath. "It's taking too long."

"Oh, for God's sake, would you—"

The cell rang, and Nick clicked in immediately. "You got her?"

"We've got a problem here," McManus said, sounding far more confused than worried.

The casing of Nick's phone cracked under the pressure of his hand. "What? What's happened?"

"You better come on in," he said. "She's not here."

Chapter 21

Jackie dabbed at her mouth with the back of her hand. The blood at least had stopped flowing. A few bumps and bruises, but nothing was hurt so much as her pride. The irony of being on the wrong side of the bars, while Chief Carson kicked back in his little office, stung more than anything else.

Nick and Shelby were not there. They would be out of town and getting McManus on the phone if they were smart. After ten minutes, things had quieted down a bit since Carson finally locked the front door to the station. After the fourth person stormed in wanting to know what Carson planned to do with those "goddamned ghosthunters," he had thrown them out and kept them out.

It was like a fucking mob out there. Her demands to be released fell on deaf ears, as did her desire to make a phone call. Hell, he had not even bothered to book her in properly, just shoved her into the cell and turned the key.

"We'll worry about those formalities later," he had said.

"You can't legally hold me here, Carson," she had snapped back. "You have nothing on me."

"Oh, we'll come up with something, I'm sure. Harassment will work. Reckless endangerment maybe? Setting off an explosive device on city property? Hell, that might even be a terrorist act." The snaky little mustache curled up, revealing a lovely, crooked array of smoker's teeth.

"It was a fucking stun grenade! And your crazy citizens were shooting at us."

"Justified," he had replied. "Protecting their own. We do that out in these parts, Ms. Rutledge."

"I'll be out of here soon enough, and you'll see what we do where I come from."

Hon, don't give that blowhard any more fodder to chew on. Just sit tight; Nick will have McManus here in a couple of hours, I'm sure.

I really hope that's fast enough, Laur. This asshole is Charlotte's lackey. He'll do any damn thing she says.

Meanwhile, all she could do was pace back and forth in the small ten-by-ten cell, up to the door and back to the barred window. Elinore sat in a state of continual annoyance, repeatedly answering the phone and politely telling all callers that Chief Carson was unavailable for comments at this time.

More worrisome, though, was the thought that Charlotte might come through that door at any time and want her blood. She was a sitting duck behind these bars, and Carson would gladly open the cell to let her in. With every passing minute, Jackie's nerves began to fray even more.

She's going to come, Laur. You know she is. What the hell do we do? I can't stand up to her. I'd have no chance in hell.

She'll just want to threaten you, make sure you leave her alone, and we have to convince her that we will. She can't afford to draw any more attention to herself. Keep to our story about Jessica. Our concern was for her safety, and that's all.

And what about Nick? That can't be good.

Laurel was silent for a moment. *No, I suppose not. I can't imagine what she's thinking about that.*

She wanted to kill him before. I get the impression that not much has changed over the past one hundred years.

You might be right, but maybe we can use it to our advantage when it gets down to it. We'll . . . The thrum of Deadworld blew in on a cold wind and washed over them. *Blessed Mother.*

"Shit!" Jackie grabbed at the bars. "Carson! I want that fucking phone call."

He walked into view with a Styrofoam cup in hand. "Sorry. You didn't say please. Politeness goes a long ways in these parts, Ms. Rutledge."

The locked front door clicked and swung open, jingling the bell overhead. Carson jumped, spilling hot coffee over his hand. The sweet, diminutive form of Charlotte stepped across the threshold. She now wore jeans and a leather motorcycle jacket, a loose curl of hair dangling across one cheek.

"Charlie," Carson said. "I wasn't expecting you so soon."

Fuck! Laur? Jackie backed away from the door to the other side of the cell. She was a rat in a trap and here came the grinning Cheshire.

Stick with the game plan, hon. Jessica is happy and healthy, so we're all good.

Yeah, except she's a fucking vampire now.

Charlotte walked with feline grace to where Carson stood and eyed the cup in his hand and the coffee dripping on the floor. "You've made a mess. Clean that up and get Ms. Rutledge a cup. I imagine she's thirsty."

Jackie took a deep breath and thrust her trembling hands into her pockets. *Sonofabitch. If she comes after me, Laur . . . if she tries . . . fuck!*

Yes, hon, I know. We'll have to.

That thing is over there, waiting for me.

But I don't believe it wants to kill you.

We don't know that!

There may be no choice. Let's focus on Charlotte.

She walked over to the cell, boots clacking on the hardwood floor, and stopped in front of the door. A corner of her petulant mouth curled up. “Ms. Rutledge. You can’t seem to leave well enough alone.”

Jackie avoided looking directly into her eyes. “You made it difficult for us to resolve our issues, Charlotte. All we wanted was to ensure that Jessica Davies was safe and free within the Thatcher household.”

The smile faded. “How did you find my sister? And why does the FBI care what a fifteen-year-old runaway is doing in Thatcher’s Mill?” Carson walked up and handed her the steaming cup. “Now, shoo. Go make yourself useful and settle everyone down. Everything is going to be fine now.”

That’s good, Laurel said. *She still believes this can all blow over and everything goes back to normal.*

Charlotte snapped her fingers at Carson, waving her fingers at him, until he handed over a key ring with a single key on it.

Jackie stared at the piece of cut steel dangling from the ring. *I’m not sure our idea of normal gels with hers, Laur.*

“I don’t know where you received your information,” Jackie replied, “but I’m not with the FBI. My team was here to investigate an unusual paranormal occurrence.”

“I see,” she said and passed the cup between the bars. “What were you investigating?”

Take the cup, hon.

Jackie sighed and walked forward, trying not to look overly hesitant. She reached out and took the cup, concentrating on keeping her hand steady. “We came to investigate the fact that Thatcher’s Mill is full of ghosts.”

The smile returned. “That it is, but what I want to know is who it is you came here with?”

Yeah, I figured you would. “They’re my research partners. Our job is to seek out supernatural occurrences and determine the appropriate actions to be taken.”

Charlotte's head cocked to the side, and she rolled her eyes. "Really, Jackie. Is this the game you want to play?"

Hon, tread lightly. Just tell her. She knows who Nick is.

"Fine. No games," Jackie said. "You want to know about Nick Anderson. Is he who you think he is? Yeah, he is. He's the same guy who tried to help you when Drake came through your town all those years ago."

"Drake?" she asked. "I don't know that—"

"The vampire," Jackie said. "The guy who came into town and slaughtered your family. The same guy Nick was trying to catch."

She crossed her arms over her chest. "Then you know what I am."

It was not a question, just a simple statement of fact, and Jackie did not care for the way she was taking that information in. "I know that you both require blood to stay alive. I know that Nick still would like to help you to deal with this situation. He has something you can drink in place of blood that will keep you from dying."

"Is that so?" Charlotte draped her arms through the bars, resting them on the metal crossbar. "And what about Drake, if that was his name? Does Nick Anderson still chase him?"

"No," Jackie replied. "He's dead now. Nick killed him."

"Dead?" She leaned back, gripping the bars. "He's dead? How?"

Jackie could not keep from snorting with laughter at that. "That's a long, complicated story. Maybe Nick will even tell you."

"So he can then kill me, too? I don't think so."

She took a deep breath. The conversation was going in the wrong direction, and Jackie was sure Charlotte had not come just for idle chitchat. The question was, had she come merely to spook her or did she have more on the agenda? "We didn't come here for you, Charlotte."

Charlotte released the bars and began to walk back and forth in front of the cell. "And yet, you've been to my house more than once, with a man who was here before and knows what happened."

Laur, I don't like the way this is going.

You need to convince her that coming here had nothing to do with her and that we'll gladly be on our way.

Trying! I don't think she believes me. "Look, Charlotte. Nick didn't realize you were here until we arrived. When we found out the Thatchers weren't supposed to have any daughters, we checked it out and discovered Jessica. But if she's here of her own free will, there's not a damn thing we can do about that."

"So," Charlotte said and stopped at the cell door. Her eyes brightened, and Jackie stared at a point on the wall over her head. "Knowing what I am, and what is going on here, you're just going to walk away? Make little notes in your research book and move on to the next?"

This would be the point at which Jackie would take a step forward, look her hard in the eye, and lie through her teeth to get the job done. Hard to do if you really wanted to take a step back and run for your life.

Do it, hon. I'll help you keep the charm at bay.

Will that work?

We're in a locked cell. We have no other options.

Jackie brought her eyes down to Charlotte's and did her best to step forward with confidence. "Yes, Charlotte. We'll just leave. We aren't the law. We've got no responsibility here."

Charlotte's eyes burned into her head, looking straight through her, searing away any vestiges of defense. After a moment, Charlotte raised an eyebrow. "Who do you have in there with you? How do you do that?"

The push from Charlotte faded from her head. *Shit! Laur?*

The truth. I think she knows if you're lying.

"It's my friend," Jackie said. "She was killed by Drake

also. As to how I do it? I'm not sure exactly. It just kind of happened."

Charlotte's eyes flared for a second and then the cell door clicked open. "How intriguing. Perhaps you can show me?"

Jackie took two steps back, hitting the bench along the rear wall. "I told you, Charlotte. I don't know how. I just can."

"So you say." She walked into the middle of the room and stopped. "Why do I feel like you aren't telling me everything? Why do I sense that you are not going to just walk away from this?"

She swallowed the lump in her throat. The cell door remained open, but Jackie knew she had no chance to get around Charlotte. The slender girl would kick her ass all over the room. "Trust me. I have no desire to remain in this place."

"But you will," she said, a soft smile on her lips. "There's a vampire in town and you researchers know how to kill them."

Jackie backed up onto the bench, towering over Charlotte. Perhaps if she leaped on her, she could knock her down and make her way out. But then? Where would she run? "We have no intention of trying to kill you, Charlotte. We didn't come here for you."

Charlotte reached into her jacket and pulled out a small ivory handle. A short blade snapped out, making Jackie jump. "You're lying," Charlotte said, holding the blade out before her, turning it over as though examining it for the first time. She sighed. "Anyway, it doesn't matter. The truth lives and dies at the Mill, Jackie. You can't leave."

We have to cross over, hon. We have to do it now.

But that thing! We can't.

She's going to kill you. We have a chance on the other side.

"Charlotte, I swear to you," Jackie pleaded. "We have no quarrel with you or your town. We came for the ghosts. That's it."

"And you shall join them," Charlotte said. "You should have left me alone when you had the chance."

She lunged at Jackie, who closed her eyes and pushed at that opening to Deadworld. With Laurel's aid, the door yawned wide, buffeting them in the cold, bone-numbing wind of the dead. The knife pricked at her skin, just above her navel, and then vanished as they stepped into the cold, gray world of the dead.

Charlotte's scream of surprise followed Jackie through and then faded abruptly. The cell door remained open in the now empty police station. Fog shifted around in swirling eddies over the floor. Jackie hopped down from the bench and checked her stomach with her fingers. There was a small tear in the fabric and her fingers came away with a dark smear of blood.

"Damn it," she said and lifted the shirt. "I think she got me."

Laurel stood next to her now and knelt to look. "It's just a small puncture. It'll be OK. We should get out of here before that Spindly Man shows up."

"Yeah," she replied. "Back to Nick's maybe—"

"Jackie Rutledge." The familiar, harsh and hollow, two-pack-a-day voice spoke from the depths of an empty cavern. "I would speak with you."

She stepped up to the cell door as the thing came into view, gliding over the floor, its long, thin arms shifting in a disjointed motion that gave it an awkward gait. The glowing green orbs, run through with pale yellow veins, stared at her, or so it seemed, as there were no pupils to give its gaze a sense of direction. Surrounding those bug eyes was an upswept coating of spines, giving its head the look of a steel-bristled brush.

Jackie flung the door closed, only to have it clang against the stop and bounce back open. The terror gripping her pounding heart told her to get out now, but common sense said to wait. It would only keep following her, waiting on the other side wherever she went. As frightening as the thing appeared, it had never actually attacked her or even tried to. It had only followed. Why? What the hell did it want? Bail or face it down?

"Hon, to Nick's! Now!" Laurel said. She stepped forward, between Jackie and the Spindly Man.

"Wait, Laur," she replied and held up her trembling hand. "Not yet."

"Jackie!" Laurel stared at her in disbelief. "No."

The Spindly Man stopped at the cell door and reached over to his right arm, plucking out one of the spines. It gripped the spine much like a knife, and its attention turned to Laurel.

She shrank away from the dark, four-inch needle, and Jackie slid over in front of her. The Spindly Man stopped and stepped to go around, but Jackie moved to block it again. "You got a fucking question, you ask me. Leave her alone."

It was a dangerous gambit, but Jackie figured that if it only wanted to see her, then everyone else was just in the way and of no real consequence. It could have killed her back in the beginning if that had been its agenda. Given the speed with which it had been following her around, that initial encounter could only have been something more cursory, like curiosity.

The thing paused turning its head toward her and then back to Laurel. Abruptly, the needle fell to the ground, clinking on the hardwood floor as though it was made of metal. Jackie looked down at the thin spine. Metal? Really? The thing grew metallic spines? The pit in her stomach grew a bit deeper.

"Laur, if it makes any kind of move, we go to Nick's," she said.

"Jackie?" Laurel clearly did not like this risk.

"I want to know what the hell this thing wants," Jackie said, trying to draw upon the anger she had over the additional fear this thing had brought into her life. "So, Spindly Man? What do you want? Who are you? What are you?"

It looked at her in silence with its unblinking, veiny green eyes. Its lanky, spine-covered body continually shifted and adjusted, as though it were uncomfortable in its own skin.

"I am Nixtchapooliomintchoktaleee of . . ."

Jackie tuned out the gibberish. She could not pronounce any of it, much less understand what any of it meant. "How about we shorten that all to Nix? I can't say any of that."

Its toothless mouth twisted around for a moment. "Acceptable."

"Why are you following me, Nix?"

"You are key," it said.

"Key to what? You don't even know who I am. What could I have possibly done to make me key to anything?"

Nix slowly raised a hand, pointing a multijointed finger at her. "Key to door. You come open."

"I'm not going to do any—"

A cold rush of air enveloped Jackie as the door to the other side pushed open and Charlotte stepped between worlds, switchblade still in hand. Her mouth was drawn down into a thin, venomous line.

"How can you—?" Charlotte stopped when she caught sight of Nix and staggered away toward the corner of the room. "You're with that . . . that thing?"

Jackie jumped toward the door, stepping out of the path between them. She knew about Nix? "We just met about a minute ago."

"I should've known," she said with a sneer, waving the blade in a wide arc in front of her. "I finally got her and you want to ruin everything!" Nix reached down to its body with each hand and plucked out a pair of spines, and Charlotte turned her focus to it. The doorway behind her began to stretch open once again. "You stay away from me, you freak!"

A soft hum, eerie in its pleasant tone, issued forth from Nix's mouth. It said something unintelligible and leaped at

Charlotte, who screamed and stumbled back through her doorway, leaving Nix to crash into the corner of the cell. The thing had moved with blinding speed, almost too fast to follow.

Jackie had had enough. If Charlotte could come through, then staying here was even less safe than before. "Laur?" She reached out to her with her hand. "Now."

Laurel clasped onto her hand, its grip dry and cold, and Jackie focused on Nick's house, willing herself toward that comfortable place before the fire. Nix turned toward them, spines in hand, an indecipherable look on its alien face. A moment later, he was gone.

Chapter 22

The sleepy little town of Thatcher's Mill had sprung to life. Shelby was forced to slow to a sane speed as they entered the town proper, otherwise she might have hit someone crossing the street. People were out everywhere, but the obvious spot was in the center of town outside of the diner. The crowd had spilled out into the road, making getting through all but impossible. Some had weapons, rifles, shotguns, shovels, and anything else they could apparently find handy. It was a mob looking for a victim.

"Maybe you should—" Nick began.

"I'll circle around behind the station," Shelby finished, sliding the car around the first corner they came to and driving down to the next block where the police station stood. There was a crowd out front there, too, and Nick was hopeful they had a back way into the station to avoid any confrontation with the locals.

"Charlotte has them all on edge," Nick said.

"Crazy," Shelby replied. "You'd think we were alien invaders or something."

"Might as well be," Nick said. "If Charlotte feels attacked, you can be sure they will, too. At least those under her sway."

"Looks like the whole damn town is out to get us."

"Wouldn't surprise me." The car came to a stop behind the station in front of the back door, and Nick stepped out. "Let's hope we don't have to go through them to get to Charlotte."

Nick did not bother knocking, exerting enough power to trip the lock instead, and stepped into the station. At the end of the short hall to the reception area, McManus poked his head around the corner and then stepped into view, sagging with relief.

"I was worried you might run into trouble out there," he said. "What the hell did you guys do here?"

Nick ignored the question. "Anything on Jackie?"

"No," he replied. "The clueless wonder-sheriff doesn't run a very tight ship around here."

Carson's voice piped in from around the corner. "Things were just fine until you city folk came in and stuck your noses where they didn't belong."

Nick stepped into the reception room and found Carson sitting on the edge of the reception desk, looking like a disgruntled child. Three strides had Nick standing in his face, where he grabbed two fists full of khaki uniform and pushed him up against the wall, leaving Carson's feet dangling six inches off of the floor.

"What happened here, Carson?" he asked, his gaze boring into Carson. "What the hell did you do with Jackie?"

Carson gasped and spluttered, grabbing at Nick's arms and kicking at his shins. "I don't know. This is assaulting an officer! I will have you arrested for this."

McManus cleared his throat. "Carson, I don't think you're in a position to be making threats, so you might want to cooperate with Mr. Anderson. I'm not sure I could get him off of you before he caved your chest in."

"What?" Carson struggled even more violently to break Nick's hold. "You federal fucks think you can just walk in—"

Nick slammed him against the wall again, hard enough to knock the breath from his lungs. "Where is she, Carson?"

"I don't know!" he squeaked. "I . . . I stepped out to deal with the crowd. When I came back in . . . she was gone."

"Who else was here?"

"Nobody!"

"What about Charlotte?" Nick focused his energies on Carson even tighter. "Did Charlotte come in here?"

"I don't—" Nick reinforced his question by pushing his fists harder against Carson's chest, who cried out in pain. "Yes! She was here, but I saw her leave alone."

Nick dropped him roughly to the floor. "Was the cell door open?" Would Charlotte have freed her? Or perhaps charmed her to walk out the back door so she could grab her outside?

"Sonofabitch," Carson said. "I'll be reporting you assholes. You can count on it."

Nick stabbed a finger against Carson's chest. "If you let Charlotte get hold of Jackie, you won't be reporting anything. Ever."

Carson tried to puff himself up against Nick, but the round gut, red face, and wheezing breath defeated his efforts. "Are you threatening me? You'll go to jail for this, Anderson."

Nick grabbed Carson's chin in his hands, hard enough to bruise it. "No, you won't." Finally, he thrust him away and stepped back. Even the smell of the man was turning his stomach.

McManus chuckled. "OK, got the picture now, Carson? You're in deep shit here. Where is Charlotte?"

"How the hell would I know? You try her house?"

Nick was about to slap him across the face when the cell in his pocket buzzed. He pulled it out and saw that it was Jackie's number. All of the rage abruptly flowed out of him. "Jackie? Where the hell are you? Are you OK?"

"Nick!" Her voice sounded out of breath. "I'm back at your house."

Her words stunned him momentarily. "What?"

Shelby was beside him an instant later. "Is she all right?"

"She's back at home," Nick said. Then it dawned on him what must have happened.

"Charlotte came after me," she said. "I had to . . . go over there."

Hell. Damn it all straight to hell. "Are you all right?" he asked again.

"I think so." She took a deep breath, letting it out in a rush into his ear, full of fear and relief. "Think you can get back here soon?"

"Yes," Nick said, breathing a sigh of relief himself. "We're on our way." He was about to click off when he put the phone back to his ear. "Jackie?"

"What?"

"I'm glad you're OK. I was worried there for a minute."

She laughed. "Not sure OK is the word I'd use, but thanks. I'm alive at least."

Nick put the phone away. "We have to go," he said.

"What's going on?" McManus asked.

"Jackie is back in Chicago," he replied, and then raised a hand to McManus's open mouth. "Don't ask. We'll explain later. Charlotte Thatcher attacked her. She had to leave."

"Hey," McManus said, sounding pleased. "She's OK, and that gives us something to work with now. I can deal with assault charges."

"That's not under your jurisdiction!" Carson yelled. "You can't have Charlie arrested for that."

McManus walked over to Carson, casually putting his hands into his pockets. He looked very FBI in his dark blue suit and tie. "What exactly is the nature of your relationship with Ms. Thatcher, Chief Carson? Can I count on you to bring her down here for questioning?"

"I'll do no such thing," he replied. "You have no basis for anything here. It's pure conjecture, and this is my town, Agent McManus. If anyone is going to be doing some arresting, it'll be me."

McManus gave him a wry smile. "Then perhaps you would like to go have a word with Ms. Thatcher and tell her that I'd like to ask her a few questions about her interactions with Ms. Rutledge."

Carson looked around at the three of them, lingering the longest on Shelby, who had merely stood leaning against the wall, arms folded over her chest for the entire time. "I'll speak to her, but I make no guarantees on her coming down here to talk with any of you."

"Mr. Carson," McManus said, "let me be clear. If you don't get her down here, I shall be going up there with the county sheriffs, who will be more than happy to assist me, given your obvious problems maintaining the safety of your prisoners."

"You have no jurisdiction in local matters, Agent McManus," Carson said. "I know the law."

McManus shoved him back into the wall. "You let someone into your jail who assaulted my former partner. This is a personal matter now. You'll deal with it or I'll throw your ass into your own jail cell and take care of it myself."

The fear and anger on Carson's face dissolved into something more like worry. "You can't do that."

"Do I look like I'm joking?" McManus said.

"McManus," Nick said, laying a hand on McManus's shoulder. "A quick word, please."

"Sure," he replied and stepped away with him to the other side of the room.

"Don't go up to the Thatcher's," he said. "Not until I've seen to Jackie, and we can get back here."

McManus smiled. "You think I'd go up to that place on my own after what you've told me? Not a chance in hell. Pernetti will have the others out here soon. We'll formulate a strategy to take her down when you get back here. Just don't take too long. I don't expect this asshole to bring her down here, but I have no plans of talking to her. If shit hits the fan, I'm getting my ass back up to Dubuque and we'll work from there."

"I'll stay here with McManus," Shelby said. "You might need my help."

Nick nodded. "Thanks, Shel."

"Go get our girl," she said. "We need to take care of this before anyone out there gets killed."

"Couldn't agree more," McManus replied. "Get out of here, Nick. We'll stay in touch."

"It will take us about five hours to get back. If Charlotte comes down here," he added, "you need to leave. Shelby? I mean it."

She smiled. "Would I try to do anything that stupid?"

Nick shook his head. "Of course you would. Just don't. I'll back as fast as I can. Call me when you're set up with everyone else."

Shelby yelled at his back as Nick walked toward the back door. "Ye have little faith, babe. I'd never do any of the really stupid stuff without you."

Nick closed the back door behind him. He had a feeling this whole thing was about to get really stupid.

Chapter 23

After three shots of tequila from Nick's cabinet, followed by another three shots of espresso, Jackie still felt jittery. The wound on her stomach both stung and itched, and she had that tweaky feeling of being exhausted but too frazzled to even consider sleep. The grandfather clock in the great room struck another quarter hour, reminding her that it had now been over ninety minutes since she had called Nick. He would be here soon, and to her surprise, she found that she was desperate for his presence.

"Would you at least try to relax?" Laurel said for about the fourth time since their arrival. "You're making me dizzy. Go soak in Nick's steam bath."

"He'll be here soon," she replied, "and I don't want to be lost in the shower when he gets here. Besides, I couldn't sit in there for one minute, let alone fifteen. How am I supposed to relax anyway?"

"I know," Laurel said, who continued to stay with Jackie as she paced around the house. They had been everywhere except Nick's bedroom. "But you should try. You just need to take a breath."

"I can't!" Jackie threw up her arms in disgust. "I don't know how to wrap my mind around what happened back there. A vampire wants me dead and some freaky alien thing wants my help for God knows what. Why does it need me? I don't get it. What could I possibly do that would be key to its needs?" She groaned in frustration. The same questions had been rolling around in her head over and over again since their return. There were no answers, only more questions.

"We can deal with Nix later," Laurel said calmly. "Right now, Charlotte is the most pressing matter. We have to figure out a way to stop her."

"I know," she yelled. "Shit. Sorry, Laur. I know we do. McManus is putting the team together. We'll make a plan, though what the fuck that plan might be is beyond me. We can't arrest her. We can't detain her long enough for her power to dissipate, since she's already shown she can cross over to escape. She knows we won't leave her alone. So, this is goddamn Drake all over again. We'll have to fill her with enough holes to make swiss cheese out of her or blow her up or cut off her goddamned head!"

"Sweetie, please. We'll figure it out somehow. We always do."

Jackie finally flopped down on the couch by the fireplace. "I don't know if I can do it, Laur. She's a bitch, a sociopathic, manipulative, egotistical bitch, but . . . hell. You saw her. She's a damn kid, a petulant little teenager who can't get her way, and I'm supposed to empty my Glock into that pouty little head? She isn't Drake."

"Let's just worry about that when the time comes," Laurel replied. "There's no point stressing over—" She stopped and looked toward the front door. "I think Nick's here."

A second later, Jackie felt him, too, the cold shifting feeling of death wrapping around her. "Thank fucking God." She jumped to her feet and made her way toward the front door.

He was walking up the front walk from the driveway, quick and purposeful, his scar-lined jaw set with determination. His eyes had a fiercer brightness to them than usual.

When he realized she was standing behind the glass of the screen door, everything eased, and his mouth relaxed into a faint smile.

"A sight for sore eyes, Ms. Rutledge," he said.

Jackie opened the door but stopped him in the threshold and threw her arms around his neck. A second later, she got the one thing her body had been craving since her return, the physical surety of his embrace. Jackie held on tight, burying her head against his chest and savored the security of those unnaturally strong arms pulling her against him. That cool strong shell of protection made those jitters fade into the background.

"Really glad to see you," she said, finally letting go. "This whole thing is getting a bit out of control."

He stepped by her and into the foyer. "So it seems. You want to tell me what happened?"

"You aren't going to believe it," she said. His silence answered her statement. "OK, you probably will, but I'm still trying to myself."

"Come on and sit down," he said. "You look stressed. You need anything?"

She waved him off and walked back toward the fireplace. "I had a couple of shots already. Didn't help."

Laurel laughed and sat down next to Jackie. "She must love you, Nick."

He paused before sitting. "Oh?"

"I tried for over an hour to get her to sit down and relax," she replied. "You did it in thirty seconds."

Jackie's fist swung through Laurel's arm and hit the cushion. "You aren't helping."

Nick sagged back into the couch next to Jackie and heaved a sigh. "Wish we could stay a while."

"McManus said things were going crazy there," Jackie said.

"Charlotte has the town in an uproar and that Carson

fellow is a useless snake, but that can wait. Tell me what happened."

Jackie told him, rolling her eyes when he stopped her to check her wound, and narrowing his own with worry when she explained what happened with the Spindly Man.

"Nix," he said, perplexed by what she had said.

"I can't pronounce what he said. It was absurdly long, and had some weird inflections I could never replicate."

"So, what could you be so important for?" he wondered. "He protected you against Charlotte and went after Laurel, but wants you. Curious."

Jackie snorted. "That's one way of looking at it."

"I think it does what you can do, Nick," Laurel said.

He leaned forward to look at her. "What do you mean?"

"I believe those spines are used to absorb spiritual energy. That's why everyone in Deadworld runs from it."

"And it went after Charlotte with what almost seemed like relish," Jackie said, recalling the odd sound it had made before attacking. "But why not me? I have the same energy."

Nick made a groaning sound, rubbing his face with his hands. "Because you can open the door between worlds," he said. "You aren't key to what it needs. You are the key."

The jittery nerves began to make a comeback. "You think it wants to come here?"

"I don't know," he replied. "Maybe. You didn't get a chance to ask."

"And I have no intention of going back to ask him," Jackie said.

"Which incurs its own problems if it's going to keep following you around."

Jackie's head lolled back against the cushion. "I know, but I can't just let it come here. Who knows what it might do."

"Agreed," Nick replied. "We can't just let it come here, but I don't want it following you around for the rest of your life."

"Me either," Jackie replied. It was going to have to remain in limbo for now. Laurel was right. They needed to deal with Charlotte immediately before more people got killed. "OK, we'll figure out Mr. Alien later. What do we do about Charlotte?"

Nick sighed. "I see only two options. We get her to turn herself in and stop consuming real blood or we kill her. Regardless, we need to get McManus and the team in on this. Planning now is pointless, and we need to get back."

As though he had been listening in, McManus called. "Nick, how's Jack?"

"Strange story and a bit shaken, but we're good here." Nick set the phone down and put it on speaker.

"Good. Now, get on that plane and get back here. We've got shit hitting the fan in Thatcher's Mill."

Nick sat up on the couch. "What's going on?"

"We've got a riot on our hands," McManus said. "People here have gone batshit crazy. County sheriff showed up and is now sitting in the station with a busted nose and probably some cracked ribs. Carson is gone, and we've had a couple of shots fired in here. People are screaming about the Thatchers being dead."

"What? Dead?" Nick asked in disbelief. "All of them?"

"Don't know, but Pernetti's team will be here in a few minutes to help us secure the station and bust a few heads if necessary, but this little jail cell isn't going to hold the whole town," McManus stated. "It gets much worse and I'm going to have to get some National Guard over here to put this down."

"That might be a problem if Charlotte is still around," Nick said. "You don't want them tangling with her."

"I understand," McManus replied, "but you have to understand we don't have the option of telling them all we're dealing with a vampire."

"We can't bring them in if we're going to try and kill

her," Jackie said. "People won't take too kindly to filling a knife-wielding teenage girl with fifty rounds."

"Jesus. Yeah, point taken," McManus said. "OK, get your butts out here. I'll meet you at the airport. I think we'll let the townsfolk cool down a bit on their own before we move in after Charlotte. I'll put Maddox up in the woods here with some binoculars to keep an eye on things and see if he spots this girl on her motorcycle."

"All right," Jackie replied. "We're heading out now. We'll see you soon. Be careful, McManus."

Nick picked up his phone. "You good for this, Jackie? After, well, everything that's happened? I don't want—"

"Nick, I'm going," she said. "This is our job. I didn't quite expect this, but we have to deal with her. That town deserves to be free."

"Yeah." He nodded. "It does."

"What?" There was that tone again, that resigned, regretful tone that she was beginning to realize all too well. Nick stood up and said nothing. "This is one of those Shelby moments, where I should come back with a sarcastic little barb, isn't it?"

"Shelby likes to come back on just about everything," Nick said. "It's part of her charm. Did you want to get anything before we go?"

"We'll grab a sandwich on the way, and you're changing the subject." She moved to get her jacket as Nick made his way to the front door. "What was with that tone of voice? Is this one of those, 'I should have done something different back then' moments?"

He stopped at the door and turned back to her. "It is. Chasing a vampire for a hundred and fifty years will provide a few of those. But this is more wishing that sometimes I was a different person, not what I did back then."

"I kind of like the person you are now," Jackie said, and wished the words did not sound so utterly cheesy. "Would a different Nick have been able to fix what happened? You tried, it didn't work, and you moved on."

He opened the door, a wistful smile on his face. "True, but a different Nick would have gone back and put her out of her misery."

She had been about to say that they were doing that now, but Jackie kept her mouth shut. It had that feeling to it on some level, of putting a wounded dog out of its misery, only this dog had turned into Cujo and took out its pain on everything it could get its mouth on, turning everyone else into rabid dogs as well. The thought abruptly brought back the image of Jessica's eyes aglow with the dead. Jackie laid a hand on his arm before opening the screen door. "Shit. All of this craziness and I forgot to tell you. We have another very good reason for getting Charlotte out of the way."

He locked the door and followed her out. "What's that?"

"Charlotte turned Jessica into a vampire, I think," she replied. "At least it looked that way before all the shit hit the fan. She had the same glowing eyes that you have."

"She's right," Laurel added. "Charlotte has apparently figured out how to do it."

Nick froze in his tracks. "Hell. That complicates matters. Now this is a rescue mission." He shook his head and kept walking. "This all makes sense now."

Jackie hurried after him. "What does?"

"The ghosts," he said. "All of the dead Rebeccas, the rotating mother and father, it's all about her family."

She got into the car and yanked the door shut, and Laurel slipped her way into Jackie's head. "She's trying to make a family of vampires?"

"Think about it," Nick replied. "How is she able to keep these people around in her life?"

"She charms them," Jackie said. "Then over time they really believe they've become a Thatcher."

Which is why none of them will move on after they're dead, Laurel said. *They've forgotten who they are.*

"And the ghosts have lost their identity," Nick added at the same time. "So they're stuck here."

Jackie tried to imagine being stuck forever, roaming a town like Thatcher's Mill, not sure who you were or why you were there. "That's a very cruel fate."

Nick swung the car out on the road and headed them toward the airport. "It is indeed, though I don't believe Charlotte would have realized what was happening until much later."

"Does that really matter now?"

"No. It doesn't. It just makes it harder to be put in the position of killing this girl, who I had a chance to help," Nick said. "She's not the monster Drake was. She wanted her family back, and her sister most of all, by the look of things."

Jackie put her hand on his leg, wanting to offer the little comfort she could. While not the same, she could understand the dilemma. Going after Detective Morgan several weeks back, knowing she might have to kill a man no longer under the control of his own mind, had pained her conscience. He had become a victim of his addiction, a harsh price to pay. Charlotte, though, had the added layer of youth. You just did not put the face of a young teen girl to the actions of a serial killer. It was too discordant.

"Nick, I'd say I was sorry we took this case, but I can't. If we didn't, then more Jessicas would end up walking the streets of Thatcher's Mill not remembering who they were, and a whole town would be left under the hypnotic manipulations of that girl. I am sorry, though, that we are probably going to have to pull the trigger on killing Charlotte. She certainly didn't deserve to be put into this situation."

He glanced over at her, a faint, wistful smile on his face. "I'm not sorry we took the case, Jackie. I'm sorry it's come to this. It pains me to know I came upon this girl in the wake of a vampire, and now we're visiting the same thing upon her again."

Jackie sighed. "I know it's not fair, but she's killed and ruined innocent lives. If there was another way—"

Nick's phone rang, cutting her off. "Hey Cyn, what's going on? We're on our way back to the airport now. Things are getting complicated. Today's paper? No, we haven't." Nick's mouth pulled taut. "That is unfortunate. We'll look it up as soon as we can, thanks. No, you should stay here. It's not going to be safe. Yes, I'm sure, Cyn. I'll call you back when we know what we're doing. Yes, I promise. OK, talk to you soon."

That did not sound good. "What's in today's paper?" Jackie asked.

"Our favorite reporter has written up some speculative fiction about our activities in Thatcher's Mill. Cyn's had about twenty calls to the office today already."

"Seriously?" Jackie groaned. "I'm going to deck that little shit."

"I may even hold him for you," Nick said. "We'll look it up on the plane."

The article not only called them out by name and put Special Investigations out there in big, bold type, but it made them look like the Ghostbusters on crack, harassing everyone in their path in the search for paranormal glory. Belgerman would not be pleased. Jackie wanted to hurl the laptop across the plane.

"I'll get my PR guy from Bloodwork on this," he said. "If we have to, I'll get the SI number changed. Don't worry, Jackie. It'll blow over."

"I'm still kicking Philip's ass when I see him," she said.

"Remember, too," he replied, "Charlotte may have had some influence over his decisions. We vampires can be very persuasive when we want to be."

His smile indicated he was going for humor, but the thought just creeped Jackie out. The whole notion of mind control disturbed her in a way she could not put into words. "Yeah, well, I still want to smack him upside the head."

Nick chuckled. "You certainly have my blessing."

The flight seemed to get quicker every time, and it was late afternoon when they touched down and met up with McManus. He waited anxiously by his car.

"Good to see you, Jack," he said. "You're doing all right?"

"If good means cranky, pissed off, and generally ready to bite heads off, then I'm doing fabulous," she replied. "Anything new down at the Mill?"

"Still no sign of the girl," he said. "There's still some rioting going on in the streets, and the sheriff's office is on my ass to get troops in there to settle the situation. Whatever we come up with, it's going to have to go down soon, otherwise they'll be down there in force to crack some skulls."

They all got into the car as he talked and were moving before Jackie had buckled her seatbelt. "We have an additional complication to deal with now," she said.

McManus smiled. "Of course we do. What is it now?"

"The girl, Jessica," Jackie said. "Charlotte has turned her into a vampire, too."

"No shit?" He shook his head. "So now we have two vamps to deal with?"

"No," Nick replied. "We have to try and get her out. She can still be helped."

McManus laughed, his voice humorless. "And you have a plan for killing one while saving the other?"

"Not yet," Jackie said. "I think we're going to need to treat this like a hostage situation."

"Except your hostage is probably going to be hostile to getting rescued."

"I know," she replied. "She's going to hate our guts."

Chapter 24

Jackie walked into their Dubuque hotel room and was immediately bear-hugged by Denny. "Jack! Looking lovely as ever."

She laughed. "God, fuck you, Denny. I look like hell."

He smiled. "Battle scars are hot. Anyway, I heard you got to cool your heels in Thatcher's Mill's jail."

"Not an experience I care to replicate, thank you very much," she said and stepped past him. Pernetti was standing by the dining room table they were using to lay out their information. She walked over to him and thrust out her hand. "I'm even glad to see you, Pernetti. I miss having an asshole around to pick on."

He shook her hand. "I asked Belgerman to hire another bitch for the team, but he didn't take too kindly to my suggestion."

They all snickered at that, and Jackie felt a pang of regret. She missed these guys. She missed the life of being an agent.

You'll be back some day, hon, don't worry, Laurel said.

We'll see. They might decide after I've been gone for six months that they don't want me back.

You're a good agent. They'll want you back.

At this point, I'm beginning to think I'm far more trouble than I'm worth.

Hardly! You're a valuable asset.

Valuable or not, if she kept getting into situations like this, they might easily want to wash their hands of her.

Shelby stepped out of the bathroom, that effervescent smile spread across her face. "You guys could always hire me. I make a fabulous bitch."

There was some uneasy laughter at that. Lust and fear made a very strange mix. Nick snorted and moved over to sit down at the table and see what they had. "Truer words have never been spoken."

She walked by and slugged him on the shoulder. "You are not going on my reference page."

McManus walked over and sat down. "Let's get down to business here, guys. This has to happen tonight. Hopefully our perp makes herself known soon or we'll be calling in the Guard to quell the rioting. Jack, you want to fill us all in on everything that's pertinent up to this point?"

"Sure," she said and turned to find Shelby with a Styrofoam cup of coffee for her. "Oh. Thanks, Shel." Jackie took a sip and began to circle the table. "You probably know a lot of this already, but I'll give you the quick rundown. We went to Thatcher's Mill to investigate a note we found by a former field agent indicating a great deal of paranormal activity. We found a town full of ghosts, like ten times what one would expect to find. It turns out most of them are likely the victims of one Charlotte Thatcher, a young woman who was turned into a vampire by our favorite bloodsucker, Cornelius Drake."

"No shit?" Pernetti asked.

"Yep, no shit," Jackie replied. "Surprised me, too. Nick realized after we got there who it was, because he came through Thatcher's Mill back in 1897 right after Drake attacked the Thatcher family." She raised a warning hand to them. "But don't ask. It's a long story. Anyway, Charlotte has been keeping this town under her thumb ever since. Most of them have been influenced or hypnotized, or whatever you want to call it, to believe she's the best thing since sliced bread. Basically, if you mess with the Thatchers, you mess with the whole town. Their police chief made that very clear after we arrived."

"He's a douche bag," Shelby said.

"No arguments there," Jackie replied. "Anyway, Charlotte has been kidnapping and brainwashing victims over the years to replace her family members, and apparently also trying to turn them into vampires as well. From what we can tell, she succeeded yesterday in doing just that. Her latest victim, fifteen-year-old Jessica Davies, has been turned."

"Jesus Christ," Denny muttered. "We have two to deal with?"

"She has just been changed," Nick replied. "She won't be a danger to us in that regard. She won't know how to make use of the power accessible to her. We need to get her away from Charlotte, however, and that is the problem we face now. I doubt she will want to leave, especially if she truly believes she is Charlotte's sister."

"So we have an uncooperative hostage, who technically may not even be a hostage by definition," Jackie continued. "We have Charlotte, who will be extremely hostile and difficult to take down, and we have the parents—also hostages like Jessica Davies—who might be dead at this point, if rumors are true. The house is situated on a hillside surrounded by adequate cover, but unfortunately Charlotte will likely know we're coming because she can sense Nick and Shelby from a ways off. They could easily be armed, but as we all know, the danger of a vampire far exceeds any weapon he or she might be carrying."

"So," Pernetti said, "are we in a shoot-to-kill situation with Charlotte?"

"Perhaps," Jackie said. "We're going to be seen as invaders

in her town, trying to take down everything she has built up over the past century. I don't foresee her handing over Jessica under any sort of circumstance, if she would even want to walk away. Honestly, Jessica will likely attempt to kill anyone who tries to take her out of there."

"That rules out a snatch-and-go possibility," McManus said. "She'll have to be subdued."

"Which won't happen as long as she's around Charlotte," Shelby replied. "We have to separate them or take down Charlotte."

"What about tear gas?" Pernetti asked.

"Doesn't have much impact," Nick said. "We can withstand it for quite a while."

"What if we burn them out?" Pernetti suggested.

"Charlotte will avoid that," Jackie said. "She can cross between the living world and the dead."

"Can the girl?"

"Unlikely," Shelby said. "She won't know how to do that yet. It's not easy."

"Actually," Jackie said, "Charlotte won't cross over. There's something on the other side that will kill her."

They all looked at her. McManus raised an eyebrow. "Something? Is this another complication we need to worry about?"

"No! God, no," Jackie said. "It's just . . ." She fumbled for words to explain. "Let's just say it's not relevant to this." They really would think she was crazy if that story got out. "The point is, Charlotte has an enemy on the other side and she won't risk running into it. So, forcing them out of the house might be an option."

"The townsfolk will be a problem," Nick added. "They see us up there, you can bet they will all come running."

The back and forth continued, everyone tossing out ideas, offering up complications, trying to resolve them, and hoping to create a plan of action that would not get them all killed. The two problems that continued to arise were the fact that Charlotte would know that Nick and Shelby were coming, and the townsfolk would likely come storming up the hill at the first hint of trouble. They all agreed the team could not initiate any kind of action without Nick and Shelby there to deal with Charlotte, so stealth in their approach was not an option. Then Laurel reminded Jackie of another issue that had not been brought to light.

What about the ghosts? she asked.

What about them?

Well, what if Charlotte can use them like Drake and Nick did, by consuming their energy to build their own? If she made use of all the dead Rebeccas in town, would we have any chance against her?

Shit! I forgot all about that. Goddammit. "Nick? What do we do about the ghosts?"

"Do? Why do we need . . . ah, of course. That could be a problem."

McManus huffed. "Come on, guys. What problem?"

Nick cleared his throat. "My apologies. It's something we should have thought of before. I can consume the energy of a ghost, the lingering essence of a person. It's the same thing Shelby and I draw from blood to keep us alive, just far more concentrated. It's that essence that allowed me to become this way. It was also how I was able to defeat Drake. You can forcibly do it, but it is difficult. If they are someone you drained of blood, however, there is a connection made, a bond if you will, which makes it far easier to do. It also works if they are willing."

"Well, that's great," McManus said. "So we have to keep a bunch of ghosts from getting to Charlotte along with worrying about a couple hundred pissed-off townsfolk?"

"Possibly," Nick replied. "The fact that so many are still in the town indicates she either doesn't know she can do this or she doesn't want to."

"But no guarantees," McManus said.

"No," Nick agreed. "No guarantees."

Jackie ran her fingers through her hair, clutching it with her fists. "We're screwed if she does that. We'd have to drop a damn bomb on her to kill her at that point."

McManus shrugged, raising his hands in defeat. "I can't deal with something like that. That's all on you SI guys."

You might be able to stop them, without destroying any of the them, hon. You did it with Rosa and her baby.

Jackie's hands fell to her sides. "Are you kidding? There must be thirty or forty of them, easy." The room went silent and Jackie realized she had spoken out loud. "Sorry. I was talking to Laur . . . Agent Carpenter. I sometimes forget . . ." Most of them gave her confused, blank stares. She waved them off. "Fuck, never mind."

"What did she say?" Shelby asked.

She sighed. More of her craziness laid out on the table for all to see. "She thinks I might be able round up the ghosts so they'd be out of the way."

"Round them up?" Pernetti chuckled. "You got a magic lasso or something, Jack?"

Shelby leaned forward over the table. "Could you do that, Jackie? Like what you did with Rosa?"

"Huh," McManus said and smiled. "What exactly did you do to Rosa, Jack?"

Really? They had to go there? "It's hard to explain."

Just tell them, Laurel said. *This is our team here, hon. They need to know everything we're capable of.*

Yeah, that's me, Jackie, the crazy, ghost-storing machine.

"Just use words us non-Ghostbusters will understand," Pernetti said.

Jackie scowled at him. "I'm beginning not to miss you already, Pernetti. Anyway. You all know that Laurel's ghost hangs out with me." She tapped her head. "She's in here with me whenever she wants, which is why it sounds like I talk to myself sometimes." She expected some laughter or at least some chuckling over that, but nobody said a word. McManus must have warned them. He merely sat there, hands peaked together under his chin, listening. She would have to thank him later for making sure they took all of the weird shit seriously. Jackie took a deep breath. "So, on the Rosa Sanchez case. This wasn't in any of the reports, but the way that we stopped her in the end was by me basically kidnapping the ghost of her baby by inviting it in, like I do with Laurel. And because her baby was more important to her than anything else, she got invited in, too. When they were ready, they moved on to wherever the hell it is they move on to."

Jackie looked around the room at the wide-eyed perhaps even dumbstruck, gazes. *Yep, crazy is as crazy does.*

They've seen enough to believe you, hon. It's just a lot to take in.

I hardly believe it's possible. They probably think they've stepped into a bad horror movie.

This is a bad horror movie. We just need to make sure we aren't the "too stupid to live" types.

Can we kill the scriptwriter then? Laurel chuckled in her head. "OK, guys, say something. You're weirding me out."

"Freaky shit, Jack," Pernetti said quietly. "I knew we were dealing with some pretty messed up stuff, but that's just out there."

"Pernetti," McManus said, "shut it. This clearly alters our initial plans. If the ghosts are a potential issue for us in handling Charlotte, then Jack needs to see if she can do this. Failing that, I think Nick and or Shelby need to see if they can get rid of them for us."

Nick shifted uneasily in his chair. "I'm not sure I'm comfortable doing that. These are the souls of young girls here, victims of Charlotte's treachery."

"They're already gone, babe," Shelby replied. "If it'll save the living, we have to if it comes to that."

"Agreed," McManus said. "I'm sorry, Nick, but keeping people alive is my primary concern. Jack? You think you can do it?"

"I can try," she said. "It all depends on them. I can't force them to do anything."

"And she'll have to be able to wander the town," Nick added. "The ghosts are all over the place."

A phone rang then, and McManus took his out. "Good. You sure? Yeah, hold on, Maddox, let me put you on speaker so the team can hear. OK, go ahead."

"Hey, guys, save me some doughnuts," he said. "And someone bring me a fucking umbrella. I'm not getting paid enough to sit here in the rain."

"What's going on there?" Jackie asked. "Anything new?"

"Our girl is back," he said. "Or someone is. Lights just came on at the Thatcher house, and surprisingly, the town has suddenly quieted down. Lot of folk milling around the diner, but looks like the violence has stopped or moved indoors, anyway. Even hicks know better than to fight outside on a night like this."

"Nice to know that we're dumber than hicks," Jackie said. "Maddox, you keep your eyes glued on that house. We need to know if anyone comes or goes. We're coming down there soon to deal with the town situation before we make any moves on Charlotte Thatcher."

"Good," he replied. "Tired of sitting on my ass out here."

"You'll probably wish it was still there by the end of the night, Maddox," she replied.

He laughed. "Yeah, I'm sure. I'll call if anything changes. Out."

"OK," McManus said to everyone. "Hopefully that means we're good to take her down, but we need to button down the town and these ghosts before we can make a move on Ms. Thatcher. Barring those two items means we're left with more drastic options, and I'd rather not deal with those unless we've exhausted everything else. So, let's figure out how we're going to secure the town and get Jack around to gather up some ghosts."

* * *

By seven-thirty, they were loaded up in three cars and heading down to Thatcher's Mill. Jackie did not bother to drive; she was too nervous. What she had done with Rosa and her baby had been born of desperation. It was that or possibly be killed. This was altogether different. She would have to talk to and convince two to three dozen ghosts to go along with her or else Nick and Shelby would be consuming them. Regardless of the fact that these people were already dead, it gave her the sick feeling to think of killing them all over again.

The alternative is worse, Laurel said.

I *know, but it still sucks. This whole case is turning into one big clusterfuck. So many things could go wrong here.* Something brushed across her hand and grabbed ahold, making Jackie lurch in surprise, but it was only Nick's hand.

"You'll make this work," he said. "Don't worry."

"And you're ready to destroy them if I don't?"

"If it comes to that," he said. "We'll do what needs to be done."

He said the right words, but Jackie was not convinced by his tone. If she failed, Nick would not want to do this. "You realize that I probably won't be able to convince all of them. You'll have to take some of them."

"I know," he said and gave her hand an encouraging squeeze. "And yes, I won't like it, but we can't give Charlotte access to that kind of power, if she's indeed able to do it, which I suspect she is."

"We should take some of them anyway," Shelby said. "We could use the extra boost against Charlotte. Actually, I wouldn't mind draining a couple pints from that ass-hat Carson. I'll bet Charlotte's been tapping him for years."

McManus laughed. "You guys are never dull for conversation, are you?"

Jackie huffed. "Think I'd rather talk nail polish."

"Now that you mention it," Shelby replied, "I need to get a good holiday color."

The holidays. Jackie rolled her eyes at Shelby and turned to stare at the streaking splatter of raindrops across the window. Christmas seemed so far away, and it was yet another routine of her life that was going to be turned upside down from previous years. She felt Laurel getting ready to say something and cut her off. *Don't. Thanks, but please, just not now.*

They arrived far sooner than she had hoped, twenty minutes flying by in what seemed like five, the convoy of three vehicles rolling into town at a casual twenty miles per hour.

"Jack?" McManus asked, pulling to the curb. "You three call me if any kind of shit hits the fan. I'm going to find Carson like we discussed and make sure these folks are settling down."

"Likewise," she replied. "We'll be close by, I'm sure, if you need us, especially if Charlotte makes any kind of move. Don't do anything regarding her without calling."

"Hey, no worries there. Farther away the better as far as I'm concerned," he said.

Jackie stepped out onto the dark, glistening street lit only by the reflection of light coming from the center of town. The flashing red light at the intersection gave the impression of blood being washed away by the rain. She hoped it was not an omen of things to come.

Chapter 25

Sensing the ghosts was not difficult. Thatcher's Mill sat in a foggy haze of the stuff. Jackie could feel them all around, but the problem was being able to zero in. Laurel walked at will through the walls of the buildings, helping their search. Jackie's biggest worry, other than failing in her efforts to keep the ghosts away from Charlotte, was that they had all moved up to the Thatcher house already.

They walked down a narrow side street behind the main row of businesses on the east side of the highway, working the part of town farthest away from Charlotte. Jackie pulled the hood of her FBI-issue rain slicker over her face a bit more. "You see any?"

"They're around," Nick said. "Some of them, anyway. Usually we see some walking around, though."

"Maybe they don't like the shitty weather," Shelby said.

Laurel came out of the building next to them, a two-story brick store, its windows shuttered against the cold November night. "There's one in here," she said. "Upstairs in an office."

"About time," Shelby replied, and marched over to the back door. The knob cracked beneath the pressure of her hand and a moment later they were inside. A short, dark hallway led toward the front of the store and a stairway went up. Shelby motioned at Jackie. "After you."

"Too kind," she muttered, and clomped up the wooden stairs, her boots echoing loudly in the stairwell.

The upstairs had a hall running to a window in the front wall. Two doors lined each side of the hallway, opposite one another. "Last one on the right," Laurel said.

They reached the door, which was unlocked, and Jackie flipped on the light to find a small office inside, little more than a desk with a file cabinet, a couple of worn, padded chairs, and a bookcase. The ghost of a young woman sat in the long chair opposite the desk, hands folded serenely in her lap, staring at the empty desk.

"Wonder why she's here?" Laurel asked.

Jackie knelt down in front of her, but the woman's gaze remained fixated ahead. "Don't know. Hi there," she said. "My name is Jackie Rutledge." There was no response. "I'm here to help you get away from Charlotte." At the mention of Charlotte's name, the girl's eyes finally focused on Jackie for a moment before returning to gazing ahead. "Do you think you'd like to leave this place? I can help you." The girl remained unresponsive. "Any ideas, guys?"

"I don't know," Nick said. "Most of the issues with ghosts I've dealt with in the past were about getting them to move on. These girls don't know who they are anymore, though, so I don't know how that effects anything."

"She thinks she's Rebecca," Laurel said. "If we assume she died from Charlotte trying to turn her—" She stopped because the young woman's head turned to face her.

"That got her attention," Shelby said.

The girl's face had shown a flicker of emotion. The slack mouth had pulled just a little bit taut at Laurel's words. Jackie reached out and put her hand in the girl's. "Rebecca, do you want to go see Charlotte?"

At that, her eyes widened, as though suddenly aware. "I miss Charlie."

Jackie's stomach tensed. So much for being straightforward. She was going to have to play against her wishes and trick the victims into going with her. So much for the moral high ground. "Would you like to see her, Rebecca? I can take you to her."

"I miss Mr. Peabody, too."

What? "Who is Mr. Peabody?"

Laurel answered. "This is Peabody's furniture store."

"He made me the cutest little doll house," the young woman said. "I never got to thank him."

Jackie closed her eyes. Could this make her feel any more like a schmuck? "We'll find Mr. Peabody for you. I'll thank him for you, Rebecca."

She smiled. "Would you? That would be ever so kind. He was such a nice man."

Was. Did that mean he was dead? Jackie had no idea. "I will shake his hand personally for you and tell him how happy you were with what he made for you."

"That would be lovely," she said. "Could we see Charlie? It's been so long."

Jackie stood up. "Laur, show her."

Laurel reached out to Rebecca. "If you come with me, I'll take you to Charlie. I'm sure she would be happy to see you, too."

Rebecca stared at Jackie for a long moment, until Jackie thought that maybe she did not understand what to do, but then the woman got to her feet and stepped into her to join Laurel. *I wonder, is she far?*

Far? No, Rebecca, she's not far at all.

Jackie let out a ragged sigh. Laurel began to talk to her, and Jackie did her best to tune out the murmuring going on in her head. Did Rebecca really have no idea that Charlotte had been around this entire time? How was that possible?

"OK, that was easier than I thought it would be. I can't believe she's just been waiting here all this time."

"Most spirits lingering around among the living tend to be pretty single-minded," Nick answered. "It's whatever they left behind that they can't let go of. That was well done, Jackie. I couldn't have done better myself."

"I'll accept congratulations after we're done," she said. One ghost was not going to do them much good at all, and what happened if they did not get Charlotte? Would she then be stuck with this ghost, in perpetual waiting to visit her long-lost sister?

We'll take them over ourselves if we have to, Laurel said.

And just drop them off. "See you later, have fun moving on?"

We'll figure it out, hon. Anything is better than this mindless waiting game Charlotte has forced them into.

They moved on and found another ghost two buildings down and then another crossing the street. It had taken nearly half an hour to find three. At this rate it would take them half the night, assuming they could find them all or even reach them all. Jackie was about to bring that issue up when McManus called.

"Hey, Jack," he said. "Just checking in. How goes the ghost hunting?"

"Three so far," she replied, "all muttering away with Laurel inside my head. This might become a problem if we have to go into someone's house who is actually at home."

"Yeah, I considered that one, too, but I think I have a solution. We have about fifty people milling in and around this diner, none of them too happy to see the Feds on their doorstep."

"No threat of violence?"

"Oh, no, plenty of that," he said, amused. "We've had to disarm a half dozen of them so far. The threat of arrest for a variety of crimes seems to be deterring them for now. It's very strange. Most aren't even sure exactly what they're up in arms over, just floating rumors about stuff happening up at the Thatchers'. I think I'm going to get a town meeting together to *explain* to them what's going on. That might be what we need to keep them out of our hair for a bit and give us the time we need to confront Charlotte."

"You got a place to hold most of the town?"

"I think that church on the north side of town will work. They'll be packed in like sardines, but it should hold them."

It sounded like as good a plan as they were going to get. "OK, work on that. We'll keep looking around for Rebeccas. If they start to get out of hand again, let me know. I don't want to be caught out on the streets if they start rioting again."

"Yep. Good luck, Jack. I'll check back soon."

Jackie stuffed the phone back in her pocket and wiped away the rain that had splattered her face while the hood was pushed back. "He's going to try and get most of the town to the church to explain what's going on, which should give us easier access to places. I want to know where the hell Carson is, though. He wouldn't be putting up with any of this."

"With Charlotte, would be my guess," Shelby said. "If the rumors about Ma and Pa Thatcher being dead are true, they'll need a story. Hell, he might be helping her get rid of the bodies."

"Laur? You around?" she called out in as loud a voice as she dared.

Laurel stepped out of a house a hundred feet down the street. Another Rebecca followed, grasping Laurel's hand. "This is Rebecca," she said. "Rebecca? This is my friend Jackie. She's going to take us to see Charlotte."

"Hi, Rebecca," Jackie replied, pasting the how-wonderful-to-see-you smile back on her face. She offered her hand. "Will you come with me? We're going to see Charlotte soon."

"You know where she is?" the Rebecca asked.

Jackie looked across the street between a pair of buildings where she could see the dim flicker of light shifting through the rain and the trees around the Thatcher house on the hill. "As a matter of fact, I do. Join me. We'll all go see her together." After the ghost joined the crowd inside her head, Jackie asked Laurel, "You think you could call out for them, announce we're going to see Charlotte or whatever and see if you can pull them all to one place? We need to conserve some time here."

"I'll try," she replied. "Where do we meet?"

"Let's do that furniture place, so we don't have to break into anywhere else."

"OK. I'll be back soon," she said.

Jackie turned on her heel and marched back through the rain toward the store's back door. "Let's get out of this damn rain."

Nick laid a hand on her arm before she had gone two steps. "Jackie? How are you doing with this?"

She shrugged away from his hand. "I feel like a fricking schizophrenic mental patient escaped from the loony bin."

For once, Shelby had no smartass remark. "I don't even want to try and imagine what it's like in that pretty little head of yours. Let's get inside."

We'll be there soon, Rebecca, Jackie said. *There are a couple of others who have missed Charlotte for a long time and would like to see her, too.*

They all talked at once and Jackie could not make heads or tails of what any specific one said. If there were another two dozen added to them, Jackie knew it would drive her batty. How long would she be able to maintain things with thirty girls, all answering to the same name, clamoring to talk to Charlie was beyond her. Once back in the store, Jackie called up Maddox.

"Hey, Maddox. Anything going on?"

"Little bit of activity," he said. "Someone walked over to

the mill and then back to the house a couple of times carrying something fairly heavy. Whoever it was, it wasn't our girl. Too tall to be her."

"Might be the father," she said, "or that damn reporter."

"Yeah, I don't know," Maddox said. "Just be glad when you guys figure this out so I can quit getting my ass rained on here."

"Sorry, Maddox," she replied. "I'll buy you a couple of shots when we get back, to warm you up."

"You getting anywhere?"

"In a manner of speaking, yeah," she said. "A little luck and we'll be situated in town here within an hour."

"Awesome, Jack. Kick some ghost ass and let's ice this bloodsucker."

Jackie hung up, thought about sitting down, but then remained standing. The girls in her head were making her feel jumpy, so sitting still was the last thing she wanted. "Looks like someone is up there at Charlotte's—hauling stuff from the house to the mill."

"So, mom and dad may still be alive," Shelby replied.

Who is the bloodsucker? one of the Rebeccas asked.

"Too dark to see," Jackie said. "It wasn't Carson though."

Are you the police? asked another.

"Shit," Jackie said. "I, um . . . I need something to write on."

"What?" Nick asked. "What's wrong?"

"Nothing," she snapped. "I just need pen and paper for a second."

Shelby walked over to the sales counter at the back of the showroom. "Think there's some here." She brought back a notepad with PEABODY'S FINE FURNISHINGS emblazoned across the top and gave it to Jackie, along with a pen.

She wrote down a message without looking at the words and handed it to Nick. *Ghosts are listening in. We have to watch what we say about Charlotte.*

Nick nodded and passed it over to Shelby. "All right," he

said." That might prove difficult with McManus. I'll step away and give him a call."

"Thanks." Jackie walked off into the store, walking among the locally crafted furniture. There were a lot of wooden chairs, tables, and benches. On one wall, perched on a pair of long shelves, were a number of dollhouses, which brought a gasp of delight from the one Rebecca.

Oh! Let's go look!

Jackie felt her begin to pull from her head. *Rebecca! Stop. Now's not the time.* To her surprise, Jackie found that her mental act of restraint stopped the ghost. *We'll have time for that later. For now, just stay with me, please. We'll see Charlotte soon.* That Rebecca huffed but remained silent.

Five minutes later, Laurel came back with four more ghosts and a disconcerting piece of information.

"Someone just drove up the hill," she said. "Most of the town though is heading toward the church."

Even as Jackie pulled her phone out, Maddox called. "I heard," Jackie said. "Anyone comes out that didn't go in, call me."

"You got it, boss," he said. "Three guys, I think, just walked in. I'm pretty sure a couple of them had rifles in hand."

"Great," she replied. "It just keeps getting better. Keep your eyes glued there, Maddox." She dialed up McManus. "McManus, Charlotte just got company, so I'm guessing she knows what's going on down here on your end by now."

"Figured it wouldn't take long," he said. "How's it going there?"

"Up to eight or nine. Laurel is bringing them to me. Seems they would all like to see Charlotte."

"Christ," he said. "Poor girls. OK, I'm guessing twenty or thirty minutes to get this place filled up before we start bullshitting them for as long as we can. I'll try and drag it out as long as I can, and will let you know when it's time to get moving."

Thirty minutes? Crap, that was going to be pushing

things. "Just stretch it out as long as you can, please. I don't know how long this will take."

She didn't know how long she would be able to handle being stuffed full of ghosts, either. Though there was no physical manifestation of discomfort, Jackie still felt swollen, almost like sinus pressure, except without the pain. At least for now. The Rebeccas, at least, were being relatively and thankfully quiet.

Nick stepped up beside her then, brushing against her arm. "Still doing all right?"

She shrugged. "Crowded. This is just really weird."

"Understandable," he replied. "If it starts getting to be too much, let me know. I might be able to help keep them quiet if it gets too noisy in there."

She offered him a feeble smile. "More vampire mojo?"

He chuckled. "Yes, something like that."

At the word vampire, the quiet murmur in her head swelled to a churning rumble of noise. Jackie sucked in her breath and closed her eyes, pressing a palm to her temple. *Girls! Calm down. Everything is fine.* The world "vampire" echoed around in her skull like a bitter, cold whirlwind.

Nick's hand gripped her shoulder, and she felt a warm surge flow into her. The girls immediately began to quiet. "Jackie?"

"Sonofabitch," she said. "Don't say the *V* word. Holy crap."

"Stirred them up, did it?"

"And then some." She let out a deep breath. "OK. I'm OK now. Thanks, Nick. That helped."

"Let me know if you need more," he said.

Jackie paced. There was little to do other than wait until Laurel was sure they had cleared the town. Another ten minutes, and she brought three more Rebeccas, then five, and then two more. After twenty-five minutes she returned with two in hand. After Jackie had let them in, she sat down on a chair.

"There are three who refused to come, but that's all I can find here in the town proper," Laura said.

"Can you show Nick and Shelby where they are?" Jackie asked. "I guess they should try to talk them into it or handle things as needed. The girls and I will wait here."

"You holding up OK, hon?" Laurel asked.

"I feel like an overstuffed Thanksgiving turkey, but for now it's all good," Jackie said. "I'm more worried about the fact that there may be a dozen others up on the hill already."

"We'll be back as quickly as we can," Nick said. "Any problems, you call, Jackie."

"Yes, Mr. Anderson," she replied, and pushed him away. "Go. We need to hurry this up." Her phone rang again and Jackie clicked it on. "What's up?"

"Agent Rutledge!" Margolin's cheery voice rang in her ear. "Back in town with your boys now, I see."

"Margolin," Jackie snapped back, "you shouldn't be here. This is not a safe situation for you to be in."

"Interesting times," he replied. "You get to check out my article in today's paper?"

"Yeah," she said. "Remind me to bloody your smarmy lip next time we meet. What do you want? You're going to get yourself killed out here."

"Only way I'm getting myself killed out here is if you guys do something stupid," he said.

Jackie clenched the phone tighter. "Philip, what did you do?"

"Me?" He laughed. "Other than keep my eyes and ears open, not a damn thing. Whatever it is you Feds are up to, though, gets to stop tonight. These people have suffered enough."

Jackie bit off her remark. "You've been chatting with Charlotte again, haven't you, Phil?"

"And she would like a chat with you as well," he replied. "Here at her house. She wants your team of ghosthunters out of her life and out of this town before sunrise."

"Christ," Shelby said. "He's up there with her."

"And what would she like to chat about?" Jackie could

hear Charlotte's muffled, young voice in the background, restless once again at the sound of her name.

"A deal," he replied, "that will allow all of us to live our lives."

Jackie waited for "in peace," but it never came. "What assurances do I have she isn't going to just kill me when I walk up to her door?"

Charlotte's voice came through clearer now. "She doesn't, but it's going to be a lot worse around here if she does not."

All of the Rebeccas erupted in a cacophony of voices. *Girls! Damnit. Hush!* She reached for the nearest piece of furniture to steady herself, her head swimming in a dizzy rush. Jackie sucked in her breath when Nick's hand gripped her arm once again and the voices gradually settled.

"Hey, you still there, Rutledge?" Margolin chided.

She slowly let out the air in her lungs. "Phil, why don't you put Charlotte on the phone."

"Why don't you quit messing with the lives of all these good people," he said. "Thirty minutes. Come alone."

Jackie slammed her thumb down on the off button. "Asshole. Nick, go find those other three. I'll let McManus know."

He gave her a hard look, and then nodded. "All right. Shel, let's go. Call if you make any plans before we get back."

Jackie snorted. "You think I'd go up there by myself?"

"No," he replied. "Even your charming recklessness has limits."

Jackie laughed. "Screw you. Let me know when you're done." Nick and Shelby headed out the back door with Laurel, and Jackie dialed up McManus. "McManus, we have thirty minutes.I just got a call from our favorite—reporter, who is up on the hill,and he told me you-know-who wants to have a chat about resolving things, or else."

"Damn," he replied. "What's that reporter doing up there with her?"

"Hell if I know. I think she charmed him into causing

problems for us. We also have that issue Nick was just talking to you about, so please be careful here." The girls were getting antsy, shifting around and whispering away. She swore there was a bucket of hissing snakes slithering around inside her head. Tip it the wrong way or kick it too hard and they would all come clamoring out.

"Yeah, I got that," McManus said. "Makes it a bit difficult, but hopefully we can work around it. I think we can be ready to move from here in twenty. I'll leave one of the guys here to spout off about the finer points of the federal government getting into their lives. We'll meet up behind that pharmacy building on the road up to the house."

"That sounds fine. Any brilliant strategies on your end yet?"

"Jack, I think our job is going to be backup and containment. If this turns into something big, we aren't equipped for it. You guys are the pros with the ability to handle the Charlottes of the world. Whatever you need us to do, we'll try to do it, but I hope we can keep it to something that doesn't pull in every news van within two hundred miles of here."

Jackie slowly let out her breath. She figured it would come to that. This had *big* written all over it. "Make sure you tell our guy in the church to be ready to bail. If things go badly, we have no idea what those people are capable of doing. She's got her web woven pretty damn tight over them."

"I figured as much," he said. "We'll have the cars running and pointing north toward Dubuque. Shit hits the fan, we run and regroup."

"McManus," Jackie said, "you realize that if we fail, it's possible we may not have anything left to regroup for." If Charlotte realized her gambit was up and her secret made public, she might just wipe the entire slate clean. Of course, she might have decided that already, and this was the beginning of her effort to end everything.

He was silent for a moment. "Yep. That thought crossed my mind, Jack. Let's see if we can get it right the first time."

Chapter 26

Having twenty anxious teenage girls in one's head was not a hell Jackie would wish on anyone. She wanted to scream. It was not that they were doing anything bad or wrong, but the simple fact was they were there and could not stop talking. They were quiet for a bit, at least, after she finally yelled at them to keep it down, but it felt like she was having the biggest sleepover ever, and the moment one whispered something, others would join in. It was twenty channels of daytime television running in unison on a continuous loop.

Nick, Shelby, and Laurel finally returned after an hours-long fifteen minutes. They had one Rebecca with them.

"The other two?" Jackie asked.

"Dealt with," Nick replied solemnly. "We moved as quickly as we could. Any more phone calls?"

"No. We should get over to the pharmacy, though. The team should be there anytime now." She stepped over to the last Rebecca and offered her hand. "Rebecca? I'm Jackie. I'm going to take you to see Charlotte if you're ready."

The Rebecca looked down at the hand and then up to meet Jackie's gaze. "Will she say good-bye?"

The question caught Jackie off guard. That was the last

thing she expected from any of these girls. “Um, if that’s what you want, I’m sure she’ll be willing.”

“She doesn’t want to,” the Rebecca said.

Jackie understood her far too well. “I know how hard that can be. We’ll talk to her together, how’s that?”

She took Jackie’s hand, eying her reluctantly. “We’ll see.”

Laurel stepped up to her then. “You need me to help maintain things in there?”

“God, yes. Please,” Jackie said with a sigh of relief. “They’re driving me insane. I can’t hear myself think, and I swear my head is several sizes larger now.”

“Need any more help?” Nick asked.

“No. I’m good for now,” she said. “If Laurel can’t deal with them then I’ll have you do that mojo thing again.”

“Works wonders, doesn’t it?” Shelby said. “You always had a knack with that stuff, babe” She stepped over and leaned in close to Jackie. “It works wonders in all kinds of ways.”

“Seriously, Shel?” Nick said. “Must you always?”

She laughed and turned toward the door. “I must, I must. We should get going. McManus’s probably waiting for us.”

Jackie had been about to offer up a snide remark to Shelby, and then noticed the look on Nick’s face. Was that embarrassment? Really? She gave him a questioning look, curious, but she was not about to ask about such things now.

Nick shook his head. “Another time. Let’s go, before Ms. Mouth over there makes another stupid remark.”

She tried to make a mental note to ask about it later, but realized there was likely no room in her head to store it. “Don’t worry; at this point, my brain is incapable of remembering much of anything.” The cacophony, at least, was beginning to die down as Laurel worked to soothe their excitement, and the one Rebecca, the last to arrive, sat silently in her little corner of Jackie’s head.

* * *

The team stood crowded under the awning that stretched over the back door of the drug store. A Ford SUV was backed up to them with its rear door swung open. Inside were a variety of crates that team members were in the process of unloading.

"There you are," McManus said. "All situated with your ghosts, Jack?"

"I'm good," she replied. "What all do we have here?"

"Well, first off, we're going to wire you up and give you a vest."

A vest was a waste against someone like Charlotte, but against the gun-toting townsfolk, it might come in handy if things turned ugly. "Nothing suspicious about that, but I guess I don't have much choice in the matter."

He smiled. "No, you don't."

Nick stood beside her, hands thrust in his pockets. "This is too risky. If she's walking into a trap, Charlotte could kill her before we even get up the hill."

"I have leverage," Jackie said, though to be honest, she had no idea how she was going to use it. It was also possible Charlotte would not care less. "And if things go badly . . . well, I have my emergency escape button."

"You think Nix won't be waiting for you on the other side?" Nick asked.

McManus paused, the wire device in hand. "Who is Nix?"

"It's that thing on the other side that Charlotte won't go near," Jackie said.

"Ah. I didn't know it had a name," McManus said.

"I can't pronounce its real name. Look, can we just get on with this please? I'm supposed to be up there in five minutes." She removed the rain slicker so that she could be fitted with the vest and wire.

We need to hurry, Laurel said quietly. *The girls are starting to ask questions.*

What kind of questions?

Like why there are all of these guns and why they share the same name.

Shit. OK, I'm hurrying. Just keep them distracted for a few more minutes, Laur. "Move it along here, McManus. My aces in the hole are getting antsy and are wondering what the hell we're doing."

"Trying," he said and tapped the top of the vest. "Video is built into the collar here. Try not to cover it up." He handed her a little ear bud. "Put this in; mic is with the video, so we'll hear and see most of what you do. Try and get us a good visual of the inside when you get there and pinpoint Jessica for us. If you can locate the others in the house for us, that would be helpful."

Pernetti hefted out a large barreled rifle from one of the crates and popped a canister of ammo into it. Tear gas would flush out Carson, Margolin, and the others, but Jackie doubted it would do much against Charlotte or maybe even Jessica. The voices kicked into overdrive when Pernetti moved toward Jackie with the teargas launcher. Jackie turned quickly away, looking up through the rain and the faint lights of the Thatcher house.

She's up there, girls. We're about to go. Just hold on a couple of minutes. "Am I set here? My leverage is going bonkers and it feels like my head is about to pop off of my neck. Just keep me informed and give me heads up when you're about to play ball."

Nick's hand settled on her shoulder, and the familiar warmth flooded into her. It was scary how soothing it was in such a short time, hitting her nerves in just the right way. The girls immediately calmed down. "Get out of there at the first sign of trouble, Jackie. If Charlotte is playing an end game here, trying to get Jessica is irrelevant. You're more important."

"So, I don't get to play the tragic heroine?"

"That's my job," Shelby said. "If anyone gets to go down

guns blazing, it's me. You do something stupid, Jackie, and I can track you down no matter where you are."

"These warm fuzzies are going to make me cry," Jackie replied. "Look, I'm going in, finding out what she wants, what the place looks like as much as I can, and using my leverage to get out if I have to. Ten minutes tops." Plus or minus the eight million things that might or could go wrong.

"You do what you need to do, Jack," McManus said. "Just come out in one piece. OK, you're up and running and good to go."

Jackie tucked one of the available Glocks in her waistband and put on her leather jacket before pulling the rain slicker over her head. She gave Nick a grim smile and walked over to one of the cars. At least it would be a short trip.

The tires of the car crunched on the gravel drive as she drove slowly up the hill. Her hands were getting slick on the steering wheel; she tried to wipe them off on her pants, but they were damp as well from the rain. Her head was bouncing, or at least it felt like it was, as many of the girls recognized the house as she pulled into the circle drive in front. The conversation was a garbled symphony of voices.

Hon? We may need to be a little wary here, Laurel whispered to her, away from the others.

No kidding. I feel like the damn fly in the spider web.

Not that. One of the girls here, the quiet one at the end, is definitely not excited to be seeing Charlotte.

OK. Why should that make me more wary than anything else going on here?

Just that she might try something after we get in there. I'll help you keep the girls here as much as I can, but the hard part is going to be containing them all.

Girls! Jackie shouted. *Please listen up for a second.* The babbling continued, only marginally quieter. "Hey!" she shouted out loud. This time it had more effect. They stilled enough to where she could actually distinguish voices. "Charlotte is inside, but so are a couple of men who may not be nice guys. I want you to stay with me until after we get inside. If you have a question, I'll try to ask Charlotte for you. Do not leave me until I tell you it's safe. OK? Do we all understand each other?"

There was a murmur of assent, so Jackie opened her car door and stepped back out into the rain. The porch light did little, other than cast a slick, yellow haze over the front steps. In the front window, the curtain pulled back a few inches before falling back seconds later.

"Maddox?" Jackie said. "Anything?"

"You look clear from here, Jack," he replied. "Someone peeked at you out the window, but I think everyone is in the house."

"McManus?"

"You've got three of us coming up the hill now; should be in place within two minutes."

"OK, sounds good," she replied. "I'm moving in then; tired of getting rained on."

Jackie half expected Charlotte to open the door and step out before she even knocked, but apparently she decided going through the formal hassle was worth the effort. On the second knock, Margolin answered the door.

"Ms. Rutledge," he said, "I figured you the type to refuse negotiations."

Jackie stepped up to him and elbowed her way into the entry, satisfied with the painful grunt she received. "Circumstances require a certain bending of the usual rules, Philip. I'm sure you get that much, even if you are stupid enough to be here right now."

He rubbed at his stomach. "You're a real bitch sometimes, you know that?"

"Glad we're on the same page. So—"

"Jackie Rutledge," the familiar voice of Charlotte said with demure charm. She stepped through the living room archway and into the entry. "You look surprisingly well given the last time I saw you."

She tried to smile and keep from wincing at the effort it was taking her and Laurel to keep the girls in check. They clamored over one another to talk to Charlotte. *Nobody is going to say anything until you're all quiet!* "I'm alive," Jackie said, "no thanks to you."

Charlotte stepped closer. "You should be more polite in my house." Her head cocked curiously to one side as she studied Jackie. "Your friend is with you. I believe I said to come alone."

Jackie steadied her breath, avoiding the itch to reach for her gun and trying to keep her eyes away from Charlotte's. "Do you see anyone else around?"

"Jack," McManus whispered in her ear, "try to get out of the entry. We need to see more of the house."

Charlotte's head cocked to the other side, staring intensely at Jackie. "You're different today, more . . . powerful. How interesting." She finally broke off and turned to Margolin. "Philip, why don't you go bring the tea into the living room so Ms. Rutledge and I can have a chat."

"Sure thing, Ms. Thatcher," he said and hurried off.

Jackie watched him walk off through the opposite archway that opened into a dining room and then turn toward the back of the house. Then her heart jumped into her throat when a gray, translucent figure stepped out of the wall—another Rebecca, who ignored her stare and blithely drifted by them and into the living room.

"Come," Charlotte motioned. "The least we can do for the moment is be civil. I am certainly curious about how you can do what you do, Jackie. It's quite extraordinary, given that you're, well, alive and all."

And I'd like to keep it that way, thank you very much. "Honestly, Charlotte, I'd like to discuss the issues at hand."

She stepped into the living room and was immediately greeted by Carson and a man she did not recognize seated in a pair of antique Victorian chairs by the front window. Each had a rifle laying casually across their laps.

"Where's your cronies at, Ms. Rutledge?" Carson asked, his mouth twisting into a sneer. The man had tissue stuffed into his nose, and one eye was nearly swollen shut.

Jackie smiled. Someone had clocked him good. "Little trouble with the townsfolk there, Carson?"

"No thanks to you, missy," he said. "Be glad when you're gone, bitch."

"Elton! Language!" Charlotte's voice barked out so harshly that Jackie had to look and make sure it had actually come from her. "You will behave while in my household."

Carson looked away from them and replied in a hushed voice. "Yes, ma'am."

Well, if there was any doubt about who ran this town, that made it abundantly clear right there. Even the girls murmuring in her head cringed and hushed at Charlotte's voice.

"You do seem to have them all under lock and key, Charlotte," Jackie said. It was rather impressive, she had to admit. "Though, I guess a hundred years gives you plenty of time to work things out."

"Yes, it has," she said with a pleased smile. "Everyone in the Mill puts in their time, isn't that right, Mayor Compton?" She gave the other man a sardonic grin. "Come, let's sit by the fire."

A dark, quiet voice spoke over the murmur of the girls in her head. *Even after we're dead.*

Charlotte stopped and looked back at Jackie. "Excuse me?"

Damnit, girls! You need to be quiet. It's not safe yet. "Nothing, just muttering to myself."

Margolin walked in then, carrying a tray with a teapot, three cups and saucers, and a sugar bowl. "Ah, there we go," Charlotte said. "Thank you, Phillip. Just set it on the table there, please."

Jackie rounded the sofa facing the fireplace to sit in the chair opposite Charlotte, ignoring the chattering of the girls, who were all excited at the prospect of tea time, and placing her back to Carson and the other man. She stopped abruptly at the sight of Jessica reclined peacefully on the cushions.

She stirred sleepily, blinking at Jackie. "Sis?" she asked, struggling to remove the quilt and sit up.

Charlotte reached over and put her hand on Jessica's shoulder. "Right here, Bec. Our guest has arrived."

The sleep evaporated as her mouth pressed together into a thin line. "The one who wants to ruin everything?"

Great. What a nice way to situate things. "Hello, Jes . . . Rebecca. Despite what you may think, I did not come here to ruin anything."

Charlotte leaned forward and poured tea into the cups. "And yet, here you are, Jackie, doing your best to ruin everything after I finally got my sis back." She smiled sweetly over at Jessica and gave her an affectionate squeeze.

"You—" Jackie stopped at the sudden outburst in her head. Tiny starbursts of light danced before her eyes.

"Jack?" McManus's voice piped into her ear. "Don't sit with your back to those guys. Not good."

"Sonofabitch." Jackie pressed her hands to her temples. Questions and demands from the girls assaulted her from everywhere. *Laur! Help!*

I'm trying.

She tried to push back against the onslaught, with a surge from Laurel to back her up, but it was quickly becoming too much to handle.

"Ms. Rutledge?" Charlotte asked, curious. "Are you . . . you . . . what have you done?"

Jackie tried to focus on Charlotte who had risen to her feet. "I haven't done—"

She had pushed them all back, quelled the growing shock and outrage, except for one, the stern and silent Rebecca who broke free, taking hold of Jackie while she struggled to contain her.

"That is *not* your sister, Charlotte Louise Thatcher!" The voice spewing forth from Jackie's mouth was not hers.

"You drank your sister's blood a hundred and ten years ago and sold your soul to Death. How many have you killed to bring me back, Sis? How many?"

Jackie pulled on Rebecca, trying to force her back within the confines of her mind, where the rest now watched in stunned silence. Even with Laurel's help, she was proving to be recalcitrant.

"Bec?" Charlotte stood up, eyes wide in shock. "How?"

"Jackie!" Nick called out. "Get out of there. You've got the real Rebecca with you."

No shit. Rebecca! You've got to stop now before it's too late. Her efforts along with Laurel's, were slowly pulling her back, but Jackie had little practice in doing this kind of thing, and it was proving far too difficult.

"All of that blood on your hands! You don't deserve to have me back."

Charlotte was in Jackie's face now. She grabbed a handful of rain slicker and leather jacket in each hand and shook her. "Bec! You've been here? This whole time you were here?"

"I've lingered here, Sis," she said, "waiting for when I could say good-bye to you without all of this getting in the way. So, now I'm here. I loved you once, but no more, not after what you've done, what you've become."

"Bec!" The violence of Charlotte's strength snapped Jackie's head back and forth. "Come out of there. Please."

Rebecca's will to force herself over Jackie's own began to wane. They were pulling her back, but now Charlotte was reaching in, her eyes aglow, attempting to do the same.

"Good-bye, Sis. I hope you find peace."

With that she withdrew back into the recesses of Jackie's mind, slipping away from Charlotte's probing power.

"Bec?" Charlotte grabbed Jackie's chin in a bruising grip. "Becca! Come back!" Her stare refocused on Jackie's, who was barely getting her vision back. "Where is she? What did you do with her?"

Jackie felt her feet lifting off the ground. "She's here with me, along with all the other Rebeccas."

"Jack," McManus hissed into her ear, "get out of the living room, if you can."

"You aren't going anywhere," Charlotte said, and twisted Jackie's head sidewise. "Got your boys waiting out there for you, Jack?" She reached up to pluck the earbud from Jackie's ear, as Jackie reached up to grab hold of Charlotte's arm. Her arm jerked away and she slapped Jackie a ringing blow across the side of her head. The blow stunned Jackie momentarily, and the next thing she saw was the earbud pinched between Charlotte's fingers. "You bring my sister back or I swear to God, I will crush your head with my bare hands and dig her out of there myself." With that she ground the earbud between her fingers and dropped it to the floor.

"Sis?" Jessica asked, standing beside her now. "What do you mean? I'm right here."

Charlotte turned and pushed her back to the couch. "Sit down and be quiet."

"Well, well," Margolin said from the living room archway. "Stuck your hand in the tiger's cage, didn't you, Rutledge?"

Jackie took advantage of the distraction to slam her steel-toed boot into Charlotte's shin with as much effort as her dangling body could manage. Inside her head, the muddled confusion was starting to focus into a hard, cool anger. The girls were beginning to realize just what had been going on for the past century in Thatcher's Mill.

Charlotte cried out and dropped Jackie to the floor. "Ow! You bitch!" Her tiny fist flashed out with prizefighter speed but missed its mark because Jackie was stumbling backward after dropping awkwardly to the floor. Charlotte's fist struck her, instead, high up on the shoulder, sending Jackie spinning sideways over the end table next to the chair.

She fell to the floor, her shoulder throbbing. So much for in and out in ten minutes. Her leverage had abruptly turned into a significant disadvantage. She got the bad feeling Charlotte might even try to make good on her threat.

"Elton! Stanley!" Charlotte called out. "Get out there and deal with whomever is waiting outside. Philip, get to the church. Go!"

Damn it all to hell. Jackie turned and reached for the Glock. She would dive out the damn living room window if she had to. The team would be making a move at any moment, given what they had heard, and she did not want to be standing around in here when the bullets started flying.

The team, however, was apparently ready to make their move sooner than even Jackie had anticipated. Suddenly the living room window erupted in a shower of glass shards, and Jackie heard the familiar hiss of the tear gas canister as it tumbled across the floor.

She rolled away from the spewing smoke. Jessica began to scream. Elton and Stanley both swore and brought their weapons to bear on the front window. Charlotte kicked the end table so hard to get it out of her way that her foot went through it, splintering it in two. Jackie had maybe two seconds to bring her weapon around to face Charlotte before she would be on her.

The look on Charlotte's face spoke volumes. End game or not, her intentions looked damn clear to Jackie. She was going to kill her.

Cross over, hon! Cross over! Laurel's voice yelled at her.

But the girls were in the way, interfering with her ability to do much of anything in that regard. She could not get the door open that quickly. Jackie raised the Glock to fire as Charlotte bore down on her, and watched in disbelief as it flew from her hand in a shower of blood. Her blood.

In the archway, Margolin stood with a shotgun in hand. "Not this time, Rutledge," he said.

Jackie's arm flopped across her stomach, chunks of flesh now missing from her forearm. She was too stunned to even cry out or curse. Charlotte loomed over her, a wicked grin on her face. Behind her, Elton and Stanley began to open fire on the team outside. *Shit, Laur. Fucked that up.*

"Come, Sis. Hurry and drink. This blood may be special, and you'll need the extra boost." Charlotte smiled down at Jackie with a humorless flash of teeth.

Nick and Shel are on their way. I can feel them coming.

Laurel's words offered no encouragement. Jackie realized in that split second before Charlotte's pretty black shoe connected with the side of her head that they would probably be too late.

Chapter 27

Nick's stomach wrenched in knots when the words came out of Jackie's mouth. For a second, he thought someone unseen had entered the room with Jackie, but the voice had been far too clear and close to be anyone but her. Only the voice had not been hers at all. What she said sent a chill through him. Shelby realized it at the same time he did.

"Oh, my God," she said. "It's the real Rebecca."

"What the hell?" McManus asked. "Who is that?"

"It's the ghost of the real Rebecca Thatcher, and she's not happy with her sister." Nick grabbed the mic from McManus. "Jackie! Get out of there. You've got the real Rebecca with you."

When Charlotte leaped up into the camera, blocking their view of everything, all three of them startled. When the camera view began to shake, Shelby stepped out of the SUV. "OK, enough bullshit. We've got to get her out of there now."

"Just let her go, Jackie," Nick said quietly. "It's not worth it."

McManus queued into the team. "Pernetti, we've got shit going down—get ready to launch that gas."

They flinched at the sound of Jackie getting slapped. Nick hopped out to the pavement. "We're heading up."

As he ran out into the street, Nick heard McManus telling Jackie to get out of the living room. Shelby was already fifty yards ahead of him, nearly at the end of the street starting up the drive to the Thatchers'. Then McManus's voice ordered the gas launched. Nick heard the distinctive shatter of glass. That should have been the tear gas going in. Any luck and it would disable everyone except Charlotte herself.

Nick had not bothered to holster either of the Glocks McManus had given him. He barreled full speed up the hill, powering his legs with the extra energy of the dead. Shelby was still fifty yards ahead. There was no plan now, other than getting to Jackie before Charlotte could kill her. Of that he had no doubt. With Rebecca showing up to condemn her sister, the one-hundred-year charade would now be collapsing into ruin. Charlotte would want to get her sister back at any cost, and he figured she would go to any lengths to get her out of Jackie or kill her trying.

A gunshot rang out as he topped the drive, low and harsh. It had to be from a shotgun blast. Where had the shotgun come from? Jackie's view had not revealed one, and the chief and the Mayor had been carrying rifles. Who was wielding the gun, and more importantly, who had just been shot? Nick had little time to ponder, as bullets began to fly out of the living room window.

Maddox's voice piped in about Jackie, followed by McManus's voice yelling into his earbud. "Do not fire on the living room. Jack is down in the living room. Repeat, Jack is down in the living room."

Shelby crossed the circle, running straight for the broken window. Charlotte was still in there somewhere. Nick could sense her, as well as Jessica, who was far weaker at this point. Through the window, he could see the two men, one of them Carson, who had spotted Shelby as she sprinted for the house.

He had caught sight of them when they crested the drive and was bringing his rifle around to bear down upon them.

Shelby ignored that fact, racing up behind Jackie's car as partial cover before using it as a launching pad. The car sat a good fifteen feet from the edge of the house, but that space was nothing for either of them to deal with. She put one foot on the near corner of the bumper, stepped across to the edge of trunk on the far side for leverage and flew across the open space and through the busted window, taking out a fair chunk of glass in the process as she crashed into Carson. Nick could not tell if she had been hit by the one frantic shot he got off before she disappeared through the flutter of curtains and into the living room.

The other man, whom Nick did not recognize, took a surprised step or two back from Shelby's attack. This allowed Nick to take a more direct approach. The window frame was a good six feet wide, which was more than enough space for him to plant his hands on the sill and swing his feet up and over, much like hopping a fence. Only, at his current speed, there was no opportunity to look for an ideal place to grab the sill. Nick planted both hands on the far right side, knowing but not feeling the bite of broken glass slicing into the palms of his hands, and swung up and over. His momentum made it more of somersault, but it got the job he wanted done. Nick's body tore down the curtains, but his boots connected with the other man and sent him sprawling backward, where he crashed into a bookcase next to the archway leading into the entry.

Nick landed on Shelby and Carson, who had tumbled into the chairs situated before the window. The Mayor was out cold, but Shelby struggled to extricate herself from the jumble of bodies and furniture.

"Damn it, Nick! You big oaf." She pushed to her knees, lifting Nick up along with her. "Get off."

Nick stood up, grabbing a handful of Shelby's shirt to bring her upright with him. On the floor, not ten feet away, Jackie lay unconscious, blood pooling around her. Jessica sat back on her heels next to her, shocked by their entrance, a glistening sheen of blood painting her mouth. Charlotte was nowhere to be seen but she was definitely near at hand.

"What have you done, Jessica?" Nick said, springing over the knocked-over chair to land beside her, grabbing her by the collar of her dress.

"Sis said," she exclaimed, and tried to pull away. "She said to!

Nick shoved her away, sending Jessica sprawling over the broken end table to land on the couch. He squatted down next to Jackie to examine the mess of her forearm. It looked like half the flesh had been ripped away, and blood was flowing from a broken vein.

"McManus!" he barked into the mic. "Get a medevac up here. Jack—"

He stopped at the unmistakable sound of a shotgun being cocked.

"What, Nick?" McManus replied. "What's happened?"

"Don't touch my sister, Marshal," Charlotte said.

Nick caught her out of the corner of his eye, standing in the middle of the entry with a double barrel in her hands. Shelby had begun to move at the sound of her words, but was a split second too late as the blast of both barrels went off.

The spread of shot, tight at such short range, caught Nick high on the side, under the right shoulder blade and knocked him over Jackie and into the wall beside the fireplace. It burned like a sonofabitch.

Shelby let out something like a banshee cry, which was followed by the sound of more shattering glass. Nick shook the cobwebs out of his head, pushing energy toward the wound to staunch the bleeding.

Jessica yelled. "Charlie!" She leaped from the couch and landed on Shelby's back.

Jackie still lay unmoving next to him. How much had she bled out already? Nick pushed himself back to his feet, feeling the warm rush of blood soaking his shirt. He needed to get Jackie out of there. If only Shelby could hold off Charlotte for a few seconds.

The thought ended almost as soon as he had it. Shelby flipped Jessica off of her back, sending her upside down into the wall beside the front door.

Charlotte's eyes got very wide, her nostrils flaring with rage. Twenty feet away, Nick could feel the surge of energy welling up around her. She blocked Shelby's left cross, lunged in, and grabbed a handful of leather jacket with both fists. He launched himself toward Charlotte, a long leap aimed at taking her out at the knees, but Charlotte was too quick. He hit her, dropping Charlotte to her knees, but not before she had spun a quick 270, hurling Shelby through the front door, blowing it off its hinges in a crackling splinter of wood and exploding glass.

Charlotte cried out, more in anger than pain and brought her elbow down hard against Nick's shoulder. There was an agonizing pop as the blow tore through ligaments and separated his arm from its socket. It was then, rolling away from the stinging shot, on the shifting air created by the hole where the front door had been, that Nick picked up on a faint, familiar smell. Propane.

That odor had not been noticeable from the outside, which meant somewhere in the house a propane source was bleeding gas into the house. Would she really be taking that route, blowing them all to hell? No, she couldn't be.

McManus shouted into his ear. "We've got a church full of people running toward the hill."

Nick could hear shouting in the background. "I'm coming up. Get Jack out of there now!"

Charlotte had turned to check on Jessica, who groaned and whimpered in a heap against the wall. Shelby was out on the front porch, struggling back to her feet. He hoped she had heard the call from McManus to get out. The smell of propane was beginning to overpower. The kitchen likely had a propane stove. If that was the case, one nice spark anytime soon and the whole north side of the house would turn into kindling.

"Head out back to the garage," Charlotte said to Jessica. "It's time to go."

Nick reached for one of the Glocks that Shelby had dropped when she attacked Charlotte, but even his swift reactions were no match for hers. She swung the barrel of the shotgun around in a swift arc, knocking the pistol from his hand as he tried to bring it around on her. It skidded toward the front door, where Shelby looked to be back in control of her senses.

Charlotte raised the shotgun to fire, and Nick had the sudden, horrifying image of Jackie getting buried alive in the rubble of the house. "Charlotte! No! You'll blow us all up."

"Just now figuring that out?" Her foot flashed out, the two-inch heels puncturing through Nick's already lacerated hand. She yelled at Jessica, who was coughing her way back into the kitchen where the fumes were likely still strong. "Go, Sis. Run!"

There was a breaking sound from out front and Shelby was gone from the doorway, having leaped through the wall of the screened-in porch. At the point, gunfire began to erupt from the outside. Blood blossomed backward in a spray from Charlotte's shoulder and then her side.

"Cease fire," Nick called into his mic. "Cease fire! There's a gas leak in the kitchen."

Charlotte cried out, more in rage than pain by the tone of it, and sprang for the relative safety of the living room, where the protective shield of Jackie lay on the floor, bleeding to death. Nick lunged for her as she flew over him, but caught nothing but air. He did not have the advantage of a dozen or more other Rebeccas fueling his reserves.

Shelby had come in through the living room window again and was diving for Nick's weapons, still lying on the floor by the fireplace. She reached them, but a second too late, as Charlotte was on top of her before she could raise the guns. The butt of the shotgun came down with swift precision against Shelby's head, who collapsed to the floor with the sickening sound of cracking bone.

Nick launched himself at Charlotte again, just as she was wheeling around to meet him, swinging the barrel of the gun in a lightning quick arc. He had guessed high this time, a fortunate move that brought the muzzle of the shotgun under his outstretched arms. The detonation of the shell so close to his head deafened him for a moment, and somewhere below, the shot connected, ankle or foot, he could not tell, as he slammed into Charlotte and crashed into the wall, shattering plaster in an explosion of dust and debris. They both dropped down on top of Shelby's prone body.

If his shoulder had not separated before, it definitely was now, and Charlotte dug her hand into the flesh there, shoving him off of her legs. Nick kicked at her knee as she got to her feet, but his positioning was awkward and he landed only a glancing blow, pushing her sideways, but not back down. He attempted to roll away from her well-aimed toe, but turned instead into Jackie, whose face, he realized was looking very ashen.

The blow from the point of Charlotte's shoe caught him across the jaw, not quite enough to dislocate it, but something cracked and he felt a warm gush of blood in his mouth. The momentum of it carried him over onto his other side, and he was forced to attempt to push himself up with the one good arm he had remaining, which lay pinned beneath him.

Several more shots rang out and Charlotte screamed this time, drowning out part of what McManus yelled in his ear. ". . . almost here. Everyone, in the cars, now!"

Nick tried to laugh and coughed out a spray of blood. "Not happening."

"Couldn't stop the vampire before, could you, Marshal?" Charlotte said, her voice full of menace. Nick turned to see her looming over him, the quaint, Victorian chair held up in her dainty hands. "And you certainly can't now."

Charlotte brought the chair crashing down, and Nick lifted his separated arm to ward off the blow. In that moment, before things went dark, something unexpected brushed up against his leg. Jackie.

Chapter 28

Voices surrounded her. Dozens of people milled around, crowding her space, whispering with excitement, agitation, and fear. They poked, pushed, and prodded at Jackie, urging her to move. She did not want to, however. A listless lethargy consumed her, a cold comfort that made her limbs far too heavy to lift.

Hon! Jackie! Come on, sweetie. You have to wake up, Laurel said.

Why? I don't want to move. I'm so cold.

Charlotte is killing Nick and Shelby. We have to get out.

The haze began to coalesce, taking on the form of girls, a dozen of them perhaps, all crowded around her. One of them held her arm, stroking it, a gray nimbus of light enveloping her hands. Jackie realized then that something was wrong with her arm. Chunks of it were missing, shredded skin surrounding the wounds. The memory came back to her in a rush. Margolin! The bastard had shot her.

The Rebeccas' hands sank into Jackie's skin as she continued to rub over the wound and gradually continued, until her arms had somehow buried themselves in her wound. She smiled at Jackie. *You can't let her win. Whatever you must do, stop her.* With that, the Rebeccas continued to vanish into Jackie's arm until she was gone. The ripped flesh around her wounds shrank. The huge divots taken out had receded back to something approaching a normal-looking arm. It looked like Jackie had done little more than burn herself in several places.

The ghost had just fueled her healing, like she was a goddamn vampire. *Wait! What are you doing? Rebecca? No! I don't want to take you for this. It isn't right, damn it! I'm supposed to save you from her.*

The real Rebecca came forward then, settling beside her. *I'm sorry, Jackie, but you have no choice. Charlotte has used us for a hundred years to fuel her twisted dream of bringing me back. We've lingered here, unknowing, because she took who we were away from us. Give us the dignity of a worthy end. Let us help you stop her.*

I don't know that I can.

Let us help, Jackie. Your friends are going to die if you don't try.

Nick. They were coming in to get me.

They're here, Laurel said. *And Charlotte is winning. You have to do this now.*

Did she have a choice? Could the dead ever matter more than the living? What it really came down to, though, was could she willingly let someone sacrifice her soul for justice? She would, so how could she say no to someone else?

OK. Rebecca, let's do this. I'm not sure what I'm doing, but we have to try.

With the open invitation, the Rebeccas swarmed around her, pressing in until she felt smothered, shouting encouragement, crying for vengeance and freedom. They seeped into Jackie, their energy dispersing and filling her body, and the cold, dead weight that had been dragging her down began to lift. Only the real Rebecca remained at the end, waiting.

Different sounds began to drift into her awareness. Faint pops, a scream, and Nick's voice. He was close. Jackie's eyes fluttered open to the grunt of his voice and the splintering crack of wood.

Charlotte stood above her, blood splattered across the side of her face. Something had torn a hole in her left cheek. Next to her a chair lay in a broken heap, beneath which legs protruded out against her side. The cowboy boots were all too familiar.

Her voice croaked. "Nick?"

Charlotte's livid gaze focused on her. "Jackie. You've . . . well. Look what you've done."

She reached down and grabbed Jackie by the jacket and jerked her up to her feet. "Hello, Sis. You in there?" Charlotte shook her hard enough to snap Jackie's head back and forth. "I can feel you in there."

Holy hell, she's strong. Jackie grabbed onto Charlotte's wrists, letting the power given to her flow through her arms and into her hands. She was not exactly sure what she was doing or how to do it, but Laurel helped guide her efforts. Her fingers dug into the tendons on Charlotte's wrists to the point her short nails began to break the skin.

"She's says it's time for this to be over," Jackie said. "You can't do this anymore, Charlotte."

"Jack!" It was McManus's voice calling from outside the window. "Charlotte Thatcher! This is the FBI. Your house is surrounded. You need to release our agent and come out with your hands on top of your head."

Charlotte glanced out the window and a moment later, Jackie heard something crash through the remains of the window. McManus swore.

"Get everyone back, McManus!" Jackie said.

"Half the town is coming up the hill, Jack."

Shit. "Just stay back." She began to twist her hands, attempting to pry Charlotte's off of her. "It's all over, Charlotte. Let your people go." Blood was seeping out between her fingers now.

"You can't arrest me," she said, her voice now strained

with the effort of keeping her grip on Jackie. For the moment at least, it seemed the amount of power they possessed was close to equivalent. "And you know you can't, so let's pretend we're both smarter than that, shall we? You mean to kill me. It's the only way to stop me."

"It doesn't have to be that way, Charlotte," Jackie replied, losing some of her grip as Charlotte lifted her off the ground.

"You can't let me walk away and you can't arrest me," she said, the cherubic smile back on her face. "So, that leaves you one option, and I think you knew that coming in here. I really hate being patronized." With that, she tipped forward and dropped Jackie to the floor, where the air rushed out of her lungs in a dizzying whoosh.

Jackie brought up her arms to deflect away Charlotte's effort to grab her by the throat, and brought her elbow across to slam into Charlotte's jaw where it had been torn open. Charlotte grunted and then laughed, blood staining her teeth in a devilish grin. She reached down and grabbed a broken table leg from the shattered end table. "You never liked to fight fair, did you, Sis?"

The jagged edge of the leg whipped down and Jackie caught Charlotte's wrist just before it hit her left eye. Inside, both Laurel and Rebecca gave a startled scream before recovering to help Jackie hold the weapon back. Charlotte bore down, using her weight as leverage, and Jackie realized that she would not have the strength to hold it back for long.

A shot rang out, close enough to momentarily deafen Jackie's ears. Blood sprayed across her face as the table leg blew apart from Charlotte's hand. Jackie was able to then leverage her legs to knock Charlotte over to the side and scramble back to her feet. Nick lay on his side beneath the broken chair, the Glock in one hand. A sheet of blood covered him from jaw to neck.

"Here," he said, and flipped the gun to her.

Jackie picked it up and tried to bring it around on

Charlotte, but from the position on her side, she brought her pointy-toed shoe around and sent it flying before Jackie could even get a shot off. Shouts outside could be heard now, unfamiliar voices. The townsfolk were arriving on the scene. Somewhere in the background, Jackie also heard the rumble of an engine. Jessica had started up the motorcycle.

A swell of energy began to fill the room. Jackie rolled away from Charlotte and sprang to her feet. To her right by the fireplace lay the shotgun and one of the Glocks. Another was a few feet away toward the broken window. She could dive for one and be firing in two seconds, even with a burst of speed. Outside people were calling out for Charlie.

"That all you got, Sis?" Charlotte asked. "It was more fun when you were alive."

Pistol by the fireplace, Rebecca said. *Now.*

Jackie jumped without thinking twice. Charlotte lunged as well. She landed next to Shelby and slid forward by the fireplace that still crackled with glowing embers. Jackie brought up the Glock to find something huge and dark swinging through the air toward her in a swift, downward arc.

Jesus Christ! Jackie reflexively turned away, raising an arm to shield herself from the sofa that whirled around and slammed her into the wall at the corner of the fireplace. Her skull cracked against the brick mantle of the fireplace and everything exploded in a momentary, blinding flash, dropping Jackie to her knees.

An immediate flood of cool, dead energy washed the stunning effects away, and Jackie found herself buried under the sofa. More worrisome, though, was the greater chill of energy that was enveloping the room, filling everything around her. Her head still throbbed, but she worked her hands up under the couch to throw it off. That was when the first disturbing groan and crack sound echoed through the room.

"Was it worth the wait, Sis?" Charlotte yelled at her, her voice full of rage and tears. There were more cracking sounds, and Jackie felt the floor shift subtly beneath her. "You betrayed me!"

The house had literally begun to shake. Jackie shoved the sofa aside. "Nick? We have to move." He had pushed the chair aside, but Jackie could see now that he wasn't running anywhere fast. A shotgun blast had torn his foot all to hell. Shelby still lay crumpled on the floor behind her, blood oozing out of her hair and running across her neck to soak into her shirt.

"Get out of here," he said, "while you still can."

"Damn it, Nick," Jackie replied and then had to dodge to the side to avoid a piece of plaster falling from the ceiling.

Charlotte had already moved. She stood in the entry, shotgun back in her hands. *Jump right,* Rebecca said. *She's going to shoot.*

"Good-bye, Sis," Charlotte said and raised the gun.

Jackie leaped as the shotgun went off. The strength in her legs sent her over the coffee table that sat in front of where the sofa had been, and into the other chair, tipping it backward and sending Jackie tumbling across the floor to the back of the room. When she stood back up, her leg burned like someone had jammed a hot poker into her thigh. Jackie began to run back when the living room ceiling split in half, a crack in the plaster opening up like a fault line running the length of the house. Sections of ceiling began to fall. The windows behind her, looking out into the back, exploded in a shower of broken shards as the frame abruptly went trapezoidal with the shifting house.

Nick was trying to pull himself back to his feet with one leg. The foot on the other dragged at an awkward angle, leaving a smear of blood across the floor.

Jackie reached him and pulled him up. "Out! Now." She let him go and stepped over to Shelby, finding her body quite easy to pick up in her dead-fueled arms. Then the wall on that side of the house buckled inward, knocking her forward into the room and into the broken sofa. The chimney, unable to withstand such a change in structure, collapsed somewhere above, sending bricks down the flue and into the fireplace. A shower of sparks and tiny embers showered the living room floor.

Fire. Jackie struggled back up to her feet with Shelby, seeing the smoking orange lights scattered over the room, most of them on the area rug that sat beneath the chairs and sofa. Nick limped toward the window, only a few feet away from being able to jump out.

"Nick, you better jump—"

The end of her sentence got cut off by the sound of another shotgun blast. An instant later, the north end of the house filled with flame, and Jackie could see that it would likely billow right on through to their side in a second, maybe two if they were lucky. She crouched and sprang forward, hoping to dive the fifteen feet she had left to get through the broken window in the front of the house, but never made it. The first floor walls buckled under the concussion of the propane blast, and the window, once five feet high, folded in on itself, and Jackie crashed to the floor, landing against the mayor's body.

She cradled her arms around Shelby's head, closed her eyes, and focused everything she had on keeping the second floor from crushing them to death as it pancaked down on top of them.

Oh, Sweet Mother of us all, Laurel said.

No! Rebecca screamed. *She cannot get away with this. No, no!*

No, she could not. Charlotte and Jessica could not get out of this town. Likely, they would never see them again, and they would set themselves up in a new place and start over, creating a new Thatcher's Mill. Charlotte enjoyed running things too much to just live quietly in the background sipping on the blood of the occasional wayward person unfortunate to get on her radar. The team was out there as well, unless McManus had been smart enough to get the team out, and now a couple hundred townsfolk were gathered around, wanting their pretty little leader to be safe. Of course, half the house had just blown up. There could be a bunch of dead or dying people out there now. Jackie turned her focus inward and opened the door to Deadworld.

Hon, what are you doing? Laurel asked, worried.

The only option they had left was what she was doing. The door between the living and the dead opened wide, and as she expected, Jackie saw the familiar, alien figure standing there.

"Hello, Nix," she said, trying her best not to sound scared shitless. "I need your help."

Chapter 29

"Jackie Rutledge," he said, in that hollow, nasally voice that made Jackie think someone was speaking through Nix via a speaker from somewhere else. "I have awaited your return."

"I'm sure you have," she replied. "Look, I need your help. You want to come through my door? I'll let you through if you get that girl who came here and attacked me earlier, and you save my friends."

"Save?"

"A house just fell on us," Jackie said. "Get us out and stop the girl. If you agree to do that, I'll let you through and open whatever stupid door it is you want me to open."

Laurel gasped. "We can't let that thing through. Who knows what it'll do."

"Laur, we're doing this," she replied. "No options left. Nick and Shelby are dead if we don't, and Charlotte will be gone."

"It might kill everyone there."

Jackie looked back at Nix. "No, I think it just wants me for something. At least I hope that's all it wants."

It stared at her with its unblinking, green orbs for so long that Jackie was not sure it had understood her. Finally it nodded once. "Agreed."

Jackie stepped away from the house, on the south side where the garage stood off the back corner. "Here. You'll have to act quickly. She's about to leave." *Now get the hell over here before I lose my nerve.* Jackie opened the way back. "After you, Spindly Man."

Nix walked over, reaching across himself to pull out a pair of spines from each arm. He stopped at the door and Jackie swore he sucked in a huge breath of the living energy that came through. The lipless crease of its mouth curled into a smile and it jumped through the door.

"I have a bad feeling about this," Laurel said.

"Can't be any worse than everyone dying out there now," Jackie said. How could it?

She stepped through, coming out in the drive just as Charlotte gunned the motorcycle out of the garage. Jessica crouched low in the sidecar. Nix stood out in the gravel drive no more than twenty feet in front of them, crouched low with its spines held ready. It looked like a freak-show ninja.

Charlotte's eyes went bug-eyed with terror. She swerved the motorcycle away, sliding the motorcycle across the gravel. People standing in the drive, apparently safe on that side of the house from the explosion, scattered and dove out of her way. Some were already fleeing from the monster that had suddenly appeared before them.

With a smooth, catlike grace, Nix sprang, arcing through the air a good thirty feet before landing on the motorcycle, one foot in the sidecar, the other on the back of the motorcycle. Jessica, who had been trying to wield the shotgun, got off an errant shot, screaming in the process. Charlotte yelled out as Nix attacked, turning the motorcycle hard to the left toward the mill building. The momentum tipped the motorcycle up on its side, throwing her and Nix off into the puddled gravel drive.

Charlotte did not even have a chance to get back up before Nix was on her. Jessica crawled out of the sidecar as Charlotte beat furiously at the alien, who ignored her powerful punches, batting away her blows until his long, thin fingers finally clamped around her throat. Jessica sat up on her knees bringing the shotgun around to bear on Nix, an action Jackie knew would doom her.

She called out to her. "Jessica! Don't!"

Nix turned, flinging his one free hand toward her. The gun went off and Jessica staggered back and fell on her butt. It was too dark for Jackie to see, but she had obviously been hit with one of its spines.

The crowd backed away. Either they knew better or Charlotte's charms did not include messing with monsters. Her pleading became garbled under the pressure of its fierce grip. Nix plucked another spine, and despite Charlotte's frantic punching and kicking, plunged his hand through her defenses, burying the spine in her chest.

The warbled scream that came out of her mouth made Jackie cringe. "N-n-no. Please." She screamed again. "Sis . . . nooo."

Jackie turned away. Just like that, it was over. Inside her head, Rebecca sobbed quietly. It was not the end they were hoping for, that's for sure. She moved quickly around the corner, hoping to see Nick at least lying on the ground. There were dozens of people down, some not moving, others groaning and crying in pain. "McManus! Damnit, get your ass back up here." Red tail lights were backing up the drive as she said it. They were going to need ambulances for twenty-five to thirty people at least. People were also screaming for reasons other than pain. Seeing a real, live monster tended to do that.

She turned back to Nix, who stood up from Charlotte's lifeless body, eyes so bright they set the ground out in front of him aglow. Jackie raced up to Jessica before it could step over to her and found her staring up into the rain, blinking away the drops that hit her eyes. The spine protruded from her neck, where blood was dribbling out on to the ground.

"Damn it, Nix. I didn't want you to get her, too. She's innocent in all this."

Something sounding like a sigh escaped its mouth. It bent over and grabbed the spine between two of its fingers and eased it back out. Jessica spluttered and whimpered, trying to say something, but quickly fainted. The spine then took on a faint, green glow, and Nix held the tip in the wound for a moment before finally taking it out. The wound was gone.

"Live, perhaps," Nix said. "Friend?"

Jackie pointed at the house. "No. In there. They're trapped."

The SUV slid to a stop as it reached the circle before it could run into anyone trying to flee. McManus stepped out, Glock swinging out over the open doorframe. "Jack! What's—?" He stared wide-eyed at Nix.

"Help the injured over there. Nick and Shelby are trapped inside."

"Shit. They still alive?"

"They better be," she replied. "Just . . . go handle the injured. I'll deal with this thing here."

"Is that . . . ?"

"Yeah."

Pernetti had stepped out of the car as well, but he looked like he was about to piss himself. The Glock braced over the frame of the door shook in his hand. Jackie could not blame him for that feeling. "Pernetti, it's fine. I think. Just go. Wait! Actually, get Jessica there in the car."

"Fucking-A, Jack. Seriously?" He stared at Nix's spiny, glowing form and did not move.

"He's not interested in you, Pernetti. Get over yourself and get Jessica in the car," she snapped back. "Nix? We have to clear this rubble to get to my friends." She pointed at the collapsed wall, where the wood had splintered and broken into pieces and lay half buried in bricks from the chimney. On the north side of the house, smoke still billowed up into the drizzling rain. "Maybe we can get in through the front window if anything is left there." Nix gave her a blank stare. "Come with me."

It followed Jackie around to where the living room window had once been. People still standing in the circle drive in front of the house scampered away, but Jackie did not have any more time to soothe their fears. She had wasted enough already.

The front wall had fallen inward and the second floor had fallen down on top of it. Only the lower edge of the window could be seen in the ruins. "Nick!" Jackie shouted. "Nick, can you hear me?"

She strained to hear something, anything to give a sign that he was alive in there. Several seconds passed.

"Friend?" Nix asked.

"Friend," Jackie replied.

Nix stepped forward and surveyed the ruined wall, his eyes illuminating the wet wood with a reflective, green light. "Insufficient structure."

You think? "Can you just hurry, please?"

It bent down, looking up under the crumpled second floor, now at shoulder level, and then stuck its head through the squashed window frame. "I smell it there."

It? "What are you talking about?" Jackie asked.

"Friend," Nix replied. "Its essence dissipates."

Jackie felt a chill run through her. Was Nick dead? The way it was talking about him creeped her out. "Can you get him out or not?"

Nix carefully placed one spindly leg through the remains of the window and squatted down, placing the palms of its hands up under the second floor. Jackie eyed it with disbelief. Seriously? It was going to just lift the damn floor up? Her eyes widened with incredulity as it did just that, its body beginning to glow all over. Wood splintered and pieces of plaster split and fell, but inexorably, the floor eased up off of the broken walls of the first floor until it had hoisted it back up over its head.

How many thousand pounds had it just casually put over its head? Jackie closed her open mouth. "Holy shit. How'd you do that?"

"Friend?" it said.

"Right," Jackie replied and walked up to the shattered opening.

The front wall had folded over and in, a broken heap of wood, insulation, and plaster. Jackie stepped into the broken window and then straddled over the wall. Carson was on the ground next to her, a cracked chunk of plaster laying over the upper half of his body. A few feet behind him, the plaster shifted and moved, and then Jackie heard a familiar voice groan and then cough.

"Oh, thank God. Nick!" She crouched down and made her way forward, pulling aside hanging pieces of ceiling to get to him. He was covered in dust and chunks of plaster, pushing up onto his elbows, when she knelt next to him. "Can you move? Is anything broken?"

He coughed again, wiping dust from his mouth. Blood was smeared across the back of his hand. "Where's . . ." His gaze froze, focused behind her on Nix. "Damn. It's here."

"I know," Jackie said. "Desperate measures and all that shit. Let's get you out of here."

"Shelby?" He coughed again, spitting out blood across his hand, and made a pained sound as he got to his knees.

She lay a couple of feet further back from Nick, a few pieces of plaster and wood lying across her body. Her body was perfectly still. "She's behind you." *And please be alive.* "Still unconscious."

"Get her first," Nick said. "I'll be all right."

"You're coughing up blood," she said. "You're not all right. Can't you just . . . fix that or something?"

He nodded. "Get Shelby."

Jackie stepped around him and pulled the debris aside. "Shelby? Can you hear me?" She still lay in the fetal position formed when Jackie had wrapped herself protectively around her during the house's collapse. She reached down and touched Shelby's face, finding it colder than it usually was. She could not even tell if she was breathing. Laurel gasped.

"Oh, hell," Jackie muttered and hooked her hands beneath Shelby's arms. Drawing upon the energy still coursing through her body, Jackie found it quite easy to move her, though the low ceiling made it awkward.

She's still alive, Laurel said. *She's still there. Oh, Jackie! Hurry. Get her out.*

"Trying," Jackie huffed. Nick had half limped and shuffled his way to the opening and was pulling himself out, stumbling to his knees as he made his way over the debris. "Have to be careful here. Don't want to bang her on anything."

She was forced to sit on the pile and swing one leg over in order to get the leverage needed to pull Shelby out of the opening. Her feet flopped lifelessly to the ground after Jackie got her out. Jackie dragged her a good ten feet away before setting her down on wet gravel of the drive. Behind her shouts and cries continued to echo in the cold November air. Once she was clear, Nix stepped out from under the ceiling and let the second floor drop, toppling it down even further onto the first floor. If Carson or the Mayor had been alive in there, they were not likely now.

"There were others in there, Nix," she said.

"Friends?"

"No, but—"

"Then agreement done," he replied. "Is friend living?"

Jackie tried for a pulse, but could not find one. "I don't know. Her head got bashed in."

Nix stepped over and squatted down on the balls of his bare, elongated feet. "It is linked to other side like dead one."

"Don't you dare do anything to her," Jackie said, jabbing a finger at it. "Kill her and our deal is off."

"Already gone," Nix replied simply.

"What!" Jackie cradled Shelby's head toward her chest. "No, wait. She can't be!"

Nick limped over to her, placing his hand on Shelby's cheek. "Shel? Come back, girl. It's not time yet." He closed his eyes and then swore quietly. "Damn it, I don't have enough left to get her."

Jackie tried to feed her some of what she had, but she did not know how to do such a thing, not when the other person was unaware.

I'm crossing over, Laurel replied in a tearful voice. *I'll make her come back.*

Can you do that?

I'm going to try! Damn her.

A moment later, she was gone, and Jackie was left with Rebecca, who to this point had retreated into silence since her sister died. A girl, one hundred years dead, and a freaking alien who she had agreed to help if it helped her, but she had been too late. She would've dropped the stupid Nix idea and let Charlotte go, if it meant keeping Shelby alive.

I'll go help her. It was Rebecca. *You helped me get my peace, Jackie. Let me try and help you.*

Won't that mean the end of you, Rebecca.

I'm at my end. I'd like to go out doing something good, instead of what my death helped bring to the living world.

Rebecca, you aren't to blame for—

I know. Good-bye, Jackie. Thank you. I hope you too find peace in your life.

Rebecca's energy flowed out of her and into Shelby before Jackie had a chance to respond.

Nick pulled his hand away and looked at Jackie. "Did you do that?"

She shook her head. "No. Rebecca did." Jackie placed her hand over the spot of cracked, dented skull, and did her best to focus on helping Shelby come back. In the distance, Jackie could now hear the wail of sirens.

"How is she, Jack?" McManus called out to her.

Jackie had to swallow hard to make her voice work. "Not now." She closed her eyes and focused on the soaked, bloody hair beneath her palm.

A moment later, Nick's hand closed over hers. "She'll come back," he said. "She's not ready to go yet."

"She better not be." Jackie tried to laugh, but it came out as a half-sob. "Who's going to kick my ass when I act like an idiot?" Nick gave her hand a gentle squeeze but said nothing. "Come on, Shel! You actually want to miss out on seeing Nick and I together? I can't believe that for a second."

Whether she actually heard or not, Jackie likely would never know, but she felt the doorway open. The familiar ghostlike quality that both Nick and she had began to fill up Shelby's body once again. Rebecca's presence was gone.

Nick smiled and leaned over to kiss Shelby on the forehead. "Thank you, Rebecca."

Shelby's breast pushed into Jackie's stomach as she drew in a lungful of air and Jackie laughed. "Ha! She's back, Laur! She's back." Laurel was back with her a moment later, tearful and laughing with relief as well.

From above them, the disturbing hollow voice of Nix echoed down. "Friend lives." His head cocked to one side, peering at Jackie with apparent curiosity. "Resourceful. Agreement completed, yes?"

Jackie nodded. "Yes, Nix. You completed your agreement. Thank you. I guess that means I get to help you." Her joy at Shelby's living evaporated into the damp, night air.

Nick gave her a wide-eyed look. "What did you agree to, Jackie?"

She gave him a helpless smile and a tiny shrug of her shoulders. "Said I would help him if he helped me."

He stood up and turned to look at Nix. "Help him do what?"

"I'm, um, not sure exactly," she replied.

A pair of ambulances arrived then at the top of the drive, along with a fire truck. McManus's voice could be heard over the din. "Sonofabitch. Maddox! Go hold them off. Jack? You need to get that thing the hell out of here. Now."

"And put it where, McManus? Jesus Christ." Jackie gathered Shelby up in her arms. "We need to get her out of the rain. Nix? Stay right there, please. I need to put my friend someplace safe. I'll be right back."

"Agreement?" it asked.

"Yes, agreement. Wait." She took Shelby over to the SUV where the emergency personnel were gathering behind it. Nick limped after her, not quite as badly as before, but his body was slowly improving. At least the horrid-looking split along his jaw was now closed. "Hello, gentleman. This here is your first casualty. She's got a nasty blow to the head. We'll bring more over. Just stay over here. There's a propane leak, and we're trying to get everyone moved to a safe place.

A grizzled, scruffy fireman stepped up to her, glancing over Jackie's shoulder at the scene beyond. "What in Sam Hell happened here?"

"Local gathering," Jackie replied. "Something set off a propane tank and blew the house to hell. A bunch of the townsfolk were gathered here in front when it happened. I think there's some fatalities and at least a couple dozen injuries. Maybe . . . um . . . I was thinking the mill over there might be a good spot to get people moved to out of the rain so you can look them over?"

His narrowed eyes looked suspiciously across the front of the yard, at the men in FBI jackets, and the sprawl of injured and likely dead people on the ground and then back at Jackie. Finally, he shouted at this men, "OK, boys. You heard the girl. Let's see if we can use the cover of the mill there to help these fine folk. I'll go check—"

Jackie knew where he was going and cut him off by shoving Shelby toward him. "Here. She needs help now, and this guy needs his ankle bound up. I'll go check on the others." Maddox gave her a smirk before she spun on her heel and tried not to run back to Nix. When she reached him, Jackie tried to keep herself parked in the line of sight. "Nix, let's go over here, away from the crowd."

Hon, is that safe? I don't like the idea of being alone with this thing.

Me either, but I don't want this fiasco any more public than it already is. Jackie walked around a pile of rubble that had been the front porch and stopped, mostly out of view of the firemen.

"OK, Nix. This is good. What is it you need my help with?"

It looked back out at the chaos and then turned to gaze at Jackie. As much as the spines freaked her out, the eyes were by far the most unnerving aspect of Nix. You could not tell if he was looking directly at you or not or what it could even see with those veiny, pupiless eyes.

"Test," Nix said.

"Test?" Jackie did not understand. "What do you mean? Test what?"

It gave her that odd little head-cock, which gave Jackie the feeling of being the bug in the scientist's little Petri dish. "You test."

"You want me to test something? I don't—" She stopped when Nix reached down and plucked a spine from its chest. It rolled the six-inch needle between spindly, multijointed fingers. Jackie got a sudden panicky feeling in her chest. "Hold on. What is this?" She tried to back up, but the crumbled remains of the house lay behind her, giving her nowhere to go.

Jackie, get out of here. Run! Laurel said.

"Test," Nix repeated and reached out to grab Jackie by the chin, the short, thin spines cover its palms digging into her skin. "See if prepared."

Jackie squirmed, losing traction as Nix pulled her up onto her toes. She latched onto its wrist, trying to break free of its grip, but she was obviously no match. Its body swam in the energy of the dead. Hundreds if not thousands of souls coursing through its body. Nix raised the needle between them, the end of it beginning to glow with the familiar green hue of its power.

"Wait!" Jackie tried to say, but her mouth was distorted by the fierceness of its grip. "No, don't. What are you doing?"

The tip poised dead center over her chest, and Jackie tried to jerk free, thrashing until she could feel the pins in its hands digging into her face. *Oh, my God. It's going to plunge that fucking thing right in my heart. Laur! Laur, help me.*

"Test," Nix said, one final time and thrust forward with the spine.

Jackie felt the first pinch of pain against her skin and tried to open her mouth to scream.

Chapter 30

Her voice would not work. Jackie's mouth moved, but everything inside her had frozen. With her head twisted upward by Nix's spindly fingers, she could only see his arm inching forward, until its fingers pressed against her chest between her breasts. Oddly enough, it did not have the piercing pain of a knife, but instead, the fiery burn of dry ice. Her chest felt like it was freezing into a solid block. A maelstrom of dead energy was turning her blood into syrup and locking her muscles into rigid pieces of stone.

Laur! Oh, my God. What do I do? He's going to kill me.

Laurel did not answer. Jackie could not even tell if she was with her.

"Jackie!" It was Nick.

"Interfere and you die, souldrinker," Nix said.

She tried to say his name, tried to shake her head to tell him to back off, but no part of her body would respond. She was a thousand pounds of ice with the howling wind of the dead whipping through her.

Jackie could only see Nick's dust-caked, rain-streaked face and shoulders, but there was no mistaking the Glock that raised up to eye level and pointed at Nix's head.

"Put her down, Nix," he said.

"Test," Nix said.

Nick stood his ground, the Glock about two feet from its head. "I don't give a fuck what you're doing," he said, in a cold, harsh tone Jackie had not heard before. "I'll give you to the count of one to let go of her." Nick's lips barely moved. "Then I'm emptying this clip into your head and we'll see how quickly your souls help you."

Nix's head turned slowly to regard Nick, and Jackie felt her heels touch back to the ground. The spine slid out of her, an icicle of steel. The thing had to have pierced her heart. There was no way it did not. The needles digging into her skin released and Jackie immediately fell to her knees.

"Test done," Nix replied. "Not ready."

Nick lowered the gun and knelt next to Jackie. "Hey. Are you OK?"

Jackie pulled up her shirt, expecting to find blood pouring from the puncture wound, but there was little more than a bright pink spot on the skin where Nix had stuck her. The bitter, burning cold was fading quickly.

"I think . . . I think so. Yeah." She sat back on her heels and sucked in a deep breath. "Spindly little fucker caught me off guard. I had no clue what the hell it wanted."

"Test," Nix said.

"Yeah! I got that," Jackie snapped back. "What the fuck did you do?"

"Test. Not ready," it said once again.

"Not ready for what?" She slapped Nick's hand away from her chest. "It's OK, I'm fine, more or less."

"You're shaking," Nick replied.

"Not ready to help," Nix replied. "Come back when ready."

"What do you mean, I'm not ready?" Jackie said. "Ready for what? What is it you need me to do?" she yelled.

Nix's spindly fingers dug through the spines on its head, as though trying to get to an itchy spot. "Need to wait. If ready, will tell." It turned and surveyed the crowd, which had backed well away from them toward the emergency crews, those who were able to see at least." Explore this place." It took in a deep breath, sounding like a wheezy asthmatic and then said something in the language Jackie found incomprehensible.

"Wait! Here?" Jackie started to stand but then had to grip Nick's shoulder for balance to get herself up. "You can't stay here. You have to go back."

Nix looked back at her, the thin crease of its mouth curled up in what had to be a smile. "Living world," it said. Nix held up the spine it had removed from Jackie's chest and then tucked it in, point first, among the bristly strands on its head. "Back when ready." With that, Nix turned and began walking away, stepping carelessly among the dead that lay strewn around the front of the house.

Jackie reached down for the Glock in Nick's hand. "We can't just let it go." Nick's grip was too tight for her to break.

He stood up next to her. "I don't think we have a choice, Jackie. We've got no way to fight that thing."

"But . . . fuck!" Her hands knotted up in her hair. "Nick, what have I done?"

"What you needed to do," he said. "Nobody can blame you for that."

She pointed a shaking finger at Nix's back as it disappeared into the darkness going down the hillside. "That thing is way worse than Charlotte. You've seen what it can do."

"I don't think we know that yet," Nick replied. "It'll be back."

"Not encouraging," Jackie replied. *Laur? You there? You can come back now.* Laurel stepped through and appeared beside her.

"That can't be good," she said.

"No, it can't," Jackie replied, and finally tore her gaze away from the wooded hillside. "We need to help whoever's left here." She began to move, and found her legs were still barely strong enough to stand. Nick grabbed her by the arm to steady her.

"Maybe you should go sit down," he said. "Let the emergency crew do its job now." She tried to shrug away from him, but his grip tightened. "Jackie, please. Go rest. Perhaps Jessica is able to talk."

"Don't patron—" She cut herself off and jerked her arm away. What an unmitigated disaster this had turned into. How many people had been killed in this fiasco? Was this all worth it in the end? At the moment it sure as hell did not seem like it. "Fine. Sorry. I'm just . . . look at this. I fucked it all up." She blinked away the tears pooling in her eyes.

"You saved Shelby's life," Laurel said. "The town is free. The price, well, it was a heavy price to pay."

Nick put his arm around her, hooking his hand under the opposite arm. "Come on. What's done is done, Jackie."

"Not with that thing out there, it isn't," she said, but gingerly followed along and let him lead her back to the SUV.

Jessica was not awake, but appeared to be sleeping, wrapped in a blanket, her head leaning against the window. The scruffy fireman walked up to them as Jackie was getting ready to get in.

"Mind telling me what in hell's name that was out there?"

"Don't ask," Jackie said. "Trust me, you don't want to know."

McManus came over as the fireman was walking away, shaking his head. "Do we have something new to be worrying about?"

"I don't know, McManus," she replied, and sat down on the edge of the seat. The cushion felt really good on her backside. "We don't really know anything about that . . . whatever it is."

He ran a hand over the short brush of his wet, reddish brown hair. "Can't lie here, Jack. This is one hell of a mess we've got. It's going to be a PR nightmare."

"I'll help with some of that," Nick said.

McManus smirked. "Nick, no offense, but you look like a PR nightmare all on your own."

"I'll have a little talk with everyone I can find here," he replied. "Convince them that what they saw really wasn't real."

"Ah, that's right," McManus said. "I forgot about that nifty trick. Well, don't worry about the townsfolk for now; just focus on the emergency personnel."

"Just give me a few minutes," Nick replied. "My reserves are running a bit low after all of that."

That made McManus laugh humorlessly. "No kidding. I'll be very interested in reading the report on this."

Jackie pulled herself into the car and out of the rain. The engine was running and the warm air from the vents felt like bliss. Whatever Nix had done to her, she still had a chill, beyond the damp, night air. Curled up in a corner of the backseat, leaning against the window and wrapped in a blanket, Jessica slept, undisturbed by their presence. If Nick could suggest away what had happened to the important players in this night's events, it just might not blow up in their faces.

Laurel moved into the car with her. "Hon, you doing all right?"

She nodded. "Cold, but warming up finally. What happened back there? You were gone in like two seconds."

"Less than that," she replied. "He blew me right out of you and through to the other side. You were flooded with a massive amount of spiritual energy, hon."

"Why? What could it have possibly been testing me for?"

"Maybe to see how you handled it? I don't know. Whatever it is, it's beyond my knowledge, or comprehension for that matter. I'm just glad it doesn't want to kill you. That saved all of us tonight."

"A lot of people it didn't save tonight," Jackie said and leaned back against the seat, closing her eyes for a moment. She got a precious few seconds of rest before a familiar voice had her jerking her head back up.

"Chief Martin? Philip Margolin, *Chicago Tribune.* Can

you tell me what the casualties are here? Do you know anything about a botched FBI raid on this house tonight?"

Jackie shoved the car door open. "Motherfucker. I'm going to kill him."

"Jackie," Laurel said. "Don't. It's not worth it."

"Oh, yeah it is."

Nick beat her to the punch, though. Literally. He came from the door of the mill, his cowboy boots across the wet gravel and barely showing the limp. Margolin saw him coming and started to back up, but he had nowhere to go.

"Mr. Anderson." He laughed nervously. "Looking a bit worse for the wear." He kept backpedaling. "Hey, if you have a complain—"

Nick did not stop. His fist plowed right through Margolin's upraised arms and smashed him in the face, dropping him like a stone. "As a matter of fact, I do." He stood over Margolin for a moment and then limped back toward the mill. He turned to the fire chief as he walked by. "Might want to have him looked at."

Jackie smiled at his retreating figure. "Almost as good as I would've done."

Laurel huffed at her. "That didn't serve any useful purpose."

"The hell it didn't." Jackie turned back toward the warmth of the car. She was already starting to shiver again.

Chapter 31

They brought Shelby home from the hospital the following day. Some people, according to the doctors, just healed with incredible speed. Or, as Jackie suspected, took a sip or two from some cute doctor who happened by the room. Regardless, she could hardly have been more pleased to see someone, having thought for a few moments at least that she might be partially responsible for her death. The lipstick-smearing kiss from Shelby sealed that thought. Saving a life when it happened had always been one of the biggest perks of her job.

They had got a hotel in Dubuque for the night to be nearer Shelby, and it gave McManus direct access to them while things in Thatcher's Mill got processed. He told them to keep as low a profile as possible, and Jackie was more than fine with this arrangement. By the time they had checked on Shelby in the hospital and got checked into a double bed hotel room, it had been well after midnight, and Jackie was asleep in the ten minutes it took Nick to shower. It was eleven AM by the time she woke up to the smell of coffee and bacon.

Nick's sowing of confusion among those on the scene had done its job and it was going to take days or longer to sort out exactly what had happened. So McManus told them to just head home and wait, which was great news until he added the part about Belgerman meeting them at their office for a debriefing on the events. When they arrived, and sat down around the conference room table just before dinnertime, Jackie was surprised by the extreme lack of anger coming from him.

Jackie sipped at the wonderful coffee Cynthia had made for her. After a couple days of diner and hotel coffee, it was like heaven in a cup. "I was expecting the Belgerman scowl," she said, with a flippant smile. "This did not go down exactly like we had in mind. We're sorry for that, sir. Six casualties is unacceptable."

"Given what you were up against," he said, "I don't believe casualties were to be unexpected. Unfortunate, but not unexpected. It would have been worse had you failed, Jack. Honestly, it was just lousy timing. If those townsfolk had arrived just a few minutes later, we might have avoided casualties entirely."

That was true, but still, casualties of any kind were not acceptable in Jackie's book. "They didn't deserve what happened to them."

"We're lucky that whole town didn't go down," Shelby said. "That girl may have looked cute and cuddly, but she was a tough little bitch. We had to play at a disadvantage, too, but that's beside the point. And Jackie here should get a fucking medal. She saved my ass."

"Miss Fontaine," Belgerman replied, "you don't have to cover for Jack, not this time anyway." He smiled at Jackie's disconcerted look. "We'll get things covered well enough on this one. Nick, you did wonders for us with whatever it is you do. There are so many conflicting stories about the events that nobody will ever be able to sort out truth from fiction."

He gave a little shrug. "Least I could do, considering. We'd both be dead and Charlotte would be gone if it hadn't been for Jackie's big gamble."

"Speaking of gambles," Belgerman said. "I want to know about this thing that got brought back from the other side. What are we dealing with here?"

Jackie sighed. "Wish we knew. It's not dead, that's for sure—or human for that matter."

"So, we have an alien presence walking around Iowa somewhere," Belgerman said.

"If it's still there," Jackie said. "Nix said he was going exploring."

"Nix?" Belgerman cocked an eyebrow. "You spoke with it?"

"It's been following me since I went to Deadworld," Jackie replied. "It wants my help with something."

"You?" He sat up straighter in his chair. "What could an alien being want with you, Jack?"

"Wish I knew. It thinks I'm the key to opening something, but apparently I'm not ready to do it."

Belgerman frowned at her. "I don't understand."

She shrugged. "I don't either."

"We need to track that thing down, then, so we can keep an eye on it," he said.

Nick, Shelby, and Jackie all snorted with laughter at that. "Sir," Jackie said, "the only reason to know where it might be is so that we can stay as far away from it as possible."

"Just how dangerous is this thing?"

"It makes Drake look like a trip to Disney," Jackie replied. "But it doesn't appear to have any sort of agenda here."

Belgerman raised his eyebrows at that and nodded. "I see. Don't poke the caged tiger, in other words."

"I still wouldn't mind knowing where it's at," Nick said. "We'd know when it was coming back then."

"I'll look into that," Belgerman said. "Regardless of how dangerous you believe this thing to be, we can certainly locate it without engagement. Shouldn't be too hard; just follow the news reports."

"I wouldn't," Jackie said. "Let the damn thing explore.

Someone gets on that thing's bad side and they are dead, no questions asked."

Belgerman gave her an *oh, really?* look. "Jack, if you were in my shoes and had an alien on the loose, would you sit back and let it just wander around?"

She huffed. "No. Still a bad idea. It can do . . . things, you wouldn't think possible." She gave him a wan smile and absently reached up to touch the tiny scar in the middle of her chest.

He gave her a concerned look. "What things?"

"I'll put it in the report, sir," she replied. It was not something she wished to relive at the moment. "I will say it pretty much lifted a house off the ground to save Nick and Shelby."

"Jesus."

Nick nodded in agreement. "It's more than we can handle, and then some."

"OK," Belgerman said. "We'll make sure to leave it alone, but I cannot let it just be out there in our world, when we don't know what it is or wants."

It only wanted her, and Jackie hoped it would stay that way. "Understood."

He folded his hands together on the table and gave Jackie a hard look. "Why do I think this concerns you even more than anyone else here?"

Jackie cleared her throat. "Because . . . it's hard to explain, sir. Let's just say I have a better sense of what it can do more than anyone else and leave it at that."

Belgerman put his hands down on the table. "All right. You all are probably ready to get home and sleep for three days, though I doubt McManus will let that happen."

"We're done?" Jackie wondered, a bit baffled by the brevity of the meeting.

He shrugged. "Investigation is still ongoing. We'll have more meetings, I'm sure, but honestly I just wanted to see how you were doing and hear about the green-eyed alien

McManus was rambling on about. I wanted to know just how serious this was, and now I do." He smiled and got to his feet. "Go home. Try to rest. We've got a good couple of weeks of this stuff to deal with."

Jackie walked him to the door, where he stopped and put a hand on her shoulder. "I mean it about the rest, Jack. Get some. You look more than just beat."

"I'll get some," she replied. "Thanks. It was rough."

"I can see that," he said. "Your team did a great job with an impossible situation, Jack. I know we lost some people, but you should be proud. This is what your team is all about. Let's hope the next one isn't quite so bad." He chuckled and gave her shoulder a fatherly squeeze. "We'll talk again soon. Good night, Jackie."

"Night, John. Oh. What about the girl, Jessica? What's happening with her?"

"We have her in a secure location for now," he said. "At this point I'm not sure what's going to be done. Nick's company is giving her that synthetic blood, and I believe Tillie is going to try and work with her."

"Guess that makes sense," Jackie replied. "I hope she will be OK. I wish her the best, though at this point, I don't think she appreciates that too much."

"In time, perhaps," he said. "Hopefully Tillie can undo some of the brainwashing that poor kid went through."

"If she can't, maybe Nick can, with his, you know, powers and such."

He smiled. "Yes, and such. I'll make sure Tillie is aware of that option. Take care of yourself, Jackie." He waved once and stepped out through the door.

Other than generating a lengthy report, which thankfully Cynthia took on the task of actually writing up, Jackie did nothing but rest for the next two days. She curled up with Bickerstaff on her couch, sipped on tequila, and slept through half a dozen movies. The only consolation they got over the next couple of days was a retraction article from Margolin, claiming his original story had come from poor sources and not been accurate. Of course, he'd left the actual accuracy of the story out of his follow-up.

Each night, she thought about Nick, picked up the phone to call, and played out the conversations in her head, but Jackie could not bring herself to go over to his house. She wanted to, but everything turned into visions of Hyperventilation Girl and yet another episode of Tales of Bad Sex.

Tillie called on the second day, two different times, and left messages, wanting to know how Jackie was doing. Belgerman had informed her to some degree about what had happened. The terror of Nix, however, was not something that she felt was even in Tillie's realm to deal with. Jackie dreamed of it, though, with its long glowing needle, watching it inch its way into her chest, piercing her heart. She would wake up gasping, hands pressed to her chest. After the second night, Jackie thought that maybe chatting with Tillie would help soothe the nightmares or at least she could get some good meds that would make them go away.

The third day was the first trip back to Thatcher's Mill to talk with some of the county law enforcement. It was to no one's surprise that they were upset about the lack of a coherent story. When people died in your jurisdiction, you wanted the facts to make sense. Jackie, Nick, and Shelby did not do a lot to help their cause, following up the ghost hunter story with how they'd uncovered some weird inconsistencies in the town, like the Thatcher girls not existing, and then getting in over their heads as they tried to expose the girls as fakes, finding out Jessica may have been kidnapped, and then calling in their FBI friends for assistance. It was not a great story, but nobody else was offering a contradictory story to go against them, so they stuck with it.

That night Shelby had Jackie and Cynthia over for dinner, with the topic of conversation being Christmas presents. How could the woman even be thinking Christmas after the recent events they had gone through? They spent the evening eating hors d'oeuvres—little puff pastries filled with crab that Jackie decided she could eat until she got sick—singing Christmas songs, and decorating Shelby's tree. Why they had to do it in the middle of the week was beyond Jackie, other than Shelby saying they would have done it Thanksgiving weekend, until all of that "vampire shit" got in the way.

At some point, after a dozen crab puffs and a couple glasses of wine each, they got around to the what-to-get-Nick question.

Jackie responded to this as any sane person would when asked what to get a guy who had been around for nearly 200 years and had millions of dollars stashed away. "How the hell would I know what to get him? The guy has everything he wants about ten times over. How about some new boots? I think his got trashed by Charlotte." That actually sounded like a decent idea to her. "You know what size shoe he wears?"

Shelby shook her head. "No good. He gets them handmade by this guy in Italy. Nothing compares."

"Of course not," Jackie replied. "OK, I'm out of ideas."

Pfft! Shelby waved Jackie off. "You suck. Get creative. Think out of the box. What kinds of things did you get Laurel?"

Laurel chuckled softly. "Why don't we move on to another question?"

"Hey! I got you things . . . most of the time." What had she got her for last Christmas? It was something small, like jewelry or something.

"Most of the time?" Shelby looked shocked. "You mean you actually forgot to get Laur a Christmas present?"

"It only happened once," Jackie started to say. Laurel held up two fingers. Jackie frowned back at her: *Really?* "OK, twice. I just . . . I don't know! I don't pay much attention to holidays."

Cynthia made a *tsk-tsk* sound, and Shelby looked like her eyes were going to explode out of her head. "How the hell do you not pay attention to Christmas? It's the best fucking day of the year. It's goddamn glorious! You get to celebrate all of those you love the most on one day and eat freaking fabulous food until you're comatose, and sing songs, and you get to unwrap pretty little presents given to you by those you care about the most."

Jackie looked away from them. Well, who was the biggest loser in the room now? "Jesus. Guess I'll figure out a damn gift for Nick."

Shelby laughed. "You're trying too hard, babe. There's only one thing our cowboy would like for Christmas, and that is you."

Jackie felt heat flushing into her face. "You're all bitches, you know that? Totally unfair."

"Hey," Shelby said, grinning ear to ear, "when you forget a Christmas, you're indebted for life."

"OK, I get it," Jackie replied. "I'll figure something out. What about you guys? What do you all want for Christmas? And don't you make me come up with shit out of thin air. Give me ideas."

"Go to Ethereal Lane," Cynthia said. "Anything you find there will be lovely."

"I'll make it easy on you," Shelby said. "Go to Ernesto's—you know the place?"

Jackie nodded. "Yeah, hard to forget."

"Tell Ernesto that Ms. Fontaine would like a bottle of his glorious red. He'll know what you mean."

"I can do that." Jackie looked up from the sofa at Laurel, who smiled affectionately at her, and Jackie's positive mood plummeted into the muck of memory. "Laur? I'm sorry. I have no clue. I wish I could get you something."

"I don't need anything except what's here right now," she said. "That's enough."

No, it was not enough. Jackie knew exactly what she

wanted, seeing how Laurel looked at Shelby when Shelby's smile turned upon her.

"Love you, baby," Shelby said and blew Laurel a little kiss. It was as close as they could get without crossing over, but even that was not quite there for them.

Watching Laurel blow the kiss back, Jackie had an abrupt flash of what she would give Laurel for Christmas.

"What, hon?" Laurel looked at her curiously. "What's that look for?"

Jackie smiled. "Nothing. Just figured out your Christmas present, I think."

"Oh! What is it?"

She laughed. "Really? No way I'm answering that. Besides I'm not sure I can pull it off, so we'll have to wait and see."

Shelby pursed her lips at Jackie's words. "Now I'm intrigued. What could Ms. Anti-holiday have in store for you, sweetie? A shiny, ripe apple perhaps?"

Jackie chuckled along with them at that. She had it coming. "Up yours. Maybe I'll change my mind now, if you're going to give me shit about it."

"Can't go back on it now," Shelby said pointedly. "It's out there. You put it out there, so you have to get it."

"Yeah, we'll see how it goes," Jackie said. *God help me.*

Chapter 32

The Thatcher's Mill case had come to a close, as much as they were concerned with it anyway. There would still be questions asked, but reports had been filed, and the Omaha branch was now handling anything on the FBI's end of things. Margolin had become respectfully quiet about the entire affair. Perhaps the broken jaw would keep him quiet for a long time.

Tillie prescribed Jackie some sleep medication for the Nix nightmares, and offered her sympathies, but as Jackie suspected, there really was no relief from such a violation other than time. The nightmares would fade and time would heal at least that part of her wounded psyche. Meanwhile, Jackie got to wait for Nix's eventual return when she was deemed ready, whatever the hell that was. The nightmares would never end until that day arrived, and Jackie was not sure which would be worse.

Nick called every day to check on her, since they were doing nothing Special Investigations related until after the holiday. No, there was no sign of Nix. No, she did not feel like doing much of anything besides letting life settle back down so she could regather herself. He made it quite clear that he would be more than happy to help her settle things back down, but Jackie only thanked him and took a rain check.

Shelby took her shopping every other day it seemed. The woman was a Christmas whore, likely responsible for keeping half the businesses in Chicago afloat during the holiday season. She had a list of people to shop for and things to buy that must have been three pages long. Jackie was sure that Shelby only brought her along to help carry the bags out to her car when done. Still, after a while, Jackie found times when it was actually fun, and Shelby made sure to give her no end of shit for it.

Shopping with Nick for Shelby and Cynthia was a one-day affair and may have been on Jackie's list as a top five best days of her life. They went to six area spas, testing out services from each, and by the time they were done, Jackie was loose, relaxed, scrubbed, buffed, exfoliated, and smelling better than she likely had in her entire life. They stopped by Ernesto's for dinner, where they were fawned over like royalty, and Jackie was sure they would walk out somehow engaged. At the end of the night, though, Jackie chose to go home instead of accepting Nick's invitation to come over, where the inevitable expectation to stay the night would occur, and Jackie would have to figure out how to have sex without freaking out again.

For his part, Nick did not pressure her at all. He seemed all too happy to spend the time together that they did, but the subtle interest was made apparent on a regular basis with an arm on the shoulder or a squeeze on the hand or if they had dinner, the kiss goodnight at the end. It was in those moments that Jackie knew his interest was not going anywhere. Nor was hers, for that matter, but her reluctance made her feel guilty. Nick deserved something. At some point she would have to suck it up and either try again or just break it off. She could not leave him dangling in the wind. It would not be fair. And as much as her cowardly self wished to tuck tail and run, Jackie had a feeling Shelby might actually track her down and kill her for it..

Tillie had told her, during their talk about her nightmares, that the less she worried about it, thought about it, and stressed over it, the sooner she would feel capable and want to try again. Problem with that, of course, was that every time she was alone with Nick doing anything—filling up the car with gas, having a beer, or helping him clean the damn kitchen after cooking her a meal—the thought was lingering there in the background. Jackie figured it would get to the point where her wants overcame her nerves. She hoped.

Also on her mind was her Christmas present idea for Laurel. She didn't know how it would work or if Laurel would even want it, but it was the best thing she could think of doing for her and something Laurel deserved, which made it an ideal gift. By any normal standards of gift giving, however, it was an absurd present. When she ran the idea by Cynthia a week before Christmas Eve, when it was only them in the office, Cynthia started bawling.

"Oh, Mother of us all! That's the sweetest thing I've ever heard," she had cried out and jumped out of her chair to hug Jackie. "You have to do it. You have to!"

"It's not weird?" Jackie wondered. "I mean, it's me, not her."

She shook her head. "Won't matter one bit." Cynthia plucked a Kleenex out of the box on her desk and dabbed at her eyes. "That's the best gift ever. It'll only . . . will you be able to tune things out if you want?"

Jackie shrugged. "I can, for the most part."

"But what if—"

"Yeah, I know. That might be awkward," Jackie said.

"Hmm." Cynthia rubbed at her chin in thought for a moment. "Next time Laurel is with you, we should work on that. I can help you work on blocking it all out. You need to learn how anyway, in case something like what happened before happens again."

"Yeah?" Not that she hoped anything like being filled with ghosts would happen again, but it would likely be good to get better at handling these problems before they occurred again. "Thanks, Cyn."

"Hey, we're a team. We work together and all that stuff." She smiled at Jackie. "So, how about Nick? Any plans yet for Christmas?"

"Not really," she replied. "Still working on it."

Cynthia waved Jackie off. "Not to worry. You've still got a whole week to figure it out."

Jackie offered a feeble smile. It might as well have been a month or a year for all the great ideas she had not come up with so far.

The days leading up to Christmas Eve were thankfully occupied for Jackie. She decided to do a little prep work for the new year, and continued to sort, classify, and eliminate leads from the FBI files. Cynthia spent the afternoons with her and Laurel working on blocking out, which became easier each day, but regardless of how much effort she put into it, she could not completely block out Laurel's presence. The best she could get was a barely audible murmur, but it was a far cry better than the difficulties she had handling the girls in her head from before.

Shelby had a tree put up in the reception area of the office, and stocked it full of presents, which they took the Friday before Christmas to open, while drinking rum eggnog and listening to classic carols. It was odd, but it kind of felt like family, or as close to one as Jackie was likely to get. She left for the weekend feeling warm, full, and humming Sinatra. When was the last time she had felt good enough to hum a song? Shelby was rubbing off on her.

Saturday was an FBI office party that Jackie felt a little weird attending, but it was wonderful to see everyone, even with the difficulty explaining what she had been doing with her time away. Thankfully, most everyone there wanted to keep the conversations as far away from work as possible. Toward the end of it, Tillie pulled Jackie aside and handed her a small, wrapped gift.

"It's just a little something," she said. "I saw it while I was shopping the other day and thought of you."

Jackie took the small box. "Tillie, I didn't get you anything."

"Not expected or needed, dear," she replied. "I just wish you a pleasant and wonderful Christmas, and hope the best for you."

She smiled. "Thank you. You didn't really need to get me anything."

"Only people I care about," she said. "Now, go on, open it."

The wrapping was crisp and pristine, white with gold embossed little wreaths, and done up with thin, gold ribbon, flowered up into little curlicues on top. Jackie could hardly bear to open the box. "It's so perfectly wrapped. Did you do this?"

She grinned, cheeks rosy from the evening's drinks. "Hidden talent."

Jackie chuckled. The woman could probably do anything perfectly if she set her mind to it. Trying to be careful, she pulled the ribbon off and tried not to tear the paper while Tillie huffed at her impatiently. Inside was a black, velvet jewelry box. Inside, Jackie found a simple, carved crystal hung from a silvery chain.

Tillie laid a hand upon Jackie's arm. "Now, I know you don't really wear jewelry, dear, but I was hoping you might reconsider. This is an amethyst; it's a stone of protection, healing dreams, and transformation. I thought it might suit you. And, I had it strung from a platinum chain, for strength of course."

Laurel drifted over and gasped. "Blessed Mother. Tillie

got you an amulet of protection! Oh, that sweet woman. Hug her for me."

She gave Laurel a sidelong glance but thanked Tillie and hugged her, whose embrace was soft and warm, and Jackie felt a rather large lump in her throat she had to swallow down. Six months ago, she would have scoffed at such a gift and stuffed it in a drawer somewhere out of sight and out of mind. Now? Who the hell knew? It just might give her some added protection and healing dreams, and God knew she needed them.

"It's just what I needed, I think," she said, hoping not to sound choked-up. "You want to put it on?"

She held up the necklace to her, and Tillie took it. "Gladly, dear." She stepped around and strung it around Jackie's neck, clipping it behind. "Wear it well, and I pray it works for you."

Jackie took a deep breath and let it out slowly to keep the tears from spilling over. "Me too. Thank you, Tillie. It means a lot, really."

"Such a wonderful woman," Laurel said. "Wish her Merry Christmas for me."

She did, and whether it was because Tillie's gift had made her feel so good or if it was the amulet itself, Jackie slept peacefully that night for the first time in weeks.

The day of Christmas Eve, Jackie was a bundle of nerves. She had to turn down a quiet dinner with Nick so she could deal with Laurel's present, but without telling them why, her decision had annoyed them both. Other than telling Laurel the present was personal, she was not going to give either of them the satisfaction of ruining the surprise, even if it ended up being a bad idea. It was a gift Jackie felt she had to give regardless of whether it was accepted or not. Laurel deserved no less.

By the time dinner came around, Jackie downed the first

glass of wine within five minutes. She nearly dropped the glass because her palms were so damp.

"Babe, what's the deal?" Shelby asked, standing before her after setting a dish of candied yams on the table. "You blow off Christmas Eve dinner with Nick to bring Laur and me a present, and you show up without a gift in hand, and you're more jittery than a seventeen-year-old on prom night."

Jackie grabbed the bottle of wine off the table and poured herself another glass. She laughed nervously. "Yeah, I know. The present is . . . um, special, and I don't know if you two will want it or think it's just a crazy-stupid idea or something."

The perfectly plucked eyebrows arched with curiosity. "Really." Shelby pulled out one of the dining room chairs and sat down. "OK, then, let's get this out of the way so we can enjoy our dinner, because having you like this all evening will drive me bananas. Laur? Oh, there you are." She had come out from the kitchen at the sound of their conversation.

"I'm here," she replied. "So, what's the big surprise, hon? I've been excited all week, and Cynthia has been a total ass taunting us with it."

"I even threatened to take her presents away, but she refused," Shelby said. "Bitch would not crack one bit, so this must be good."

Jackie smiled and took another large gulp of wine. She held the glass with both hands to keep it from shaking. One would have thought after all of the shit she had been through that something like this would be cake.

"Laur," she said, "you've been my best friend for almost ten years, and I can't say that, during that time, I was as good a friend for you as you have been for me."

"Oh, nonsense," she said. "That's—"

"Stop," Jackie said. "It's true. I'll admit it. Hell, I was probably a downright bitch half the time, too self-absorbed in my own shit to care about the person who has been there for me through everything, good and bad. I never really realized until you were, you know, gone, what you meant to my life, how you kept me sane and whole. Without you, I'd have been kicked out of the FBI a long time ago."

"You're too good an agent to—"

"Let me finish," Jackie interrupted again. "I owe you more than anything in this world." She wiped at the tears pooling up. "And I never really had a chance to give you what you deserved." The tears began to fall, and she finally gave up trying to keep them at bay. "Hell. I knew this would happen."

Shelby leaned forward and grabbed Jackie's hand. "Babe, it's all good."

She shook her head. "No, not really. My best friend is dead. I couldn't save you Laur, and I have to live with that every day for the rest of my life. But," she said, sniffling, and Shelby handed her a napkin from the table, "thanks. I do have one thing I can give you though, the only thing I actually have to give you."

"What's that, sweetie?" Laurel asked, kneeling down beside Jackie, her cool hands closing in and around Jackie's.

She gave them a feeble smile. "Me."

"What?" They said in unison.

"My present," Jackie said. "It's me. Laur, you can have me for tonight, so you can be with Shel for Christmas."

"You . . . really?" Laurel said, flabbergasted.

"Holy, fucking hell," Shelby cried out, clapping her hands together with a loud pop that made Jackie jump.

"If it's too weird or inappropriate—"

Shelby leaned forward and grabbed Jackie's face with both hands and kissed her hard. "That's an amazing gift, babe, and I don't give a shit if it's weird or inappropriate, because I'd give just about anything to have a real night with this beautiful woman right here."

"Hon, are you sure?" Laurel asked.

Jackie nodded. "Thought about it for a while. It's what I want, if you'd like to."

She looked at Shelby and laughed. "More than anything. Oh. Oh! You sneak. This is why you were practicing blocking with Cynthia."

She laughed. "Yes. I figured I might not want to be aware of everything that went on."

Her eyes got wide. "So, you're saying you don't care if, you know, we actually sleep together?"

Jackie let out her pent up breath. This was going to work. "We have to be at Nick's by ten for brunch and presents and whatever else there is. I'll need to run home first, so I need my body back by eight. That gives you about fourteen hours to do whatever you want to do."

"Really?"

"Yes, really," Jackie replied. "Just leave me in one piece, that's all I ask."

They all laughed at that, and then Shelby got to her feet. "Well let's eat first, so we can get this show on the road." She was bouncing on the balls of her feet. "Oh, my God, I'm so excited. Jackie, you're the best."

Laurel's cold lips brushed her cheek. "I love you, hon. It's the best Christmas present in the world."

Jackie beamed. That was all she needed to hear. Christmas was officially all good now.

Morning came around, and Jackie returned to a sleepy, worn-out body. On the plus side, she had already showered. Twice. She had been able to block out most of the night's events, but when things became too intense, which seemed to happen on a fairly regular basis, it was impossible to block out everything. Shelby did things Jackie had never thought of before, and Laurel savored every moment of it. Jackie just wished she had not cried so much. If she could have sex half that good, she would feel pretty damn good about herself. Good tears or not, it stung to know how much Laurel had missed out on because she had been stuck with her.

She left around eight, was kissed good-bye perhaps a bit too appreciatively by Shelby, and left Laurel with her while they basked in the glow of their first real night together. Walking out to her car, Jackie felt stiffness in muscles she didn't realize could be stiff. It was worth every last painful twinge though.

Jackie arrived at Nick's a few minutes after ten, but Shelby had not arrived yet. He greeted her with a kiss and a smile, taking the three gifts she had held in her hands. "Merry Christmas to you. How was your evening with Shel and Laurel?"

"It was good," she said quickly, hoping he would leave it at that. "I think my gift went over rather well."

"Excellent. Shel and Cyn are on their way," he said. "I'm just finishing up brunch so we can eat when they arrive."

"OK. Can I help with anything?"

"Nope. Just a couple things to do. Coffee?"

She smiled. "Make it mud, please."

"You'll be able to stand a spoon in it," he replied and headed for the kitchen.

"And Merry Christmas, Nick," she added. "You all have made it the best Christmas I've ever had."

He stopped and stepped back over to her. "You deserve no less." His kiss this time was deeper and longer lasting. "And we still have all day to make it better."

And it was better than she could have hoped for. *A Christmas Story* marathon ran on the television in the background under threat of death from Shelby, who insisted it was the best holiday movie of all time. Brunch left Jackie so full she could barely move, with eggs Benedict, waffles, raspberry puffs, fresh fruit with homemade whipped cream, all washed down with coffee and mimosas.

Flopped on the couch with Nick and a coffee, watching Shelby hand out gifts, Jackie felt rather happy for the first time in a long while. The alien death, guilt, and self-doubt were all successfully pushed into the background, for at least a little while, and damn it all if she was not going to enjoy it while it lasted.

When they were all settled in, Shelby held up the card, which was all she had received from Nick. "A card, Nick? This doesn't count as a present."

"Why not?" he asked. "You need it put in wrapping paper?"

"And a box, with ribbons and a bow," she added. "You suck."

Still, when she opened it, she gasped and grinned. "A year-long pass to Four Seasons Spa? Jesus Christ, Nick. How much? Oh, never mind. This is awesome. Thank you."

Cynthia had the same gift, which would allow them to go together. Jackie found that she had a similar card in hers as well. Shelby took immediate offense.

"You got her the same gift as us? What's wrong with you—"

"She hasn't even opened it up yet," Nick said. "You don't know what it is."

"Well, you wouldn't tell me, so I can only guess it is."

"Telling you is like sharing a secret with the whole world," Nick replied. "You can't handle it."

Shelby huffed. "Bullshit. I can too. Fine. Open it already, Jackie. Let's see what Mister Boring got for you."

Jackie opened up the envelope, curious now, since it was apparent that she had received something else, not that the spa would bother her. She had not minded her trip there at all. Inside was what looked like a postcard, with the picture of a showroom piano on the front. "Ooh, that's pretty," she said. "I wouldn't mind having one . . ." Jackie turned the card over, where a simple, *Merry Christmas, Jackie* was written in large script. Below it, it read, *Scheduled for delivery, December 29th, 2 PM.*

"Well?" Shelby said, impatiently. "What is it?"

"A piano," Jackie said. "Wow, Nick. This is a Steinway, isn't it?"

"It is," Nick said. "You'll really notice the difference over the one you have now."

Shelby snatched the card from her hand and looked it over. "Well, I guess you're excused on this one, babe. That's lovely."

God. It was a twenty-thousand-dollar piano, easy. It sure put her present to shame, not that Nick needed a new piano or much of anything else for that matter. "I don't even know what to say, Nick. It's beautiful."

"Just promise me I get to hear the first song played," he replied.

She leaned over and kissed him. "You can have the first hundred songs." She watched him pick up the gift she had gotten for him at the suggestion of Shelby. "My present isn't anything close to that."

"It's not about the money," Laurel said. "It's the thought that counts." She gave Jackie a big, cheesy grin with that, and Jackie felt heat rush to her face.

"OK, fine. Cost doesn't matter."

Nick opened up his painting, or actually a print of an oil painting, which he recognized before she even said who the artist was. "It's a Remington!" He sounded genuinely excited. "I love his work. There are a couple of them up in the library."

"I thought maybe for your office," she said, hopeful. "It's not the real thing, but it's hard to steal from a museum."

"It'll look great up behind the desk," he said. "This is great, Jackie. Thank you." He kissed her again. "It's a perfect gift. Really."

Not next to a grand piano, but she had to convince herself

that the cost of the gift really did not matter. Her gift to Laurel cost no money at all.

They continued around, opening the remaining gifts, and then lounged in their seats watching a full round of the movie before eating leftovers, playing pool, and switching from mimosas to hot buttered rum. As evening rolled around, Shelby and Cynthia began to gather up their gifts and help clean up, and Jackie found herself struggling to stay awake. How many drinks had she had over the course of the day? How much sleep had she actually gotten the night before?

Hugs and kisses good-bye went around, and Shelby whispered in her ear. "Planned on staying, didn't you?"

"If I can stay awake," she muttered back. "How late were you two up last night?"

"Oh," she said, "kind of late. Sorry, babe. Get a nap in for later."

Yeah, right. If she fell asleep now, she would never wake up until morning. Except that is exactly what she did. Nick put on *It's A Wonderful Life* for them to watch, and with the fire going to warm the bottoms of her feet, and the soft crook of Nick's shoulder to cradle her head, Jackie was gone before the opening credits were done.

When Jackie stirred from her comatose state, it was dark, and she was lying down, smothered in a thick layer of blankets. Nick's arm was around her waist and she was spooned up against him. It felt too good to move.

"There you are," Nick said, amused. "Good morning."

"Morning?" Jackie groaned. "Damn, what time is it?"

"Three-thirty or so," he replied. "I was going to let you sleep on the couch, but when the movie ended, you muttered, 'Let's go to bed.' I had to carry you, but you weigh 110 in the pouring rain."

She halfheartedly threw an elbow back at him. "One twenty-four, thank you very much."

Nick chuckled. "I was close. You need anything? Glass of water? You want to get up?"

"No," she replied and relaxed against him. "This is good just like this." Settling in more solidly against his body, Jackie could tell that he was good with it, too.

His head lifted up next to hers and his lips pressed softly to her neck. "Agreed. Might be stuck here all day at this rate."

Jackie felt him grow even firmer against her backside, settling between her cheeks. It occurred to Jackie then that she was indeed naked. "Nick?"

"Hmm?"

"I have no clothes on."

"I noticed," he said. "You undressed yourself when I set you on the bed last night."

"Oh." She had thought about it, had been considering it for the past two weeks, but the actual implementation of it? The thought had knotted her stomach with fear. "I guess that's OK. Did we? I mean, last night."

"No," he replied. "I did take the liberty of settling in here with you. If that's all right."

Jackie smiled. Actually, it was more than all right. When was the last time she had actually woken up in the morning with a guy still next to her? "Yeah, this is good. I like this arrangement."

"I'd hoped so," Nick said. "I could get used to this."

Jackie shifted her hips against him and turned her head back to look him in those depthless, softly glowing eyes. "Me too."

Nick's hand slid up her torso, cupping a breast, and brushing the palm across her hardening nipple. His mouth came down against hers, pulling her body tightly against his. What he wanted was readily apparent, and Jackie knew that she wanted this, too. The time was right. Fear had drifted away to an inaccessible place. She lifted up her leg and draped it over his, allowing Nick's cock to settle between her thighs. A subtle move of his own hips and a moment later he was inside her.

Jackie gasped and moaned against his mouth. There

would be no hyperventilating this time, no panicked, racing heartbeat, and no urge to just hurry up and get it over with. They had hours here, and Jackie felt no compulsion to get out. He wanted her, every single neurotic cell of her if his hands and mouth provided any indication. The time was finally right, and for the first time in her life, Jackie made love to a man she truly cared about.

It did not last all day, but Jackie heard the clock chime two PM before she finally crawled out of bed and into the shower. Her mouth appeared to be stuck in a perpetual smile. The nerves had crept in at times over the course of the morning, but Nick was so casual and at ease with her in bed, that they would recede into the background once again. So many things to do and try, many of which she might have actually done at one time or another, but tequila had stolen all of those memories. It was almost like learning about sex for the first time, and Mr. Practical had been just as willing to talk about sex as actually perform it. It had gotten to the point, at one stage, where she tried to see if she could fluster him with absurd sexual requests, but he took everything in stride.

"We'll try it all," he had said, implying that this would not be the last night they would be in bed together. Her biggest fear, that he would not find her at all interesting in bed, had been assuaged right then and there.

Now, the clear, bright December sky lit up the windows of Nick's great room, and Jackie sipped on her coffee while Nick fried bacon down in the kitchen. The smell of it had her stomach growling. She sat at his desk and logged into her e-mail to check on messages, hoping to find more Christmas messages. Who would have thought the holiday spirit could fill her so completely?

Shelby, not surprisingly enough, had sent the first message.

How'd it go? Tell me it ended up being the best Christmas ever!

Jackie hit reply and typed,

It was, in more ways than I can count. Thank you.

There was a note from Cynthia, too, a message from Belgerman and from Tillie, and even Hauser sent her an e-mail, oddly sent to her as a forwarded reply. What stupid Christmas shit had he sent along to her? Jackie opened it up.

Hey, Beautiful! Hope your Christmas was awesome! All the guys in the geek room send their love ;-). Anyway, this caught me off guard, so I wanted to zip it to you right away. You remember, way back in the early days, when we had no gray hair, I still had hopes of getting you into bed, and you gave me a name to put in to see if it pulled anything up on the database? Well, guess what? It finally got a hit! After all of these years. I don't even remember why you said you wanted to know, but the name hit on an Indianapolis newspaper. The article is attached. Happy New Year, gorgeous. Keep kicking ass. Hauser.

The headline of the article was innocuous enough: INDIANAPOLIS MAN ARRESTED IN FRAUD SCHEME. The picture and name of the accused was not. Jackie sat up abruptly, sloshing coffee into her lap. She swore and set the cup on the desk. All of the warm, contented feelings swimming through her body evaporated in an instant. The man's name was Bradley Jenkins, a.k.a. Carl Peterson. Carl the Cop had been caught.

Jackie's stepfather had resurfaced into her world once again.

Prologue

A misty rain swirled down into the darkness between the two brick buildings. Flattened against one cold wall, Archie Lane huddled next to a stack of sagging cardboard boxes, peering out of the narrow alley at the sliver of sidewalk illuminated by a nearby streetlight. This was not how he had envisioned running away. There had been no envisioning to speak of, really. All he had wanted was to escape the smack down going on in his parents' living room, where Dad had the leg up on the cursing scorecard and Mom was on pace to set a new "thrown objects" record. Now the midnight sounds of Chicago's suburbs were frightening him even more.

They were not strange sounds. Archie recognized most of them, from the sounds of tires on wet pavement to the screeching yowls of two cats duking it out, but in darkness, all things magnified in the wrong direction. Every shadow contained lurking doom. Body parts lay rotting in every container. Every passing car was his dad hunting for him. Surely, he was destined for the belt with this one. That threat had been very explicit after the last time.

The problem was where to go? Every friend he knew would have parents who would turn him over and make a phone call. His grandpa would let him stay, if only he could remember how to get there. He was also a thirty-minute ride by car. On foot that might take all night, if he even knew what direction to go in.

Archie's concerns had turned more immediate as the rain began to fall. It was getting cold. His long-sleeved shirt offered piss-poor protection, and, worse, he was starving. Where did street kids go when they were hungry and wet?

Archie hadn't the slightest clue. He did not know a single street kid. If he could find one, maybe they could tell him. At worst, maybe he could find a store to hang out in for a while, maybe steal a candy bar or something to fill his rumbling stomach. There was a Kroger not far from his house, but the darkness had confused his sense of direction. It was not on the old downtown strip where he found himself now. It was . . . somewhere else.

Archie thrust his hands deeper into his jeans and ventured forth. He would just have to ask someone. It couldn't be far, and it was open twenty-four hours. He could wander around until the sun came up and maybe, if he was really lucky, sneak back into his room without anyone being the wiser. Mom and Dad would be passed out by sunrise. As long as Dad didn't come in to kick at the foot of his bed to see if he was sleeping, all would be good.

At the alley's opening, Archie stood at the corner and poked his head out. There were only a few cars parked on the street. Further up at the corner, a couple walked quickly down the opposite sidewalk, huddled under an umbrella. Boy! They were in a real hurry, looking back at something, but Archie could not tell what. The intersection ahead appeared empty. Not fifty feet down the sidewalk, a car door opened, and a man stepped out. Nice car. Nice suit. He popped open an umbrella and looked up in Archie's direction, eyes hidden behind dark, round glasses.

Archie ducked back into the darkness and watched as the man began to walk toward him. He hardly looked dangerous, but what Archie found disquieting, what spawned a gnawing worm in his gut, was that the slick-looking car eased along the edge of the street, matching him step for step. Archie took another step back into the darkness, just in case.

The man hummed a tune, some old-fashioned-sounding thing Archie didn't recognize. His footsteps were silent upon the wet cement. When he got close, Archie held his breath, freezing every muscle of his body, willing it not to begin shivering. There was no way the guy could see him there, melded flat to the brick wall, right? He continued to walk, stepping across the alley's opening, one step, two, but at the edge he stopped.

Archie's heart leaped in his chest. The man, not ten feet away, paused and then turned, the umbrella resting lightly against his shoulder. He looked directly at Archie.

"I dare say, young man. Whatever are you doing out on a night like this and dressed like that?" His voice was old, reminding Archie of his grandpa, but it had a smoothness to it that belied the man's age. "And huddled in that rotting, forsaken alley. Surely you must be cold?"

Stranger at night on a nearly empty street. Archie knew better. These weren't the sorts of people you talked to when alone. "Pervs will snatch you right off your own street!" his mother had been fond of telling him.

"Just, um, hangin' out," Archie said. "I was on my way home actually . . . from a friend's house."

A corner of the man's mouth curled up beneath the shadows of the umbrella. "I see. No ride home from your mum or dad? It's awfully late. Bad sort of folk out and about this time of night, Mr. Lane." The blue car came to a stop behind the man, its windows cloaked in glossy, rain-splattered darkness.

"It's okay," Archie said, the worm in his gut now chomping gleefully at his insides. "I'm good. I don't have far to go." If he was quick enough, he might be able to bolt past the old guy. If not, one of those gloved hands could easily get a handful of shirt. The man's words suddenly sunk in. "Hey. How'd you know my name?"

"I know your mother, Archibold," he said, the other corner of his mouth twitching up to reveal a ghostly smile. "We met at the mall just the other day. I believe you were at the candy machines getting yourself a treat."

Archie nodded. "Oh. Yeah." His stomach rumbled at the thought of the handful of gummy worms he had gotten last weekend.

"Would you care for a ride home, Archibold?" When Archie remained silent, the man knelt down. "You ever ridden in a Rolls-Royce before?"

Archie shook his head. "Nope. It's Archie, by the way. I hate Archibold."

A deep chuckle rumbled out of the man's throat. "Archie it is. I've got soda inside, and I believe there might be something you could eat."

A ride in that car would be cool, no doubt. Free food and drink would be good, too. The worm paused in its hungry gnawing to shake its wary head. Don't ride with strangers. You just never knew, did you?

"I don't know. Actually, I think I'm good. My house isn't far at all."

He stood back up, looking down the street from where he'd come. "Almost two miles, Archie. That's a bit of a walk on tired feet."

"You know where I live, too?" Archie pulled his hands from his pockets. The worm was telling him to run, and the idea was making more sense by the second.

"Of course I do," he said, kneeling back down. A gloved hand reached up to pull the glasses down the bridge of his nose. "I could not have followed you here if I did not, now, could I?"

Archie froze, his body and mind coming to an ice-encased standstill. "Whoa, dude. Your eyes are glowing."

"They are." A black gloved hand reached out toward

him. "It's a special trick. Can you see anything in them? If you look hard enough, you will see something very special indeed."

One step, followed by another. Archie felt his hand reach out to take the strange man's hand. There actually was something in the glowing, irisless eyes. Shadows, gray and swirling like fog, danced around inside them. Archie began to shiver.

"They look like ghosts," he whispered.

The man stood up, his hand clasped tightly around Archie's. "Very good, Archibold. You can see the other side. Would you like to go?"

The door latch clicked open, and Archie stepped toward the car. "Are they all dead over there?"

"Every last one, my young man," he said and pulled open the door. "You see, they are my ghosts, but to join them, you must be one as well."

"Oh." The comforting warmth of the inside of the car beckoned. It felt so good against his wet, shivering skin. "Don't you have to be dead to be a ghost?"

The gloved hand gently pushed Archie in the back, easing him into the black cave of the car. "But worry not, Mr. Lane. I shall take care of that."

The door slammed shut, and a moment later the Rolls eased back into the street.

Chapter 1

Beneath the serene, protective canopy of maple leaves, a boy reclined against the trunk, withered and bloodless, his skin two sizes too big for his depleted body. It was death in all the wrong ways.

Jackie Rutledge squinted at the chaos from the parking lot, frowning at the milling gawkers. A gaggle of reporters and cameramen huddled around their cluster of vans waiting to pounce on the nearest unwary law-enforcement officer. She absently rubbed at her throbbing temple. There should have been laws against committing crimes on Mondays.

The drifting scatter of clouds taunted her by blocking the late September sun only to laugh at her seconds later. Her sunglasses provided little relief from the pain induced from last night's bottle of tequila, and Jackie hoped that luck would bring a thunderstorm and send the crowd running. There was no luck to be found in this park however. Death had sucked it all away.

The enormous maple, its branches drooping nearly to the ground, was completely encircled with crime-scene tape. Some of the crew were walking around, combing through the grass. The local police looked to have been put in charge of crowd control.

Jackie walked over to her partner, Laurel's, car and accepted the triple-shot latte and four Tylenol. "Thanks for the wake-up. Why can't killers keep better hours?"

"Off shifts pay better," Laurel said and reached up to brush off some lingering sand from the dangling ruffle of auburn hair on Jackie's forehead. "How was the lifeguard?"

"My thighs still hurt, so I'm guessing it was good." Tequila shots blurred out everything beyond last night's walk on the lake. The guy was long gone when Laurel had pierced Jackie's skull with the seven AM wake-up. Plopping the pills into her mouth, Jackie swallowed them with the lukewarm coffee.

She took the FBI jacket offered by Laurel, who was now scanning the crowd past the pair of television vans parked at the curb of the parking lot, her blue eyes narrowed in concentration. Her voice was distant. "Wish my thighs hurt."

"So is this the same MO as the Wisconsin woman?"

Laurel did not answer. Her eyes were closed, and Jackie knew better than to keep talking. Laurel had her psychic radar on, checking for anything out of the ordinary. If this was related to the Wisconsin victim, odds were there would be something. Even with the length of time that she had been dead, there had been a "taint." For Jackie, some demented prick had drained the woman of her blood. Period.

She finished off the last of her latte and waited for Laurel. She was ready to get moving, more so to avoid the media that looked to be wandering in their direction.

"Something is off here," Laurel said, her voice barely a whisper.

Jackie cringed. Of course there was. "Not off in a 'spiked your morning coffee' sort of way, I hope?"

"There's some bourbon in the trunk." Laurel didn't smile at the humor. She was too intent on something out in the crowd.

"Great. Off to a fabulous start already," Jackie said, but

Laurel was shuffling across the grass to the other side of the parking lot where the crowd had gathered. Something had tweaked that little psychic nerve of hers, and Jackie knew when to leave well enough alone. She waved. "Go find your bogeyman, Laur." Turning around, she made her way toward the overhanging tree before any media might notice she was standing by herself.

The blanket of leaves and limbs pushed and swatted at Jackie until she found herself standing in near darkness, thin shafts of light shining down on a boy seated neatly against the trunk of the tree. A couple members of the crew were already milling around in the shadows.

"That you, Jack? Glad you could join us."

Jackie's mouth creased into a frown. Pernetti. He would be the one detailing the victim. As if her headache didn't already feel like someone cranking screws down into her skull. "Don't even start with me, Pernetti. I'm not in the mood."

"Boy, did you get laid or something? You're bright-eyed and bushy-tailed this morning."

For a moment, Jackie thought he might have actually noticed, but then common sense took over. Pernetti was not capable of noticing anything like that. "Kiss my ass. Just tell me what we've got here."

He knelt down next to the body. "Archibold Lane, age twelve. Some sicko sucked the boy dry. There's ligature marks on the wrists and ankles. Funky marks, though. It looks like zip ties. Other than the hole in the arm, there's nothing else visible on him. Scene so far is weirdly spotless."

Twelve. What was wrong with people? "Spotless? That's doubtful." These days, everyone left something to track. Unless of course you knew how to clean up after yourself, and knew how forensics worked, but even then, it was unlikely.

"Clean so far, Jack." He shrugged, pointing at marks on the boy's wrists. "Other than the marks and the hole, he's got a couple bumps and scrapes that anyone might get when they've been out and about for a couple days."

"Two? He hasn't been dead that long."

Pernetti stood back up, thrusting his hands into his pockets. "Runaway, according to the sheriff. Fled from Mom and Dad beating each other up and not seen until this morning."

She doubted very much that Mom was doing any beating up on Dad. It hit her then, a brief flash of a twelve-year-old running away from a "domestic dispute" nearly twenty years prior. Mommy certainly had not been doing any of the beating. Jackie took a deep breath. The smell of death was doing little to wash the residue of memory away. "Anything else?"

"Nope. Area still being gone over. Bowers and Prescott are out canvassing, but it's looking a lot like that Wisconsin woman we brought in a couple months back."

Jackie shrugged and pulled out a pair of latex gloves from her jacket pocket. "Maybe. Okay, move, Pernetti. I want a look." She didn't want one, really. There was almost nothing she would see here, she could tell already. The perp had been clean and careful. Even the ground around the body looked undisturbed. Still, she would end up lead on the case, and, if anything, she needed to verify Pernetti's own observations.

"Think we should track down those parents and see what they have to say. Let them know their son is dead because they can't bitch at each other like other civilized folks."

She did not bother glancing up at him. "Go away, Pernetti. You're distracting me."

Thankfully left in silence, Jackie gave Archie a quick look over and found nothing out of the ordinary. He seemed almost peaceful, if one could ignore that fact that he looked like a pasty, deflated version of his former self. The thought sent a shiver down Jackie's spine, and she decided she had seen enough for the moment. Putting her sunglasses back on, she stepped back out from under the tree to find Laurel seated on the hood of her car smoking a cigarette. That was the first sign of trouble right there. A healthy girl by nature, Jackie knew if you hit the stress button hard enough, Laurel would be reaching for that security blanket in the bottom of her purse.

Jackie knew any shot at the day getting better was vanishing with each puff of smoke.